Rachel Urquhart is a former writer at *Spy*, *Vogue*, and *Allure* magazines. Her non-fiction has appeared in *The New Yorker*, the *New York Times*, *Tin House*, *Elle*, *GQ*, *Harper's Bazaar* and *Vanity Fair*, among other publications. She received her MFA in Fiction from Sarah Lawrence College and lives in Brooklyn with her husband and two sons.

THE VISIONIST

Massachusetts, 1842: Fifteen-year-old Polly Kimball sets fire to her family farm, killing her abusive father. With his fiery ghost at her heels, Polly and her young brother seek refuge in a nearby Shaker community, The City of Hope. Polly has much to hide from this mysterious society of believers, with the local fire inspector on her trail as well as the ever-present demons from her past. But when she is hailed as a 'Visionist', the first the community has known, she is subject to overwhelming scrutiny. Despite being fiercely protected by a young Shaker sister named Charity, a girl who has never known the outside world, Polly finds herself in danger from forces on both sides of the City's walls. And in a world where faith and fear co-exist, safety has a price . . .

RACHEL URQUHART

THE VISIONIST

Complete and Unabridged

CHARNWOOD
Leicester

First published in Great Britain in 2014 by
Simon & Schuster UK Ltd
London

First Charnwood Edition
published 2015
by arrangement with
Simon & Schuster UK Ltd
London

A catalogue record for this book is available
from the British Library.

ISBN 978–1–4448–2353–0

Published by
F. A. Thorpe (Publishing)
Anstey, Leicestershire

Set by Words & Graphics Ltd.
Anstey, Leicestershire
Printed and bound in Great Britain by
T. J. International Ltd., Padstow, Cornwall

For John, Theo, and Simon

Prologue

The City of Hope
1902

It is not uncommon, when one is young, to think that life is simple. In my case, I reasoned, it would require little besides discipline and effort. If I labored well, worshipped, confessed, and shunned all carnal desire, my soul would find sure and brilliant its path to Zion. And if I held faith as the brightest star in my firmament — and thus the easiest by which to chart my course — the universe would fall into order. Order, after all, means everything to a Shaker, and a Shaker is what I am.

But if we are to be sincere, then we know that we are not made for perfection. However we may try to fit the pattern, it pulls and bunches like a poorly sewn waistcoat and we exhaust ourselves with the fruitless smoothing of seams. I know something of this struggle, and now that I am old, I realize that my youthful presumptions about the way forward were based on a fundamental misunderstanding: I thought life was simple because I thought I was simple. On both counts, I was mistaken.

What I could not know was that, even in societies as steady as my own, life-changing tumult can be born of a single happening. And though, when first I heard of it, the event may have felt as unconnected to my daily existence as a sigh breathed in a distant land, it transpired that nothing would be the same after the day in August of 1837 when six young sisters received signs from the world beyond.

The communication took place in a settlement far from my own, after the resident schoolteacher had died of a sudden ague. My caretaker, Elder Sister Agnes, who had once lived and taught in the enclave, was summoned north while community elders searched for a permanent replacement. She was gone several months, and as she had been the one who raised me from birth, I missed her. I was barely ten years old at the time, and Elder Sister Agnes was the closest thing to a mother I had ever known.

A child will despise anything that deprives her of her beloved's attention, and I viewed the miracle of divine contact — for that is what it was — as an interloper and a thief. Once I had won my eldress back, I was determined to banish from my thoughts the cause of her absence. Perhaps that is why the import of what she had witnessed was lost on me until later. Certainly, I understand now how foolish the passions of a child truly are, how such willful blindness cannot last.

Yet, however little I allowed the remarkable day to mean to me at the time, the story threaded through and bound us all as believers, passing from community to community until there was no one who did not know of it. My

2

eldress told me the account herself as though it were a parable from the Bible whose lessons she had yet to discover. She glowed as she recalled even the smallest details of the wondrous day. How faint breezes blew the smell of tomato vines through the open windows and carried songs sung by the brethren as they brought in the last of the summer hay. How the girls in the schoolhouse — young as ten, old as fourteen — struggled with penmanship that day. How their ears rang with my eldress's exhortations to keep their letters evenly spaced, cleanly drawn, pure and unadorned as the beliefs we are taught to hold dear. I knew how the studious sisters must have felt, listless and hypnotized by the droning of flies in the late-afternoon heat, for I, too, was a schoolgirl.

From this most ordinary of scenes erupted an episode the likes of which had never before been experienced. For all of a sudden, as my eldress described it, the girls' fidgeting ceased — a moment of calm before the room rang with the sound of furniture scraping the wooden floor, a crash, the crack of a desk toppling, and then, once more, silence. Virgie Thompson, one day shy of her eleventh year, jumped to her feet and began to sway. What Virgie saw my eldress could not say, but her blue eyes were fixed hard on a point in the distance directly in front of her. She made no sound at first, yet her lips moved ceaselessly, forming strange syllables that seemed to stream from her mouth. Her hands fluttered and twitched by her side as her head cocked from shoulder to shoulder, quickening until her hair had loosed itself into a tangle and it seemed her thin neck might snap.

'Virgie?' my eldress asked. 'Are you all right, child?' The others were afraid to look, eyes glued to their careful writing. *Do All Your Work*, the lines read, *As Though It Were To Last 1,000 Years And You Were To Die Tomorrow*. I knew the saying well — indeed, I had copied it countless times myself. It was one of many left to us by our Beloved Mother Ann Lee — founder of all that we believe, equal in Heaven to the Lord Jesus Christ, sufferer at the savage hands of the World's people. Dead more than half a century at the time, Mother was yet as powerful from the beyond as she was when she walked this Earth, and my eldress had asked that the girls scratch her words over and over onto the pages before them, in the same blue-black ink with the same tidy hand.

The rattle of wood on wood, louder and louder as Virgie's feet trembled against the leg of her tumbled chair, filled the room. Her narrow hips began to jerk while her arms shook and went limp, sounds now issuing forth from her mouth full and loud. They began deep in her throat and recalled no utterance made by human voice, but rather a deep growling that rose to a moan and then to the high-pitched keening of an eagle, her eyes wild, expressions of bliss and terror, woe and relief passing across her features, my eldress said, like the flicker of shadows in candlelight.

'Virgie, come back, dear,' Elder Sister Agnes implored, kneeling before her, trying to stay her movements by enveloping the child in her arms. To regard a young believer so lost to the Spirit disturbed her. She had seen grown men lament their sins, weeping and rolling in the mud outside the meetinghouse. She had watched Brother Eleazer Howell get down on his hands and knees in mortification to lick the floor clean where he'd stood. She had heard Sister Thankful Brice confess, wail over wail, to the carnality of her previous life. Such gifts occurred during Meeting, and such passions were commonly made manifest only in the adults of the society. Yet there before her, little Virgie would not, could not, be still.

From another corner of the room came the sound of singing. A strange, warbling tune unlike any my eldress knew. Divinity Brown, meek and dark-haired, had assumed a pose of beatific serenity as song swelled forth in great balloons of melody. Some of the words were familiar. She spoke of Heaven, of honey and a golden light. She called again and again to Mother in choruses that sounded as though a full choir was singing, so richly and tunefully did her voice weave the verses.

But then Divinity tumbled into other noises, eerie yowls that made no earthly sense. She chanted with the deliberateness of a three-year-old, *O sari anti va me, o sari anti va me, vum vum vo, vum vum vo!* Twirling, stamping her feet, she danced faster and faster until her skirts whipped into a great bell-shaped billow from which her thin, youthful figure emerged like the knob on a child's top, spinning without cease.

5

The incantations, repeated then varied, seemed to swallow her body as she quickened the rhythms, and her broad smile made it appear as though her face were being twisted from inside as her nonsensical Latin verse continued to drum forth. *I co lo lo san ti rum, I co lo lo san ti rum. Vive vive vum vum vum. Vive vive vum vum vum!*

Elder Sister Agnes rose from her place at Virgie's side and did her best to stand calmly by, then walked to the front of the room with her head raised and her eyes focused upon the black-painted canvas chalkboard in an effort, she told me, to hide her face from view. Why had Mother chosen to bestow such gifts inside the orderly confines of her schoolroom? How wild the Spirit World! The young sisters were lost to it, and my eldress feared for where they might have gone. Compared with the languidness of the summer day, the din was indescribable, and by the time she had wiped her countenance clear of confusion, she heard yet another strange sound as a body thudded to the floor — ten-year-old Hannah Whithers writhing at her feet, the child's fingers clenched as though pleading. Holly Dearborn then erupted into a fit of the jerks, flopping about the room with her arms and legs as loose as a scarecrow's. Severe and solitary at fourteen, Adelaide Hatch fell to her knees, praying in feverish foreign tones. And finally, Bridey White, the lone girl to remain seated at her desk, commenced howling like a dog.

My eldress sat down and drew her hands into

prayer, lowering her head. The room resounded with the clamor of an asylum, but she resolved to wait and pray until the moment passed.

On their way back from the workhouses and barns, the settlement's sisters and brethren could hear the commotion inside the school. Later, my eldress said, they assembled around the stepping-stone in front of the gray-green door, sisters to one side, brethren to the other. The elders began to sing and pray as they listened until well after sunset to the noise from inside, and though it was said that the older believers spoke quietly of the event as a miracle, those who were newer to our kind wondered in hushed tones if something had gone terribly wrong.

As the moon rose and the night became heavy with the scent of sage from the drying racks inside the herb house, the girls began to quiet themselves. Elder Sister Agnes gathered them together, and one by one, her pupils emerged pale with exhaustion, shuffling along the stone path that led to the yellow clapboard dwelling house. No one spoke as they passed — indeed, all pulled back in awe. The sight of the students in such a stunned, blank state after so many hours of commotion gave the impression that they had traveled far, that while it was unto their souls alone that communications from the Spirit World had been bestowed, an important sign had fallen before all of the believers.

★　★　★

Word of the goings-on spread quickly, and it was said that Mother's hand had begun guiding other young sisters into similar states in settlements to the north and south. My eldress's charges may have been the first instruments chosen to carry news of the Second Awakening, but it was said that ministers traveling between the Eastern villages in the months following that day recorded many related stories in their journals. Not all of the happenings involved such dramatic display. A young sister in Hancock drew luminous trees on paper and inscribed in perfect hand their brightly colored leaves with poems of peace and love. Visionists — for that was the name given to Mother Ann's chosen instruments — were allowed to make things that were not simply functional but beautiful, for they had created them under divine inspiration. The rest of us worshipped as we always have, through the songs and dances we performed in Meeting, through our industry, and through our belief that — save for the Visionists — no one blade of grass stood taller than any other in the verdant fields of our faith. We knew that order was dependent on union, even in the face of heavenly chaos.

Elder Sister Agnes felt that the day she described marked the beginning of an extraordinary time, a time of great wonder. Why else would there have followed talk of renaming the settlements? Not Hancock, nor Tyringham, nor Watervliet any longer, but *The City of Peace, The City of Love, Wisdom's Valley*. Why else would the sacred rites have begun, each on designated hilltops near the Church Family

8

buildings? Why else would the elders in the largest of the villages have begun to forbid the attendance of Sunday visitors from the World to Sabbath Meetings, the better that our ecstasy might be expressed in private and seen only by those who could understand its meaning?

My eldress never forgot the miracle she watched unfolding in the souls of girls who, just hours before, were naught but little chatterers, a flock of tittering sparrows — just as common and without care. Still, it was several years before a Visionist came to The City of Hope. She appeared on a day that dawned as bleak and searingly cold as a metal blade left in the snow. And in such humble form. How could I have fathomed that her presence in our small, remote sanctuary — as unforeseen to her as to anyone — would change everything? At least, for me.

Polly Kimball

Ashland, Massachusetts
October 1842

She darns her father's socks without needing to watch her work. Just as well, for the kitchen is dim save for the light thrown by the old Argand lamp, a relic from her grandfather Benjamin Briggs's time, a better time, a time she never knew. She feels the rough wool, the stick of her wooden needles as she weaves a net from shore to shore of the gaping hole. On the floor beside her, the pile of clothes needing mending is as high as her waist, but there is this: When her father is gone, the house is peaceful, and she and her mother need never speak of him.

Even so, he will be home soon. In the gloom of late afternoon, Mama's face is melancholy and the blue of her eyes is that of a willow-painted plate, scrubbed too hard, too often.

'Ben,' she says to her young son playing with his bits of string and birch twigs by the fire. 'Pick up your things now, there's a lad. It's coming on time for supper and your father . . . ' She looks up with a doe's sense of impending danger as the door swings wide then bangs shut, the sweet apple smell of early fall gusting in from the orchard.

'Come 'ere!' Silas Kimball growls at the boy, dropping to his bony knees, pinning him to the floor. Silas thinks he is playing — cracked boots encrusted with manure from the cows and pigs, cold hands, beard smelling of cheese and whiskey.

'No holding me down!' Ben cries. 'No holding down!'

But though Silas leans harder on the boy — his skinny six-year-old frame laid low as a sheep for shearing — Ben manages to wriggle free and runs across the boards to hide in Mama's skirts.

'No better'n a runt hog, my son,' Polly's father says in disgust. 'Worthless half-wit.'

Polly hangs her head. *Whose fault is that?* she thinks, remembering the day she'd left Ben asleep in his cradle so that she could run and feed the milk cow before he woke. From the barn, she'd heard a scream and, bolting back towards the house, saw Silas holding the baby's head in a bucket full of water as Mama tried to wrench Ben from his father's slippery grasp. He'd wanted a son for years, one who could help him on the farm. But Mama's womb was weak and she had lost child after child until, by the time she finally managed to birth Ben, Silas had become so crazed with rage and the burden of never-ending debt that he saw the boy as naught but a drain, one he'd rather see dead than struggle to feed.

Whose fault is that? Polly would never forgive herself for letting Ben out of her sight. Though she had been but a nine-year-old girl at the time,

11

Mama had trusted her to take care of her new brother. And the water? It changed Ben. After that day, no matter how he might grow in other ways, he would never be more than a sweet, vulnerable child. Silas had tried to murder him, but it was Polly who'd failed to protect him. *Whose fault . . . ?*

After the outburst, all is quiet except for the rasping of her father's breath and the child's muffled sobs. Mama stirs the stew pot with Ben clinging to the skirt beneath her apron. Polly's needles click as she watches. She is always watching. Motes of dust dance in the grease-scented air, swirling as her mother moves around the room. They make a mockery of her, for Mama tends to her cooking and tidying as though she wishes not to disturb, as though she wishes not to be present at all, yet still the dust flurries about and makes a fuss.

Silas springs up and storms outside to drench his head beneath a gush of icy water drawn from the well. Polly can hear him hawking and spitting in the yard. How she despises him. He hasn't it in him to be kind, not for as long as Polly has known him. He consumes life, sucks it dry. She pictures him coughing up debris like an irritable barn owl, his pellets laced with tiny bones.

'Not a penny of credit left at the Dry Goods,' he says as he comes in from washing, his hair dripping, his troubles tumbling forth like rocks down a hillside. 'And here I am, thinking you and the girl been making bonnets while I work myself sick in the fields every day.' He takes a step closer, and though Mama will not look away from the supper she stirs, Polly can see her shoulders stiffen.

'What is it you do all day, tell me that.' His voice has become soft. 'Why, it's close on winter and I don't see the dairying done,' he says. 'I don't see the potatoes dug. I don't see nothin' but two whores and an idiot settin' by in my house.'

Then he turns on Ben and makes to kick at him, wanting Mama to look his way, knowing she would throw herself between harm and her boy in a minnow's twist. She twirls round and takes a step towards him, pushing Ben behind her. Polly puts down her mending and half raises herself.

'That's better,' Silas says, lifting his arm. 'You'll look to me when I talk, I'll learn you that much right now.' Polly sweeps in on her brother and pulls him to her, hiding his face as her father swings the back of his hand at Mama's head and smacks her so hard that she falls against the hot iron pot.

'That's for being lazy,' he says, brown gravy seeping up the bodice of Mama's faded green dress. He wallops her again. 'That's for being the child-whore I married. That were my biggest mistake. Tyin' myself down. And for what? A litter of runts? Hang from my belt like hairless possum pups, that's what you three do. But things are going to change now. You watch and see.'

He scans the darkening room. Polly wants him to look her way, to see the fury that burns inside her, but he will not. Her strength, she wants him

13

to feel it. But tonight, as on so many nights, all she can do is watch, watch and cover Ben's eyes and ears.

This night is different, she thinks. The feeling flashes through Polly's mind though she can't say why. Not an hour had passed since the boy's singsong voice had filled the kitchen. Now, Silas picks up the knife Mama uses to cut carrots and field onions and brandishes it like a child playing pirate.

'Another thing,' he says. 'Something I heard from a gentleman I been talking to. Something about wills and land being left to little girls. You know anything 'bout that?' He draws closer to Mama. 'Your papa weasel 'round me like that? Don't you lie. I never thought to be worried on it before now, but his talk got me wonderin'. Seems there's a fair number of boys left high and dry by their dead fathers. Wives' dead fathers, too.' He laughs. 'Seems a man isn't to be trusted no more. We *leave*.' He imitates a whiny complaint. 'We *drink*. We *got notes against us*. Better to pass everything on to you women, that's the story I heard.'

Beneath the anger, Polly senses a strange elation coursing through him, quickening his movements. Her heart pounds as she studies him. He is in debt to every saloonkeeper in town, but it's clear he's not been denied his fill at one or another of the taverns on this particular day.

He is an outcast. Who would have spotted him a belt or two? And there's the look in his eyes. They glisten with something close to glee. Usually, she can see the signs — she has learned

14

to take meaning from a clue as common as the sound of his boots on the step outside — but she does not know how to read him now.

'See, I care 'cause I been thinkin' I might like a little time on my own, sell this land — *my land* — set myself up pretty somewhere. Just like Mister Fancy Coat told me,' he says. 'Rest up without you and your waste. It wouldn't be so difficult to manage now, would it? Gettin' so's I could be alone, I mean. Things happen after all, am I wrong? Takin' sick, disappearings — like they say, twist of Fate.' He pushes Mama towards the table and lays down the knife. Even in the thin light of the lamp — its wick running low — the gleaming blade catches Polly's eye. *Mister Fancy Coat.*

'I seen whole families go,' Silas continues. Kicking Mama's feet out from under, he glares at her as she buckles to the floor and covers her head with her arms. 'Death come easy here,' he says. 'It's livin'. *That's* the struggle.'

He walks away, taps his hand over the tops of the cupboards in hopes of finding a forgotten bottle of cider; with his back turned, he cannot see Polly as she rises and guides Ben gently into her chair. She moves quickly and reaches out, her fingers barely grazing the cooking knife's handle before she pulls away and slips quickly back into her place. He has found his prize, uncorked it, and he guzzles the liquor as he turns back to face the room. 'Problem is, can't do much more than slap you up 'til I know what's mine,' he slurs, yawns. 'Tired now, that's what I am. But tomorrow? Tomorrow, we sort this out.

We make sure your daddy didn't leave me out of his prayers. We make sure — just like Mister Fancy Coat said — that you tell me the truth 'bout any dealings between you. Give me a nod,' he orders, kneeling to grab Mama's chin and shake her head up and down. 'Yes . . . that's right,' he says, still pulling at her. 'Yes, Silas.'

Silas stands unsteadily and looks at Polly, a queer smile hooking up one side of his mouth. 'Lucky for you I met up with this little friend,' he says, holding up the bottle, then pulling it to him like an infant as he shuffles across the kitchen floor. 'Lucky, too, that I'm in need of a lie-down.' One boot then another falls as he makes his way towards the room where he lies with Mama every night. 'There's always a tomorrow, ain't there? Can't count on much, but that's for certain.'

Polly hears him tumble into bed.

⋆　⋆　⋆

She knows the stories about her father's kin. His parents had been born of a bad lot — just two of a hundred ruffians, townspeople said, all descended from one drunk Dutchman up by the New York Lakes. He was — would always be — Silas Kimball, the son of stoop-backed, black-toothed marginals. Smelling like smoke and animal fat, mongrel skins for warmth, teeth ground down to nubs: talk had it that the three of them appeared as savages when they walked the path to town in need of a trade. His mother made dolls tied from sticks and corn silk and tried to barter them for food and cider, but the

16

figures scared people with their haunting look and she couldn't raise much. When Silas came, she bound him to her with hemp cord and fed him in plain view, not a thought given that she was baring herself for all the town to see. Wild as skunk cabbage, living in a makeshift shack in the woods, stealing from the fields of nearby farms — in most people's opinion, as Polly heard it, the Kimballs were barely human.

Benjamin Briggs, Polly's grandfather from Mama's side, had been different. Wealthy, they said, an educated merchant and gentleman farmer come out from Hartford. But he couldn't work alone the land he had tamed and there was no help to be found in town that wasn't already at labor in the fields. So it came to pass that when young Silas showed up at his door — not long after the boy's parents went missing — Polly's grandfather gave him work and a roof over his head. Whether the vagrants were dead or just set to scrabbling in some other place, no one knew. But with them gone, Silas walked into a brighter future than ever he could have imagined. Or so it might have been.

Mama was ten-year-old May Briggs then, the sole kin left to a man widowed and mourning a wife and son lost in childbirth. Polly imagined her as a girl struggling to fill a woman's shoes and a man's empty heart, a child depended on for tending to everything from chores in the house and barn to minding the count. It was only right that if her father saw fit to take in this strange new boy, May should strive to make him feel welcome. It was surely what her own mother

17

would have done, wasn't it? So she fed Silas and taught him how to care for the chickens and find the eggs they'd hidden in the yard; how to milk the cows with a gentle pull-and-squeeze so as not to get kicked and have the pail knocked dry; how to speak so people could understand him and stop thinking of him as half-boy, half-animal. She did this for her father, that he might have one less thing to trouble over.

Polly never understood how such simple lessons could have led where they did. How the townsfolk could have whispered that young May Briggs broke her father's heart when she married Silas in secret at thirteen. How a farmer as careful as Benjamin Briggs, with a barn tight and new, could have gotten himself killed by a falling loose beam. How, according to gossip, someone had to have worked the joint. How there was but one person who'd want such a decent man dead.

Silas. They say he'd grown to hate Benjamin Briggs as dreams of owning the farm himself began to fill his head. He assumed, by all rights, that the land would go to him if he married May. He didn't know about law. He figured property just passed from man to man, as it always had, so he'd good reason to want Benjamin Briggs dead. Still, no one could say for sure what really happened. 'Accidents' are like that. Plenty of suspicion, no investigation, case closed.

May was only a girl when Benjamin Briggs died — married to a boy just two years her senior, pregnant with his child, alone in a life that must have seemed turned on its head. And though Polly had asked in every way she could

18

figure how it came to be that such a strange incident stole her grandfather from her, Mama would never say. Just stared, frightened-like, then turned away. Fact was, Polly had seen the back of her mother so many times that she had begun to think it was *she* who'd cursed the farm, for she was the seed Mama carried when everything went wrong.

★   ★   ★

She feels his weight in her dreams. So many nights, his acrid stink has covered her — blocking out her senses, taking her from the world she can see and hear and feel. His flesh is cold, his black hair prickly; he is sure and quiet. She does not scream or fight. As he pins her arms over her head with one hand, she looks beyond him. She hears a babble of voices over his chuffing. She accepts a thousand kindnesses raining down upon her from a crack in the ceiling. His beard scratches her cheek and her ear is filled with the wet roar of his breath. Still, her mind rises to pass throngs of angels misting round her like whirling clouds. They spin. They call out. How they dance across the night sky. Though his thighs bear down on her, she will not be restrained. She cannot breathe or move, and yet, as she takes leave of the angels and travels miles and miles from the heavens, she imagines she is running through a field of wildflowers, her arms spread wide and her face turned to the sun. She is vanishing beneath him, dividing into twin spirits that join hands as they fly far away.

This is what nighttime feels like: an odd cleaving of body and soul as she goes where he cannot follow. But she is lonely and imagines herself walking, elbows brushing, with a friend. She conjures the sound of chatter and nonsense song. She will sing and dance the sun to its cradle. She will talk with the wisdom of an old towering oak. Her fingers will shimmer the air like leaves. She longs to tremble free of this dirty life. She is fifteen.

Quiet Polly, seated by the fire with her long straight frame carried high, awake now, her gaze steady. She thinks of the daylight hours. Day upon day, after coming home from helping Miss Laurel at the schoolhouse, she says little, save to offer assistance when the chore is too hard or heavy for her mother to carry out alone. Together, they fill the washing tub and carry pails of milk from the barn. Together they slop the pigs, toss grain to the chickens, fork hay into the manger. Seeing sweat at her mother's brow as she churns the butter, the blue-gray circles that color the loose skin beneath her eyes, Polly takes the old dash from her callused hands and recommences the slow, resistant work. Ben is the doll both of them dress and feed. He smiles, laughs, sings, and his noise is a language from another land.

How she would like her father gone. The fire snaps. Her ears ring with the memory of Ben's cries. She wants to hold the boy tight to her always — as if they could be one — but in her gut her hate glows like coals. How she would like her father gone.

Sister Charity

The City of Hope
Albion, Massachusetts
October 1842

I have never answered to a name from the World.
I am Sister Charity and thus have I grown up in
The City of Hope, setting down roots so deep in
our soil that my sisters and brethren imagine me
to be a tree of great strength. We are 118 all told,
and I know something of most everyone
— apart, of course, from the leering hired men
who come from the World to help at harvest time
and the stragglers who arrive with the bad
weather and leave with the good, those we call
'winter Shakers.' I did not arrive in childhood,
like the orphans who come by the wagonload
when one of our ministers buys their freedom
from a home. Nor am I like the children whose
mothers and fathers are alive and, not wishing to
become believers themselves, abandon their
young and must be flushed from our midst like
crows from a cornfield. Though I am barely
fifteen years old, I can shoulder the burdens and
responsibilities of a believer twice my age. For I
am different, and therein lies my gift.

I say this not because I think myself to be
above my sisters — certainly not now, given my

21

affliction. But I was delivered as an infant, less than a month old — left without kin on a stone step at one of the entrances to the meetinghouse. I never knew a relation of the flesh. It is my Shaker sisters who have informed every thought, every action, every skill I possess. Thus, besides my regular chores and the duties I perform preparing curatives in the healing room, I am often called to the aid of the Elder Brothers and Sisters of the Gathering Order and trusted to care for new girls without overly indulging their anguish. It falls to me to wash and cut their hair and pull their dresses — tatty or fine — over their heads in exchange for a simple striped blue cotton frock in summer, a brown woolen one in winter. It is my duty to unlatch lockets from around their necks and pry beloved dolls from their clutches, for no such vanity or plaything from the World is allowed by our kind. This may seem hard-hearted but I ask: What good does it do a girl to hold on to a heart-shaped keepsake of her flesh parents who must, by our covenant, be banished from her thoughts? And what joy is it to play at mothering a doll when, as well by our covenant, she can never in her life with us experience such a bond?

As to my mothering, it would have been truer to our way for me to have been raised by all the sisters present at the time of my appearance — fed by some, bathed by others, soothed and clothed and learned by more of our number still — but because I was an infant I was placed in the care of a single believer. Thus it came to be that my upbringing was entrusted to Sister

Agnes — as she was known in those early years — a believer held in great esteem by everyone in our settlement.

A glance at my caretaker — she is *Elder* Sister Agnes now — would not reveal the tenderness she allowed herself to visit upon me when I was young. Her blue eyes shine hard and are quick to spot clumsiness and an idle hand. And though she is far from aged, she combs back her graying hair in a tight bun and creases her brow such that it seems permanently set into an expression of disapproval. Who could imagine her chafed red hands caressing my baby cheek, or her upright bearing crouched low behind a cupboard in a game of hide-and-seek?

Yet in the privacy of our rooms, she sometimes sang and bounced me on her lap with the devotion a flesh mother might have shown a beloved son or daughter. She was patient as she taught me to dance our dances and sing our songs, the better that I might worship well in weekly Meeting. When I was older, she told me stories about the first Visionists, wishing that I might someday witness the miracle of Mother Ann's chosen instruments for myself. Of course, I do not know what she truly thought of me, nor what she might feel about me now. And, to be sure, for every one moment of intimacy there were ten, twenty, one hundred when she appeared driven only to raise me up as a dedicated believer. I was the chore assigned to her.

I suppose that when one knows nothing of one's origins or whether a soul on this Earth truly cares, it is natural to scavenge what love one can find — watching, waiting, always on guard for the dropped morsel. I read and read again the hearts of those around me and so find sustenance in the more generous aspects of their natures. That is how I have come to know that there exists a softness beneath the hard attitude my caretaker presents. She can indeed be formidable, but she is not so dissimilar from the many others in our settlement who carry secret wounds. Often as not, those who find this place seek it out for the balm of its routines, the haven a life of unquestioning worship can provide.

In near twenty years of service to Mother Ann, Elder Sister Agnes has become perhaps the most well-regarded sister ever chosen to oversee those of us who find their calling in The City of Hope. She did not always reside here, having first made herself known in the place we now call Wisdom's Valley. A young bride, bruised and rejected by all of her kin — she told me about her past. When she was sixteen, she married the only boy she'd ever known — a farmer's son from down the road. They were happy at first — as a steadfast Shaker, she had difficulty admitting it, but it was the truth and my eldress does not lie. Time passed and her husband inherited his father's farm. He needed children, he told her; she'd best get on with birthing them. Elder Sister Agnes tried to give him what he wanted, but her body forced out the fruit of his seed the way winter's frost heaves up stones from a field. She could bear him nothing but misery so he began to hit her. It didn't matter to him that her milk money kept the farm going. It didn't matter that the yards of palm bonnet trim she braided bought them food and fuel and grain all the year long. What mattered to him was that she could not give him a child.

I cannot recall what prompted my eldress to tell me all this. I can only think that she did so because some sadness in me reminded her of her own difficulties. I have never been a popular sister. Respected and favored by the more senior members of the community, I enjoy a position that is unique. But such good standing comes at a cost, rendering me the object of jealousy among the younger sisters. The snubs have always been small. Taking my place at the dining table, I feel the sting when the sister next to me turns purposefully — if by minuscule degree — away from me. Picking up my knitting, I am jostled so that the skein falls to the floor and I am left to scramble after its unspooling yarn. There are whispers and sudden silences when I enter the schoolroom. I am that strangest of creatures: a celebrated outsider.

My eldress is not blind to my troubles. Especially when I was young, she wanted me to know that cruelty can be overcome. She said that she ran from her husband only to find that every neighbor's door was closed to her. She sought shelter from her mother and father only to find that they, having thought themselves rid of a costly mouth to feed, would have nothing to do with her.

'Do you see how threadbare is the family tie?' she asked me, for no story was worth telling

25

unless it had a lesson to teach. 'I had heard of other women who'd gone over to our kind. At least there would be food and a roof over my head. At least I would be safe.'

When she shuffled, cold and battered, into the village of Watervliet — it was known by its World name then — she had little idea of the refuge she would find. The Shakers welcomed her. They fed her, dressed her welts and gashes, gave her clothes to wear and a bed to sleep in. Then, most glorious of all, they offered her confession, and when she was done, they made her to understand that her barrenness was a gift, that to bear children — to engage in carnality of any kind — was the utmost sin. They took the thing she most despised in herself and made it her salvation.

In these later years, Elder Sister Agnes has won admiration not by virtue of her warmth or humor but rather by her devotion. She demands that her charges strive to mirror her zeal, and her expectations of me in particular amount to nothing less than that I should follow in her footsteps and become a prominent eldress — with Mother's blessing of course. To this end, she taught me our work long before I was of the age most sisters have attained when first they come to live with us. I was barely as tall as the back of one of our chairs before I learned to spin the swift and wind our newly dyed yarns into skeins. Standing high on a stool, I washed pot after pot in the kitchens and, in the dairy, strained cheese enough to feed an army. The brethren made me a tiny ironing board so that I

26

could labor at my eldress's side in the laundry, pressing handkerchiefs and napkins. In spring, summer, and early fall, I followed along as the older sisters collected herbs and flowers from the fields into white tow sheets for drying — only one specimen each day, lest the plants be mingled by mistake and cause a fatal error in the mixing of remedies. In a game devised to teach me the work I now perform so well, I chanted the names of the leaves, buds, and tree barks, matching them with the curatives they would become. 'Touch-me-not, lady's slipper, wild hyssop,' I sang. 'Dropsy, nervous headache, worms.'

One could imagine that I was young for such toil but I never felt it to be so. The chores I performed made me a stronger believer. That, over all things, is what I desired. Purity. Industry. Chastity. Faith. Kindness. Union. Elder Sister Agnes may have been stern in her teachings but she was never unkind. Indeed, I do not think that she was capable of such behavior towards me. For though I would never discuss the matter openly, my arrival brought with it the mantle of motherhood as much as it did the opportunity to fashion a perfect Shaker. I was a gift to her. I was her gift to them.

I knew myself to be fortunate in this regard, for on occasion, I saw cruelty operated upon my younger sisters by those who should have known better — older believers who came to us with twisted hearts, believers in name only, whose souls had already been too much infected by the evils of the World. One such history has lodged in my memory. A sickly sister named Clarissa — she had attained perhaps twenty-four years in age — took into her charge a young novitiate answering to the World name of Daisy. The child, an orphan, had come from privileged circumstances and bore all the marks of an easy life. She was well fed and clean, and Sister Clarissa — who had never before known luxury — often warmed her cold hands by thrusting them down the back of Sister Daisy's dress, and sat across from her on bitter winter evenings with her feet buried beneath the child's skirts, resting them in the heat of the young girl's generous lap. As Sister Clarissa became increasingly ill — her eyes burning feverishly bright and her skin taking on an unruly flush — the meaner corners of her soul revealed themselves and her charge bore the brunt.

One day, she took up young Daisy's hand. 'Such a plump little bun!' she exclaimed. 'I wonder what are its juices?' A pair of scissors lay nearby, and snatching them up, she pressed the sharp edge against the child's skin and forced a crimson line of blood. It was shocking to behold, yet as Daisy was brave and thought this to be a test of her nature, she neither flinched nor complained, and I remember thinking well of her for it.

Not so Sister Clarissa. 'Silly little toad!' she cried. 'Did I not affect you?' Daisy remained silent, peering into the livid face of her caretaker. I left in search of Elder Sister Agnes, who came upon the scene soon enough and reprimanded the sickly one sharply. Nothing more was said.

Indeed, Sister Clarissa died of her illness soon thereafter and the believers excused her strange behavior as nothing more than an unfortunate symptom. Thus was her passing noted with due respect, though it was generally felt that in death she had entered a realm better able to bear with her singularities.

I speak of this only because there are times when the deep goodness of believers is fragile as the wing of a damselfly. Sister Clarissa was damaged before her arrival in our midst. I, on the other hand, have felt neither spiritual nor material hardship in my life, and so I count it as my work to accept and forgive. I see that every day, we give and work and worship, humbling ourselves through deep and heartfelt bows before the eternal spirits we encounter in Meeting. All of this we do to subdue our carnal natures, to conquer that which is the inevitable result of time spent living alongside the filth of the World, to create a second Heaven here on Earth. Not every soul can withstand such sacrifice.

★ ★ ★

It does me little good, however, to idle in the past — especially when I am faced with such troubles as plague me at present. Last week, as I was washing, the first blossoming bared itself, curled into a pink, fern-shaped welt over the ribs on my left side. As I have never known such decoration — no believer had ever come to me in the healing room and asked me to erase her skin — the sight surprised me. With the passing of every hour, the whorls became redder and soon covered my stomach and the tops of my legs. When finally they reached up my neck and over my high collar, I could hide them no longer.

They frightened me — they were so clearly Other. I could find no name for the condition, no mention of it in the medical journals we have kept for decades. I tried to calm the lesions myself, smoothing pastes fashioned from the pounded leaves of figwort and sheep sorrel. I wished my white skin to return, but the sores would not leave and they have since become angrier — strange paisley forms swirling about without reason. Indeed, not long after they made their appearance, young Sister Columbine screamed at the sight of a perfect sample snaking across my hand and told our Elder Sister Agnes that I had been visited by the Devil. Such a thought did not please my eldress and her orders were sharp.

I wonder what it is that disturbs her more: the hideousness of my infection or the evil of the power that has so defaced me. Can it be the contrast I present to the miracles that seem to have blessed so many of our neighboring settlements? It is the time of the Visionists after all, and though we have yet to welcome one here in The City of Hope, their songs, dances, even the strange drawings they pen — are known to us all. Whatever the explanation for my eldress's disgust, she has separated me from my sisters and confined me to the healing room for a time uncertain in length. I have never resided in the place where I spend so many hours curing others. I wonder, *Who will tend to me?*

The answer was not long in coming. When I had been quarantined for three days, Elder Sister Agnes paid me a visit. She found me alone, for no sister dared rest in my presence. Even my meals were left outside the door, my dinner bell a sharp knock followed by a scurry of footsteps down the hall. I rested in a long, narrow cradle bed, its slanted wooden sides up close against my arms. I lay as if already inside my coffin. I may have been learned for my age, but I found burgeoning womanhood to be a trial and had already suffered many humiliations of the flesh. How I longed for a simpler time, beating my very breasts to push them back inside me! Now, to add to my shame, the Devil wrote upon my skin when it pleased him and I felt despair descend more heavily upon me with every passing day.

Elder Sister Agnes has come to help me, I thought. *She has faith enough for the both of us. Can her goodness prevail where mine has failed? Has she come to drive evil from my being? Does she stand before me because she alone believes in my virtue?* She looked barely a moment at me before she spoke.

'You cannot know it,' she said, straightening the bottles of tinctures already in perfect alignment along each shelf. 'But in the days since you have been ill, I have spent many a beseeching hour in prayer. I find myself full of wretched self-doubt, for surely I have erred in my teachings. Why else would you have been possessed in such a manner?'

She came closer. 'If *this*,' she said, pointing at

my mottled skin, 'be a sign of evil within you, then how can I not bear the blame? *I* raised you. Your faith has grown from the seeds *I* planted. If your goodness be false and rotten, then how can my own be true?'

I saw tears falling down her cheeks before she spun quickly away, drying them on a corner of her apron then breathing out as she set straight her shoulders. I had never seen her cry and it twisted my heart to know that I was the cause of her sadness and thus could not comfort her. She turned once more to look at me.

'It shall be my baptism to cleanse you myself,' she said. 'I will not be afraid of whatever it is that afflicts you. I will not lose you to the Devil just as I will not lose myself.'

Listening to her make twins of our miseries, I felt sure she could cure me. I did not understand what she meant to do, for I had tried everything I could think of and still the markings left their stain. But I did not question it when she asked me to rise from my sickbed and remove first my apron, neckerchief, and white linen cap, then my collar and my worsted dress, then my winter petticoat, my knit stockings, and, finally, my chemise so that I stood naked before her. And though I wept for the shame of it — while in my sickbed, I had lain fully dressed until the tolling of the night bell told me that my brethren and sisters were readying themselves for bed — she did not look away or attempt to assuage my humiliation. Quite the opposite, for my condition caused her to gasp. Winding across my body, the sinister loops and fronds were frightening

— in their strangeness of course, but also in their beauty, for they looked painted upon me with a most delicate, if determined, hand.

She pointed to a table on which she had placed two sheets and directed me to lie between them. I concealed myself gladly. With a strange silver tool she looked long into my eyes, my ears, my throat for signs of the Devil's presence. I imagined she might glimpse wicked spirits in the cavities of my flesh like maggots in a corpse. I feared she might speckle me with leeches or try to cup and blister the bad out from under my skin, but I needn't have worried. Instead, with the sheet still covering me, she ran her hands down the length of each of my arms and legs, first in stroking movements then clenching and unclenching as though she were molding me out of clay. She pressed her fingers round my stomach and tapped along my ribs as I have seen the brethren do along a bend of wood when they wish to make certain their work is sound. Then, in a motion that I found most difficult to endure, she bent her head to my narrow chest and laid her ear upon my bosom.

If Elder Sister Agnes did not scare the Devil, then she succeeded in scaring me. I could hear her breath — it came in short exhalations — and I felt its warmth blow over my ribs and stomach as tears ran down the sides of my face and wetted the sheet beneath my head. At length, a sob choked forth from within me and she rose with a look of some confusion. It was as though I had awoken her from a dream and she moved quickly away, walking the length of the healing room, lost in thought. Such was her intensity that I imagined she had found the Devil after all, that he lurked somewhere deep within me, beyond the reach of even so devout a believer. Certain now that I would be sent away, alone for the rest of my days never to see The City of Hope again, I began to cry.

Elder Sister Agnes approached me once more. Placing her hands in the clefts where my arms met my chest, she lifted me to sitting. I could not stop my sobbing — it came out in great hiccups — but she was tender now and careful not to let the sheet fall from my body as she perched herself on the edge of the table and wrapped her arms around me. I had not been held like this for many a year and the shock of it stopped my crying more quickly than if a hand had covered my mouth and nose and I had ceased to breathe. She held me and rubbed my head, ran her palm down my back over my long hair, which I had loosened the better for her to pore over the all of me. I sensed I was melting from the warmth that flooded my insides and I wondered if this was goodness spreading through me, fighting back the Devil and his evil hand.

I held fast to my eldress when I felt her begin to pull away from our embrace. I wanted to make last the glow that had enveloped me when she took me in her arms. But she had remedies to prepare, and as I listened to the slop of water from a nearby bucket, I searched within that I might replace my need with Mother Ann's presence. I prayed silently that one as faithful and true as Elder Sister Agnes could rid me of my cross. From what I knew of the circumstances surrounding her own mortification, I imagined that one who holds so fast to perfection would have found it difficult to confess her sins and thus purge them from her soul. Only a trial similar in hardship could rid me of my markings, but I felt ready.

I remember mostly the sharp stubble of the brush as she passed it round and round, circling over my body until the prickling scream of my skin faded into numbness. When she had scoured near every inch of me, she left without a word and I slept. I had held myself tightly for days and now, to feel the sting of the brush's bristles was to believe that I had been cleansed of all signs of the Devil. In my dreams, I thought I saw straight through to Elder Sister Agnes's sad heart, for surely she could not have hurt me so much without suffering herself.

I awoke alone in sheets that were stippled with blood. Rising from the table, I pulled the covering away but it clung to my wounds as though armored with the hooked thorns of spring meadow rose. My reflection in the looking glass stared hazily back at me and I felt I might faint, for beneath the angry red rings made by Elder Sister Agnes's brush, the markings decorated me still. In the flickering of the candle I viewed my naked self, unhealed and stamped with whirls of paisley that appeared golden in the dancing flame. They dared me to find the good in Mother Ann's strange teaching. They dared me to see that She — The Woman Clothed With The Sun — had allowed the Devil into my soul as a test of my devotion and that I could prove myself only by carrying the burden bravely. I understood then, as I blew out the candle and stood in darkness, that to attempt to deny my cross, to crawl out from under the weight of it, was only to render it heavier still.

Polly

It had been but a few hours since her father had threatened them. Had he come at Mama with a shovel? Crept in and dropped a fieldstone so close to Ben as he sat on the floor that his fingers had near been crushed? Was this the night he'd swiped at them all with a broken bottle and left a gash the length of a hare's ear on Mama's arm? Polly often found it difficult to separate his rages one from the next.

But as bad as those times were, this night frightened Polly more. *Mister Fancy Coat*, her father's strange elation, his sudden suspicions . . . *Things are going to change*, she thought. Her father had a plan, she was sure of it. He'd as good as spelled it out: rid the farm of the three of them, then sell it. *Death come easy here*, he'd said, and Polly knew he was right.

Why, when she thought on it now, she had seen Silas leaning on a gatepost not so very long ago, talking to an odd-looking man who was all puffed up and dressed in frilly city clothes. *Mister Fancy Coat*: a mill agent sure as she was a drunkard's daughter. She'd watched her father point towards the fast-running river that poured down the wooded hillside — the only forest of white pine, chestnut, ash, oak, and sugar trees for miles around. The water emptied out into a cold, clear pond at the other end of which a dam quickened the flow once more before it slowed to a meander and lost itself in distant fields.

Polly imagined the future. Close to the Post Road and surrounded by land well suited to the slow birth of a working town, their farm was the perfect site for a paper or textile mill. She remembered seeing the stranger nod and clap Silas on the back, his coattails whipping in the wind like the trappings of a well-dressed scarecrow. *Mister Fancy Coat*. He was no farmer.

Once a welcoming place, now, like stink round pigs, her family's farm echoed only the poor, dirty lives of those it sheltered. The house her grandfather Briggs left behind had long passed into another world. His fine parlor might have been filled with company if ever Polly's mother and father had visitors. But with no one venturing out their way, the silent space felt to her like a trinket shop full of bric-a-brac from a past life. The odd setting of pretty china, a brass compass, her grandfather's books, many of them moved up into the attic as much to stop cold from seeping through the cracks as to keep Silas from using the volumes for kindling. These were the things she studied when there was a moment's peace, the few objects her mother had managed to save from the happier days of her childhood.

Grandfather Briggs's snake-rail fences were still standing, though there were gaps where wooden posts had fallen and never been set right, and along the tracks he made neat, milkweed and juniper had staked their claim. Except in the plots where Silas planted his weed-choked crops, Nature had begun to take back the land, and everywhere, even inside the little house, Polly sensed the encroaching wildness. Her father struggled behind the seasons as he did his plow: It was all he could do to sow corn and alfalfa soon enough after the long winter to replenish their stores and keep the animals fed. When he drank too much and forgot to read the skies, whole pastures of cut hay lay to rot in the drenching summer rains. And though he knew enough to let his fields go fallow from time to time, he grew impatient with thinking about what had been sown where, planting the earth over and over until he had laid waste its soil and was left with nothing but stunted stalks and patchy grass that refused, in spite of his fury, to grow full. He exhausted Nature as he exhausted everyone else.

The farm was overgrown or empty; there was no between. Polly's bedroom — where, as a child, her mother had nestled under soft covers each night — was now a cold, barren space beneath the eaves where she and Ben slept on narrow pallets full of night-biters and ancient barley straw. In the great room just below, Silas and her mother shared a bed and a beaten old wardrobe, little more. Piece by piece, they had sold off most of Mama's furniture and possessions, and what was left — save for the treasure in the parlor — was crude, overused, and out of date, made largely from worn wood, threadbare cloth, and old straw.

Some things, of course, changed little with time and circumstance, like the heavy old cooking pots and the gun above the door and the blades, scoops, and prongs of the farming tools her father left leaning against the gray clapboards. But Polly knew that her house had lived two lives. All summer long, it weathered and opened to the warming sun. Now, buffeted by cold winds and surrounded by a glittering frost every morning, it seemed to shrink against the coming winter, and Polly felt the beams bracing themselves, as did she.

Shaking her head free from thoughts of the past, she snapped to and stared about, unsure of what to do. Slowly, it came to her. Silas would be the death of them, whether tomorrow or the next day. Poor enough, drunk enough, greedy enough, mean enough — he was a poison fruit grown ripe. Silas would be the death of them. She knew it.

Mama did, too, but then, she always had. She'd lived so long with the shame of being helpless, she would never raise a hand to him now. She'd seen what he was capable of, understood that the hitting and the screaming and the visits in the night — they were not the worst of what Silas had in him. Polly let out a long-held breath and closed her eyes. She wished it was different, wished there was someone she could turn to. But he'd beaten them all. All, save one.

She rose and walked out of the house into the

40

night air. Inside the barn, whispering soothing words to calm the startled animals, she felt her way through the darkness, tapping her hand along the sides of the wooden pens and unbolting the gates as she went. There was little more she could do for the weary beasts. She hadn't time to flush them out and it would be noisy, besides. She could only hope they'd take their chance at freedom when the time came. In a stall at the back, the old bay nickered as Polly reached out to stroke his velvet nose. He might have been a fine horse, had he been allowed — as Benjamin Briggs intended — to be raised for young May to ride about town. But Polly's grandfather Briggs died just a few weeks after buying the colt, and so Silas whipped him into plowing stony pastures just as soon as the animal could budge the blade. Were it not for May's taking trouble in secret to dress his lash marks, blanket him in winter, and feed him warm gruel when his lungs rattled, he'd barely have lived out his first year. Were he not Silas's only horse, he'd have been given his rest long before now.

Even so, with May in particular, the bay was gentle and loyal. More than once, Polly had seen him prick up his ears and run back and forth along the paddock fence, snorting and whinnying whenever he heard Silas yelling. He was May's horse — just as Benjamin Briggs had meant for him to be — and he seemed to know that if they were to survive the curse they shared, they would need to watch out for each other.

'Quiet now,' Polly whispered into his ear. 'You'll let me harness you up easy, all right?'

41

Groping for the leather bridle, the collar, and the breeching, taking each from its hook, she laid the pieces across the horse's dark, sleek body and fastened them round. Then she backed him out from his stall and led him to the wagon. In no time, she had the traces hitched, the bit loosened, and the horse muzzled, half his handsome face immersed in a feed bag.

'There, boy,' Polly said as she patted his warm neck. 'I'll be back soon enough.'

In the house, she moved about surely and softly, gathering clothing, bedcovers, anything she could pile into her arms and carry out to the wagon. There was some brown bread and hard cheese on a shelf in the kitchen. She wrapped them in a piece of cloth alongside a few apples and stuffed the food into a basket. Then she took it outside, packed it, and tried to imagine if there was anything she had missed. Walking slowly back to the kitchen, she counted out the tasks that lay before her. She would collect Ben, wake her mother from where she slumbered in the rocker by the fire, give her a moment to bid farewell to the place where she'd grown up. Then . . . the horse, the wagon, the road out. Her head spun just trying to keep up with a future she could not begin to envision, and she took a deep breath to steady her nerves before walking through the door.

Moments later, Polly was ready. 'Mama,' she said, touching her lightly. Dressed in a heavy shawl with Ben asleep over her shoulder, Polly stood beside her mother holding the old lamp, her wrist aching under the weight of its wooden base and etched-glass shade. Mama opened her eyes and cried out with a start.

'Hush,' Polly said, putting a finger to her lips. 'Bring your things and come silent.' Mama nodded. Nothing more needed to be said. She seemed to understand that Polly was leading them away.

Keeping the light low, Polly watched her mother rise, ready herself, and move soundlessly into the parlor. She walked past the shelves, running her fingers lightly over pictures, bowls, a locked wooden box — objects so fiercely kept it was as though they existed under some sort of a protective charm. Dusted free of grease and ash, even in the most desperate times, they had never been sold for food or clothing. *They remind Mama that she was loved*, Polly thought. *I remind her that she was beaten and forced.* How she wished she could be an easier souvenir.

She watched as Mama reached the far corner of the room, hesitating before she bent down quick and slipped her hand into a gap between an old cupboard and the wall. From it she pulled a thin envelope and tucked it into the folds of her dress. Then she continued her silent tally of all that had bound her to this place — the house given form by her father's hands, the kitchen where she had lost so much life. Shadows flickered dimly on the walls. It was, Polly thought as she opened the door, as if Mama were already a ghost in this place.

'Take Ben,' she said, struggling on the threshold with the lamp and the shawl and the sleeping child, near to dropping them all. 'Take

43

him to the wagon and wait.' As Mama embraced the boy's warm bundle, Polly slid her arm gently out from under and clutched the lamp with two hands.

'It's all right, Mama,' she said. Standing in the bracing cold under a bright curl of moon, every inch of her existed for one sole purpose: to save her mother, her brother, and herself. But there was something else she had to do. 'Stay,' she said, pushing them towards the wagon and turning to run back into the house.

She passed through the kitchen and towards the room in which her father lay sleeping. In the doorway, she stopped, shielded the lamp's dim light with her hand, and breathed deeply. Why had she come back inside? She approached his bed. She had never seen him like this, so vulnerable. She could do anything in this moment. She realized, staring down at his ravaged face, that he was hers. She squinted hard. He had once been a child. His cheek had been smooth and soft. His pudgy fingers had struggled to pick up acorns just as Ben's had. How could he have turned so mean? Her hands shook around the base of the Argand.

Though there was no time to stand by his side a moment longer, she found herself rooted to the spot. The heat and smell of the lamp made her dizzy. Would she be able to keep Mama and Ben safe? Surely such a man would track them down. Not because he loved them or would miss them, but because he wanted to own them as much as he did the dilapidated farm. He would hunt them if only to prove that much. Her eyes

44

traveled the length of him, down the buttons of his ragged blue shirt, over stains on his soiled work pants, tallying his gnarled, yellow-nailed toes. To stare at him without fear was to see his power drained away. How easy it was to feel nothing. Her mind cleared, its thoughts unfolding logically with each steadying breath.

Suddenly he coughed, bolting up wild-eyed to stare at her a moment before falling back on the bed. Polly jumped, stifling a scream with one hand as the lamp slid from the other. It fell, her father flopping onto his side away from her, asleep again in the silence before the crash. The sound of breaking glass was all she could hear as flames rose up in a roar from the puddle of spilled oil. *Death come easy*, said a voice inside her head, her body frozen until the time for doubting had passed.

She turned and scrambled through the house and across the yard to where Mama and Ben were waiting. She heard Mama gasp; the horse shifted and tossed his head so violently that Polly had a time of it loosening the feed bag and untying the reins. She looked back towards the barn, where she could hear the animals panicking at the smell of smoke. She wanted to help them. *Run!* she screamed in her mind, hoisting herself atop the driver's bench and slapping the leather reins over the old bay's back. The cart jerked into motion. There was nothing more she could do.

She prayed the blaze would fade once it had consumed her father, but a single glance told her she'd lit more than a funeral pyre. How quickly the past is made gone. Fire roared up through the windows, the inferno wrapping round the house as she drove away. In the fury of flames Polly could see the blackness of her father's gaze just as she could feel the force of his will in the suck of their heat. She could find in her heart no space for pity.

Later, there would be time for them to decide what to do. Perhaps there would be mill work in one of the bigger towns, for the noisy factories seemed hungry for young women like herself, girls with nimble hands and sharp eyes. Mama might be able to find employment as a domestic, once she became well again. Polly shook off the hope that they would encounter much in the way of charity. If life had taught her anything it was that trusting Fate to human kindness was like leaning on the wind.

With the turning of the cart track just ahead, she allowed herself to look back once more. The fire was hypnotizing, but then . . . Were her eyes playing tricks? Though she could not be sure, she thought she saw a smaller blaze spat from the larger, moving, running, falling to the ground and rolling over and over, then up and running again. She closed her eyes against the thought, for surely it was a mere twist of the mind. The flames had been too hot. Not even a man possessed of such evil as her father could have survived. Could he?

She faced forward and concentrated on the road ahead. The horse was blowing hard, breath steaming from his chocolate-colored nostrils; every so often when he turned his head at the sound of dry leaves whispering in the trees, he revealed the whites of his eyes and a flowering of foam at his mouth. *The old boy wants to leave as sorely as we do*, Polly thought. *If only the way were not so difficult.*

Cold. It was cold on the wooden cart bench where she sat bone to bone next to Mama, Ben still asleep in his mother's lap. They turned onto the Post Road, a worn track leading away from town. It was several miles to a neighboring cluster of houses round a small common where townsfolk grazed their fat cattle and held meetings when there was something of a communal nature to discuss. How separately they had lived from the people of this world. Polly went but once a week, to bargain for what they could afford by offering what they could live without. Eggs, butter, cheese — during the good months, they could spare a little of each, enough for dried beans, a pot of lamp oil, a jar of pitch molasses. Otherwise, she only left the farm to help Miss Laurel with the children who attended school on the outskirts of town in a building much like the one they were passing now, dark and empty as it loomed over the road. Her father allowed her to go so that she might learn how to do her sums. But the count is easy when you have next to nothing, so Polly told him one thing and did another, losing her troubles in the task of teaching the younger boys and girls how to read. She would miss the hours she had spent with Miss Laurel. She would miss the books filled with stories of a world so much bigger and more wondrous than her own.

Silver clouds blew across the sky. In blackness, the countryside around them disappeared until the thin moon, unveiled, revealed once more the track, the trees, the school, the slant of the horse's haunches, all of it bathed in a spectral wash. *Am I really here?* Polly wondered. Her father's fiery ghost was at her heels. *Have I left my life forever?*

She shuddered, pushed closer to her mother. They rolled through the town, and in the windows of the neat houses no lamps were lit; not even the bark of a dog pierced their invisibility. Polly felt they were slipping away from all she had known. Who was she now? They had no family she could recall, no friends to take them in. They were reckoned to be folks best left unto themselves. Who were they to be left unto now? These were night thoughts, she knew, the kind that come when sleep will not, the questions no one can answer, least of all a young girl in the dark.

She knew about the dark; Mama had left her to face it alone for years. Polly had often wondered: Was this her punishment for failing Ben? Her mother never stopped Silas, would not even try. This Polly learned early when, the morning after that first endless night, she asked her mother: 'Why am I bleeding?' She was standing barefoot in her chemise, the sun outside just a slit on the horizon. 'He climbed into my bed and hurt me in the night.'

Mama turned slowly from scraping the sides of a porridge pot and stared. She took a small step to steady herself. Polly recalled that, for what seemed an eternity to a ten-year-old girl, the only sound in the kitchen was the bubble of boiling water set up for washing in a cauldron over the fire. Then, a faint rustle of skirts and Mama went back to her scrubbing — harder, faster.

'You'd best not speak of this again,' she said, breathless from her exertions. 'Little girls think all sorts of things are true when they're not, and you've nothing to fear from something that only happens in your head.'

A thin trickle of blood ran between Polly's thighs. *This is not happening in my head,* she thought angrily. But then she remembered how terrifying were her father's rages — how murderous was the look in his eye when he'd tried to drown Ben — and she spoke of it no more. From then on, when he came to her, she lost herself in other thoughts — good dreams to cover the bad, visions of saviors, scenes of heavenly beauty, the sense that she was being lifted away by gentle hands, taken to a golden land and laid upon cotton clouds. She came to know the place well, to trust that its gates would remain open to her if ever she should need to enter. In this way, Polly heeded Mama throughout every dark sleep and lost herself not in the nightmare but in the dream it forced her to summon.

The wagon lurched. Her mother's head bobbed against her shoulder, and Polly could feel the tears. She wondered why Mama was crying. For the farm? For the father who had been killed? For the boy she married? It could

49

not be for the man he became.

'Was he right, Mama?' Polly asked, clucking at the bay. 'The farm. Was it his or no?'

Mama sniffed and raised her head. 'Was it his?' she said. '*His?* No. It wasn't his. Nothing was ever his.'

'Well, then whose was it?' Polly asked. 'Whose *is* it?'

Her mother looked around as though realizing for the first time that she was free. If she felt any relief, however, it was fleeting, for Polly saw her face cloud over as she receded once more into her shawl. 'That's a matter to be settled once we're . . . once you and Ben are safe.'

Polly urged the horse to move faster. 'Once Ben and I are safe?' she asked. 'What about you? You'll be safe too, right? You'll be . . . '

'Hush, girl,' her mother said. 'You don't need to worry about me now. You did a big thing back there — perhaps more than you intended. It's you I'll be thinking about for the moment, 'til we're sure what's what.'

Polly nearly pulled the bay up short, but her mother leaned over and pushed forward on her hands to keep the reins loose. 'If it's the fire you mean,' Polly said, her voice rising in panic, 'I don't even know . . . '

'Quiet!' Mama snapped. 'Now you say nothing about the fire, you understand? That's for me . . . ' She paused. 'That's for me to worry about.'

Polly was not used to the tone her mother had used. She'd spoken sharply, with force. She'd said she wanted both of her children safe. How long had it been since Polly had felt protected? Could she trust Mama to make things right?

★ ★ ★

She could turn to no place in her mind and find peace. She hoped Silas was dead; she feared she had killed him. Should she expect the constables round every bend? Surely a fire-reader would come to the property, a man whose job it would be to parse the devastation. He would pull from the wreckage a record of the past. Perhaps he would conclude that the blaze simply happened as such things often did — an accident of shattered glass and lamp oil. But if he knew from truth, then he would see it plain as day: her hatred spelled out in smoke and ash. Could her mother keep her safe from such scrutiny?

A red fox screamed — a horrid, womanly sound from somewhere deep in a ravine. *There will be time*, she thought as she tried to allow the road away from the farm to erase her worries. *There will be time for a better life once things have settled.* She yanked on the reins to slow the horse as they reached a pitted stretch where the ruts were deep. The carriage swayed and creaked, rolling sideways then down, its wheels at the mercy of the frozen track. She feared they would tip and be stuck here in the cold, for the way was new to her and she did not know where the nearest town might lie. But then the road became dry and smooth again and the horse quickened his pace as though he too wanted to flee the unforgiving ground.

Hours later — it must have been hours, though Polly could not be sure — they paused to let the old bay rest in the shelter of a stand of giant white pines. With trembling hands Polly handed round the hard hunks of brown bread and cheese. In the vast darkness slowly lifting, they had come to a crossroads, but she found herself too tired to think which way to turn. A new land surrounded them, and the hills and craggy ravines that had loomed so menacingly were behind them now. How long had she been driving? How far they must have come. One way revealed a road that seemed to lead into emptiness, but as she peered down the other, she could make out the white lines of neat, straight fences and tall houses sitting upright in the gloom like well-behaved children.

'Where are we, Mama?' Polly asked. Her mother raised her head but refrained from answering, her features thickening as they often did when she resigned herself to performing a difficult task. When finally she spoke, it was as much to herself as to anyone else.

'Far from where he can find us,' Mama said, reaching over to take the reins. Yanking them sharply to one side, she clucked the horse forward and they pulled gracelessly onto the track once more. Polly watched her mother direct the cart down the road that led towards the tight little settlement. Her mind was numb with cold and fatigue, but when a warm breeze washed round her body she knew the spirits were close. She could feel their featherlike caresses.

Go unto my mother, Polly pleaded silently.

Minister unto my mother.

A cock crowed. A bell sounded in the gloom of early morning. Mama had taken charge. How did she know where to go? Polly nestled in closer. Ben was waking now as dawn began to brighten the sky behind a slant of frosted hillside, and she pulled him to her as she stared across the stubble of fields puzzling the valley before them. What lay ahead she could not know, only that every creak and turn of their wheels put the past farther behind.

Simon Pryor

Hatch, Massachusetts
October 1842

Give a man too much time to think and he will entertain the wildest of notions. I, for a sample, was considering tossing aside my *Ashland Gazetteer* on this particular Sabbath Day and attending church. Do not mistake my meaning. God makes as little time for me as I do Him, and His is a house to which I afford wide berth. However, faced with a lull in my caseload, I could not deny the benefit of venturing onto hallowed ground to root about for work. Sunday morn, though quiet in other respects, is an ideal time for the flock to pore over its faults and missteps. And, in such heightened states of repentance or resolve, to whom do its members appeal once they have squared themselves with God? Why, as it turns out, to me.

Permit me to engage in the niceties of introduction. After all, one can't very well play the cynic without giving up a detail or two for some other cynic to hang his hat on when the time comes — as it always does — for the observer to be observed. I am Simon Pryor, and it is my profession to watch and listen without attracting notice so that I might know more, perhaps, than I have a right to know, and share more, perhaps, than I have a right to share. I nose around fires as an inspector for the county, but of interest to me as well are the smaller — and often equally incendiary — mysteries of human behavior. Mind you, I am no altruist. My craft is valuable and, like that of a cobbler, takes time to learn — for a fee, I will take on anything and all.

In the Great Cities, I might tend towards self-aggrandizement and crown myself an 'Expert in Incendiaries' and a 'Private Investigator,' but in the small towns that serve as mazes to me, I am known rather less grandly as a 'sniffer.' I do what I do because there is a demand for the keen senses of a bloodhound and the canniness of a scoundrel — the latter, a talent I acquired in my youth while apprenticed to a local solicitor named Mister Hiram Scales, Esq. He was not the most upright of gentlemen, which rendered him a fine teacher for the line of work in which I find myself at present. He, wicked man, could identify a loophole in the Shroud of Turin and saw it as his duty to enlarge such careless dropped stitches into opportunities sizable enough to thread through with a draft horse.

Not that I was proud to be his messenger, his scribe, his eyes and ears in the alleyway, the forger of his very name. Far from it. But there are moments good and bad that determine one's path and I am afraid that I experienced one such flash — of the unfortunate kind — when I was but a lad of sixteen.

Alas, who has time for the past? Shall I tell you

instead of the scant mysteries I faced as I contemplated spending Sunday morn in rare company with my Maker? Charles Dugsdale, sure that his wife visits the town butcher more times than the meat on their table would suggest is necessary, would like to know what it is she does with the man. In his heart, like most people who find themselves in this position, he knows all too well; still he desires proof, as though it might bestow upon him the power to lure her home. I asked (only to be met with the sullen attitude of the cuckolded man): *When has a poisonous truth ever rekindled love?* But as he will not let the matter fizzle of its own accord, his wretchedness is money in the bank for me. Miss Elvira Drean, a rich spinster of twenty-seven, seeks information regarding eligible male companions. She pays me to ferret out honorable men who have not yet attached themselves and who therefore might find her an attractive prospect. Here again, I have tried to convince her that I can be of no assistance, for there is not an honorable unattached man within a hundred miles of Hatch. Whether it is local or universal I cannot say, but this is the bald truth concerning romance in our fair county. Either you get married young, or you leave. Either you leave young, or you get married. But you only flee on the flimsy wager that you might find something you don't already have, and you only marry on the silent prayer that life might, somehow, be miraculously transformed. Miss Drean's romantic notions — that domestic bliss awaits just round the next bend — have little to do with the coldhearted world she inhabits.

Why so hard on love, you ask? After all, a young man such as myself at twenty-four years of age might be just the sort of person Miss Drean — for there are so many Elvira Dreans — would consider a worthy companion. I make a decent enough impression, being of a spry if not overly impressive build and possessed of good teeth and a head well-threaded with dun-colored hair. My green eyes have yet to rheum over from excessive vice, and my skin is not so pockmarked as is my conscience. There, of course, I might need to kick a little dirt around to cover certain details of my life so as to conceal from her gentle soul some of my less worthy endeavors. But I am, at heart, a good enough man. And my work, though not as commendable as that of a doctor or magistrate, is undertaken much of the time in service to honest people in need of honorable counsel. The hitch in the rope is this: Though I was once an openhearted boy — with an impractical tendency to view everything in an optimistic light — I notice nothing but misery around me now. I trust no one and have little desire to seek a bond that can only, in the end, bring disappointment and despair. I once expected the world of the world, but no more. It is far simpler, I have found, to dive into other people's problems than it is to sort out one's own, and my work provides me ample foxholes. For that, I am ever grateful.

My personal prayer book? The *Gazetteer* and similar town penny sheets full of pleas for help, if one reads between the lines. After all, the stories contained therein — each at its core — hold an almost biblical truth. In simple typeface, the complexities of human passion, greed, generosity, and desperation are laid bare. One need only wipe clean the magnifier and train it on another's sad history to find a mirror of one's own unfathomable existence. Not to mention, the potential for employment.

★ ★ ★

As luck would have it, moments after I had blown the dust from my Sunday topper, a sharp knocking at the front door spared my soul the Lord's forgiveness. It was a messenger — one I knew well — and I could not help sighing as I took the paper packet he pushed my way and showed him into my study.

Elwyn Cramby. The mere sight of his tortured frame unnerved me, for he hailed from Burns' Hollow, the town where I resided when I was young. We had shared little but the schoolhouse and our unequal attempts to survive the bullies it sheltered; still, I am not proud that I turned a blind eye to the humiliations Cramby suffered at the hands of a boy who was, in those long-forgotten days, my friend. One James Hurlbut.

How I wish now that I'd known well enough to take Cramby under my wing. But as a youth, he shriveled in the face of human contact and could not meet another's gaze were a pistol pressed to his temple. The tic rendered him difficult to like and thus to defend when he became James's target. While I made excuses to absent myself from such sport, I knew that on any given day, Cramby could be found hanging by his britches from a high branch, or covered in hogs' filth — which, when it was too cold to wash, soiled him for days at a time.

Misfortune struck us both in the winter of our sixteenth year. It came at different times and for different reasons, yet our miseries are linked. My past will be made plain enough when I've a mind to spell it out. As for Cramby, his most dangerous brush with James Hurlbut occurred when he was lured into a sleigh and driven far from town, dumped on a wild stretch of road, pushed into a snowbank, and left to tramp the miles home through darkness and bitter cold. The trick nearly killed him, and for months after, no one saw skinny hide nor lank hair of him. Then, with the blossoms of April, Cramby reappeared. His illness had made of him a walking corpse, and from the way he laughed at odd times and spoke feverishly to himself, people assumed he'd been touched in the head. In a move worthy of his father, Amos Hurlbut — the town's chief puppeteer and architect of my initial indenture to Hiram Scales — James pretended to play the benevolent and bestowed upon Cramby the dubious honor of becoming his messenger. Almost a decade later, it was a post he still held.

The envelope I accepted from his clawlike fingers was secured with the ornate Hurlbut family seal, and beneath my name, PERSONAL & CONFIDENTIAL had been penned with great flourish. (Who but the rich — ever certain that their affairs are of interest to one and all — would send a private missive by errand boy labeled in such a manner as to beg inspection? Of course, the canniest lad in search of employ as a messenger always professes illiteracy, for it lends him a frail immunity. As one might expect, however, the boy unable to recite the alphabet during daylight hours can be found poring over the finer points of Machiavelli's treatises by night. And I say good for him.)

Popping the seal, I read without enthusiasm, for though I was in need of a case, I would have preferred that it come from anyone other than James Hurlbut. He wrote of an incendiary that had broken out the night before on the outskirts of the town of Ashland. As the Hale County fire inspector, I would of course eventually have been apprised of the tragedy, but Hurlbut wanted me to visit the farm as early as possible so that I might 'sift through the wreckage before it has been disturbed by clod-footed constables.'

That a former friend-turned-traitor had me at his beck and call galled me beyond description, but his order did not surprise me. After all, my job as a fire inspector was no coincidence. James's father had made sure I was named to the post as it afforded him — and now his sons — access to land that might become available to them at a favorable rate *under the right circumstances*. Need I spell out that having a man like me in your pocket goes a long way towards creating such a happy outcome?

I skimmed the rest of the note. I was to show

60

him my report just as soon as I'd finished it — long before making its findings official. The size of the purse I could expect would be dependent upon my ability to massage the truth in favor of my master's desires. This was our standard agreement. If revenge was his goal, a finding of arson pleased him best. But if it was a sought-after piece of land that had caught his eye, then declaring the situation an accident was what I was expected to do.

This property was known as 'the Briggs place,' though its owner was a farmer named Silas Kimball. Any Ashlander, he wrote, would be able to point me in the right direction. He hoped my investigation would go smoothly and signed his missive 'Ever your devoted patron.'

My patron indeed. How I longed to crush the paper in my fist.

One thing puzzled me: why James Hurlbut would be intrigued by an incendiary so far from his fiefdom, and one that had consumed but an isolated farm at that. But his plan would reveal itself soon enough. Writing that I would set out immediately and cast an eye over the premises, I felt a familiar heaviness. Was there no escaping the shackles of the past? I handed my reply to Cramby and nodded a silent farewell. As he set off down the path that leads towards town, his singular stride was crooked and purposeful, a rickety wagon on a rutted road. Messenger. Puppet. How little difference there was between us.

⋆　⋆　⋆

Whether out of carelessness, revenge, or fraud, it is a plain fact that buildings burn and are burned with alarming frequency in our hamlet. After all, the greedy and insane thrive as well on country air as they do on the sooty atmosphere of the Great Cities. Delinquents with too little to occupy their time, drunks, hotheads raging over everything from politics to the property rights of loose-running chickens — these are but a sampling of the reprobates who find reason to set entire livelihoods to flame.

And I've yet to even mention the driest fuse in the box where incendiaries are concerned: insurance. Nose long enough round any fire and, like as not, you'll smell banknotes as sharply as you do burnt timbers. So common are opportunistic arsonists among us that a local tippler once asked whether my skill in exposing their crimes grew from having set a building or two to flame myself. I aimed a dazzling smile at the fellow and responded that I had settled upon my calling only because when presented the opportunity, my matches had been wet. One must, I have found, meet foil with foil and make a game of it when strangers pry.

Truth is, I cannot claim such breeziness when faced with carrying out my duties, for the job is a difficult one. Time and solitude are the greatest of accomplices to the common country arsonist. He inhabits a vast emptiness as compared to the bustling streets of Boston or New York, where witnesses abound and bad news travels quickly. Why, a single day will see a fire set, extinguished, and solved in even the largest cities, while a week may pass before news of a distant incident is brought to my attention. By the time the fire wards dump a single bucket, the property will have been destroyed. Bad luck — perhaps — for its proprietor, and worse still for anyone with an interest in determining the cause. With everything reduced to ash and the boot-prints of constables and curious neighbors, it is only Mother Nature in her greatest fits of pique that can hinder the rural investigator more effectively.

Thus, the sooner I take note of all evidence, the better. And the quicker I can question anyone within a mile or ten, the less likely I am to be fed a string of exaggerations: Yesterday's fire becomes today's Vesuvius of destruction, such is our addiction to the misfortunes of strangers.

'What can you do,' I was asked by one beleaguered farmer, 'when all that's left is a pile of ashes?'

'Resurrect it,' I said. For even the tiniest grains of soot must add up to a flaming torch on one side or, on the other, an honest pan of grease placed too close to the hearth.

Divining truth requires instinct and, of course, more than a few broad assumptions concerning human nature. One must know, for a sample, that men will tell you *where*, women will tell you *what*, and a sharp-eyed child will fill in everything between. *The dog was tied up there, the old well used to be here, the hog pen opened down-valley to soften the stench.* So says the Mister, whoever he may be. As for his wife, she chirps on about berry cobbler, children dressed in tatters, cups and saucers handed down from distant kin. And their boy? Just let him think he's got it figured and you'll have advanced your inquiry beyond measure.

Notes are fine where detective work is concerned, but when looking at the scene of a fire, a set of crude sketches takes the advantage. Approach a recalcitrant neighbor with a book full of questions and you'll knock against lips pursed tighter than those of a dead scold. But show him, with apologies for your artistic ineptitude, a few scratches depicting where you *think* the stove might have been, and he's yours. The more you get wrong, the more he will set you right, for there is hardly a person alive who can resist correcting another man's mistake. From this, one could infer humankind to be uniquely helpful as a species, but I suspect that it all boils down to the deep pleasure we take in showing up one another for the fool.

Of course, in the end it's witnesses that are the real problem when it comes to a country fire. In the city, it is quite common that a man living just across the street will never have met — or even know the name of — the person who has suffered or caused the nearby incendiary. Being a total stranger, he will offer up his testimony without the slightest hesitation. The rural lands are different. You cannot reside in the country and reside alone. You rely upon one another in times of hardship, celebrate in times of plenty, and are known by name to everyone with whom you conduct business. Friend, banker, merchant: They will all have formed a close attachment to whoever is under suspicion of setting a fire. A companion knows that he will lose a valuable neighbor should he give voice to his doubts, just as a businessman with debts to collect knows he will not get paid should his customer be convicted.

What's a decent fire inspector to do? I shall tell you. He must find and fasten on to one Mrs. Bumby. That's right — you are familiar with Mrs. Bumby. There's one in every hamlet the world over. She's the busy bee, the sage sure to answer the questions on everyone's lips, including your own: *Who, how, and why.*

Mrs. Bumby knows. She belongs to all the social groups, attends church every Sunday, listens in at the baker's and the bank and the Dry Goods. Listens and talks and then listens again. What's more, she remembers. But she must not be hurried. Mrs. Bumby has a yarn to spin and she will do so after her own fashion. 'Well, I don't know a thing about the man,' she will say, staring through the steam that rises from her cup of tea. 'Except . . . '

Except. Who knew such an unremarkable word could be so entrancing? Oh, she'll flutter her eyelashes, knot her kerchief, and sigh before protesting that she is only guessing. *Really, I don't know a thing. Except . . .* That's Mrs. Bumby, bless her hollow heart.

Have you heard enough? Fear not. I've a tragedy to examine and so my lecture must come to an end. Somewhere an hour's gallop or so to the north there are ashes to be read like tea leaves, and it would seem I am just the gypsy for the job.

Sister Charity

In the days after Elder Sister Agnes came to me it was decided that I would be released from confinement. She had been unable to scour the markings from my skin. But as she had found no contagion, I was deemed harmless enough to rejoin my fellow believers. To be sure, there were changes with which to reckon: With my body claimed by the Devil, I was no longer fit to serve as my eldress's assisting sister, and in my absence, all of my effects had been moved and replaced with Sister Columbine's. She would now sleep where I had lived for as long as I could remember — in a small chamber above the meetinghouse hall, next to where Elder Sister Agnes resides. I lied and told myself that I understood — I wanted to save my eldress the pain of having to comfort me even as she pushed me away — but truth be told, it broke my heart to have been exchanged and I hated my markings most of all for the love they cost me.

It happened so seamlessly. My belongings had been packed into a blanket box and placed in one of the smaller rooms on an upper floor of the North Family dwelling house. Though I knew there had been tittering among the younger sisters, the decision to move me had taken place behind closed doors. Nothing official was said, and on the surface, life continued as though I had always been just another believer. I was just another believer and to have thought otherwise had been my undoing. My newfound deformity was my rightful comeuppance.

I hung my dresses and placed my things in the cupboards built into the walls of my new chamber. The little notes and samplers I had received from my elder sisters over the years; my quill and ink pot; my embroidery ring, thread, and thimble; my knitting needles — inside every room in every building, the painted cupboards hold a multitude of artifacts, personal and otherwise. In the sewing room, they are fitted with drawers in which spools, extra pins and needles, scissors, and patterns lie ready for the general making and mending of clothes and linens. In the dairy, they are lined with marble so that they might stay cool on the hottest of summer days, the better to keep sweet our milk, butter, and cheese. Why, in certain of the chambers — though this reveals a matter of some delicacy — they are lined with tin and vented into the chimneys: small enclosures made to hold our chamber pots and air them to the outside.

Dirt in any form — the foul smells of stale breath and body, the dust of laziness, the grime that conspires in corners, beneath beds, even jammed into gaps between the floorboards — is a sure sign of sin. It identifies an idle mind and an unclean soul, and no sister or brother will suffer it here. Indeed, from my labors as a nurse to the sick, I know that filth shows itself in many guises including the demon, Disease. In the Great Cities of the World — or so I have been told by those who once resided there — such smut flows in the streets and through the minds of the inhabitants that whole populations are smitten down by illness born of imprudence and moral depravity.

We believers live in close quarters — I have but a second empty bed in my chamber, while to either side of me there are rooms with three, four, even six sisters apiece. Still, we do not take ill as do the people of the World. Good health is a reward hard-earned: Our fastidiousness protects us. That, and of course our faith. I see the occasional ague or pox in my work in the healing room, but rarely — unless it is consumption — am I not able to contain and cure it. Indeed, save for when a sister or brother has been mortally wounded in an accident, or comes to me coughing up blood — the sign of one of the worst afflictions brought in from the World — I have seen but three believers die of anything but the natural winding down of their earthly lives. Be that as it may, though it is a step out of union to say it, I am glad that for the time being I am to sleep alone. To mind another's habits can become tiresome. And though we are all well schooled in the ways one should live as a good believer, some sisters are better at following the rules than others, especially when it comes to showing kindness and mercy to the afflicted.

I may no longer be the sister closest to Elder

Sister Agnes, but I pass only a single day in my new surroundings before she calls me back to the Church Family for assistance. Doubtless it is because she wants me to learn the young sisters in the North Family workshop. The carding, the spinning, the dyeing of wool, the retting of flax in warm water to rid the fibers of their toughness and ready them for scutching so that we might weave them into linen — all must be taught. The toss and pull of the great loom is the work of elder sisters, but there is simpler weaving to be done. And then, the mending, always the mending of tears and lost buttons from a summer spent toiling in the fields. So many chores to study to perfection. Patience and constancy, I tell the new girls. Patience and constancy win out in the end.

I ready myself for the walk to my eldress's workroom above the meetinghouse hall. Once I have received her bidding, I shall make my way back down the hill to the buildings of the North Family, for as we are only a small community of believers here, we divide ourselves into two groups — the Church Family and the North Family — each with its own dwelling house, barns, and workshops. The Church Family, where I used to reside, is the larger and holds those who have committed fully to our ways and signed our covenant. It is to their meetinghouse that all believers come for worship on the Sabbath Day.

Otherwise, we do not see one another frequently, for the North Family contains within it the Novitiate Order — those who, having

69

recently arrived into our faith, require much teaching and purification. Most will sign our covenant when they are ready, but some find the righteous path too narrow and difficult. Entrenched in the wicked ways of the World, they refuse all efforts on the part of our elders and eldresses to purge them of their sins. I have seen many a husband leave his wife, many a mother and father abandon their children, all because the allure of the World's excesses is too great. Of course, even when a family comes whole before us, we explain that they shall never know each other in the same way again. In our midst, they shall be brothers and sisters — children, like the rest of us, of our Holy Mother Ann and Jesus Christ.

I smooth my hair under my cap and pull my warm cloak and hood about me. Nature may have colored the leaves of autumn with an untempered palate of orange, red, and yellow, but we are less frivolous in our ways. Our buildings are painted in order that, no matter which community a believer visits, the houses might easily be recognized for the function they serve: Yellow is the color of the dwelling houses, gray-green marks the school, mustard brown for places of work, white for the ministry and the meetinghouse where we worship — this last with its inside ceiling beams painted the pale blue of Heaven. Nothing here exists to satisfy the senses. Even our roses, picked in high summer to make rosewater, must be clipped cleanly beneath the bud lest a wayward sister attempt to pin the flower by its stem to her frock and distract a brother from his work. Of course, rarely do I reflect so fully on such details — only when called upon to teach the young girls who come under my guidance. Then the full mystery of our way is revealed to me anew and I am awed by the completeness of our worship.

Though the morning has barely begun, all are busy at work and I am relieved to meet no one else along the road as I make my way. Passing the brethren's workshop, I hear one of the elder brothers speaking quietly to a group of young believers, teaching them about coopering or some such skill. His voice is so calm that his words seem like an incantation afloat on the morning breeze. The boys are learning trades their flesh parents most likely would never be able or willing to teach. They are not unhappy. I must remind myself of this when I witness the initial pain of separation, kin from kin.

Just across the carriageway stands the meetinghouse. I enter from the west, through the sisters' door. Inside the cloakroom, I feel under my feet the gleaming wood planks that line the bright room and make not a creak beneath my weight, their sheen and fit a sign of our steadfastness to Mother's Way. I know well the floor upon which I stand, for through my infancy and childhood, I crawled and walked it every day of my life. No longer, save in worship, I suppose. How life has changed since the warm days of summer, since before the markings appeared.

Up the narrow stairs I climb to Elder Sister Agnes's workroom, lift the metal latch on the door, close it quietly behind me, and walk in.

71

Then, gasping at the shock of it, I nearly trip over a small huddle of people. Visitors are normally to be welcomed in the office of the ministry, but if these poor wretches came to us in the middle of the night, the meetinghouse would have been the first building they encountered.

'Sister Charity,' my eldress says to me, 'we have two new believers. Take them — they are tired from their journey, and their mother and I have their indenture to discuss.'

Such are the only moments in my earthly life that I can hardly bear, for even when the gathering is over, it resounds in my memory with an unfathomable emptiness. I tell myself that the children will be full again, that they will smile at the privilege of an afternoon spent sledding, they will laugh as they gather berries for pie, they will grow to be strong and steadfast. Time makes it so — I know this to be true. The passing days and weeks and months and years. Again and always, it is time and slow forgetting. And yet.

Only the older girl pulls back when I enter. The mother and her boy — so gray in dress, so pale in countenance — are weeping. It surprises me that my eldress has stood their misery for so long before becoming stern. She had no doubt been soothing at first, when the ragged threesome shuffled in. She would have assured the children that they would be cared for, kept safe and warm and well fed by a new Mother here, our own Mother Ann Lee, who shines Wisdom and Love down upon us from Her place in the Heavens. But there is, though I daren't express it aloud, the stony truth of the matter: A spiritual Mother, no matter how perfect, cannot hug her young charges to her or wipe away their tears with kisses. How the sight of their misery makes me glad for my abandonment: The gift I was given in the first days of my life is that I need no one like those children do their broken kin.

I nod in answer to Elder Sister Agnes's request. My feet feel as though they have been nailed to the floor. Like so many before them, the girl and her brother will be made to renounce their family of the flesh and submit to mortification before an elder brother or sister — such horrors as a child can possibly confess, the filching of an apple perhaps, a pinch in school for which another was blamed. Then they will swear themselves against the filth of carnal relations. For days — weeks even — having come to a corner of their hearts that is cold and hard, they will shuffle from place to place like the walking dead.

I do not question our way. Still, I imagine that I see a stoniness pass across the little boy's face, blotched and swollen from crying. No matter how poor, how sickly they seem, no matter what food and warmth and medicine they stand to receive, the price of losing their mother is the dearest they've known.

And what will happen to their only kin? After greeting the worn woman kindly and sending for her horse to be watered and fed, Elder Sister Agnes will have told their mother that she must sign away all claim to her children, that only in their eighteenth year will they be allowed to choose either to enter their names by their own hand into our covenant or to leave and follow their fortune in the World. Until such a time, my eldress will have informed her, they must remain separated from all blood relations.

No mother or father, daughter or son, hears such news gladly. Why, this woman — such a wastrel she is — already looks askew to me, as though the mere thought of such a severing were enough to bring about a troubled state of mind. Mothers cannot easily comprehend what seems, on its wintry surface, such an unnatural farewell.

The boy suddenly screams, grabbing hold of his mother's skirts so that as she tries to walk to the door and leave her children with me, he is dragged on his knees, then his stomach, as his grasp slips down the folds until finally he must let go and fall to the floor. He jumps up and hurls his body into hers once more.

'Ben,' the mother implores, bending down to him, 'here you'll not go hungry anymore, or wake up crying from the cold. Oh, Ben, I promise . . . I'll watch over you from . . . '

She is unable to finish comforting him.

'You must know,' Elder Sister Agnes tells her gently, 'that you can stay with us. Why do you flee? You are tired and unwell. Take shelter here, at least until you are stronger.'

The mother wipes her tears away and shakes her head, looking at her daughter. 'No,' she says. 'I have . . . business to which I must attend. I have heard tell that you take in the unfortunate. That is why we are here.'

'And from what misfortune do you flee?' my

74

eldress asks. 'Are you alone in the World?'

The mother has not taken her eyes off her daughter. It is as though she is talking only to her kin, with no thought of explaining her situation to anyone else.

'My husband left us — I know not where he went,' she says. 'Perhaps to the city. Perhaps to seek his fortune in more generous country. He will not be back, of that I am certain.'

'And why do you say that?' Elder Sister Agnes asks. 'No child can be signed into indenture with us if the father does not agree to our terms.'

The woman finally looks away from her daughter and directly into my eldress's eyes. 'Because I know him, Madam. He will not be back.'

Elder Sister Agnes regards her closely before nodding slowly. Hers is a history that is not unfamiliar. 'And your home? What has become of it?'

'It was never ours,' she says, holding Elder Sister Agnes's gaze. 'It was my husband's, and I suppose it shall remain in his possession until such a time as he chooses to dispose of it.'

I have been watching the girl. Her expression is blank but I can tell that she is listening intently. I have the sense that she was not expecting her mother to leave. That is usually the case, for how could the woman have persuaded her children to give her up? They have already been abandoned by one parent; losing another would be unthinkable.

'I want only that my children be safe,' the mother says, looking back to her daughter. 'They and I will be better for it.'

I watch the tall, thin girl clench her fists. She and her mother lock eyes once again, a message passing between them. She stands so straight that a board might have been slipped down the back of her simple frock, and as she walks towards where her kin are so miserably entwined, her steps are silent. It is as though some part of her has left the room. I cannot explain it except to say that an absence inhabits her, as though she has become a specter, her soul rising above the sadness. Kneeling, she puts a hand on her mother's shoulder. 'It's all right, Mama,' she whispers. 'I'll do it. I'll take him.' But as she tries to wrest the boy's arms from around his mother's legs, her raw knuckles turn white.

Elder Sister Agnes stands and nods impatiently at me. She is telling me to step forth, but again I resist. It is perhaps the boy's will that gives me pause, or the girl's strange dignity. And the mother, I wish she would stay. I have a bad sense of what the World will do with her.

Putting aside my doubts, I cross the floor, bend down to force the boy's hand from his mother's leg, and clasp it firmly in my own. Then we rise as one, stepping aside as the mother moves quickly towards the door. *Please don't look round*, I think. She stops with her back to the room, a shaking hand upon the latch. Lifting it appears to require the strength of David. Then, with a click and a swirl of her soiled skirts, she is gone. Elder Sister Agnes's heels thud dully as she strides across the room and follows the mother

76

out into the stairway. The boy's hand jerks madly in mine, his lower lip trembling, while the girl stares ahead with a countenance blank as a sheet.

Their mother will find her cart full of baskets of bread, jugs of cider, warm clothes, blankets, and feed for her horse. We do not send away the poor, the weak, and the weary with nothing. Yet, I think, even Elder Sister Agnes fears somewhere inside her heart that the woman is empty now, empty and alone until the end of her days.

Simon Pryor

The roads beyond town are possessed of an eerie atmosphere. One passes, of course, the occasional sheltered valley farm, fields clean and tidied for winter, buildings robust and orderly, nothing shoddy about the place. But riding farther one encounters the less fortunate, those whose newer pastures look to be veritable graveyards of stumps, whose farmsteads are empty and neglected, forgotten by all but the seasons. I passed forlorn lots where the houses and barns appeared little cared for, surrounded by rings of refuse tossed from every window, weed-choked yards ruled by roving swine and flocks of crows.

Some properties — tied to their absentee owners by title alone — are little more than overgrazed hillocks and random fields of rock, juniper and milkweed gone brown and dry. It takes a tenacious breed of farmer to resist the fertile promise of Ohio and Illinois, leaving behind the hardship of our meaner climes. I cannot blame them. It feels somehow colder in the hinterland, with everything given over to an air of life at its least forgiving — the soil rockier, the sun less generous, the wind gusting more harshly.

I journeyed along the Post Road, searching for the track leading down to the Ashland farm. A shop boy in town had pointed me in the right direction, though clearly he thought my destination an odd one.

'Why're you lookin' to visit him?' he'd asked. 'Crazy. That's what he is. Everybody knows it.' Unwittingly, he'd given me as valuable a clue as any other. My investigation had officially begun.

Just as the boy had described, the turnoff to Silas Kimball's farm was marked by a singular tortured birch rising up over the road, its white bark flashing in silver shafts of afternoon sun. I had passed a river along the way and heard water trickling down the hills that bound this section of road. Indeed, the way down to the site of the fire appeared more like a streambed than a passable thoroughfare. I put the tree's forbidding shadow behind me and attended to new concerns that my horse would break a leg on the uneven rocks and clumps of grass.

A final twist in the track revealed sooty clouds wisping from the few beams that remained upright. My mount behaved skittishly, shying at the smell of fire still heavy in the air. The buildings — a farmhouse, shed, and barn — looked to have been laid out nicely on the land, which at one time must have presented a pleasing prospect of fertile fields, a forest of tall trees in the distance, a cattle pond, and an orchard. In all, it was a neat little package gone to seed and turned hellish by sudden misfortune. Ash covered the leaves of nearby maples and oaks while smoke still puffed from patches of lower vegetation that had not yet given up the last of their coals. Though I had encountered many such scenes of ruin, I wondered at the strength of the fire that must have blown through and left such desolation in its wake.

I dismounted and tied my horse upwind. The remains of the farmhouse were charcoal and dust now, beams protruding like the bones of a huge carcass. I peered into the old shed and noted tools, a plow, and bits of old machinery whose parts would have been harvested for making repairs. The wreckage included pitchforks with prongs bent in the heat to resemble the unruly coif of a restless sleeper; and scythes, sickles, hoes and ax heads whose wooden handles had been consumed by the fire. I discerned the twisted metal wheel strakes and ashen timbers of what looked to have been a log cart, but saw not a trace of what might once have been a wagon. No farmer, I thought, lives this far from town without a nag and a trap.

A herd of pigs ran squealing from the ruins of the barn. The bodies of the beasts trapped inside — cows and oxen by the look of it, a sheep or two — were still smoldering, but that hardly seemed a deterrent to the rooting swine. I wrote down the deaths in the margins of my sketchbook. No sign of a horse.

No cart, no horse, and, as yet, no human remains. The outline of a story began to form in my mind.

Flesh burns with a cloying sweetness, and even in the crispness of the day, the air felt sticky and ghoulish as I retraced my steps to the farmhouse.

Walking across what had been a small porch and into the space that had held the kitchen, I noticed no footprints in the ash inside the house — a fact I found odd at first given the usual neighborly scavenging that goes on. Upon further reflection, however, I began to wonder if the Kimballs had been a family nobody wanted to get close to, for pariahs give off the scent of their misery just as foul air harbors disease, and persistent misfortune cannot help encouraging fear of the curse at its origin. I bent down to pick up the crude blade of a charred kitchen knife. However lowly and isolated their existence, this family lived in a world of their own and my work would be made all the easier for it.

Away from the animals, cold air helped to mask the worst of the fire's atmospheric effects. Indeed, granted say in the matter, I would choose every time to suffer the frozen-fingered toll of inspecting a winter blaze. The putridity of a summer burn often lasts for weeks, muddling the senses of anyone forced to linger. Standing among these ruins, I felt blessed to be able to think with some clarity. That is when I noticed a rifle lying on the ground to the right of what had once been the threshold. No doubt it had previously hung above the entryway, but its inclusion in the wreckage indicated that there had been someone present at the start of the fire. Why? Because assuming he has had time to plan his exit, a man rarely leaves home without his weapon. Even a farmer sowing corn in a distant field knows that there is a chance he might shoot a meaty hare for his supper. In my experience, a gun laid upon its hooks signals that the man in charge is at home.

I bent down to study the fallen rifle more closely. An arsonist would purposefully leave it to burn if he thought it might reinforce his story: that the fire roared up so quickly and with such force he'd had no time to salvage even his trusty Springfield. Why then had I not found the farmer Kimball waiting for me when I arrived, wringing his hands and shaking his head over his apparent lightning strike of bad luck? His talk would have been of claims-to-be-filed and his manner — though convincingly exhausted — that of an eager assistant to my investigation. This was a vignette I'd witnessed before. But there was no sign of him.

I turned away from the gun and began my inspection of the kitchen. Kimball still cooked over a hearth in old pots and pans, which lay neatly piled near the stones. He had no stove. But none of the cooking vessels was tipped haphazardly on its side as though it might have spilled a greasy stew that fed the fire as effectively as, no doubt, it inflamed the gut. Only a single cauldron stood apart, a blackened glaze baked within. In a corner, the outline in ash of a table lay across the ground like a carpet. Broken plates and forks were scattered round its edges. I picked up a shard of china. It was decorated with a pretty pattern, one that somehow seemed too fine as compared with the rest of the objects I could see. Where had it come from?

The table had been set for a number of people. And with such a complete if primitive kitchen, it seemed clear that Kimball had had a wife. Children, too — though as babies will sit on their mother's laps at mealtime, how many I could not tell. Where were they? A convincing fire-setter would have had his family in tow when I arrived, the better to impress upon me their abject misery and need. I scribbled these details along with a quick sketch, noting that the incendiary might well have taken place in the evening, perhaps in the midst of preparing what had so charred the inside of the lone used pot. Several heavy brown bottles lay shattered about the room. That I did not find them all together told me that they had been secreted away in nooks and crannies, a suspicion that suggested the presence of someone who needed a drink more often than others might have wanted him to have it. Again, like the false distress of an arsonist, I had seen this pattern before, and usually it pointed to darker facts.

The room I passed into next had been some sort of parlor, and the charred remains of its contents were of a different nature entirely from those I had found in the kitchen. Indeed, as I mentally reconstructed the room, it seemed to be as out of place as had the fancy china in the kitchen. Small, ornamented brass locks suggested keepsake boxes; an ash-pile of shelf upon shelf of books was apparent. A brass compass — glass shattered and face melted away — appeared to have come from some faraway land, for it was inscribed with symbols oriental in nature. This room had been kept in perfect order — I could tell by the arrangement of fallen objects peeking out from the dust. To the untrained eye they represented tragic disarray, but to me they exemplified the ordered chaos of a wealthy man's study. It was strange, I thought, as I made a list of my findings. Books, but no chair in which to sit nor lamp by which to read them. Not so much as a candleholder either, the likes of which I had noticed in the detritus near the hearth.

In the hallway, I could barely make my way through the wreckage. A second story had come down, and by the looks of the ash, it had been full of the kind of material that burns quickest in a fire. Cloth, straw bedding, and — what was this? Books again? Their presence made little sense to me. Other than the strange set piece I had seen in the parlor, this farmhouse did not strike me as an abode full of people with time to edify their minds by reading books. It felt like a poor and lonely place, with fences left to mend and barely enough livestock to get a small family through the winter.

I made my notes and moved into the last room — the space in which the man and woman of the house must have slept. A barren chamber it was, more in keeping with the kitchen than it was with the strange parlor. I sketched the outlines of the wardrobe and wrote that it had held very little, for the mark left in the ashes did not indicate that it had burned as hot as it might have had it been stuffed with finery of one sort or another. The ash print of a bed signaled the only other piece of furniture that had occupied the room. All was as I would imagine save for two things: the charred ground beneath my feet sloping ever so slightly near where the bed had stood, and the unmistakable sound of grinding glass beneath my boots.

This is where the fire had burned longest. I could tell by the extent to which the floorboards had been eaten away. This is where it had begun. But how? And why did the shards upon which I stood appear to derive from two different vessels? The glass of one was coarse and broke only under heavy tread. The other was fine and took barely any weight at all to crush into slivers. I bent down and picked up the mouth of a cider jug — the only part of a drinking vessel you will find intact in the wreckage of a fire, for the glass or potter's clay is thickest at the neck. The finer shards were more difficult to identify. Delicate as the pearlescent inlay of a shell, they did not fit with the sparse nature of the room in which they lay. I stared round, leaning down to pick up a heavy chunk of wood. It alone had survived the heat of flames no other wood could withstand. Dense in nature — a solid block of burled fruitwood, perhaps — it was the sort of material from which fine possessions are carved. I turned it in my hands until its purpose revealed itself: the base of a handsome lamp, a lamp whose delicate glass shade lay in pieces beneath my feet, a lamp with no business illuminating so bleak a chamber.

Walking outside once more — of course it was all outside now — I stopped to inspect the well. The pump handle had been pushed down even though most people know to leave it up after they've drawn water, thus making it easier to loosen should the arm of the mechanism become stiff with rust during a period of disuse. I also noted that the ground around the well appeared less charred than elsewhere, indicating that someone had tried, however uselessly, to draw water at some point before or during the fire. Where, I wondered, was the bucket? I searched the blackened grass closest to the house and found nothing. Strange. Then, expanding the sweep of my gaze outward towards the edges of the cornfield, I saw the pail lying on its side.

I had not noticed initially that the stalks were newly trampled where the bucket had been dropped. Someone had moved carelessly through them. I walked back towards the house tracing a faint line of indentations in the ash-covered grass and surmised that whoever had run from the fire had stopped next to the well, perhaps found the metal handle too hot to work properly and continued on, tossing the bucket aside just as they reached the field. Disturbingly, the tips of the dried leaves on the cornstalks were singed. I quickened my step, following the trail of scorched vegetation towards the cattle pond at the field's edge.

Water. The swift-flowing current ran into the pond at one end, then over a small dam at the other. Along with its proximity to the Post Road, the property's location at the edge of a river would have made it ideal for sale to one of the many mill agents who roam the county in search of land upon which to construct their mills. Here, burbling before me, was the reason for

Hurlbut's interest in the dilapidated farm. No doubt he sought to buy it cheap at auction, then dip into the deep pockets of a mill owner and sell it at a profit. The waterway rattled small stones as it churned. Industry, I thought, is nothing without a source of power to make it chug and clang.

But a more gruesome find awaited me on the banks of the pond, for there lay a blackened body. By the size and shape of the corpse — as well as the charred form of a belt buckle and what was left of a pair of tough leather farming boots — I knew it to have been a man. Indeed, judging from the path I'd followed through the field, I was near certain that it was the farmer Silas Kimball who lay before me, unless he'd had a grown son he'd managed to keep with him on the farm. This changed everything. I could see Kimball running in flames through the field, falling just shy of the water that might have saved his life. He had endured a tortured end, the bones of his hands curled into fists, his head thrown back, his jaw agape — a posture of agony. 'Crazy' as he may have been, I could not help feeling for him.

I sat beside the body, noting and sketching the details. I drew a map of his futile scramble and described what was left of him, taking rough measurements with my tape and estimating his size and build. He no longer had an identity beyond what little I could salvage, and I could not help thinking how bare we are in death, how quickly our bones join a field of broken sticks, how life's end strips us of everything that makes us unique. Our history remains, but even there, the mark we leave is dependent on the impressions of others.

With the last of my notes and drawings complete, I turned my mind to the story I would present in my report. Whatever 'official facts' I submit, I always write down what I imagine actually to have happened. My reasons are not the least bit admirable, for one can only tell a believable lie when armed with the truth. If Silas Kimball was dead, then who had set the fire? I thought back to the rifle. It was more likely that a woman running from a blaze would leave the gun behind. With the lives of her children in danger, a mother has no thought of future protection; she concerns herself with the peril of her immediate predicament. The table had been set and the charred substance I assumed had been the family's supper made it likely that Kimball's kin had been at home on the evening of the fire. Yet the horse and cart were missing. Someone had successfully run from the scene, never, perhaps, to return. My wager was that it had been Mrs. Kimball and her children. As to the nature of the crime — if it was a crime: It was distinctly feminine. A man would have employed more brutish instruments to set a blaze, while the use of a fancy lamp — my best guess as to the source of the flame — suggested a lady's touch.

I suppose it is a weakness of which I should be ashamed, but I am never glad when the evidence points to the woman. It's an irrational bias. After all, the world is replete with cruel and devious females. But hardship plagues the country wife, and in my experience, poverty and drink do not a gentle husband make. I thought back on the shop boy's comment and the crude brown cider bottles in the kitchen and by the bed. Somehow, though I could not begin to guess at the details, the circumstances surrounding this fire reeked of desperation, not greed.

Polly

She woke in a room not her own. Her bedclothes, crisp and white, smelled nothing like the lard soap she had scrubbed over slatted washboards at home, hard enough to bloody the joints in her fingers. Here, the clean sheets were folded under a mattress lumpy with shredded corncobs and tucked so tightly across her feet she could not turn to look about.

At what? Where was she? She lolled her head to the side. She was resting in a narrow bed across the room from someone — the girl who'd led them away from Mama. It was dark out. Night or early morn, she could not tell. But the moon that had lit their way still shone brightly through the panes of the large window between the beds.

Mama! Mama! She heard the screams so loudly in her head. Ben screaming, *Mama!*

The scene came slowly back to her now. The stern face of the woman who opened the door of a white building and urged them to come out of the cold; the crisp white cap she wore atop her head; her dark dress. A simple woman with a heart big enough to take them in. Polly had reasoned then that Mama directed them to the house only because it sat close to the road and seemed to enjoy a position of prominence in the compound. But it turned out that Mama had known about these people, these 'Shakers.' Had she planned to abandon her children here from the moment Polly set the house aflame? Had she realized that they would be separated from her? Tears pricked at Polly's eyes. Strong as her mother had seemed as she spoke to the woman of leaving her children where they would be safe, Polly could not forgive her this new betrayal. She squeezed her eyes shut. After all they had been through, how could she have left them?

Putting a hand to her hair, she felt that it had been pulled tightly from her forehead and fastened at the back. It smelled different — washed, medicinal — and her scalp pulsed with the blue-bruised feeling she remembered from when Mama would take a comb and peck into her tangled tresses, every sharp tooth pulling out nests of hair that blew free into the fields around their house.

Their house. Their house in yellow and black flame. Their house a plume of smoke in the cold night air. She could still feel Ben curled beside her on the cart bench — where was he now? He should be nestled up against her here, on this narrow pallet, under the tight-woven warmth of this blanket. She wanted to cry out, call him in for supper, in from the rocks in the grass where he used to sit, making piles of pebbles and sticks and clover leaves torn from their stems to look like hearts.

But the severe woman had tried to talk him

away from her — as though a child could stand to hear what she had to say:

Bid good-bye to your sister, Benjamin, for she is no longer as you have known her. You are a Shaker boy now, and your kin are the children of Holy Mother and Jesus Christ, our Holy Father. One day, your name shall be Brother Benjamin and you shall not be called other. Come now and meet the brethren. You shall know happiness and the contentment that hard work can bring if you labor in the name of Mother. Go now, boy. Go.

Again, Polly heard his screams inside her head, but this time they were for her. Mama had gone, a door closing and the air in the room suddenly wholly different. The girl who now lay across from her had held out a hand strangely decorated with graceful red curls. Somewhere, Polly could hear the echo of Mama's sobs as she waited for the older woman in a room close by and yet so far away.

The girl with the paisley hands had halted before opening the door to lead them outside. 'Shh now,' she said to Ben. 'Try not to cry.' And before Polly could move to stop her, she knelt down and held out her arms. Polly felt sure Ben would recoil but he did not. Instead, he hugged her, burying his head into this stranger's neck and whimpering softly. She held him a moment — how it had ripped at Polly's heart to see her little brother find comfort in the arms of another

— then rose again and led them outside along the pathway through a village whose houses were all shaped alike. It had been very neat and trim, very quiet. Even at a later and busier hour, Polly could not imagine children shouting or herders whistling. No clop of horses' hooves. No harping shop-women, no tuneless drunkard's song. Only silence.

Where was everyone? She had thought they might be the only people for miles around until a door into one of the buildings opened and a young man in dark clothes and a white shirtwaist stepped out and walked towards them. He nodded. 'Good day, Sister Charity.' Charity. What a strange name, Polly thought, for one complicit in such a cruel separation. She watched as the girl refused to meet his gaze; they exchanged no further greeting. It was as if they were afraid of each other.

'This is Brother Andrew,' the girl told Ben. 'He will care for you now. There, take his hand.' Ben had looked terrified and spun round to run for Polly, crying her name over and over. She, too, had reached for him, but the girl stepped between and held Polly back as Brother Andrew took the child gently by the hand and pulled him towards the door from whence he had appeared. Once they had gone, Ben's cries became softer by the step, as though he were vanishing farther and farther into the depths of the building, never to return.

Polly remembered shaking and clutching her arms about her. *No, no, no, no, no, no* . . . The word kept filling her mouth, and though she had

93

never before known herself to protest aloud in the moments when her mind spun away, she felt an agony so old and deep, she could not be silent. She had lost sight of Ben once before and he'd nearly been murdered. *No, no, no, no, no, no* . . . She had lost sight of him, and the moments her father had held him under water had changed him forever. *No, no, no, no, no, no* . . . He was just a sweet, simple boy. What sense could he have made of his abandonment? With Mama gone, Polly was all he had left. She looked around her, falling slowly — so slowly that she wasn't sure if it was she or the world around her that had slipped away. The ground was cold as she crumpled to the stone path before hitting her head. Then, nothing but blackness.

Back in the chamber, the girl opposite stirred and shifted. She wore her hair woven into a long, thin braid. The color of ginger cake, it wound across her back and over her shoulder like a serpent. Above the collar of her chemise, her skin looked red and beaten. Did they hit people here? How long had the ginger girl been in this place, and how had her time been passed? In happiness? Despair? She looked to be close to Polly in years, but with a face so still in sleep, she seemed doll-like, almost ageless. Had she, too, been left here by her mother? Had arrangements been made so that she could be taken from the one who had borne her? Polly watched closely as her eyes opened wide, suddenly large and glistening, fluttering out of sleep in an instant.

'You are finally awake,' the ginger girl said.

94

'You fainted yesterday morn, and though you are not heavy, it took myself and another sister to carry you here. I made you drink a sleeping draught. To calm you. You were dirty and your hair was full of lice. We washed you — scrubbed and picked until you were clean of all life except your own.' She sat up, smoothing the covers over her legs, making the bed neat around her. 'As you may have heard, I am Charity, but known as Sister Charity to all within this place. You, too, will be a sister soon, after your confession. Sister Polly. Sister Polly, the new believer.'

Polly heard the girl's voice coming to her from afar, as though each of them stood atop her own mountain calling into the wind through cupped hands. Confession? She wanted to lean forward and cry, *What? What is it you are saying? Tell me again!* But she was lying down, bound beneath her bedcovers, and she found herself clinging to each sentence in her mind just long enough to card it into meaning.

'I do not know where I am,' she said, afraid of the sound she would make in this stark new place.

'You are in The City of Hope,' the girl answered. 'Your home. You must forget all that you have left behind, for your life begins now. Soon you will hear the bell and we shall rise and wash. It is Sabbath so we shall go together to the meetinghouse this afternoon, and you will be able to see all the believers who live here.'

'Shall I see my brother then, too?' Polly asked. She felt her heart awaken, beating inside her ribs as though it wanted to get out. 'Will Ben come to the meeting place?'

A veil dropped over the ginger girl's face. 'I cannot deny,' she said, 'that you will see young Benjamin, but he is nothing to you now, nor you to him, and you must look through one another as if you were naught more than apparitions. You must see into the spirits of the believers *behind* him and draw from their purity, for you have no flesh kin now.'

Polly looked up at the ceiling. It was smoothly painted. No cracks through which her angels might come to rescue her. She closed her eyes again. *The City of Hope.* Where was the hope in losing everything and everyone she had ever known? How long would she be held here? How would she find Ben and whisk him away? Away to . . . where?

'Why must I pretend that my brother is not my brother?' she asked. She no longer felt afraid of this stranger. Nothing moved her anymore, not love, not worry, not even sadness. She had become as hard and dry as a winter seed.

'Mama said she had business to attend to,' Polly said, not intending to speak her doubts out loud. 'Perhaps. And yet, how could she have left us in a place where there can be no love?'

The girl let out a sigh. 'There is love here, you will see. Brother for brother, sister for sister. But flesh bonds are forged in the fires of carnal sin. Your Ben, like you, was born of a filthy act. Here, that filth will be lifted. You shall see for yourself, if you are willing to renounce your blood ties and confess. Should you refuse, then you do not belong among us.'

The room was quiet as Polly tried to absorb what the girl was telling her. Certainly there had been evil in her old life. But there had been tenderness as well, hidden in the instants when she and Mama brushed hands while picking berries, or looked up and smiled at each other having finished a particularly burdensome chore. Tenderness tucked away into the time she spent chasing Ben through the barn in fun or coaxing him from his secret hideaways. Had not Mama glowed proudly at the sight of Polly poring, in secret, over the books in her attic room? Had they not shared many such small but rebellious alliances? The luxury of a sweet from the Dry Goods. A soft pair of mittens Mama knit for her — privately, of course, so that Silas would not punish her for using up valuable wool. Such flickers of love had sustained Polly when all else seemed hopeless and cruel. How would she survive without them now?

She had no choice. She and Mama might have found work once they'd left the farm, but who would have looked after Ben all day? And there was the danger that they might be chased down and tried for arson — perhaps even murder. Or else, discovered by a man — her own father — who wanted them dead. Without her children, Mama would find it easier to hide from the law, perhaps even to begin her life anew in another town, under another name. Without them, she might even be able to slip free of Silas. Polly shuddered. What wheels had she put in motion when she set their house on fire?

97

The obvious dawned on her: *She* was the reason Mama had left them here. It was *she* who had laid waste their home, perhaps even killed Silas. What choice had she left Mama but to take the blame should the truth about the fire come out? She'd no right to be angry, but she was.

Closing her eyes, Polly tried to will the angels to her side but they, too, seemed to have abandoned her. She and Ben had nowhere else to go. They would have to stay in The City of Hope, hide there until Polly could be sure that the world beyond its walls was safe — whatever *that* meant. How, then, to stay in the good graces of these strange people?

Work. Polly realized that industry was all that could save her now. She would work until she could work no more, toil like she had never before toiled, make of herself an indispensable . . . *believer*. Labor would ease her sorrows and fears. Exhaustion would be her solace. She had discovered herself to be a fighter when it came to those she loved. In this new place — so foreign to her in every way — she would walk among strangers, pliable as dough. She was a lone traveler. She was no one now.

Polly rose and mimicked the ginger girl's every move, pulling on a borrowed brown woolen dress and slipping her feet into worn leather shoes belonging to a sister who, it seemed, no longer needed them.

'How could it be,' Polly asked as she ran her fingers over the soft, well-woven cloth, 'that a girl could find no use for clothes such as these?'

Sister Charity pursed her lips and regarded

her sharply. Had she been foolish to be so inquisitive?

'You wear the dress,' the sister said, 'of one who was offered a life of fullness and purity here, but chose instead to run away. She has joined the filth of the World from which you have just come. She did not deserve the attention we gave her.'

Charity yanked the quilt from her bed and shook it. 'We shall see if you are different,' she said. 'Then, when you prove yourself a good believer, you shall have your own set of clothes, made for you and no one else. Why, the sisters will even make you a cap, for you are comely and of an age when your hair and the nape of your neck could distract the brethren.'

Polly put her hand to her head. How strange these Shakers were! Did they not have more to concern them than the attraction between a boy and a girl? She had never before given a single thought to her hair or the nape of her neck. Where she came from, no would-be suitor ever so much as glanced her way.

Sister Charity had turned her focus to airing out the sheets on her narrow bed before making neat its cover. Polly thought it best to do likewise, so she let billow her own coverings before pulling them tight and tucking them smoothly under her mattress. Nothing looked askance in the room where she had spent her first night. Brooms, hanging from pegs on the wall, bore mute witness to the girls' efforts. The white basin on the washstand gleamed. The warp and weft of the woven cotton rug lined up precisely with the floorboards. All was as it should be as Polly joined her new sister in silence and crossed the hall to air out and sweep clean the brethren's quarters, waiting for the second bell to summon them into the company of believers.

Sister Charity

A miracle has taken place and the telling fills me with such joy that I can barely speak! But I shall catch my breath and attempt to calm myself, for if I do not, my words will tumble forth, meaningless.

Where to begin? She had been so unremarkable since awakening on the morn of our holiest day. Polly, the new believer, of course. Clothed in the borrowed dress of a backslider — one who has forsaken us to rejoin the World — she said nothing as we readied ourselves to take part in the Sabbath Day Meeting. From our neckerchiefs to the soft shoes we wear to dance, we sought to make ourselves a perfect reflection of Mother Ann's way. Throughout, she watched then copied my every move, though she hardly seemed present. Indeed, as we walked side by side into the sisters' entryway, I had the feeling that she might float away, like fluff from a dandelion. In the vestibule, there was the usual swish of cloaks being hung and bonnets made loose, for the start of every Meeting is hectic however obediently we try to keep order. The new believer's presence caused me to ponder the strange, small ways in which we begin to abandon ourselves before worship. Perhaps we are preparing, in some unknowing fashion, for the wondrous disorientation visited upon us by divine spirits. Perhaps it is nothing more than the shedding of encumbrances on a cold day. All the same, peace won out eventually as we took our places in the large meetinghouse hall, where the sisters and brethren settled themselves in several lines on opposite sides of the room.

I motioned that my charge should bow her head as Elder Brother Caleb read his sermon. How strange to think back upon it now. That *I* told *her* how to worship! But what did I know of her then? Only that she might need instruction, like so many new girls, and that I was the one to give it. We bent our heads before our elder, who did not presume to offer his own thoughts as do so many ministers in the churches of the World, but trusted instead that the Bible was the last and only Word, and was thus without need of prideful elaboration.

Still, I will whisper here that I sometimes find myself wishing for the last and only Word to make good on the promise of its description, and pass quickly so that we might begin our dances. For the past week, we had gathered every evening after dinner in the North Family dwelling house to learn the steps of a new labor, one that had been seen by a Visionist at Canterbury and brought to us by a visiting minister. Its movements were simple and beautiful in the humility they showed before Mother. We bowed, we turned, we reached our hands aloft to receive her blessing, then swung them low to spread her Word. We danced and were made glad.

Brother Caleb ended his sermon and we began, bending down and lowering ourselves again and again — first the sisters, then the brethren, faster and faster until the room appeared to rise and fall like waves upon the sea. Our breath came quicker, too, our faces filled with the pure joy one feels when caught up in the fullness of worship. We smiled — why, some were even taken with what we call the Laughing Gift, their merriment catching everyone up in its sway. Before long, the hall rang with such mirth that it was impossible to imagine that any spirit — divine or otherwise — could be oblivious to our elation.

Then we set to circling, sisters holding hands and turning in the center, brethren to the outside. We circled to the right — never left, the way of the Devil — faster and faster. After many revolutions, we became so dizzy that when we let go of one another's hands, we each stumbled in place, falling this way and that like lost souls. In this manner, we celebrated the strength we show in union, all joined together, all moving in the same direction. And we showed the waywardness and confusion of a believer left unto himself.

But even the most inspiring dance must come to an end at some point, and as our heads cleared and the dizziness left us, we formed lines again and began slowly marching in place. It was then that I heard our labors to be accompanied by a strange noise, a moan so mournful and otherworldly that I felt sure a sudden wind had come up round the corners of the meetinghouse. As I ceased in the dance, I looked upon my fellow believers and found that they, too, had stopped to listen. I could not see Polly, for our places had shuffled, and I wondered what she must have made of such an odd occurrence. Even I, who cannot remember a time when I did not dance and sing, found it frightening.

'It's a haunting cry that greets us, is it not?' whispered Sister Lavinia, standing so close that I could smell the clove she had tucked into her cheek. 'I've not heard anything the likes of it before. What a tortured soul it is that visits with us today.'

I nodded and leaned in closer. 'The spirits have spoken quite freely of late, though none sounded so fast upon us.'

Sister Lavinia looked nervously about her. Then, as her eyes settled on Elder Brother Caleb, she placed her hand on my arm to signal his intent to speak.

'Lo, is that Satan we hear?' he asked. 'Or can one of the eternal spirits be calling to us?' His deep voice rang out against the howl. 'Mother, show thy vessel that we may better understand.'

We searched the room for an answer, but the sound only grew higher in pitch as the expressions on the faces of those around me began to change from curiosity to fear. Surely no man or woman could give voice to such a pure translation of misery. We were in the presence of a warning spirit, one who had something of the gravest importance to tell us.

Then, I saw her.

Who could have imagined such a transformation? The new believer, standing apart from the rest, swaying with eyes closed and fists clenched, dancing — a slow, mournful shuffle — alone in a sunsoaked spot. Under the blue, blue beams of the ceiling, her hair ablaze, the whiteness of her skin giving off a light all its own . . . I can only say that the sight stunned every believer in the room into stillness. But her song — its sounds spoke of suffering without ever sinking into words. In her wails and cries resided all the Earth's pain and sadness, yet she appeared so radiant, like an angel warrior delivered into The City of Hope to help us fight against the doom she embodied. The utterances and look of her were singular indeed, and we stood in awe of the gift before us.

She began to speak. 'I am in light,' she chanted. 'The only light. Still, he paces round my angels — look! They flit in and out! He moves faster, he moves faster, and his feet pound the floor around me, so loud, in rhythm with the raging thunder, in rhythm with the rain that I might not hear him steal up behind me, to the side of me, in front of my face — so close, so close!'

She froze and opened her eyes, whirling about to stare at the circle of believers who had gathered round. She was as stunned by her outburst as were we, but though few among us had ever seen a Visionist, we knew enough to recognize that one stood before us now. To be sure, I never expected the vessel chosen by Mother Ann to lead us into grace would manifest torment over hope. The miracle had finally come and such is the power of Holy Mother Wisdom: ever surprising and never diminished, even when passed down through the frailest of believers.

The Visionist's expression suddenly turned fearful, as though she were scouring out the Devil among us. For who else could 'He' have been? Her shoulders drooped, her fists loosened, and she began to tremble. Yet the presence of her terror after so forceful a display did nothing to dampen the wonder that lit the features of my sisters and brethren. All had seen the new believer for what she truly was. All had felt her worship fill the meeting hall with the Gospel Spirit, and the knowledge set many of us to shaking. We broke from our lines and, entranced by Mother Ann's glory, began again to sing, each raising a voice to the Heavens that was at once unpracticed and in perfect harmony.

'Listen!' one of my sisters cried out. 'She has come! The Book of Revelation tells us:

And there shall appear a great wonder in Heaven; a woman clothed with the sun, and the moon under her feet, and upon her head a crown of twelve stars.'

It was Sister Margaret who spoke, one of the older and more sober believers. Passion had been aroused even in her quiet soul. 'She warns that the Devil is near! Though it has cost her much pain, she is come to save us! We must move as blades of grass on a wide plain, sway as one,

106

blown by the winds of faith and love. Dance with me now, my brethren, my sisters! Show Satan the strength of our souls!'

We began to move and bend, our bodies rocking gently from side to side until we danced in union, our movements increasingly expansive even as they remained filled with the grace of leaning, reaching, undulating upwards. Everywhere on the faces of my fellow believers was etched an attitude of peace and contentment, and it was only after many minutes had passed that we abandoned the great prairies to which we had traveled in worship and moved into the ways we knew by rote. Though forever transformed, we had been led back to ourselves.

I felt that hours had passed with the fleetness of a falcon's dive. We were breathless from our quick dances, from turning fast on our feet to show Evil our backs, from raising our hands to give and receive gifts from the Gospel Spirits in Heaven, from shuffling our feet along the righteous line we walk in Mother's name. Throughout it all, the Visionist stood apart. She did not move or sing. It was as though she were drained of all life, and when her eyes met mine, I felt that she was beseeching me to come to her. I pushed through the rapturous throng and caught her as she fell against me. She shook as she watched the commotion around us. There was no triumph, no glow of renewal in her gaze. Bleached as a river-stripped branch, she did not seem to know where she had been or where she stood now. I placed her arm about my shoulders and bore the full weight of her as we turned to walk across the floor. Guiding her, I looked to Elder Sister Agnes for her blessing, but she and the new believer seemed locked in silent communication, scrutinizing each other with expressions more difficult to read than if they had been made of mist.

I had erred to think that she was like any of the other novitiates I have known. Those who giggle and make fun of our ways, ignorant of the bareness of their souls before Mother. They do not know that She watches them from on high, Her countenance dark, Her will unstoppable. But it has been made clear that the Visionist is different. Indeed, the power of Spirit lying hidden within her ragged soul had lifted all the sisters and brethren in The City of Hope and made us strong.

I led her so quickly from the Meeting that we did not stop to put on our thick wool cloaks, leaving them instead to hang limply on the row of blue pegs inside the entryway. Even so, the cold did not pierce the skin on our faces or the soft cloth of our dresses. We were, I knew, under the protection of Mother, and the warmth of Her gaze beaming down on Sister Polly filled me with heat. *Sister Polly:* By virtue of her gift, she had earned the title even before formally confessing, and now it was *I* who had become *her* student. There was so much to ask. I wondered how it felt to be entered by the Divine. Was Mother Ann's presence convulsive, like gulps of White Vitriol? Or, as I have imagined, did She pour through the body smooth as springwater?

'You have shown something few save Elder

Sister Agnes have seen before,' I said, trying to keep my speech steady though my heart was pounding hard in my chest.

'I have done nothing,' she answered, tired. 'I am nothing. I heard the sounds of your dances so loudly and felt the heat of the sun, and inside the meeting hall, the smell of so many bodies brought back memories I could not push away. I was begging for deliverance. That is all.'

Her step was light over the frozen ground. Walking fast as though to distance herself from the clamor of our worship, she looked neither right nor left through the tears that ran down her cheeks.

'You are mistaken,' I said, unsure whether to touch her with my bedeviled hand. But she pulled me close, and I was forced to entwine my arm round hers in order to bear her weight. 'You have filled the vessel of your body with the Word of Mother. She chose you, do you not see?'

Suddenly, I realized the truth about my markings. They made of me a leper because I had dared to think I was different. And here before me was my trial: to lose myself in teaching Sister Polly the full extent of her gift, to celebrate one who deserved to think she was different and thus sublimate my own foolish pride.

'I have done nothing,' she said again, fixing me with her pale blue eyes, red from crying. 'Not even here, where everyone is good, can I be saved. Someday, you will realize that I speak the truth. Someday, perhaps, you will even task me for it.'

I refused to believe her. Color had begun to

shade her cheeks, and when, in sadness, she softened her gaze, I felt as if I were leading an angel.

She put her free hand on mine and tried to smile. 'Thank you for holding me up,' she said. 'I keep thinking I have known you before. Not in nightmares like those that came upon me just now. But in the dreams that saved me again and again, before I knew you even walked this earth . . . '

'You had the Visions then, too?' I asked. I wanted her to come back to me. 'Mother found you even then?'

She stopped walking. 'No one found me then,' she said. 'I was alone.'

I knew in that moment that she was true, for she had humility in the face of such closeness to the Divine. Others, when they have been moved to dance and labor well in Meeting, are ecstatic afterwards — I might even say prideful. They crow the news of their enlightenment. But Sister Polly was modest in all things, even the acceptance of friendship. By Heaven, she was grateful for it! Was she to become my redeemer? I felt sure the answer was yes. Why else would Mother have sent her to me? In the blaze of her visions, my markings would fade, of that I felt sure.

I pulled at her sleeve and looked down in order that I might better follow the paved way leading us back to the warmth of the dwelling house. Safe in the embrace of all who could see her for who she was, she would find herself. And I? I would love her, my close companion, my Faith Incarnate.

Polly

'You will tell me, please,' Elder Sister Agnes said, 'what happened earlier.'

It was evening on the Sabbath Day of Polly's first meeting, and while sitting in the dining hall and eating her supper, she had been summoned by Sister Columbine to the eldress's quarters. Before her, Elder Sister Agnes now stood in front of the window, clasping her hands and rubbing one over the other. Polly heard them chafing — a dry whisper. Nose a-twitch, eyes wide, ears assaulted by the most commonplace of sounds, she felt like a cornered animal in the small room; its upright ladder-back chairs and writing desk, its orderly oval boxes and baskets full of tasks yet to be completed — they all appeared steeped in moral rectitude. Somewhere, a clock ticked down the minutes, seeming to push time forward as purposefully as it did its pointed hands. A log crackled inside the small stove, and Polly jumped, looking up at Elder Sister Agnes and her stern, watchful stare.

'I am not wholly certain, Elder Sister,' Polly answered. 'I hardly remember it, though it was just hours ago. I think back and . . . '

Polly paused, her mind flooded by the

111

memory of the believers advancing and retreating like soldiers, their turning in ever smaller interlocking circles, whirlpools of skirts, a dirge of song, the cloth-clad feet beating fast — their commotion and noise mixed with the sounds of her mother crying, the *creak-creak* of the stairs leading up to her bed, his hideous grunting, the suffocating darkness. Before she could stop, she'd heard herself moaning, felt herself rocking and gazing upwards into the shaft of light that seemed to fall just where she stood, as though a chute in the Heavens had opened and from it poured all manner of terror. This was not salvation. It was him again. In the rhythms of the believers' worship, she heard his hoe hit the earth, his kick that sent the hens fluttering, his angry roar. Over and over, back and forth, he came at her, left her weak, made her sick with nausea: the knowledge that, inevitably, he would touch her.

'You think back and . . . ?' Elder Sister Agnes prompted.

Polly kept her face purposefully blank. How could she tell this woman that she had not seen anyone's devil but her own? She had envisioned something nobody in this peaceful place could understand.

'I hear only noise, smell only smells, and heat . . . that's all I feel until . . . ,' she continued.

'Yes,' said Elder Sister Agnes. 'Until?'

'Until my angels come,' Polly answered. 'Then my soul is taken away from that which frightens me and I . . . escape.'

Elder Sister Agnes held her chin high, her

112

lined skin stretched taut over her face. With her neat gray hair, high cheekbones, and straight nose, she might have been pretty once, if there had ever been a time when she allowed her expression to soften. Polly gazed into her hard, pale eyes and tried to imagine what the eldress saw in her — a gaunt figure dressed in a stranger's ill-fitting clothes, her face drawn and sickly. The older woman's regard was not unkind, but she hid her emotions well. She was to Polly as solid and impassive as a rock.

The eldress looked into her lap, holding the silence between them for a long time. 'Why did you come here, child?' she finally asked.

'I came because this is where my mother brought me,' Polly answered. 'You know that I did not choose it. You were there. You know that I did not seek the attention of your believers.'

'It is not something one 'seeks,'' Elder Sister Agnes said crisply. 'Or it shouldn't be. They think you are a *Visionist* — that is the term we use. It is an honor, bestowed without warning. Do you understand the consequences of your behavior today? The believers — many of them — think that you have been chosen to speak for Mother Ann. Their faith is a weighty responsibility. If you've anything to confess, child, now is the time. A single outburst can be easily explained. But if this continues, their belief in you will become impossible to contain.'

The eldress fell silent, then added in a kinder tone: 'Tell me your secret, Sister Polly, for I sense that you — like so many who seek peace here — come to us bearing a heavy burden. I once took shelter here myself, you know. I realize that the World holds many a reason to make a girl run.'

Polly gazed down at her feet. How she yearned to talk and never stop. To tell Elder Sister Agnes everything she had never been able to say to anyone else. But what did she know of this woman? Only that she scrutinized her with little but suspicion. Hadn't Mama made it plain that Polly was never to say anything about Silas, about the fire? She would be foolish to even consider trusting this stranger.

'I cannot explain what happened in Meeting,' Polly said. 'And as to any secrets I might confess, they are commonplace enough to be of little concern to anyone but myself.' She met Elder Sister Agnes's gaze.

The eldress paused before speaking again: 'You stared at me as you departed the meetinghouse. What did you seek?'

'I suppose I looked for what I could not find in the faces of the others. Wisdom. Something that might explain to me what I had done to cause such a commotion.'

The faintest of smiles played across Elder Sister Agnes's lips. 'Well, 'tis true that your episode caused a mighty stir. But surely, this cannot be the first time that you have been possessed by such wild emotion?'

How to answer this? No, not the first. But it was not the same here, for Polly was no longer alone. She spoke her fear. Her angels had flitted about her head, urging her on. Falling into consciousness as the tumult quieted, Polly found herself surrounded by beatific faces flushed with ecstasy, eyes so moved by the Spirits that they glinted. To be sure, it had been a strange enveloping, and she was grateful when Sister Charity took her by the arm and led her away from their fervor. In the midst of such an intense display, she had been frightened and confused, but she had not felt alone.

'It was,' she said, 'different before.'

'How?' demanded the eldress.

'Here, I was not . . . in danger,' Polly answered. 'Demons descended upon me despite the presence of the believers, but my angels did as well.' She sighed. 'Even so, I would be lying if I did not tell you that every ounce of my being wanted to flee.'

'And what is it you were fleeing?' Elder Sister Agnes asked.

Be careful, Polly told herself.

'I believe that I was fleeing the past, Elder Sister Agnes,' she said clearly and, she hoped, without a trace of nervousness. 'Is that not what everyone runs away from?'

'I cannot argue with you there, Sister Polly,' the eldress answered, 'but I am warning you that my responsibility is to protect the believers from harm. And as I know as little of you now as I did before you stepped into my chambers, I shall be watching you closely henceforth. Perhaps you are precisely what the believers think you are — a Visionist. Perhaps not. I suppose only time will tell. Now go. Take your rest and may morning bring you clear-sightedness and peace. You will, you realize, be made to confess everything to me if you are to stay with us. Not even a Visionist can escape that.'

Elder Sister Agnes took up her sewing basket and commenced her work. Her stitches were tiny and perfectly spaced. Polly had never seen a woman so deft and sure. *What can the eldress,* she wondered, *have possibly needed to run from? When will I be made to confess? And to what? That I failed to protect my brother from harm? That I have had 'carnal relations' forced upon me since I was ten years old? That I set my home on fire? That I may have killed my own father?*

Revelation seemed impossible, but she had to stay in The City of Hope, for its isolation from 'the World' made it possible for her to vanish. Wasn't that what Mama had wanted for her children? At least until she had tended to whatever it was that needed tending? Polly was still confused about the change she had seen in her mother once they'd left the farm. She wasn't sure that she trusted her to remain strong.

Lying in bed later that evening, she thought about the eldress's warning. One thing was certain: Her past would have to remain secret. Her safety depended on it and now so did her reputation — as a *Visionist*. No matter where she turned, life held its threats. The goodness of the believers aside, it was no different in The City of Hope, and the unceasing menace exhausted her.

★　★　★

Too soon, she heard the tolling of the first morning bell. Ben must be waking to its dull, rhythmic chime as well. Who was with him? Had Brother Andrew discovered that he was different — that his words came out more slowly than did those spoken by other boys his age, that he needed time to understand what was being asked of him, that he had demonstrated but two emotions in his short life: sweetness and fear? After Silas plunged his tiny, swaddled body into a bucket full of water and held him under, the light in his eyes had changed forever. He grew, same as any child, but he appeared to view the world around him through a haze.

He was good at helping round the farmyard. He could calm any animal, weave nets from wild vines for catching fish in the pond, coax fruit and vegetables from the most blighted trees and seeds. His fingers were dexterous and strong, his eyes and ears sharp as a hawk's. But with horizons known only to him, Ben's mind remained a mystery, and Polly prayed that he would not be punished for its peculiar constraints.

She closed her eyes, mourning the loss of him. She had failed him as a baby — Silas had moved silent and quick as a catamount to steal him away when her back was turned. Now that she'd let Ben be taken from her again, she felt the full extent of her culpability.

The bell rang and rang. Polly covered her ears. She would take her brother back. She had to. She owed him that much.

'Up we get!' piped a cheerful voice from the

bed across the room. 'We've so much to do!' Sister Charity's tone could not have been more different from the one she had used the morning before, when she had sounded like a short-tempered old maid. Polly stared at her — she looked so happy. Radiant, even, beneath the magical markings. Stranger still, the transformation was catching. No one had ever before gazed upon Polly with such unguarded devotion. Under the warmth of Charity's hopeful regard, Polly's doubts melted away.

Something was changing.

What was it? Lifting her covers, she peered down towards her toes. Even in the thin gray light of dawn, she could see that nothing about her long, sharp-boned body was different. And yet, heat flooded her. Each muscle — strung so tight just a few hours earlier — went soft as she lay in the gradually brightening gloom. She sat up, swung her feet to the floor, and turned to face her new friend, half smiling.

Hope. In spite of all her pain, it brightened inside of her just as the sun began to fill the small chamber with its weak morning rays. Basking in the dawn of a new day, Polly pushed Elder Sister Agnes's words from her mind and allowed herself to wonder if she might actually possess something like the powers ascribed to her by the believers. Might she have been a Visionist all this time and never known it? After all, her waking dreams were not false. She saw and felt — had always seen, had always felt, however wordlessly — the power they had to transform. Perhaps when she was alone, the spirits spoke only to her, lifted only her soul from inside her body and stole it away until all danger had passed. In this new place, she could find her voice because she was no longer alone. Even if she did not understand their reaction to it, the believers acknowledged her suffering — not even Mama had done that. Surrounded by brethren and sisters who hoped to see beyond the bleakness of their own earthly lives, might she truly be able to show them into a world — her world — full of angels and the miracle of what it felt like to be saved?

Clearly Sister Charity was convinced of her destiny, for later that morning, when they had finished washing the dishes from breakfast, she looked at Polly and reached out to touch her arm. 'We are going to the sewing room,' she said. Her smile was so open and kind that Polly, once again, found her gladness to be contagious. The sister's tone was teasing as she continued to speak. 'After all, it will not do to clothe a Visionist in the vestments of a backslider! Come! Shall I tell you of the bounty that awaits you?'

They left the dwelling house and walked where the sun shone brightly and there was no risk that they might be overheard by another believer. Sister Charity pulled Polly along the pathway, humming softly beneath her breath in a manner that was not somber or prayerful but girlish.

'Gowns, gowns!' she trilled. 'One worsted, three winter! One white, three summer! Two light-colored, three cotton! Oh, and cloaks and petticoats and palm-leaf bonnets! Aprons upon aprons! Shoes, socks, and stockings! Oh, yes! And caps and collars and neckerchiefs and all that goes beneath . . . '

Then, as suddenly as she had begun, she stopped, dropping Polly's hand as though scalded by it. 'I forget myself,' she whispered, staring at her own marked hand. 'And who it is I am with. Please, will you forgive my foolishness? I meant no . . . '

Polly smiled. 'Whom do you take me for?' she asked. Seizing Sister Charity's hand, she could say nothing more. And why? Because the expression of all that she felt would pour forth and the sheer force of it would bring her to tears.

You are my friend, she thought in wonder. *And I cannot lose you.*

She took a deep breath. 'Now show me where we are going,' she said. 'I have yet to learn the nooks and crannies of this place.'

'Then I shall guide you,' Sister Charity answered, pulling at Polly's hand once again and leading her towards the sisters' workhouse.

It was a dull-colored building on the outside, plain and severe in its lines. But inside, everything seemed to glow in the light that poured through the windows and illuminated the bright-yellow walls. They entered a spacious room furnished with chests full of drawers, some tiny, others wide and thin, and more still that looked large enough to hide a small child.

Polly's thoughts flashed on Ben, and for a moment all color and light faded as she felt her heart plummet into her stomach. The smallest glimpse of him at Meeting the night before, the

120

sight of him in clean clothes, under the care of the young Brother Andrew, had been of little comfort. *It should have been me looking after him*, she thought. But instead, Ben had looked on in terror as she slipped into a state over which she had no control. Her *Vision*.

She looked up and caught Sister Charity watching her. 'You are thinking of young Benjamin,' the sister said. 'I can read it on your face.' She took up Polly's hands in her own. 'I promise he is being watched over by a kind soul. I wish that I had better comfort to offer than that.'

Polly looked down, squared her shoulders, and drew in another breath. She would need to accustom herself to such stabs of memory — at least, where her souvenirs of Ben were concerned. That the pain would never abate was as certain as the fact that she could not let it keep her from embracing this new life. Her survival here would depend upon her ability to shift emotions as easily as a curtain billows and falls in a changeable breeze. *Hasn't it always been like that?* she wondered. How else could she have moved from night into day?

She shook off her dark thoughts and looked up. The two girls had caught the young seamstress by surprise. One minute, she was sewing quietly in a chair near the window, the next leaping from her place so suddenly that her basket of thimbles, needles, pins, hooks, and buttons fell to the floor.

'I'm sorry,' she said, dropping to her knees to gather up her dainty tools. 'I did not expect to see the . . . ' She looked fearfully at Polly, who had knelt down to help her. 'I did not know you would be coming to the shop today. It was silly of me. I should have . . . '

'How could you have expected us?' Polly asked. 'Sister Charity has had time to do nothing besides keep me from making mistakes in every instance possible.' She was surprised by the ease with which she carried on. Indeed, so new to her was this side of her character, she felt she was watching an actor in a street play.

Still, Polly spoke the truth. She'd even had to rely on Sister Charity to educate her on the matter of dressing properly. To brush and fasten the right side of her hair before the left, to attend to the right side of her gown before the left, to pull on her right shoe before her left. For the left was, in all things, the Devil's domain, and righteousness must always be tended before evil.

The seamstress smiled and looked down. 'Oh, I doubt that you can have required as much correction as all that, Sister.'

'The new believer is being modest,' Sister Charity chimed in. 'As she is in all things. Now, should she not take off her dress and stand in her petticoat on this stool so that you can pin the form properly?'

'Of course!' the young girl exclaimed, jumping to her feet and setting her thimble a-tumble once more. Polly watched it roll under a chair. 'I have the muslin cut already,' the sister continued breathlessly. 'All that needs doing is the fitting. Would you mind? Could the Visionist step . . . ?'

'Please,' Polly said. 'What is your name?'

'I am called Sister Eugenia,' the girl said softly.

'Sister Eugenia, then. Please, call me Polly. I should recognize myself much better that way. Or — if you must — *Sister* Polly.' She knelt and swept up the thimble. Smiling, she held out the finger cup to the young girl. 'If you are to pin me, you shall no doubt have need of this.'

'Thank you, Sister,' the seamstress stammered. 'Sister *Polly*, I mean. The stool, yes, if you could stand . . . That's right. Oh, the sun makes this so much easier! You must have blessed the day.'

Polly looked round at Sister Charity, who appeared not the least bit surprised by the young girl's enthusiasm. Turning back to the seamstress, she said, 'Sister Eugenia, I have no say in the travels of the sun. Indeed, I have no say in any of the events that happen here.'

The seamstress was quiet now, bent at Polly's feet, her mouth a pursed line of pins. 'Mmmm. Mmm, mmm,' she mumbled as forcefully as she was able.

At this, even Sister Charity broke out giggling. The room was peaceful. With only the three of them present — not a cluster of believers — there lacked the bustle of industry Polly had noticed while going about her kitchen chores. It was quiet, save for the rustling of the muslin and Sister Eugenia's soft, regular breathing as she pinned the dress form to fit the lines of Polly's body.

When did I last feel so at ease? Polly wondered. In this single moment, she feared nothing, neither watched nor braced herself for his tread upon the boards. She was free. With her

123

arms held out, staring through the window in front of her, she felt as though she might be flying. Her mind's eye took in the rooftops of all the buildings in The City of Hope, and the straight stone pathways that connected them, and the backs of the brethren bent over in the brown fields, and the bell tower and great barns, all of it surrounded by the neatest walls she could ever imagine. Only the mill ponds expanded beyond the boundaries of the settlement, feeding one into the next, dotting the land as far as she could see. Polly realized that the believers sought to make a miracle of the earth around them, and every inch was as tidy and well tended as the insides of their houses — indeed, as perfect as their very souls.

'If you would turn just a bit towards the door, Sister Polly,' said the seamstress meekly, awakening Polly from her reverie. Having run out of pins, the girl had rediscovered her capacity for speech and she gave a nervous laugh. 'I shan't stick you, I promise. There's just the bodice left, then you can rest your tired arms.'

At the sound of the girl's voice, Polly's thoughts returned to the room in which she stood, her gaze alighting on Sister Charity. She had not asked about the vinelike marks that twisted around her new friend's hands and arms. *How did she come by them?* Polly wondered. *And why, when they are so beautiful, is she ashamed?* Even in her short time in The City of Hope, Polly had witnessed the pains the other young sisters took to move awkwardly round

Sister Charity for fear of brushing against her. She had seen them staring, and noticed the shame it caused her new friend.

Subtle though their cruelty may have been, Polly bristled at the fact of it. She thought back on the moans and wails she had uttered in Meeting and could not fathom why such miserable sounds would be held in reverence here while such a wondrous manifestation as Sister Charity's markings could be despised — especially in one who was so obviously good. *I shall take her into my embrace and show her that I am not afraid*, she thought to herself. *I shall see her for who she is.* For Polly realized suddenly that earlier, in the pale gray dawn, Sister Charity had performed no other miracle than to bathe her in love. Such a small thing, yet how it had changed the world.

Looking around her, she noticed a set of darning needles stuck into the heel of a thick wool stocking that lay on a table nearby. An image flashed before her eyes — her father's threadbare socks — and it was then that the truth struck her. Love? What did she know of love? What was she, after all, if not the embodiment of its opposite? Had she not been born of violence? Was she not raised on secrets, lies, shame? Unless Polly confessed everything about her past, her friendship with Sister Charity could be born only of duplicity. Yet the impossibility of confession . . . It was enough to make Polly teeter and sway.

'You've gone pale,' Sister Charity said, walking quickly to Polly's side and catching her by the waist. 'Are you all right? Do you need water?'

She steadied herself, stepped down, and breathed her fear away, concentrating on the weight of her feet on solid ground, conscious of her heart's thrum. 'Yes,' she answered faintly. 'A glass of water would make me feel better. I'm sorry. I must have been shaken by standing for so long at such a height.' She watched as Sister Charity moved quickly across the room and filled a cup from the pitcher that stood in the corner.

Then she looked up and willed the angels to her aid. *Please*, she pleaded silently. *Please deliver me from my past that I might deserve this one person.* Eyes closed, she waited, and to her amazement, they came. Ten, twenty, she could not count the soft caresses of their wings as she stood with her face raised to the Heavens. They sang and filled her with hope. They told her nothing for certain. Their gift was to transport her soul, and now, as she felt their delicate presence, her mind was cleared of doubt. Faith infused her so powerfully that she began to smile as she opened her eyes.

'Look!' Sister Eugenia exclaimed. 'Look at the Visionist now!'

Turning towards the fitting mirror that the young girl held before her, Polly felt overcome with amazement. For there, with the light from the window shining through the whiteness of the muslin dress form, she glowed from within, the lines of her petticoat ringed with what seemed a gown made of gold.

'Surely now,' said Sister Charity, 'you can see

your gift. It is just as Sister Margaret said in Meeting. You are cloaked in raiment made from the sun. You have only to gaze upon your reflection to know that what we say is true — that you are a Visionist. *Our* Visionist.'

And in the stillness of the moment, Polly found herself unable to speak. For if ever grace had made its presence known to her, it did so now.

Simon Pryor

No matter how many times I reread my notes in the days after my visit to the Ashland farm, I knew in my bones that a crime had been committed — one I had been hired to hide. Though not a situation unfamiliar to me, it rankled, and I resisted writing the false report. True, I wanted to claim my full fee as soon as possible — in such lean times, there was my living to consider — but the nagging sense of shame at being paid to tell a lie was the stone tied to one leg; the need to protect that lie by tracking down May and Polly Kimball (Silas's wife and daughter, as noted in the town records) was the other. A well-doctored arson scene is difficult enough to achieve. Combing the countryside to save the arsonist from herself — and thus, preserve my findings — was an extra effort I vaguely resented.

In his letter, James Hurlbut had demanded that, once written, my report be withheld from county authorities so that he could submit it for approval by Mister Scales, my former mentor, the solicitor who served as both front and rear guard when it came to Hurlbut's business dealings. He wanted me to declare the fire an accident because he knew that the criminal investigation following a finding of arson would be a drawn-out affair, and he hoped to buy the property quickly and cheaply when it came up for auction.

He also knew that he would not be the only interested party, and he needed time to position his pieces. Aside from the odd poster seeking information as to May Kimball's whereabouts, there was little evidence of any serious investigation. Doubtless, Hurlbut had paid the law to ignore the law — this was how things usually worked. As far as proper society was concerned, the family was a marginal one, a family for which the hamlet likely had little use. Taxes on the farm had not been paid in full since Benjamin Briggs had owned it, and the municipality stood to earn whatever monies came from the auction. Debtors would be paid and coffers would be filled. Financially, everyone stood to win — save for May Kimball and her daughter.

Why did I assume that the woman would not fight to save her farm from being taken away? The family did not — as I discovered in a pro forma inquiry — have insurance on the property, so there was no obvious monetary incentive. Furthermore, if I had found it so easy to suspect her of setting the fire, I was certain that a less knowledgeable official would come to the same conclusion; it made little sense for May Kimball to voluntarily involve herself in an investigation that would likely incriminate her for arson as well as murder. Indeed, she would be a fool to return to the scene of her crime. Barring the appearance of a distant relation — Ashland's town records had yet to provide information regarding the chain of inheritance, but I'd not finished searching — the land was ripe for the plucking.

Still, crime is a heavy burden on those not accustomed to committing it. Who knew how May and Polly Kimball would respond to being questioned by the law, should they be tracked down by the Straight Arrow — that imaginary figure who made complete my crookedness. I could not count on them to be capable liars, and if their versions of the truth veered even slightly from my own, we would all pay dearly for the discrepancy — me with my purse and reputation; them, quite possibly, with their lives.

I have yet to divulge how my investigation ended. Having determined for myself what I thought to be the real cause of the incendiary, I was left to juggle the facts to suit my master's interests. I have said that my motive was born of the need for payment in full, but that is not the whole story. When executing a job as distasteful to me as those I perform for James Hurlbut, the desire to relieve him of as much money as possible is never far from my mind. I've neither the time nor the inclination to explain myself at present, but the truth will come out in the end. It almost always does. For now, I offer only this small but closely held belief: A guilty conscience should be as expensive to the man who perpetrates it as to the one who must live with it.

What to do with Silas Kimball's body? I

wondered. Within hours of my leaving, animals would pick clean and scatter his bones, rendering his disappearance a mystery to be solved should anyone decide to check my work. I have learned over time that I must be thorough in my craft, allowing for that rarest of men: the honest constable, my Straight Arrow.

If the fire was to be declared an accident, clean and simple — with no obvious heir to claim possession of the land — there was but one course of action to take. I wrapped Kimball's charred skeleton in the blanket I keep rolled at the back of my saddle and carried it to where his bed had once been. Laying him in the ashes, I took a candleholder from the kitchen and placed it on the floor close by. Once I had gathered up the fine glass shards of the lamp shade and returned them — along with the wooden base — to the parlor from whence I was certain the lamp had been taken, the dirty work inside the house was nearly done. Another bottle neck from the kitchen, a few more pieces of coarse, thick glass, and the picture of a drunken man who had left his candle burning and set himself alight was complete.

A few handfuls of water splashed upon the banks of the pond erased all traces of Kimball's body. I took care to pick the ends of the singed leaves from the cornstalks and imposed a more random trampling through the field. I did not worry about my footprints — my job as inspector explained them away easily enough. I had been delicate in my placement of the corpse, but even there I needn't have troubled myself too much. The ash would dust and blow when the wind picked up, and before long no one would be able to discern the layout of the rooms, much less the bed of a dead drunk.

I had done my job well and, by placing Silas Kimball in plain sight, had ensured that a critical detail was resolved beyond doubt. An accident. That is how my report would read. No arson. No murder. Just tragedy in the middle of the night, an occurrence commonplace enough to go unquestioned. I had simply to put it into writing for my version of the truth to be complete.

My version. That was the only sticker in the pot. I am not such a beast as to have mounted my steed and trotted away from the Kimball farm with a clear conscience. *Would the lies never cease?* I wondered. My life had been built on deception for so many years that I no longer trusted in truth. After all, one cannot say that it partners easily with compassion — to wit, I have found the relationship to be quite the opposite. I often wrestle with the question: Who is the better man? He who seeks truth or he who seeks understanding? I had a history of meddling in the fates of others when it would have been so much safer to turn my back and allow life to follow its heartless course.

Had I not learned a single lesson from the ice at Biddle Pond, the frozen shards that made me who I am?

Sister Charity

I do not know why I took it. I never give a thought to the keepsakes, the diaries, the dolls, the slingshots, the balls made from old socks stuffed hard with wood shavings. I bundle them together and give them to the brethren to burn. Like the clothes and blankets alive with fleas and bedbugs, such objects from the past can only cause a persistent sting. Our new believers, whether rich or poor, lose their belongings along with their old lives. Only then can they be cleansed and born anew. In the case of Sister Polly and her kin, even the departing mother had been urged to bathe and exchange her tattered green dress for a set of clean petticoats and stockings, a worsted wool gown, decent shoes, and a cape.

'She cannot know what awaits her in the World,' Elder Sister Agnes said, once Sister Polly had been tucked away that first night. 'The least we might do is arm her with the trappings of decency.'

The memory of my eldress's kindness makes my duplicity all the more wicked. But you see, it was after the Vision that I saw it peeking out from under the great stone carriage lift where

Sister Polly and her family had dismounted from their rickety wagon. Since then, knowing what I did of my new friend's gift, I could not help picking up the thing and slipping it beneath my apron.

The thing. You see? I can barely give it a name. It was a book, bound in red leather, too perfect to be thrown away. Although I have known a sister or two to keep notes in a secret diary, reading and writing is forbidden here unless it is a compendium of songs or prayers or rules to aid us in worship. Ministry elders and deacons keep careful record of all that we make, harvest, sell, slaughter, and consume. They write daily journals that describe the weather, meetings of note, who has died or taken ill or eloped in the night. And of course, like the kitchen sisters who commit to paper their recipes for meat pie, elderberry wine, and sweet cakes, I add my own curative formulas to a well-thumbed journal of healing. All to say, I know better than to cast my eyes over idle words. For the Devil resides in books, where only sin and fantasy can be set forth.

All I can say is that selfsame Devil must have pushed the rule out of my mind for the handful of heartbeats it took to snap up my prize. Why I allowed him to hold me in his sway I cannot say. Perhaps it was because I knew that the book — its leather smooth and cool in my hand, the embodiment of my waywardness — belonged to her.

I said nothing for weeks, tucking it beneath my mattress in the hope that I would forget its existence. I am well aware that the road to Hell is paved not with good intentions but with the smallest of sins — a contrary thought, a lie, a careless stitch left uncorrected. I suppose I was waiting for Sister Polly to become so entrenched in our ways that she would lose all desire to glance at anything from the World. Then I might be able to rifle through it and, seeing it for the dross it was, feed it by the page into the fire of our little stove. But something in me knew better. Something in me knew that the time would come when, as her friend, I would want her to have it.

'Here,' I said one night before extinguishing the candle that stood between us. 'I found this not long after you arrived and could not bring myself to burn it.'

Her hand shook as she reached out to take it from me. *'Far from Home,'* she said, almost as if she were talking to herself. *'An Englishman's Voyage to Worlds Unseen.* How strange. I hardly remember stopping to . . . ' She looked up, suddenly secretive. 'That this should be the only object I took not in service of keeping us fed and warm. And that it should be the only one to survive . . . ' She looked up quickly and smiled. She had stopped herself before telling me something.

'Survive what?' I asked.

She flipped through the book's pages without answering me, and while the fluttering sound sent chills down my spine, her face glowed with pleasure as her eyes scanned the words. How I wished she would put it away.

'I don't even know why I chose it,' she said, looking up at me. 'Just grabbed it blindly, I suppose.' She turned it over in her hands. 'It's an account of a journey. A distant one at that. If ever you wanted to know about the World you so despise, then this' — she stared at the author's name — 'this Horatio Wolcott seems a good man for the job.' She lifted the volume to her nose and breathed in the scent. 'Here, smell it. It won't poison you.'

I hesitated, then found myself bending down as if to kiss it. The book smelled of milled wood and leather harnesses, and though I knew I should be disgusted, the effect it had upon me was calming. We expect the things that are bad for us to give off some sign of their malignancy, but instead the little red book pulled me in. It promised something.

I drew back. Here was the Devil's temptation pure and clear, for I had never before thought of allowing myself to be distracted from my steadfastness as a believer.

Sister Polly laughed at the look of alarm on my face.

'I . . . I should never have kept it,' I stammered. 'I have told you that books are forbidden, and yet I offer you this. What must you make of me?'

She put it in her lap and gazed at me in silence. As I had never before shared a sleeping chamber with another sister, I had known nothing of the soft whisperings exchanged between girls when it seems as though the rest of the world is asleep. I had come to prize such time spent with my friend. Indeed, there were moments during the day when I could think of nothing else. Was this, too, the Devil's work? I knew not, nor did I much care, for another fear loomed larger in my mind. Would the presence of the book ruin our nights? Would a souvenir from the past put an end to us?

'I make of you,' she said slowly, 'that you are kind and brave to have rescued this for me. Shall we look together and see what wisdom it holds?'

'No!' I said. I felt a surge of panic, as though the book's leather cover encased a box full of demons we might never be able to push back inside. 'No!' I begged again, covering my ears. 'Please, do not open it or look at what it says. You cannot be sure that it doesn't hold all manner of . . . oh, please, Sister Polly. Put it away!'

Her regard was not unkind. 'If it frightens you, then of course I shan't open it. Here,' she said, sliding out from beneath her covers and tucking the book under her mattress. 'I would give it back to you, but then I'd worry that, should some prying soul discover it, you would be blamed for the kindness you have done me. Don't lose a moment's sleep now. It is done — hidden and gone and never to be spoken of again.'

The candle sputtered into darkness of its own accord, and without its glow, the room went black. I closed my eyes, and while I remember thanking Mother for my sister's grace, I fell asleep in the midst of promising that I would not let joy weaken my resolve to follow the narrow path. Please, Mother, I prayed as I traced the raised outlines of my markings, I shall remain in union with my sisters and brethren. I shall be better. Do not punish me further.

* * *

She must have heard my plea for mercy, for she answered it with the gift of true happiness. In the kitchen the following day, where Sister Polly and I had been told to remain after the breakfast clearing, I felt a lightness of spirit such as I have rarely known. There was Deaconess Eileen across the way, making mince for the pies, but it was not she who excited in me this tumult. Quite the opposite, for she is, I must say, a mean old wretch. I know that it is not right to judge another of my sisters, but Deaconess Eileen twists her pinches so fiercely on the young ones who do not heed her bidding that they are marked for weeks with rose-shaped bruises. I have tried to soothe them with hogs' lard and comfrey. Even so, they stay and stay. Such long-lived remonstrances they are! The poor girls fairly jump into nearby cupboards to avoid the woman's nasty hands. I have even heard them say that she sometimes appears by night at their bedsides to whisper into their dreams.

In the cool of the side room, however, there are only my Sister Polly and me, busy in our work to make the daily bread for the believers as well as for sale to the World. The money we earn allows us to buy what we cannot make for ourselves. Hence, we prepare extra stores of medicines, cloaks, bonnets, blankets, and seeds — all of them known to be of superior quality and thus well desired beyond our walls. In this way, we profit from the rich, the better to aid the poor and saved.

It is pleasant to labor in the dim light of the pantries and store-rooms, to be surrounded by good smells and the presence of the kinder sisters who, under the darting eyes of Deaconess Eileen, rule the ovens with capable hands. Most of us change jobs every few months so that we may join in all of the chores that help to make The City of Hope a place of peace and equality. But some sisters are so practiced in their positions that they are kept on as teachers to help the rest move well through their work. Save for the Deaconess, the sisters of the kitchen are as sweet and soft as the cakes they bake, and other than the solitary hours I spend in the healing room concocting curatives and treating all manner of ills, I am at ease here as nowhere else, even in my bedeviled state.

Sister Polly and I. Together we measure into slant-sided dough boxes small mountains of flour tossed with sprinklings of salt and yeast. I whisper to her of the Deaconess's faults. We pour milk heated with butter and sweetened with sugar into holes we make with our fingers. She laughs and feigns a stern look, reminding me that I am never to grow wicked, that I am to be good enough for the both of us. Then, it is to kneading that we give ourselves over, and we do so in time to a song my new believer has learned in Meeting. Such a pretty thing it is, too.

I have a little plum cake
A pretty little plum cake,
Will you eat a piece of it
Says blessed Mother.
'Tis my love and blessing
For my dear children
O how I love you so
I will be with you.

Soft and high, Sister Polly's tone is clear. Indeed, I feel that she was made to sing, that it is as new a joy to her as to a young song sparrow, as new a joy to her as she is to me. I never saw what a somber life I led before, spending day after day in the company of old women who know much and young girls who know nothing at all. I take from one and give to the other, and rarely have I had the time or sense to wonder at my isolation. That Sister Polly should come to me at the same time as the Devil himself — this is the most blessed miracle I have ever known.

I have said that we are a group of believers, living in union. True, but when I think that we are also human, then I see us in another light — brighter and more beautiful in some cases, harsher in others. Sisters my age are clever at joining together when they are in the presence of one who — for reasons she will never understand — was left on a doorstep as a babe to grow old amongst strangers. To these girls, I am an oddity because I have known neither the World nor the sort of mother who lives in it. I am naught to them but a walking, breathing book of rules. For though the sisters of whom I speak are the silly ones, their experience of the World binds them like an unspoken oath. They know to laugh at the same foolish sights, to whisper when I enter a room and then quickly look back at their work when they are certain that their mean-spirited stares have hit their mark.

Of course, the children are different — yearning to be loved, comforted, lauded, coddled. In moments of weakness, I wonder why no sister ever fussed over me as I do them. It is not that I am ungrateful for Elder Sister Agnes's stern teaching. Indeed, I know that I am more capable of love for never having taken it for granted. But I also know enough of human nature to have noticed that one behaves towards others as one wishes to be treated oneself. My eldress was kind in her way, loving within the bounds of what is accepted here. That has always had to be enough.

Such thoughts are of little matter now, for my Sister Polly has chosen me as her dearest and there is none here who can turn her. Why, just last week, when Sister Columbine took her by the arm to pull her from my side and into some whispered intimacy, she turned back and caught me by the waist.

'You are kind, Sister Columbine, to invite me into your company,' she said, 'but as I am only half myself without dear Sister Charity, you must take us as one.'

Sister Columbine forced a smile, and it was not long before she found an excuse to be on her way. How glad I was that my Polly and I were alone again, two parts of a whole.

Look! In the messy mixing of the dough, the Visionist has become covered in flour and the sight delights me. She is adept at many things but they are the coarser labors — the clabbering of cream, the scouring of pots, the carding of wool — such work as is done on farms that are too poor to have occasion to make fine-flour breads and spice cakes. In the kitchen, her delicate hands are clumsy as a colt's hooves, and I must stop my work and bend double at the sight of her as she struggles with sticky strings of dough.

'You shall be wearing the midday meal long before it can be placed near the oven for rising!' I whisper, laughing. 'Your face is white as a phantom's!'

The older sisters often include me in their quiet merriments, but this feels different. Indeed, I am dizzy with happiness to be standing near to one who accepts me so completely.

'Well, then you too shall be dressed!' she cries. 'A line here, another there . . . ' She is running her powdery finger along my cheeks. 'Three across your brow. There. You are an Indian spirit now, just like those we heard in Meeting. Shall we sing the song of Tecumseh, as did Elder Brother Caleb?'

Quo we lorezum qwini
Qui qwini qwe qwini qwe
Hock a nick a hick nick
Qwini qwi qwo cum!
Hack a ling shack a ling
Hick a chick a loreum,

Lal a ve lal a que
Qwi ac a qwo cum!

She is winsome, my dear friend, one who has become lighter with every passing week. It is as if her gift — though it has shown itself but once in its full glory — has lifted the sadness she used to know and replaced it with a child's innocent pleasures. Indeed, the only time when I cannot reach her is when she catches sight of young Ben. It is not that she worries for his happiness — since his first miserable days, he has expressed nothing but great merriment as he speaks with Brother Andrew or makes mischief with the other boys. No, I believe that she pines for a time when she could hold his hand and be the person to make him laugh, when she existed to protect his innocent nature from the menace of the World. As she is not allowed to speak to him, and as there is no evil here from which to shield him, she has become someone he hardly notices. I believe that it is his indifference that breaks her heart.

On this morning, however, we laugh and dance, keeping our play secret from the Deaconess. Polly takes her arms and raises them above her head in the manner of Elder Brother Caleb, her feet jigging in a spritely fashion to the beat of the Indian song. She is smiling, and each time she whirls and catches my eye, her blue gaze fixes me. It cannot be, such elation! It cannot, and after several such turns, I am suddenly frightened, as though a dark spirit has walked across my conscience.

'We must stop now,' I say, touching her shoulder so that she ceases in her dance. 'Deaconess Eileen will pinch us as she does the little ones. Let me wipe your face. Hold still.'

Polly freezes and makes blank her expression, eyes closed like a child awaiting a good washing. I cannot help staring upon her beauty — the way her face falls in soft pink slants from her cheekbones, the fine arch of her eyebrows, the thin pink of her lips. As I lift the corner of my apron to wipe clean her lovely skin, ghostly no more, she opens her eyes and pins me once again.

It is rare to look closely at another for a long time, to hold oneself in that tumble. No one has ever stared at me like that before — *into me* is more like the truth. But Sister Polly and I are frozen, and without a word passing between us, we make a game of it. I shall not blink, nor shall she. We stare and stare until tears fill my eyes and I find my mind has begun to wander. *What lies within her?* Her eyes alone show every emotion. As to what she can possibly glimpse in me, I cannot say, for though I know of certain aspects of my bearing, I have never held a mirror to my heart. Only to my faith, which has shone back unassailable. I break away and turn from her at the reminder, brushing the flour from my bodice, shaking hard my skirts. Straying from my purpose, I know I have been pulled close by an invisible hand, so close that I can feel the warmth of her breath on my face.

I look back at her cheeks and rub the corner of my apron gently over her skin. Then I tilt her head to the other side and do the same, setting her straight again.

'Why, thank you, Sister,' she says, curtsying and backing away.

In a twist of perception, she seems to sense my discomfort. 'We must work this dough before it dries,' she says evenly. 'Here, I'll cleanse you of your Indian stripes.' And with quick hands, she wipes my face — skin on skin, licking a fingertip to rub clean a stubborn spot below my right eye.

She turns back to her kneading while I burn in the place she has touched and I recognize her power of spirit, that truly it is Mother who has caressed me and filled my heart. Mother Ann warms me from within. Mother Ann teases my brain into spinning. Mother Ann rules me. I step beside Sister Polly at the stone counter and begin the push and pull. We are in time, and as it is I who taught her the rhythm of kneading, we turn and pat the dough with flour in tandem, as though caught up in a dance. Push, pat, pull — like good believers, we labor as one.

When each of us has kneaded enough, we roll the mounds of dough into logs and break off equal-sized bits to make loaves — forty of them! Then we shape and set them on shelves near the ovens to rise. It is skillful work, and best of all, the Deaconess has left us free from bitter comment.

Taking up our towels and dipping them into a bucket of water we have warmed by the hearth, we wipe down the stone counter and make clean the workroom. We do so in turns, but then a game becomes of this as well and we race to the pail to see who can reach it first. There is much splashing, though we stifle the sound of our laughter as best we can, turning our faces into the sleeves of our dresses. Of a sudden, it is now Sister Polly who goes silent. She can barely breathe, so quickly have we moved in our diversion.

'I am blessed to have found you,' she says as soon as she can steady her voice. 'You are the only one who has stayed by, who has not flown away.'

All is quiet about us, for our amusement has filled my ears with such clamor that a sudden silence pulses and rules the room. My heart hits hard and I cease all exhalation as she takes my face gently into her hands.

'Sister,' she whispers. 'My sweet Sister Charity.' Then her lips brush mine so lightly, it is as though a moth has fluttered close by before retreating into darkness.

Simon Pryor

Charred ruins, frozen ponds. What, you might ask, could the two possibly have in common? Though it happened long ago, the death of young Millicent Hurlbut has never ceased to haunt me. After all, it was responsible for not only my fated tumble into the bosom of the Hurlbut family but also an irrevocable separation from my own. I am telling you this — before I describe the weeks and weeks that followed the submission of my report — because it seems only right that I should attempt to explain the genesis of my corruption.

I knew James Hurlbut to have been a complicated youth, for we were schoolboys together. Kind in one moment yet quick to conjure mischief whenever boredom threatened to slow the empty hours, he lived in constant conflict with his better nature. I can barely stand to admit it now, but I liked the fellow and he liked me — even sought to impress. You see, where he was rich and born into the powerful family that had founded Burns' Hollow, I was smart and embodied a kind of moral confidence that was foreign to him. In that still-innocent time, I think he understood that like apple trees possessed of a sour harvest when grown from the seeds of fallen fruit, each generation of Hurlbuts had germinated meaner and more profligate than the one before. As it turned out, he and his brother, Calvin, were no exception, but I did not know that then.

Their father, Amos, was perhaps the cruelest of the line, and James suffered mightily under his reign. The patriarch sensed his youngest son's disdain and treated him all the worse for it. Forced to wear the foppish vestments favored by his forebearers, James worried ceaselessly about the punishment his father would devise should he soil his clothes. Amos tested James's filial loyalty by making him deliver threats of all sorts to the families of his schoolmates. And I can still recall the fine spring day when his father came upon him as he attempted to woo an innocent schoolmate. 'We've a maid prettier than that slut!' Amos bellowed as he and Calvin passed by in the family carriage. James, color rising in his cheeks, looked away from the girl with tears in his eyes. He was terrified of his father.

Two lives changed the afternoon Millicent died. Two youths were transformed — one choosing to walk the despot's path and shun any notion of moral decency, the other accepting a life of servitude as punishment for a tragedy he failed to prevent. James's telling of a single lie changed both of our destinies.

I can remember as if it were yesterday. I close my eyes and the frozen surface between us is slick and gray. Millicent's coat is pale blue — so blue that it appears to be made of sky. She

148

trembles on legs thin as my arm at its wrist, and the woolen stockings that bind those stems are the white cream of fresh-churned butter. She stands in tiny brown leather bootlets that have left imprints no larger than a deer's hooves. And her mitten, crimson against the dull gloom, sears into memory, reaching towards me always, even now, in this very instant. She is six years old.

Calling out from a treacherous spot at the center of the pond — where underground springs make for thin, undependable ice — she begged for help. And how could I not heed her cry? How could I not spin in my boy's agile mind through every possible plan and then watch the marble roll to a stop on the one I chose?

Perhaps I chose wrongly. Perhaps I could not judge the frailty of such a tricky, cold membrane as ice. I trusted the crust would hold, and even as it cracked beneath me, I did not believe it would disintegrate and merge forever the worlds of life and death it had kept so perfectly separate just moments before.

I am haunted by her like the ghost who beckons to village children from inside an empty house on a lonely cart path. Haunted like the farmer, one Ebenezer Goodson, who has come to me five times now to request my services in proving the existence of an aquatic creature that bursts from the depths of Lake Cullen and pulls his best cows to a watery death. Haunted as so many people are by the twisting of their short, small lives.

James was with me that day.

'It cannot be known that I was here,' he said, his eyes flitting back and forth between his sister and me. 'My father . . . he will never forgive me for letting her out of my sight.'

It was true: He should have been looking out for the little girl. After all, he'd known that she'd followed him as he left home for an afternoon spent skating with me. Indeed, he'd seen her playing by herself at the pond's edge and cursed her for it.

'That's not important now,' I said, aghast at the fact that his father's wrath was foremost in his mind. I grabbed his arm. 'You cannot leave. You must help me save her.'

He glanced again at Millicent before looking down. He knew full well that what he was about to do was wrong.

'Leave off, Pryor,' he said, peering to see if the road was empty of witnesses.

'But she'll die of cold, don't you see?' I was practically begging. 'It's up to us. There's no time to run for help.'

'So high and mighty. That's always been you, hasn't it?' he sniped. 'Thinking you're smarter than me. You, a printer's son. You go and get her if you're so brave. But not a word that I was here. Not ever, or I'll see to it you pay.'

He shook off my grasp and looked away. Then, he ran.

His behavior disgusted me, but I had Millicent to worry about. Her whimpers were getting fainter, and I noticed that her legs had buckled as cold and desperation set in. I lowered myself onto my stomach as I reached the center of the

150

pond. Inch by inch I crawled across the thinning ice. The front of my woolen coat was frosted and hard as it caught on the surface. My buttons scraped. How I wished I could be a serpent in that moment, just as slithery and undulating. How crude and boyish were my movements, the ice turning more and more transparent as I approached the child.

'Don't move,' I whispered. 'Please, stay still until I'm closer, until I can . . . '

Then, the crack. Millicent's high child's scream. The red gash of her woolen mitten as it raked across my sight and into the churn of gray water. Gone. She had vanished, and though I floundered to reach her, the brittle crust gave way and plunged me into the same frigid hole. I fought until I found her coat with my hand, pulling with all my might. Even if I made it out of the water and onto thicker ice, I was afraid that I would not be able to drag her to shore by myself. I could feel my blood thickening with cold, my movements becoming slower by the second.

The sight of James's back as he disappeared into the trees will never leave me, but neither will my memory of Millicent as shards of ice slashed at her face and hands. I thrashed through the water — I could see that her eyes were open, but her lips had turned a deep blue that was beginning to spread beneath her skin, fluid as an ink stain. I headed for the shore, and when I felt my chest collide with ice strong enough not to give way as I threw myself upon it, I pulled Millicent next to me. I could not stand. My limbs were frozen and I was incapable of any movement save for a clumsy tumble, the girl passing under and over me as we rolled like a barrel towards the shore.

Only when we reached the frozen ground at the edge of the pond did I allow myself to realize that she was dead. Even so, when I saw a sleigh pulling past, I yelled and screamed — a sound so desperate and primitive I hope never to have to make it again. It brought the driver to a halt; whatever happened afterwards will always be a mystery to me.

Two days later, I awoke, my mother by my side, my father standing gray-faced at the end of my bed.

'They say in the town,' he said weakly, 'you should never have crawled out on the ice by yourself. They say . . . ' He could not finish and he did not ask me if any of it was true. Just handed me a sealed note. 'This came for you the night you were brought in. A stable lad from the Hurlbut place delivered it.'

As my mother rose and began to weep quietly, he walked to her side, gently put his arm around her shoulders, and escorted her from the room. Numb of mind and shaking with fever, I opened the letter. It was a summons from Amos Hurlbut.

James had been busy after the accident, making sure everyone knew that I was to blame for Millicent's death. He admitted to being at the pond that day, but said he'd left me in charge of his sister because, worried that she was cold and would need a warmer coat, he'd run home to get her one. He put it about that I'd been careless and that when I noticed she was in trouble, I had acted in an impulsive manner to cover up my failure to watch out for her. Instead of running to town for help, I sought to look the hero and attempted to save her myself, he said. He claimed that my hubris had ensured his young sister's death, and far-fetched as his story may have sounded to anyone who knew me, no member of a town that lives by the thin strands of the Hurlbut family's approval had the courage to question it. I was branded a prideful youth who should have known better, a bad seed, the boy who all but murdered poor Millicent.

As soon as I had the strength to leave my sickbed, I went to see Amos Hurlbut. The house was large and hot and filled with things that were either too bright or too fat. The burnished wood paneling gleamed in the white winter light. Overstuffed velvet armchairs sat solidly next to even larger settees. Gilt-framed portraits of corpulent Hurlbut ancestors crowded the silk-covered walls. I had never seen such a display of wealth and I felt ill at the sight and smell of it.

'You are too bright a boy to have behaved in such a tragically stupid manner,' Amos Hurlbut said, sitting behind a desk that put acres of fine leather covering between us. He gestured towards James, who was seated by the fire. 'He used to speak well of you.'

I did not respond, did not much care what James *used* to think of me. Sitting stiffly in my high-backed wooden chair, I waited as an animal awaits slaughter: knowing something terrible is about to happen yet uncertain as to what it might be.

'Since the accident, however,' he continued, 'James sings a different tune.'

Apparently, upon hearing his son's version of what had happened on Biddle Pond, Amos saw — even through the haze of his grief — the opportunity to turn tragedy in his favor. He demanded, as penance for my sins, that I be indentured to him for an indefinite period of time. When James took over family matters, I was to serve him with equal devotion. No doubt, having lost a measure of faith in me since the accident, my parents would have little trouble believing the following story: that I was throwing in my lot with the Hurlbuts in the hope of finding my fortune, that I was tired of working with my father in the shop and cared not a whit for the trade he had taught me, that my eye was on the future — not the past — and I could no longer afford to indulge my boyish affections and notions of familial allegiance. In short, I was to tell them that I was abandoning them forever.

Back in the warmth of my own humble abode, I found that once I had opened my mouth and allowed such hurtful lies to spill forth, there was no turning back. Though it pained them to reckon with a side of me they had never before encountered, I played the scoundrel convincingly enough that my parents came to believe the worst of me.

They knew nothing of the blackmail that prompted my callous behavior, for Amos Hurlbut promised to see my father ruined if ever

I tried to wriggle free of his hold over me. My father, you see, made his wage as the printer of town penny sheets, many of which were owned by the Hurlbut family. The entirety of his meager living was drawn from that job, and if either Amos Hurlbut or his son ever took his business away, my family would lose everything. That was the chief curse of life in Burns' Hollow: So intricately bound was the fate of the town to the Hurlbut fortune, it was as though the inhabitants were but marionettes, the movement of their every limb controlled at the will and whim of a malevolent puppeteer.

James Hurlbut's lie about Millicent's death stole from me the love I held most dear, for I have not, to this day, spoken again to either of my parents. By cover of darkness, I left my home, slinking into service to Hurlbut and his brigade of crooked lawyers, constables, speculators, even ministers. His reach was all-encompassing and to find myself entangled within it made me servile as a bird dog laying carcasses at his master's feet.

It has been eight years since I left Burns' Hollow, permitting myself no more than a weekly visit in secret that I might catch a glimpse of my parents. It is several hours' ride, and as they are a quiet pair who keep to themselves, they do not know that we still live in the same county. Hurlbut ensures that my name never appears in any of the penny sheets my father might be called upon to print, so you see, I have become a ghost to them. He is bent over his box of type by the light of a single lamp, my mother knits in a chair by the window — this is how I usually find them. I can only press my nose to the glass like the boy I once was and assure myself that they are safe, that the Hurlbuts are still holding up their end of the bargain. But looking in from the outside convinces me of little else, save for the fact that my heart is broken.

★ ★ ★

The weeks passed quickly as I continued my search for May and Polly Kimball. There was little movement to auction off the Ashland farm — under the best of circumstances, things municipal in nature happen slowly. But something inside me had begun to change. No matter how hard I tried to deafen myself to its sound, a mysterious hand rapped persistently on the window of my conscience. The Kimballs' misfortune called to me, a siren's song of unhappiness that swelled with the reckless hope that I might be able to save them. Faced with such familiar bewitchment, I did not seek a mast to which I might, in the tradition of Odysseus, lash myself against temptation.

Instead, I have given in and devoted myself in earnest to finding and delivering them. I am unfamiliar with diligence that is anything but detached — even uncaring — and for the first time in my career as an oft-time wayward inspector, a case presents me with a deeper and more personal objective. Other than an unusually strong desire to see Hurlbut's plan fail, I have yet to understand my response. I am certain only that my involvement is not without risk, for in tampering with the Kimball case, I am placing my faith in fire and I cannot be sure it is any more dependable an ally than ice.

Polly

She had arrived in The City of Hope with the dawning of a crisp autumn day; now, it was early December and she had yet to have a second Vision in Meeting. This appeared to have little effect on the believers' faith in her. In their minds, she had come to them and made of herself a vessel for Mother Ann's word. Even if the miracle never happened again, she had been anointed a Visionist and would never be known as anything other. But why had her angels not come to her of late? Polly wondered. She did not miss the terror that preceded their visitations, but she wished she could feel the comfort of their presence. If only they could take away her doubts and fears. If only they could erase the evils of her past.

She worried, too, that Elder Sister Agnes continued to expect her to prove herself. The eldress's suspicions weighed on her almost as heavily as the history she sought to hide. It was a battle of wills — the eldress's scrutiny pitted against Polly's determination to follow Mama's warning and say nothing about the fire, to hide her father's rapaciousness, to air neither the fear that she had killed him nor the terror that he was still alive and would come for her. She was not sure how much longer she could hold out.

The fact that she had begun to meet with a string of ministers from other communities gave her some reprieve. They were such an earnest lot, and though she found their attention strange, stranger still was the effect they seemed to have on the other believers in The City of Hope. The settlement was small and lay well off the beaten path, rarely catching special notice from the Central Ministry at Mount Lebanon. But since Polly's Vision, everything had changed and pride seemed to have flooded the village, causing its believers to labor harder and worship more fully than ever before.

Even with dreary winter darkening the paths long before the sounding of the dinner bell, the sisters around Polly wove and cooked and mended with their faces aglow.

'By this time of year,' Charity told her, 'when the very shortness of the day makes it appear to last forever, we are a dour lot. But you have brought us light worth the power of a thousand suns. That is why we laugh so readily, and step lightly over the slippery ground.'

Charity's faith in her shone more brightly than did any light she might have delivered unto the believers, and though Polly had the sense that they would have been friends no matter what — for she knew Charity to have been the girl who had walked through the fields of her dreams — she could never have imagined such selfless love between two people. When Polly stroked Charity's arm, tracing the curl of one of her

159

markings, she cherished her friend all the more deeply for the beauty of her imperfection. She admired her strength of devotion, but it was Charity's humanity that she treasured. It made her feel that, someday, her own invisible markings — the secrets she carried inside — might find acceptance, that she might someday be able to put the past behind her.

Even so, she was often loath to believe Charity's unwavering convictions. It was true that the brethren bowed their heads when they passed, half in greeting and half to hide their shy smiles. And that the sisters, save for the few who envied the attention her gift had brought her, treated her with warmth and respect. She had nothing to which she could compare such appreciation. At home, she had been called a lazy whore-child, worth less than the dirt on which she stood. To acknowledge her influence here, to allow herself to accept that her Vision had affected others in such a profound way — oh, how happy she would be if only she could. But, unfamiliar with being at the center of things, she could not comprehend that she was the shaft around which the wheels spun.

'Sister,' Elder Caleb called to her one evening as she left the dairy, having returned to attend to some chores she had been unable to finish earlier in the day. She was late for the small nightly Meeting held in the North Family dwelling house. This was a time for learning new songs and dances, and Polly had come to enjoy the gatherings. Unlike Sabbath Day Meeting, they were light affairs — suffused with seriousness of purpose and respect for the operations to be mastered, yet leavened as well with moments of laughter between sister and brother. She worried she might miss the event if the elder kept her too long, but there was little she could do about it. One did not give short shrift to the most revered believer in The City of Hope.

'Elder Brother Caleb,' she answered, lowering her gaze. 'Good evening to you.'

He hurried towards her, his shoes squeaking on the new-fallen snow, his breath coming in rapid puffs that dissolved in the winter air. 'I shan't keep you, I promise. I have been meaning to speak to you for some time now, but you are either surrounded by sisters and ministers, or hard at work. Indeed, rarely have I known so busy a new believer!'

'I would have asked Elder Sister Agnes to bring me to you myself had I known your wishes,' Polly answered. Was it ruder to avert her gaze or to acknowledge him fully? She had learned that it was highly unusual for a sister to find herself alone with one of the brethren — even an elder — and she worried that a passerby might be shocked by the impropriety.

But Elder Brother Caleb seemed not the least bit concerned. 'Visionist that you are, I would not expect you to predict my intentions,' he said, smiling. 'I merely wanted to inquire as to how you are faring under the burden of so much attention. Elder Sister Agnes says that it affects you not a whit. Indeed, she notes that you appear to have stepped with surprising ease into your new role.'

He paused a moment as though he had arrived at a fork in the road of the conversation and was considering which turn to take. He chose the smoother path and looked all the more relieved to have done so. 'Whatever my esteemed Elder Sister says, I wonder if there might be another side to finding oneself suddenly beholden to such expectation.'

His ruddy, full face was possessed of warmth and joviality — something Polly hardly saw in the somber expressions of the other elders and eldresses. Doubtless they worshipped as steadfastly as did Elder Brother Caleb, but he alone expressed the joy of his faith so openly. It was as though he viewed his place in The City of Hope with gratitude to Mother, not merely by adhering strictly to her rules but by taking genuine delight in following them. *He lives his beliefs*, Polly thought, *as enthusiastically as he lives his life*. Had she ever lived hers with anything but survival in mind?

'You are kind to concern yourself with my well-being,' Polly said, finally daring to meet his regard. 'But you needn't worry. I assure you that the honor I feel is outweighed only by my wish to deserve the gift that has been ascribed to me. I am full to the brim with gratitude, Elder Caleb. There is no room for anything else.'

She could not help shivering at the lie she spoke. For there was certainly room in her heart for the pain she felt whenever she remembered that — in spite of all they had given her — the believers had taken Ben. And there was room in her heart to resent Mama's leaving. Why had she

162

again tasked Polly with watching over her brother when others were determined to steal him away? At nine years old, she had been too young to realize the full extent of her father's hatefulness, for he had yet to seek her out in the night. That he was a bully and a drunk who beat her mother? Yes. That he was capable of grabbing Ben when Polly's back was turned and trying to drown him? No. Here, what else could Polly do except hope for a glimpse of her brother, wondering always what she could do to take him back — and when she could do it.

'You have given us all great strength, Sister,' Elder Caleb said kindly, watching her as her mind churned. 'And for that I thank you. I only hope that you have drawn similar blessings from us.'

'To a one, Elder Caleb,' she answered, 'the believers have shown great patience and made me feel most welcome.'

He nodded. But had she detected a flicker of skepticism in his regard — just a twitch of the eye, a glance that lasted half a beat too long? Polly thought back to her meeting with Elder Sister Agnes weeks before. Did she still disdain Polly? Elder Caleb took his meals with her in the elders' dining room every day and the eldress was no actress. What effect might the constancy of her suspicion have had upon him?

They stood silently in the darkness at the center of divergent paths.

'Well,' Elder Caleb said, clasping his hands together, his voice breaking through her somber thoughts. 'I have delayed you long enough,

Sister. My apologies to Elder Sister Agnes and the others if I have made you late for Meeting.'

Polly bent into a stiff curtsy as he bowed good night and they turned from each other, walking in opposite directions. What was happening to her? She had been fairly warned of the burden that would accompany the believers' unwavering faith — Elder Sister Agnes had seen to that. Why hadn't she had the courage to confess everything when she'd had the chance? Instead, ever fearful that she would be thrown back into a world full of danger and uncertainty, she had chosen to live with the burden of having lied. *I am building a house of cards*, she thought. *What will it bring down with it when it falls?*

Morning brought her face-to-face with yet another visiting minister, another sober man who asked the same sober questions as had every sober minister before him. *Could you hear Her speaking to you? Did She direct your movements? How, precisely, did She enter your soul?* Like all the others, he was dressed in the backward style of a Shaker brother, his hair cut straight across his brow such that it sat like a lid atop his head. As she did throughout each inquisition, Polly sat bolt upright in her chair, which faced his but had been placed a respectable distance away. Elder Sister Agnes watched and listened from her seat in the corner of the room. It was like being a field mouse who knows he's been marked by a circling hawk.

She could hardly keep her mind on her answers, so deeply was she lost to guessing at her eldress's thoughts. Surely Elder Sister Agnes saw the same changes in the settlement as did Charity. Had they not pleased her? Polly shifted in her seat and gazed at her inquisitor. As she spoke of angels and the messages they brought and what it felt like to be transported away from all fear, she could not help wondering why they did not gather round her now.

Describing her past visions — without ever mentioning the horrors that had occasioned them — she could sometimes believe that she had reached another world. Indeed, Polly's status as a Visionist had even allowed her to put off the sacred rite of confession, but that could not go on forever. Elder Sister Agnes would demand it eventually, especially now that it was so widely known that The City of Hope had finally found its vessel. That she was a poor farm girl and a novitiate had caused stir enough. That she had yet to submit to mortification? Not even Elder Sister Agnes would be able to keep secret such an irregularity for much longer.

* * *

When she could push her fears away, Polly found moments of happiness. She and Charity were often together during the day. And by night, alone in their room with the door shut against the rest of the world, they fell under the spell of the red book. Though at first she had barely been able to look at it, Charity had slowly let her timidity fall away. How her voice had trembled the first time she asked Polly to read. 'Just a sentence or two,' she'd said, eyes cast down. And now, though she steadfastly refused to touch it, she did not allow a single night to pass without demanding more of the story.

'Where will Mister Wolcott take us this time?' Charity would inquire, nestling under her covers, eager as any child caught up in the spell of a good yarn.

And to be sure, they traveled far and wide with the writer. He told of ships beset by pirates; of tropical ports full of women who wore little but a cloth wound about their waists; of songs sung by drunkards in foul-smelling taverns; of beautiful court ladies dressed in sumptuous silk gowns and glittering jewels, their hair piled high above cheeks and lips reddened with berry juice. The world he described was riotous and exotic, full of forbidden lands so different from The City of Hope that it was as if a brightly colored parrot had landed amidst an affliction of starlings.

'It is as though he is describing a dream,' Charity mused. 'Can there possibly be such places, such people who do exactly as they please?' She looked at Polly, her expression suddenly one of concern. 'Surely, he will write of their punishment soon. Will he not?'

Polly liked reading. Indeed, the changes it had brought about in her friend's attitude surprised and delighted her. The stories seemed to embolden Charity, make her forget her markings, fill her with the sense of freedom that comes from allowing one's mind to wander. The rules, the constant threat of judgment, the work meant to purify their souls — all of it melted away under the hot sun of the Orient. In distant

166

kingdoms, each could find escape. These were among the loveliest times they shared, for the sisters were truly alone in their togetherness.

And yet. While slipping the little red book back under her mattress, Polly thought of how she used to read to Ben, how his eyes grew wide with wonder at the smallest detail in a picture book. The memory of his face made her want to weep, and in such moments, it was as if the little red book were beckoning. *Come with me*, it seemed to say. *Find your Ben and come with me*. Listening to its imagined whispers, Polly recognized the familiar allure of running away.

They had lived in The City of Hope for what seemed a second lifetime, during which her brother had become like a phantom to her. She saw him in Meeting, but other than staring at her in terror when she'd had her Vision that first Sabbath Day, he refused to meet her gaze. Sometimes the pain of his absence was so acute, heavy-heartedness would engulf her and she felt nothing but gloom as she looked at the believers, stamping out their sins, singing their salvation.

In the dining hall — another chance to see him — the believers would stand behind their low-backed chairs, awaiting the sign from their Elder Brother and Sister to sit and begin eating. She did not care about the food. She was searching for Ben. In the earliest days, she hunted in vain. Ben was held away from meals that first week, fed alone on account of his sorrowing. Charity said that she had heard he could not be quieted except when given an elixir made from cicely, garden coltsfoot, honey, and

Madeira wine. He was held to drink it by Brother Andrew, she said, who was kind and well versed in sympathizing with the sorrows of young new believers, and it had brought Ben peace.

The story angered Polly. Should she not have been the one at Ben's side? She had always been good at calming his fears, even when plagued by her own. Away from him, she could do nothing.

Short and tall, slim and stout — her only chance of spotting her brother was to peer through a forest of women wearing long dresses in dark browns and blues with loose-fitting neckerchiefs fastened over their chests.

'It's to hide your womanliness,' Sister Charity had said to Polly on the day she had first attempted to tie her own. *My womanliness?* she remembered thinking. *I am nothing but ribs and skin.*

But then again, Polly had been taught a thousand strange lessons each day. To cut her food into squares and never on the diagonal, for such was the slant of the Devil. To keep separate the bounty that lay on her plate, never mixing it into a hash, a habit so commonly practiced by the World's people. To eat well, finishing all that had been placed before her and then to 'Shaker' her plate by sopping up the leftover juices with the last of her bread. To waste nothing. To leave her plate clean in order that she aid the sisters whose task it was to wash up after meals. To sit still and tall. To refrain from even looking at the brethren.

Before each meal, the sisters and brethren

marched into the dining room in parallel lines without so much as a glance sideways. She had often passed Ben so close that she could smell the barn where the brethren had worked since rising at the four-thirty bell. The warm, sweet perfume of the cows as the men moved by reminded her of home. Mama. Polly could not think about Mama anymore. Not since she'd abandoned them. And Ben. What labor could the brethren have asked of so thin and frail a child? She wanted to call out to him, signal that he was in her presence once more and that everything would be as it was, only better. But she could not make a sound and heard nothing in her head except for the thud of dutiful footfalls as the believers filed into the dining hall, each keeping to their side of an invisible partition and turning to sit at opposite ends of the room.

They dance here almost as they do in Meeting, Polly thought, *though with none of the same abandon.* It amazed her — how many lines the believers could find to follow in this rigid world.

Ben never looked at her, his stare fixed in front of him as he walked in step with the brethren, each following the solemn procession with their right foot stamping just the slightest bit louder than their left. Out of the corner of her eye, she would watch him sit when directed while Brother Andrew helped cut his meat and pour his drink. Her brother barely gave his plate a glance before stabbing at his potatoes with his fork and lifting them to his mouth. What faint traces remained of the boy she remembered! On the table in front of her, platters brimmed with food. They appeared, as if by magic, in a corner cupboard with shelves that moved silently up from the kitchen when one of the sisters pulled hard on a rope that hung close by the wall. No one spoke. They were, she thought, a silent congregation of eaters.

Polly knew she had to finish her food, but there were so many times when she found that she could not. Her stomach heaved and her breathing became shallow and quick. She was becoming sick with longing and she wished that she could feel the spirits close about her, poised to take her from the pain. But they would not come.

'You appear ill, Sister,' Elder Sister Agnes said to her one day. She had stepped into Polly's line of vision as if to break the numbing spell. 'Did something you ate not agree with you?' She appeared impossibly tall as she stood and awaited her answer.

'No,' Polly said. 'I became dizzy is all. I don't know — '

'Are you well enough,' she interrupted, 'to come to my chambers after you have finished your morning chores? I believe it is *my* turn to speak again to the Visionist, now that so many others have had their fill.'

Polly could not find her voice fast enough.

'The answer is a simple one,' Elder Sister Agnes said.

'Yes,' Polly replied. 'I will come.' And with a curt nod, the eldress was gone. *Will this be the*

170

day I confess? Polly wondered. Perhaps this was her opportunity to banish Elder Sister Agnes's doubts. She had worked and worshipped with great vigor, after all. She had become a good Shaker, hadn't she? Might that be enough?

Simon Pryor

As I questioned the inhabitants of Ashland, I should not have been surprised to find such willful apathy. Though for more than a decade they had turned a blind eye to the Kimball family's misfortunes, they were happy to dole out condemnation as though it justified their lack of sympathy. There was not a bar owner for miles around who didn't angrily shake a tally in my face and declare Silas Kimball a thief, a drunkard, and a man who boasted openly of his cruelty at home. Benjamin Briggs's accidental death was lamented, but as for May, she had been a girl of loose morals who sowed the seeds of her own misery when she married so feral a specimen. Polly, the unfortunate fruit of this unholy union, was ignored by all save a schoolteacher and her students, the children she had helped to learn how to read and do their sums. One does, on occasion, come across people who renew — if briefly — one's faith in humanity.

In fact, it was the teacher who told me where I might find the man who would know more about the Kimballs than anyone else, for he had tended to their animals and was the only person Silas never ran off the place. He went by the name of Peeles, she said. Mister William Peeles.

That is how I found myself in a saloon at the far end of Ashland. Not a genteel spot, I'll say that. Dark, smoky, full of customers of the rabbling sort — the place scarcely spoke to my more refined sensibilities. Still, as there was liquor and a penny cigar to be had, it was as good a place as any to approach the man I hoped would further my inquiry.

I was glad that the wear of a dusty ride coated me in a patina of collegial scruffiness. It allowed me to slip less conspicuously from my comfortable chair by the fire into a world far grittier and unpredictable. The men who watered here bore little good feeling towards townsfolk like myself. They worked hard in forge and field and found those whose professions did not leave calluses, burns, stooped backs, missing fingers, the reek of sweat, and the dirt of real labor to be an untrustworthy lot indeed. I cannot say that I much blamed them.

My companions spoke loudly and loosely, doubtless a result of the alcoholic bilge they drank in such copious amounts. Ever since the temperance preachers had begun their self-righteous invasions, whiskey had become increasingly difficult to come by. Wherever the amber fluid flowed freely, one felt the urge to suck it down as might a man who fears he will never drink again.

I approached the bar. 'Is there a gentleman by the name of Peeles here tonight?' I asked the saloonkeeper.

'Who wants to know?' he answered with

suspicion, wariness being a requisite trait in all taverners. He weighed my request as he gave his clouded whiskey glasses a cursory wipe before putting them back on the counter.

'I was told I might find him here,' I said. 'Wanted a word concerning the Kimball family.'

'Got an eye on the land already, do you?' he asked with barely concealed disdain. 'You mill folk don't know much shame, do you?'

'I'm no mill agent,' I assured him. 'Just an inspector looking to find anyone who might have survived.'

He went back to his cleaning. 'Peeles'll come,' he said after a brief silence. 'For all I know he's already down there. You'll recognize him — he'll be the last to leave once it's over and done with.'

He nodded to an open hatch in the floor at the back of the room. It seemed to be swallowing the tavern regulars in great numbers, and though it took me a moment to jostle through the crowd, I too eventually found my way down into a pit surrounded on three sides with rough-cut boards for seating. I closed my eyes against the heat and fug. A fight was about to begin and the placing of bets was well under way.

I regard such amusements with loathing, but this was not the first time I had found myself crawling into the cramped bowels of one drinking establishment or another and waiting for the games to begin. It was neither a fistfight nor a wrestling match between men that attracted the crowd. Not a bit of it. The drinkers were in high spirits because some enterprising fellow had bagged himself a woodchuck and found someone equally opportunistic and cruel to put up a dog. The custom is as straightforward as they come: The man in the pit holds a writhing grain sack containing the wild contender — anything larger than a common cat, with teeth and claws will do — while another stands a few feet away jiggling a piece of raw meat before a cur that has been near-starved for days. As harmless as a chuck may appear, a large male is serious business when cornered. His opponent? The unfortunate creature chosen to fight an animal more formidable than a bag full of rats is usually a veteran of particularly churlish disposition, a dog no man would be sorry to lose.

True to form, the cur across the pit from me was old and battle-scarred — an underdog, as it were, against such a powerful adversary. *Oh, that the worn-out mutt might simply be left in peace*, I thought. The cruelty and brutishness of men is, on occasion, more than I can bear to witness.

So why did I stay? The work, always the work. I am used to depravity of one sort or another — indeed I have been well trained — and it is often in such a Hades that one finds men brim-full of useful information, especially once the fight has ended and the victory rounds have commenced. The well-lubricated winners are primed for indiscretion born of elation, while the losers — having spent their last crumpled notes to numb their disappointment — don't much care what they say. I am served in either circumstance. Temperance be damned — I bless the power of alcohol to transform.

Heat from tallow candles shoved into raw potatoes on the shelf that circled the room stifled any hope of drawing an easy breath. We populated a mere hole in the ground, a sort of square-sided paupers' grave — just as close, just as undiscriminating.

Trapped in such crude surroundings, the senses come under siege — the grit of smoke and pit dust assault the mouth; the smell of drink and puke and urine and sweat offend the nose; the sound of bullying and boasting, of roaring and the ripping of flesh, of bones being crushed, of pained whimpers and growls — how they deaden the ear; the push of the crowd leaning in and in, their thirst for violence, the absence of humanity, the malevolent pull of one's own curiosity — whether physical or atmospheric, these are the evils that rage against one's ability to feel. Even disgust is temporarily suspended.

And what, you might ask, of that fifth sense? What is it that occupies the eye in a pit fight? The stuff of such nightmares that I have learned to watch the battles in bits, never as a whole. The faces of the men, excited to heights of ecstasy better suited to a grunting toss under the roof of a brothel; the rippling muscles of the dog as he wrestles to overthrow his challenger; the bullish wild chuck using his proximity to the ground to flip his opponent, his overwhelming solidity of mass, his teeth and raking claws making again and again for the dog's neck and stomach; the tenacity of life when a quick death is by far the better end.

In this case, the old dog eventually suc-
cumbed; the woodchuck barely breathing but
alive and in shreds. The spectators' fun was over,
and as quickly as they had filled the earthen
theater, they abandoned it. All but one. A lone
observer, long and lean of build, with a face so
deeply lined you'd have thought the years had
been whittled into his cheeks. He wore a solemn
expression — indeed, it was clear he'd shared no
part in the other men's rapture. I watched him
approach the dying chuck, wondering if there
wasn't something strange about him. Why would
he linger in so damned a spot?

A single sharp report provided me an answer.
Smoke trailing from the end of his pistol, the rag
he'd used to catch the blood-spatter hung limp
in his left hand. Shaken, I asked, 'Why?'

'Must have put a mercy bullet in a hundred
animals since I been coming here,' he said,
looking up from the corpse. 'Can't stop the fight
when torture's all that moves some men. But the
creature unlucky enough to be left breathing?
Well, I can make short work of his misery.'

He turned to climb the stairs, and I had no
words with which to call him back. No reason
either. A man who suffers through fight after
fight only to shoot the last animal standing
— that was as strange a sort of goodness as ever
I'd known. Making my way past the carnage, I
ascended to the bar where the keep indicated to
me with a quick nod that the somber Mister
Peeles, having pocketed his pistol and cloth, had
taken his usual seat.

I sat down next to him, ordering what I

considered to be an essential and well-earned drink.

'Stake you to the same?' I asked.

'Lead a man to whiskey these days and you'll have no trouble making him drink,' he said, his voice a weary and graveled rasp that I imagined to have been born of smoke, liquor, and disgust.

'Name's Pryor.' I pushed a glass of murky liquid his way.

'Peeles,' he answered as we saluted without looking at each other, then drank down the questionable brew in a single gulp. I had learned long ago not to sip my poison in such company, for it signals softness and a sense of leisure enjoyed solely by the rich and is thus an affectation that squelches useful conversation. Besides, why prolong the agony of the burn?

'You from 'round here?' he asked, looking straight ahead. 'I never seen your like in this place.'

'Next town over,' I replied, nodding my head in the direction of Hatch and Burns' Hollow. 'The incendiary that flared over by the Kimball farm. Know of it?'

'I read the notice,' he said cautiously. Clearly, he shared the barkeep's dislike of mill agents who comb over poor farms and damaged properties in hope of securing them cheaply and without complication. They were an aggressive breed of land-grabber — land, always land at the center of men's greed these days. Brazen enough to lure young country girls from their families with the promise of good wages and freedom from the chafing rules of home, the mill agents

178

were considered lower than thieves by the type to congregate at taverns like the one in which Peeles and I now sat. And I can't say I felt any differently about them. Their noisy monuments to industry dominated once peaceful fields and turned babbling brooks into foul-smelling runs, boiling with waste and tinted whorishly by the dye-lot of the day.

'I'm not one of them,' I said quickly. 'No, I have business concerning the fire on behalf of the county. Fire inspector's what I am. But there's only so much a man can glean from ashes and I'm looking to find out more about the family. You know them?'

He paused before turning to stare into my eyes for the first time. Paused quite a while, actually, as though trying to determine if it was worth the effort to tell me what he knew.

'Yessir, I did,' he said finally, his gray eyes focusing ahead once more. I sensed a familiar struggle within him — the reluctance to speak pitted against the need to unburden himself. Most people with anything real to say suffer from it. But it was only when he eyed his empty glass that I recognized the deal to be struck. He would talk so long as I held up my end of the bargain.

I spotted us both to another round and followed suit as he tipped back his shot then placed the empty glass on the bar.

'They weren't like most, if that helps any.'

'No,' I said, 'I'm beginning to get that feeling.'

Peeles's way with animals — which explained his quiet abhorrence of the evening's proceedings and his self-appointed role in bringing them to a quick if startling close — was seen as a valuable skill by many of the country folk who live on outlying farms. He told me he ministered not only to their livestock but to their families as well. Living and dying and sickness and birth, like any doctor, he knew about all that. But he understood something less concrete as well. He understood that poverty, pride, and independence puzzle together to make a wall that rarely admits outsiders. That was why people like Silas Kimball trusted Peeles.

'I never liked goin' out to Kimball's place,' he said. 'For one thing, after old Briggs died, it weren't what anyone would call a proper farm no more. That were a sad thing to see.'

He looked up at the motley collection of bottles on a dirty shelf behind the bar. We drank another round.

'If you've talked to anyone in town, then you already know that Silas beat young May. And he weren't much of a father neither, from what I could see. His girl Polly was skinny and drawn like a ghost, and . . . Well, it's a funny thing about townsfolk. When it were Mister and Missus Benjamin Briggs living on that farm, they pulled 'em in like a flock of sheep'll herd round its own. But when Silas come along, it were as if those selfsame folk lost any interest in knowing they was alive.'

'So you knew both families from years back?' I asked. 'From before the time that Benjamin Briggs died?'

I did not need to delve so deep. But different as it was from my own tale, I felt a strange likeness beginning to bloom between the two. You might say that the troubles of my early years have taught me to climb into the skins of others. To feel myself wrap men's souls about me, pull my feet into the boots of total strangers, settle their hats firmly on my head so that my view becomes one with their own. It's a transformation I welcome, despite the attendant complications.

'Oh I knew 'em all right,' he said. 'Enough to see a wealthy man sweat out a fine farm of his own hand then die for no reason. I seen Silas 'round the time Briggs died. I knew then that things were anything but right.'

'How?' I prodded. 'How did you know?' Intuition told me that Silas was the bolt of lightning that split the tree.

'I don't put stock in rumor,' Peeles answered cautiously. 'You just happened to ask 'bout something no one else cares to know. And with that farm lost in a blaze and everyone gone missing, I figure there ain't much harm in telling you.'

He paused. I signaled the barkeep. Peeles recommenced speaking. This was our pattern.

'It were spring,' he began. 'I remember because I had calves born all which way that year. No cow seemed to be birthin' straight — no sheep neither — so I was everywhere, which means that I heard and saw most everything there was to wonder about. One day, I was walking home on the road that passes the school-house. It were late morning. No one about. The girls were in with the old

181

schoolmarm and damn near everyone else and his son were in a field somewhere. So I was surprised to catch sight of a boy old enough for farmwork. Thin and tall, maybe fifteen years on him, not many more. I knew from the odd gait he kept that it were the Kimball boy. He were quick and light as he run up the bank of the road, then down again in a kind of game. But the sun was shining my way and I'd been up half the night with a breech, so I didn't catch it right away.'

'Catch what?' I interrupted.

'The blood on him, his shirt marked with red, arms covered with it already dried brown. It nervoused me some, I'll say that. Like old Briggs, I suppose I had a soft spot for the boy in those early years before I come to know better. He 'peared smart, in a twitchy sort of a way, and though he'd never been learned more 'n a little math in school and a little farming from Benjamin Briggs, he tried to have a good manner to him when he was younger. He looked the savage that morning though, something changed 'bout him. All that blood. I couldn't hardly look at him; then I couldn't hardly let him go neither.

' "What you bin about?" I asked, but he just stared at me. 'What you bin at to be covered in blood?' says I, reaching out to stop him passing me by. 'And why aren't you out helping Briggs?'

' "He's gone now. Gone for good and there ain't no one but me and May." ' Peeles nodded for the barman to refill his glass. 'I was barely fit to speak after what he told me,' he said. 'But I

182

had to ask: 'What about the blood?' I weren't a bit sure I wanted to know, but I kept on. 'That Briggs's blood, boy?'

' 'The blood?' he says, almost like he forgot he was covered. 'That's him, all right. I tried to help him, see. Went to him right away after he was hit.'

' 'Hit by what?' I asked.

' 'Why, by the beam. It fell just like that, no warning. Just swung down and hit him square in the head.'

'I didn't believe the boy,' Peeles said. 'How things could up and change so fast. Why, I'd seen Benjamin Briggs buyin' seed not a week prior. And here's Silas, covered in his blood. Said he tried to get him up, see if he was still alive.'

Peeles swirled the whiskey in his glass. 'I thought, how's a thing like that happen? In a new barn? How's a joint get loose without a farmer like Briggs noticing?' He gulped the drink down. 'I said I'd best go out to the farm and so I did. And there he was, in a heap, dragged out from under the wood, blood everywhere.

' 'Why didn't you call upon May to fetch me?' I asked Silas. 'You know I been round before.' 'Well, sir,' he said, 'May run to school the whole way after she saw him. Just cried and run, wantin' to get away from me, I'm guessin'. Been there ever since. But we're together now. Yessir, we're married. And May's with child — my child — whether anyone like it or no.' '

Peeles sat quietly a moment. 'She can't have been more'n thirteen. Heard later that after Silas took me back to the farm, he went round the schoolhouse. Walked in the door while the girls were at their lessons. The older ones like May, they sit at the back, see, while the teacher keeps the pups up close where she can watch 'em. They say Silas stood there, quiet like, in the door 'til May looked up. They say that's when the others saw the blood and started to scream. But frighteningest thing of all was that he was just smiling and pointing at May, smiling an' pointing like they was in a game of chase and she was It. Fell into a faint, the poor girl did. Never went school-ways again that I know of.'

He paused. 'Townsfolk say Silas was a savage. Marked May for his own that day. The constables came, asked a lot of questions. But in the end, there weren't nothing they could do but call it an accident.'

'You think Briggs was murdered?' I asked.

Peeles stared at me before looking down at the bar and tapping his glass. Once filled, he tipped it back before answering.

'Silas has murder in him, that much I can tell you for certain,' he said. 'I have my opinions about whether he killed Briggs, but that were a long time ago. Don't matter much now.'

'And yet it's the reason you're so sure he was a murderer, isn't it?'

By this time, Peeles's eyes were rheumy with drink and exhaustion. 'Understand me good,' he said. 'I'd've sooner laid down in a nest full of copperheads than gone to Briggs's that day. But I felt sorry for May and the boy. That's why May knew she could trust me when her baby girl needed birthin'. That's how I came to see things

184

change, came to know how far she sank the day she hitched herself to Silas Kimball. But I'm done thinking about them, Mister. I don't like the tale — use it any way you will. Far as I'm concerned, the fire was a blessing. Just tell me this: They all live?'

'Found Silas dead in his bed,' I answered. 'Can't say what's happened to May and the girl.'

'And the boy?' he asked, looking down. 'He dead, too?'

I wasn't sure I'd heard him right. 'Boy?' I said. 'What boy?'

Peeles stared at me a moment, then looked away and clucked in disgust.

'That's a tale for someone else to tell,' he said. 'And you won't find but one or two you can turn to for the whole truth.' He stood, turned to leave, and, with his back to me, lifted his hand as if to swat me away. It was a strange farewell, but he'd had his fill of whiskey and, doubtless, of me as well.

I sat awhile, tossing back the dregs of my drink. Why was May Kimball proving so difficult to find? A family that's invisible in full view can disappear without much made of it. Still, with little ones to care for — not so easy.

She has a son, I thought to myself. Why hadn't his name been entered into the town records?

I rode home in the dark, my head swirling in a swill-fueled fog. *Where are you, May Kimball?* I asked myself over and over. In the back of my mind, a ghost was lurking, and when I fell exhausted onto my bed, stinking of drink and cheap smokes, I could hear — in spite of the

185

enduring tinnitus of tavern chatter — a child's voice. As ever, it pleaded with me, and before sleep descended — before the room stopped spinning and my mind went blank — I wagered I was lost.

Sister Charity

'Does your Sister Polly exhibit operations in her sleep?'

The question startled me, as I was lost in imagining the life of a sojourner. Until the red book, my nose never twitched at the smell of horse sweat nor spice in the kitchens nor smoke from the stove fires. Such things surrounded me, but I concentrated on *doing*. There was not time to feel, see, or hear. I paid no mind to the bright blue of a jay, nor did I wonder at how its brilliance brought out the muted world around me. The stories I read each night with Sister Polly had changed me, and though I was glad for it, I understood why books from the World are forbidden here. In a sister less steadfast, they might breed envy, curiosity, even discontent, and none of these is a friend of faith.

Fortunately, I found it simple to separate idle fantasy from the work I perform as a believer, and so I was able to will my thoughts with ease back to the gathering room in which I sat with my Church Family sisters. The sound of a single sister's voice above the peaceful burble of quiet conversation had occasioned the turning of many linen-capped faces towards mine. Such a patch of mushrooms we appear! You see? I had never before noticed it.

Sister Lavinia sat beside me, a gentle presence; not so Sister Ruth, who regarded me from across the room with cold eyes and a mouth pursed tight. She is the cruelest of us all, for when my markings first appeared, she whispered it round that the impurity of my true nature was clear for the reading on the surface of my skin. I remain inked with strange designs, but while most believers no longer stare at me, Sister Ruth seems never to cease in her scrutiny. It is humiliating, and though I try to look upon her with sympathy, I fail more often than not. Her meanness protrudes like the bones of a starving dog. Indeed, I wonder if perhaps she was born sour, for I remember her family dropping her here and leaving without so much as a glance back. She was only ten years of age at the time, but she seemed a heavy load they were eager to set down and never bear the likes of again. Standing by Elder Sister Agnes's side, I watched Sister Ruth's eyes follow the dust of her kin's retreating carriage. Her cheek twitched, then her chin, but that was the last and only sign that her abandonment had caused her pain. Looking over at her now, I chastised myself for begrudging such a forlorn soul its bitterness.

I had yet to answer the question posed to me about how my Sister Polly sleeps, and Sister Prudence, sweet thing, stared at me with the wide, questioning regard of one ever ready to supply the proper emotional display once informed as to what that display should be. Were

I to respond coldly now, for a sample, she would utter a soft *tsk tsk* under her breath, resuming her knitting while shaking her head at the insolence of the inquiry. But I offered no such answer, allowing instead the clicking of my needles to fill the silence.

'Sister Polly,' I said when I was ready, 'is as worn out as the rest of us when she lies down. She sleeps most quietly, not uttering anything like the sounds I have, on occasion, heard coming from even the daintiest of girls gathered in this room.'

The older sisters giggled — especially Sister Prudence, who never failed to look relieved when called upon to exhibit humor over contempt. They knew that though I had not shared a room with anyone save Sister Polly, I have — in my capacity as caretaker to many a new believer — looked in on most all of the young sisters here, and I could say a pretty piece about what sorts of operations they perform in their sleep were I of a mind to do so.

Pettiness aside, I was reminded of how pleasant it can be to pass an evening in this manner. The room was warm — chairs circled closely round the stove, lamplight casting a golden glow. I sighed and wound the skein of red wool that had become unruly in my lap. I had been caught up in racing through my chores so that I might arrive more quickly at the end of each day, tucked beneath my covers, ready to listen to Sister Polly read from our book. Do you know that last night, we entered into Arabia and met a king who had not one but eleven wives?

'Imagine what Mother would say about that!' Polly commented with a smile. 'The poor Sultan! To think of him here, hauling stones from the field. Much nicer to imagine him with his pipe and flowing robes and . . . '

'Stop!' I exclaimed. Because truly, I did not like this King of Arabia. The place itself — its endless waves of sand, its camels and strange islands of water in the desert sea — I was happy enough to envision that. But to hear tell about the customs of such a sinful lot . . . How could my Sister Polly have laughed?

It troubles me still that I did not ask her to put the book away. But once we had moved on from the carnality I so despised, I was able to sleep content in the knowledge that next time we ventured into the World — a World so distant that it posed little threat to the sanctity of The City of Hope — we would be in Egypt. There, I was certain, we would encounter natives of a more principled nature.

Sitting with my knitting in hand, I could not have been further from exotic lands, but I was content. Content in part because it pleased Elder Sister Agnes that I had come. She had approached me in the laundry earlier that day and asked if I might join my sisters for the evening, and though I knew Sister Polly would wonder where I was, I said that I would. The hours I spent in the company of my new friend had become cause for comment among certain of the believers. Those of a coldhearted bent whispered that I might have attached myself on account of her renown as a Visionist, for she was becoming famous. Why, not even one week ago, the Central Ministry at New Lebanon sent Brother Isaac Youngs — he who has visited all of the Eastern settlements to record spirit manifestations of one sort or another.

'Like everyone else, he asked me what it was that I saw when I fell into my Vision,' Sister Polly said when she told me of their meeting. 'But truthfully, I was relieved to encounter someone who might explain to me why such things happen. He has spoken to many Visionists . . . to many sisters is what I mean. I suppose that is why I thought he might be able to see beneath the surface of things. Do you understand?'

I had nodded at the time. But it struck me as strange that Sister Polly needed another to explain what surely was as natural an occurrence in her as is happiness or self-doubt or irritation in the rest of us.

Though I'm not certain that Brother Isaac had much of an answer for her, he did describe some of the happenings he had seen in the other settlements. In Wisdom's Valley, for a sample, he spoke of witnessing two sisters with closed eyes, unaffected by any distraction yet perfectly joined in a great variety of exercises. He told Sister Polly they sang songs that had never before been heard, in unknown tongues but also in English, with beautiful, intricate, and graceful motions, both in complete unison and perfect time, never stumbling. As well as speaking about them, he acted out the operations of other Visionists he had met before coming to The City of Hope: bowing and shaking, writhing and twisting, shouting for joy and groaning in agony. My dear friend admitted with a smile that she was taken aback by his mimicry but also drawn to its fervor, for she recognized parts of herself in the passion he displayed and felt all the less alone for it.

Needless to say, in near every Meeting, Elder Brother Caleb expresses his pleasure and astonishment over Sister Polly's gift as well as other, smaller transformations — the quick step he sees in the brethren's strides as they go about their work; the sisters' renewed enthusiasm for making baskets, bonnets, and cloaks to sell beyond our walls. Barely two months have passed since her arrival, yet she has set the world spinning faster beneath our feet. We worship with more passion, we are kinder and less impatient with one another, we perform our chores with more heartfelt devotion, and, most miraculous of all, we know that we are seen in all of our labors by a host of Heavenly spirits.

'It gives great satisfaction,' Elder Sister Agnes had said to me that very morning in the laundry, 'that our community has found its way into the close embrace of the believers at New Lebanon. But I understand Brother Isaac's task to be one of weeding out impersonators as much as writing down the Visions of the truly divine instruments.' She checked that a freshly washed white apron did not bear a stain.

I kept my head down as I turned the crank and wrung out the water from the laundered clothes. I did not want to appear to be correcting my eldress.

'Surely,' I said, 'if you'll pardon my forthrightness, Elder Sister Agnes, he would not pass so much as an hour with Sister Polly if he thought her to be false. Once a pretender shows herself, it is my understanding that he moves on.'

She regarded me a moment in silence. 'I cannot know the precise nature of the interest Sister Polly holds for Brother Isaac,' she said, her words quiet yet forceful in the precision with which she uttered them. 'But do you not ask yourself how the powers of a Visionist could have been bestowed upon one so recently come from the World? Why, you know better than anyone that there are believers who toil a lifetime in service to Mother and yet She bestows her gift on a girl whose body has barely been washed clean, let alone her soul?' A knot of wet neckerchiefs lay before her, and though she needn't have paid them any mind — they were, after all, for me to shake out and hang — she plucked them one from another, pulling each edge straight before folding it over the drying rack next to the clean aprons. 'And you, child. Do you not question how readily you have put your faith in such a novice?'

I wished I could put an end to her suspicion — it pinched like shoes that are too small. I did not want to see it, but my eldress's bitter envy was plain. If I had been chosen as a Visionist, the honor would have reflected holiness on her. Elder Sister Agnes would have been rewarded for the constancy of her own worship as well as the purity she had instilled in me. I could hardly bear the thought that so revered a believer needed such affirmation. But then, how unlike her first experience with the Visionists in Wisdom's Valley this time must seem to her. There, she was naught but a visiting teacher, an amazed bystander. Here, she has a congregation of believers to protect and guide. I feel for her, but I do not agree with her.

'Sister Polly is my charge,' I said. 'Closer to me, perhaps, than some of the others, but only because you asked that I be her caretaker. You gave me that duty, and I have tried to fulfill it . . .'

Elder Sister Agnes sighed, smiling as she laid the last neckerchief in its place. 'I did indeed ask you to care for her,' she said. 'And you have done so with great heart. But I have known you, dear Sister Charity, from near birth. You believe, without question, anyone in whom you can find some good. Any good. I, who have lived longer and seen more than you, know there can be danger in that.'

'Would you have me ignore her now?' I asked, my voice as steady as I could make it.

'I would never ask that you turn your back on a sister,' she answered. 'I request simply that you remember *all* of the people who love you here, and that you begin once more to share your daily favor with them.'

She reached out from where she stood as if to touch me, though we were far enough apart that she could not. 'Look at the marks that still sear your skin. You bear them without complaint or self-pity despite the behavior of certain of the sisters, who have not treated you as you deserve.

But there are many others who miss you in your absence. I pray with my whole being that you shall be well again, and have kept my love . . . '

Her voice faded as she stood next to the washing table with her arms hanging loosely by her sides. She appeared small and slack, as though work and discipline were the only winds that could fill her sails. I did not like to see her so feeble. It frightened me. Moving towards her, I took her hands. She spoke out of love for me, not dislike of Sister Polly. 'I have understood your wisdom well, Elder Sister Agnes,' I said. 'You needn't worry. Tonight, I shall be glad to be back with my sisters again. Then you shall know that, in the important matters, none shines before me any more brightly than another.'

She gripped firmly before letting go and straightening herself to leave. She found strength in the fact that I had not forgotten her teachings, that she had not labored so diligently only to lose me — first to my markings, now to the whims of another sister's heart. 'I shall be pleased to see you later,' she said briskly. 'It will remind me of less tumultuous times.'

She turned and left, shutting the door softly, as if she wished to be neither seen nor heard having visited me. She had no reason to hide, yet she slipped away as a shadow fades into light.

Of the sister's inquiry into the sleep of my dear friend? My answer had been a lie. Sister Polly does not rest soundly, and though she rarely makes a noise except to cry out in a manner so pleading that it breaks my heart to hear it, she tosses as wildly as if a net were thrown over her. I rise each time it happens and sit beside her, stroking her arm and uttering the most soothing sounds I know, but she holds fast to her terror then awakes with a start, regarding me as if I were the cause. Sometimes she addresses me, though it seems clear that she cannot truly be speaking to a dear sister but rather is locked in the hold of some creature she can bear neither sight nor sound of. When I reach forth to calm her, she jumps away and makes herself a crumple of limbs. It alarms me, and when she comes to, though she lets me embrace her and rock her in my arms until she has fallen back asleep, I am left with the uneasy feeling that a malicious presence lingers over us.

Her anguish will disappear, but only when she trusts that I am here to protect her. I have seen the stern glances Elder Sister Agnes flashes at me when she fears my love for Sister Polly is overshadowing the devotion and meaning in which I steep such simple acts as sweeping the floor of the dwelling house, pressing apples, pulling the fur from a raccoon pelt that it might be spun into thread and used for the knitting of mittens. Those are the moments when Mother makes Herself most visible, the better to inspire us to do our work as She would wish it. My eldress has taken a lifetime to teach me this.

But I have found that Mother resides in a rarer place still, at the center of another sister's heart. When I find Her there, She shows me that my worries are one with Sister Polly's. She teaches me that our laughter rings out more fully for being forged by the both of us, that she and I fashion a single young sister in all that we say and do. And Mother tells me that this is a wondrous thing.

I know that such attachments are to be discouraged, for they can only lead to the destruction of union. Why, even knitting a scarf for another or saving her a sweet bun from the kitchen is considered by the strictest believers to be an affront to the whole. Even the diversion of a child's affection for a pup or kitten is known by all to be against the teachings written in the *Book of Secrets*. For in that text, Mother Ann says:

> *You ought not to give your feelings to beasts more than is necessary to make a good use of them. You must not allow dogs, nor cats, to come into the house of worship, nor dogs into dwelling-houses; for it is contrary to good order . . . Remember what I say, Dogs and cats are unclean beasts, and full of evil spirits; therefore, if any of you, old or young, unite and play with them, you will be defiled. I cannot hold my peace, I am constrained to roar out of Zion against the sins of man with beasts.*

Why had my mind turned to animals? I wished that it would cease wandering, for again the sisters were talking about my Sister Polly and I knew I should prick up my ears. It was a relief when I heard Sister Eunice speak, her voice rich and wise. I relaxed my guard and kept my eyes on my work.

'I have rarely seen a sister who walks so light of step and yet can manage such heavy tasks,' she said, appearing to speak to the yarn in the sweater over which she labored. 'The other day, I watched Sister Polly lift the largest of the pickling jars and carry it to the farthest storeroom. She knew I was nearby, but she did not call out for help in her chore. I felt that Mother showed me that even one possessed of the ghostliest presence can toil with the strength of an ox in her labors.'

'Indeed,' answered Sister Regina, 'she is a pleasant girl, both to look upon as well as in her manner. Just Tuesday last, she bent to help me gather something I had spilled — what were they now? I remember fewer and fewer of life's details . . . At any rate, her face was aglow when she turned it towards mine, smiling so kindly as to make me feel as though I was blessed to have been brought so close to her goodness. It made light my heart the remainder of the day.'

This quieted the room for a bit. Then one of my younger sisters — Sister Vestia — commented that she wondered that the possessor of so light a spirit and frame could keep herself upon the earth at all, that perhaps Sister Polly had filled her shoes with stones to act as ballast.

Sister Honora, a wicked compatriot, giggled and added, 'If we are lucky, we might catch our dear Visionist rising ethereally into the Heavens from the Sabbath Meeting, for there is little room for stones in the soft shoes we wear for dancing.'

'Wouldn't that be a sight for sore eyes!' Sister Vestia exclaimed. The other sisters lowered their chins to their chests, the better to peer at one another from beneath arched eyebrows.

How well I knew such changes in the conversational weather, for this particular group ridiculed with great agility, never saying anything for which they could be chastised by their eldress yet successfully turning the tenor of an evening in such a way that no one felt in safe company. This was the case now, and as I looked up, briefly, I caught the nervous glances exchanged between the elder sisters, afraid for whoever might feel the sting next.

'How little some of you have changed since I last passed an evening here,' I said calmly. 'Stimulating talk is a temptation for us all, is it not?'

I wrapped up my knitting in a clean cloth and placed it in my basket. I displayed not a jot of irritation in my movements. Smiling and raising myself slowly out of my chair, I regarded my eldress. She stared back. We are, I think, in a game of hide-and-seek, where neither wants to show the other her thoughts.

'Good night, Elder Sister Agnes,' I said. And in truth, I wished her nothing but goodness. She did not encourage the young sisters' pettiness. Rather, I think she was made uncomfortable by it, for it revealed the sort of character she abhorred and I could feel her disappointment that the evening had not taken a different turn. She does not accept that I have never really fit in. My faith, my markings, my friendship with

Sister Polly — they hold me apart, even from her.

I finished saying my good-byes. 'Alas, I must leave the rest of you to complete your work in peace. My nights have been quiet of late and I am unaccustomed to the spiritedness you display. Good night, dearest Sisters Lavinia and Prudence. And, Sister Eunice, you have warmed my heart. To all, I trust sleep will come easy.'

In the entry hall, I unhooked my cape from where it hung alongside those of the other sisters. The pegs were numbered by chamber, but as I was a visitor on this night, mine was blank. I breathed deeply. The room had become hot and still — full of the odors of sweat and smoke from the stove — and I found myself pausing in the cool dark of the vestibule before heading outside. In the retiring room, having taken up where they left off, the sisters were laughing again.

'Had you not heard?' This from a new and very pretty young sister named Abigail. 'Our buoyant sister was spotted just yesterday, floating outside the windows of the Brethren's Workshop. She was, no doubt, seeking only to inspire those within.'

'Or perhaps to give them a vision more earthly in kind!' said Sister Ruth, her laugh as acid as a tanner's bath. The young sisters joined in her mirth and then suddenly went quiet. My eldress had doubtless thrown a withering glance around the circle. It was a look I knew well; it left little need for words.

Pulling on my cape, I pushed open the heavy

main door and stepped outside. It had been injuring to listen to my sisters mock the one I have come to believe in with such fullness. Had I done enough to defend her? Had I not, myself, allowed my mind to drift into judgment when I thought of Sister Polly and the Sultan?

I shook my shoulders loose and stood on the snowy path. Beneath such a full moon I felt the world to be generous again. I could believe once more in happenings too strange for others to comprehend. I could hear in the rattling of tree branches a language so intricate that few could glean meaning from the mysterious creaks and cracking. I moved along, glad to be walking the dark road towards the North Family houses. For there, I knew, resided one who heard and understood everything, one at whose feet I could lay all of my doubts and find not scorn but love.

Simon Pryor

I think that I have made it quite plain: I do not believe in Providence. However, I must admit to moments when it seems an invisible hand extends itself and pulls sinners like me up out of the mire. On the particular morning of my salvation, I trundled downstairs after a bath and a shave — even in the dullest of times, one must keep up appearances — to find the corner of a letter peeking out from under my door. I pulled it to me and squinted hard at the print, for though it spread tidily across the envelope — each letter as perfectly formed as the next — it appeared very small indeed.

To Neighbor Simon Pryor, it read. Strange, I thought, because never have I known a single one of my neighbors to categorize our relationship so officially.

Making my way to the study, I looked forward to an interesting morning read. I settled into the sagging seat of my chair — as clear a reprimand for my sedentary ways as a piece of furniture can manage — and slit open the missive.

Dear Neighbor Pryor,
  My name is Elder Sister Agnes and I

202

reside in a place that is referred to by your kind as 'the Shaker settlement' in Albion. You should know that we believers refer to our home as The City of Hope, and that is what I shall call it henceforth. I expect you to do the same.

I was recently made aware that a fire took place some time ago on the outskirts of Ashland. The mention in the monthly compendium of notable World events was small — just a few lines conveying little but the name of its owner, one Silas Kimball; the extent of the destruction; the fact that Mister Kimball had died; and that his wife and daughter had gone missing. You were named as the fire inspector, which is the reason I am writing to you now.

I do not usually meddle in the affairs of the World's people, but as we are an ever-growing community with a great interest in making bountiful and pure any land that appears to have, in some way, fallen into wild disarray, I have undertaken to approach you with a simple request. It is one I should like to speak about privately and in person. Also, on the chance that it might aid you in your investigation, you should know that I have some knowledge of the family involved. In anticipation of your agreeing to meet, I trust that you will be at liberty to visit me this Wednesday in the late afternoon (4 o'clock will be convenient enough) so that we may discuss the business to which I have alluded here.

Of course, I am willing to pay you a fair wage for what I ask, but more I will not say. Please pen your answer clearly and leave it in precisely the place where you discovered this letter. I assure you, it will find its way to me promptly.

In friendship,

Elder Sister Agnes

The City of Hope

The tone of her letter was upright enough, and I welcomed the opportunity to learn more about the Kimball clan — to say nothing of calling upon so mysterious a people as the Shakers. They do not often crop up in regular conversation, their ways having been deemed too strange to merit mention. Oh, and the purse promised? What do you think? I wrote that though I was indeed a busy man at present, I would find a way to meet the Elder Sister at her convenience. Then, as instructed, I slipped the envelope under my door. By the time I had finished my breakfast, it was gone.

I sighed. Not even the prompt, early morning response to a professional inquiry could save me from the bureaucratic task that lay ahead. I had tried my damnedest to avoid it, but now with a new client to please, it seemed all the more important to keep abreast of the facts. After all, who knew what the Shaker woman would have to say? If there was something I'd missed the first time I rifled through the town files — some record of a will or a far-flung heir or a child — I wanted to find it.

Property deeds and church records of marriages, births, and deaths: Does society offer up documents of a more paradoxically dry nature? They testify to our ownership of the very earth upon which we live, our most costly oath, our grand entry, and our final bow. Still, it often seems to me that they are written solely to be sorted in the wrong spot by a bespectacled clerk, pale as a grub and sporting suspenders.

In the bowels of the Ashland courthouse, dust and faded ink made an enemy of me for hours as I searched once again for something that might indicate the owner of the Kimball farm. A birth certificate testifying to the existence of May's son would have been equally welcome. A thorough perusal of the ancient rolls in a nearby church had led me to discover official proof of the death of Benjamin Briggs, his wife and newborn son, and the births of May and her daughter, Polly. But there was no reference whatsoever to Silas, nor to his son — the boy Peeles had inquired after. May's name had been entered in the flowing script of Reverend Israel Harkness, next to the elegant signatures of her mother and father, Mister and Mrs. Benjamin Briggs. I could not help noticing that Polly's entry bore only Peeles's careful print, May's shaky scrawl, and Silas's X followed by his name, which a more confident scribe had written out in full. Their marriage had been recorded in much the same manner, but those were the only official mentions I could find relating to members of the Briggs and Kimball clans. The illiterate farmer's death had yet to be noted, probably because May was not present to see it done.

With regard to ownership of the property, I could find nothing except an old deed on file in the courthouse indicating Benjamin Briggs to be the original proprietor of the Ashland farm. It almost didn't matter that there seemed to be no indication as to whether Briggs had had a will. Given what I knew of the efficacy of James Hurlbut's machinations, it was likely that the farm would end up within his greedy grasp whether or not there existed a legitimate heir. As for Elder Sister Agnes, I could not imagine what foothold the Shaker woman's pursuit of bounty and purity might gain in this slippery scenario. In my experience, greed trounces good most every time.

So what did I expect to find in this dismal, underground room? My report, provided I could find and speak to May and her children, had assured their innocence. Now, I sought a means by which I might thwart Hurlbut's plans, but seeing Benjamin Briggs's property placed firmly back in the hands of his kin would be tricky. I needed more information and I needed to find May Kimball. I packed up and hoped that my new 'neighbor' could assist me.

'Pryor?' I heard a voice close by my right shoulder. 'Simon Pryor?'

Turning to face my inquisitor, I nearly bumped into a gentleman possessed of a windswept wave of brown hair, a full face, and expressive dark eyes that advertised an earnest, intelligent mind. He was dressed like a man who brings in little more than his keep through hard work and a sharp wit, which is to say that the notches on the lapels of his well-made waistcoat had lost their crispness and the garment displayed diminished resolve to hold its shape. His style was rumpled, to be sure, but a far cry from the patched garb of the common swindler. I granted him a respectful nod.

'Simon Pryor I am,' I said, closing the registry. 'Who's asking?'

'Forgive me,' he said. 'My name is Barnabas Trask. I work as a solicitor in Ashland. I wondered if I might have a word with you about the Briggs — I mean, the Kimball place.'

'Why?' I asked. 'And how, pray, did you find me here?'

He looked down sheepishly. 'I'm embarrassed to admit it, but I have been watching you, waiting for a moment when we might speak in private. When I chanced to see you enter the courthouse . . . well, I know from experience that few people save for myself hang about in these dungeons. So I thought it a grand opportunity to . . . ' His voice faded, as though the effort of explaining himself had induced exhaustion.

I sighed. Another scavenger.

'Let me guess,' I interrupted. 'You would like to pay me a tidy sum to ensure that, when the county is ready to bang the gavel, the Kimball farm goes to you.' I turned back to the register and stared blankly at the dusty cover in front of me. It's bad business to appear overly interested in a new assignment. A world-weary manner always pulls the money in.

'You are half-correct,' he said with a self-deprecating smile. 'I am also interested in the family who lived there, but to be frank, I would like to ascertain whether there are any encumbrances upon the property. When it becomes available at public auction ... on account of the death of ... Well, you don't need a lesson from me as to how complicated these things can be — I just don't want to waste my time chasing a land sale that might turn out to be tangled in a web of legalities.' He paused a moment before asking, uncertainly, 'Have you found them? The family, I mean?'

I avoided his question. I wasn't on the clock yet, and so I owed him nothing.

'I believe I get the picture,' I said. 'You're a speculator caught up in a race to buy every bit of land you can find, especially when the parcel is as blessed by nature as this one appears to be. Well, I'll not argue — it's a lovely piece. But all I can say is, you're not alone.'

'I know.' He sounded glum. 'I rarely am in these matters. Still, what will you answer me?'

I hesitated for effect, calculating the pros and cons of his proposal. In fact, I was thrilled by the job, for it allowed me to assist someone — however shady he might be — *other* than James Hurlbut. Equally, I would line my pockets finishing a task I had already begun on my own: to find May Kimball.

Beat, beat, beat — I made him wait for my reply. No need to sound desperate.

'Of course,' I said, ruminating, 'the money would have to be good. In these parts, finding a

208

poor family — or what may be left of one — is like looking for fleas in a shepherd dog's coat. There are more than a few to spot, and for one reason or another, they're not always keen to be picked out.'

He reached into his pocket and withdrew a fat envelope of notes. 'This should be enough to get you started. And there's more, especially if you deliver a quick and tidy outcome.'

I ran my fingers through the paper, working hard to conceal my satisfaction. 'This will get me on a bit,' I said finally. 'I'll take your case. Where can I find you, should information of any import come my way?'

'I've a shingle out on the main street,' he said, relief washing over his face and making him appear years younger. 'I'm afraid the office serves as my lodgings as well for the time being, so you'll find me there whenever you come looking.'

'You're new to your trade?' I said. 'Not that it's any concern of mine.'

'New to . . . ?' He was clearly perplexed.

'I don't mean the law,' I answered. 'I mean land-grabbing. You'll pardon my saying so, but you're either green or not much good at it. Otherwise you'd be rich enough to be sleeping somewhere with a better view than that of the underside of your desk.'

He looked down and smiled. 'Yes, now I get your meaning. As a matter of fact, I am a novice in the game of chasing parcels of land. But lawyering doesn't garner me much in the way of income, so . . . At any rate, I'm hoping to be the dark horse in this race — with your help, of course.'

'Of course,' I said as I gathered up my things and prepared to leave.

I liked this man, however unlikable he might turn out to be in the end. My opinion of people changes with every new piece of information I collect, but for now, he was certainly preferable to my usual employer. What a strange and unholy trinity of clients I faced: a crook, a Shaker, and a lawyer. Was this some sort of Heavenly test? If so, then God had more of a sense of humor than I'd previously given him credit for. Not quite reason enough to convert me any time soon, but a point in his favor nonetheless.

I bade Trask farewell and climbed out of the basement towards the light. Turning as I reached the middle step, I said, 'You asked about the family — what I know so far. Well, I can tell you about as much as has already been printed. Silas Kimball died in his bed. As to the mother and her daughter, I've not a clue as to where they've gone.' I deliberately left out the mysterious son; after all, some people can't wait to tell an inspector what he's missed. But Trask said nothing. Waving the envelope, I added, 'Here's hoping this speeds the hunt.'

Perhaps it was my use of the word *hunt* that caused him to seem momentarily knocked off-balance by what I'd offered as a casual answer to his question. Looking away, he regained his composure and faced me once again.

210

'Thank you for letting me know,' he said. Then, after a brief pause, he went on. 'It occurs to me, if I might, that there may be any number of men like me looking out for the widow. As she is the person closest to the property, she'll be the one best able to attest to its legal status. You'd do well to find her quickly if no harm is to come her way.' He laughed self-consciously. 'But who am I to tell you your business?'

I said nothing in return and looked up the stairs towards a notice board where a single sheet had been pinned. Its news was common enough — a pauper auction was to be held in Burns' Hollow on the coming Saturday. Foul event. I scowled, my mind darting quickly elsewhere.

'What's that?' Trask asked.

'It's nothing,' I answered, tipping my chin at the sign. 'I don't much like seeing humans for sale is all, and there's an unfortunate lot up for auction Saturday next.' I had only to utter the words for both Trask and me to arrive at the same thought.

'Not a bad place to look for May and her daughter, is it?' he said. 'A woman and a girl with no home, no prospects . . . '

I looked into his eyes and nodded. 'The idea had occurred to me,' I said, recommencing my climb. Something about this Trask figure suddenly struck me as odd.

The notice in the paper had mentioned Silas's name. It had said nothing of his wife's.

Polly

Polly and Charity had led an interior life since she arrived. Around them swirled first the brown leaves of November, then the dry snows of December. They woke at the tolling of the early bell, crossing over to the brethren's side by candlelight to clean the men's chambers and make neat the upper floors of the dwelling house before returning to the sisters' side and going down the back stairs to the kitchen to lay the cooking fires.

It was dull work, airing or changing soiled sheets, never giving them so much as a glance. Sister Charity had taught Polly with the slightest of smiles that, as the linens had touched the brethren's bodies and were thus tinged with their scent, the intimacy might excite desire in a less disciplined sister. Morning after morning, they beat the mattresses until the cushioning rose off the rope webbing of the narrow beds. They emptied chamber pots, swishing them clean, dumping the refuse into metal pails, then placing the porcelain vessels, gleaming, back inside their cupboards. The air must always be pure, and the upper floors must shine in the name of Godliness, in the name of Mother Ann, and no sister could treat the work as drudgery. For where dirt resided, so did sin. Even the heavy labor of loading the soapstone ovens with wood and then stoking them until the flames died into even-tempered embers was a form of worship, and she and Sister Charity tried to do so with cheer at the start of each day before the older sisters began preparing the Early Meal.

But Polly was haunted by her kitchen work. She saw Mama by the stove, heard Ben singing, felt the heat of the coals, and thought only of flames. That was not all. One day, a young sister named Rebecca suffered a skirt fire. She had leaned in too close to the open hearth — the only part left of the old kitchen chimney that had yet to be enclosed. It happened in an instant, her apron aflame and her clothes gone up so quickly that Polly and the others could not douse the blaze before it had consumed her. Listening to Rebecca's wails, Polly could not help wondering: Had *he* survived a curse such as this?

The brethren arrived as quickly as they could, carrying Rebecca upstairs to the healing room in spite of her moans.

'Boil up some water,' Charity ordered them, and Polly was surprised to hear how confident she sounded as she commanded sisters and brethren alike to do her bidding — to fetch more water and ice from the icehouse, tear muslin into strips, boil barberry stems into an infusion, bruise leaves of bee balm, and pound the roots of purple coneflower. She whirled round them as they worked, showing them how to do it quicker, better. And then, after the liquids had cooled,

213

she dressed the burns with linseed oil so that the bandages would not stick, and laid the poultices over the whole of Rebecca's body. Throughout the bustle of preparation and the wrapping of skin, the girl lay on the bed, gently rocking and crying in her pain because she could not writhe or scream.

'I think she might be soothed to hear your voice, to hear the Visionist speak,' Charity whispered to Polly as she wiped the sweat from her brow and continued her ministrations.

Polly nodded, then pulled a chair close to the bed where the young girl lay. Rebecca was but eleven, an orphan who'd been left with the believers not a year before. Polly tried to speak and found herself mute, unable to do anything but stare at the burns that blazed so angrily on the sister's skin. She might have felt that she could be of some comfort if only she could touch Rebecca, but there was hardly a place on her body that had not been ravaged by fire. Strange how Charity's markings drew Polly in while this affliction terrified her. It was not that she had no sympathy for the poor girl. It was her agony, the nearness of it, and the fact that Polly was powerless to assuage it.

Then she heard her whisper. Polly leaned in and put her ear close to the girl's blistered lips.

'Mother,' she said, barely more than breathing the word. At first, Polly assumed Rebecca wanted her mother, but then she remembered that she had none. 'Mother,' she said again. 'Call . . . Her.'

Polly was silent. She did not want to pretend

214

to this child that she could do something she feared she could not, for her angels had been deaf to her pleas for some time now. And yet, to deny Rebecca comfort seemed cruel.

'I . . . I shall try,' she said. How she wished she could hold the girl's hands and offer her love in some other manner, one that didn't need to be conjured.

'Is she here?' Rebecca whispered. Polly looked away, feeling weak. What could she do?

Nearby the bed, a window had been cracked open to let the steam out of the room. A cool breeze blew in from outside.

'There,' said Polly. 'Do you feel them?'

'Who? Who has come?' Rebecca croaked. 'Is it . . . ?'

'Her angels,' Polly said, whispering into her ear. She closed her own eyes. 'Do you feel the cool beating of their wings? They are all around you. Can you hear them singing?'

'I . . . I don't know,' Rebecca said. Then her body seemed to go rigid. 'Yes,' she whispered. 'Yes, I can hear them!'

'They are Mother's angels, sent down to comfort you,' Polly told her. Her eyes were still closed, and though she'd called for them to come, she had not expected the angels to pay her any mind. And yet . . . 'They are singing, can you hear? They sing of Mother's love. They sing so that you might be healed, might feel no more pain. They are singing for you, can you hear, dear Rebecca?'

The girl's breath became steadier, and her tortured body seemed to relax. It might have been the tea Charity had made her drink. It might have been the comfort of the poultices that covered her body. Polly wasn't sure. Then, once more she heard a whisper.

'She came to me,' Rebecca said. 'You called and she came.' And with that, she drifted off.

Polly turned to find that the room had emptied. Sister Charity, having done all she could for the moment, stood nearby, leaning over a table, elbows down, her chin resting in her hands. She was staring and Polly wondered what she was thinking.

'You made her feel the presence of angels,' Charity said. 'You brought Mother Ann to her and she was given comfort that none of us here could have offered.' Her voice was soft, full of awe.

Polly dropped her gaze. She could not say what she had or had not done. She knew only that she had been prepared to fake her gift if it would bring relief. This disturbed her, for if she was willing to lie now, what would she do if she was asked another time? Then again, hadn't she too felt the gentle brush of wings? Hadn't she been calmed and strengthened by the presence of her angels? Had they not enabled her to ease Rebecca's pain?

She looked up. 'Will she live?' Polly asked.

'I don't know,' Charity said with a sigh, turning to gather the bowls and pitchers and pestles and spoons that were strewn here and there on the table. 'She will never see again, that much I can say for certain.'

Polly busied herself helping her sister. She had

become more sensitive to signs since she had come to The City of Hope, for everything appeared to have meaning here beyond its earthly significance. Now, just as she wondered whether Ben's hatred of her signaled his deliverance from the miseries of his past life, she wondered if Sister Rebecca's accident had been some sort of test.

I am thinking like Charity, she mused. But then, perhaps she had never before felt safe enough to believe in the greater implications of small things. If this had been a test, she had not failed, though she had taken a great risk in forcing something akin to a Vision. Why could she not redeem herself by believing in the power of her gifts to heal?

* * *

Polly sat nervously, her back straight in the chair before Elder Sister Agnes. They had met a handful of times now, and the eldress had pressed more and more firmly for her to confess.

'You know that it is one of our most important principles,' she said irritably, 'and yet you insist on delay. If the believers here did not put such store by your gifts as a Visionist, I would have asked you to leave long ago.'

Though Polly knew this to be true, it was a shock to hear it spoken so plainly. She looked into her lap.

'Now,' the eldress continued, 'I have heard talk of your ministrations to Sister Rebecca. Is it true that you visited her and filled her head with what

217

can only be . . . misplaced hope?'

Polly looked up. 'I do not see it that way,' she said, a flash of anger in her eyes. 'It is true — I wondered at first if I could do what she asked. But then, they came. My angels. They came and filled the air around her and gave her great comfort. How can I deny a sister who lies blind and wrapped like a mummy in her bed? Would you have had me turn away?'

Elder Sister Agnes's face softened. 'No, Sister Polly. You are right — I would not.' She paused. 'How you vex me, child! I have seen sisters — the first Visionists — taken over by the same powers you are thought to possess. I know that such gifts exist. And yet, I am well acquainted with young girls, their thirst for attention — worse still, their ability to use that attention towards their own selfish ends. How can I be certain that you are not abusing the trust that has been placed in you?'

Polly did not answer her right away. 'I cannot do more than to give myself over when the Spirits take me. And, as I have said before, I cannot explain why it is they have chosen me.'

'Then confess your sins to me that I might see to it that your soul is clean.' Her face had never looked so stern. The moment had come.

Polly spied a small leather-bound book lying on the gleaming table in front of Elder Sister Agnes. Her eyes hovered over the words embossed into the cover: *Youth's Guide in Zion By Holy Mother Wisdom*.

Looking to the eldress, she tried to discern whether or not she was meant to open it.

'Read to me, Sister Polly,' the Elder Sister said. 'Before you begin, there is a power in the Heavens with whom you should be better acquainted. She is Holy Mother Wisdom, equal to our Holy Father Jesus Christ. Her word is divine and eternal and her power is great. You must know her as do all the children in The City of Hope — by reciting her commandments and humbling yourself before her will. This is how we begin.'

Polly bowed her head and opened the cover. Her hands shook. Elder Sister Agnes held a wooden form covered by an unfinished basket, its thinly shaved splints made from the pounded branches of black ash fanning out, as yet unwoven. They made an odd sight, like stiff hairs springing from an uncombed head. *Make no mistake*, Polly thought, *the eldress will succeed in bending and weaving them into order.*

She began to read.

I am Infinite Wisdom. I dwell with the Eternal Father, and have known all things and transactions of both good and evil spirits on the earth and in the heavens, ever since the beginning and the creation thereof. I know the mighty power of God. I know the hosts of hell, and I know the greater and stronger hosts of heaven.

I also know the cunning craftiness of evil spirits, and the great influence they have on the souls of mortal creatures, and especially upon the young and inexperienced mind.

As order is heaven's first law; so must all

things that pertain to heaven be strictly kept in heavenly and perfect order.

I am Eternal Wisdom, and in my wisdom have I stated the order of souls to keep in regard to this book, and if any should break my orders, they lose my blessing, and unless they confess their carelessness, and beg my blessing to their Elders, it shall not rest on them.

Polly looked up. Elder Sister Agnes forced each shaved splint in and out of the weave. Her hands were strong, for basket-weaving was the chief work of the Elder Brothers and Sisters. The long, slim strips dipped and reared up, dipped and reared up; she was expert at pushing and curling the thin sliver of soft wood, forcing it to join the other strips until it lay, like them, pressed along the oval-shaped basket form in service to industry.

'Do you know anything of craftiness and cunning, Sister?' The eldress did not look up as she spoke. 'Were they part of your former life? The World has tempted many of our believers down such paths. I wonder if it tempted you as well.'

Polly stared at the clock hanging from a peg on the wall. The plain case was made up of a square atop a rectangle precisely two times its size. The shapes were, like everything here, in perfect balance. Only its face appeared ripe in its roundness, carefully contained within a square glass frame as if the lush curve might somehow be contagious. A fine machine, it ticked away the minutes and hours with heartless precision. 'I can say,' she answered, 'that I never behaved knowingly in such a manner, Elder Sister.'

'You were a help then, to your flesh kin? A daughter they thought to be a blessing?'

This last word — *blessing* — unnerved Polly. She had never had cause to consider the term because nothing in her life or in the lives of those around her could be called a 'blessing.' It was only here that she had heard it used, and each time it had felt like a hand on her shoulder, an exhalation of cold, fresh air.

'My mother and father did not think in terms of blessings,' she said. 'They led a difficult life, and it is not easy to reflect on good fortune when bad knocks so persistently at the door.'

This seemed to quiet Elder Sister Agnes a moment; then she directed Polly to read on.

Section IV, number 7. *Seek not to display any great talents in time; for that belongs to, and is of the children of darkness; by which they gain glory one of another; but have none of God.*

'Great talents, Sister Polly. Do you think that Holy Mother Wisdom would fault you for seeking to show such things?' Elder Sister Agnes did not look up from her basket when she spoke. 'Might *you* be 'of the children of darkness'?'

Polly pondered the question. She had not sought to display any great talent. She had only fled into her mind when the world around her — its noise, its smell, its touch — became too much for her to bear. Was she 'of the children of darkness' each time she fell into the dreams where she had so long taken refuge? The Elder Sister's questions shook her. Did the wisdom she supposedly gave to the believers exist if she could not fathom its source?

'I have not sought to mislead,' she said. 'Nor to claim attention, if that is what you mean by 'darkness.''

'And what else could I have meant by 'darkness,' Sister?' At this, Elder Sister Agnes looked up and stared Polly straight in the eye. 'Can it be that you were thinking of some other manifestation?'

Polly attempted to keep her voice steady. 'I . . . I have only known the darkness I feel before my dreams come to me, for they exist to pull me away. They are a shield. But it is different here. My mind fills with angels and other voices both when I am happy and when I am afraid. And they come when I feel the need for them in others, like Sister Rebecca. I do not take them lightly, Elder Sister, if that is what you fear.'

'Read,' the eldress replied.

Section V, number 6. *The true cross-bearer forsakes the pleasures of time, and curbs the strong desires of nature. Such souls feast upon the love of God, and taste the sweet pleasures of eternal life in the world to come; yet dwell in a house of clay.*

'And what do you make of that verse, Sister Polly? Is it possible that you can envision 'sweet pleasures' because you have tasted them yourself?'

This Polly could answer quickly, and she did so with some annoyance. 'I have never tasted 'sweet pleasures,' nor had any need of curbing desire. Indeed, when I behold the believers pass the Horn of Plenty in Meeting and laugh to receive its bounty, I envy them. For they know what I do not, and that is pleasure, even if it is of the holiest and purest kind.' Polly spoke without regard to what she was saying. She could not stop herself. 'As to desire, I imagine the taste of such a thing to be bitter and disgusting beyond words. No, Elder Sister, I can envision nothing of what is written here.'

Her answer was met with silence, but Polly had the feeling that the eldress was listening to her words with something akin to sympathy. 'Go on, child,' she said, waving her hand.

Section VI, number 22. *A record is surely kept of the lives of all souls; and ye whose names are entered and written in the book of life will be tried by the record of your own lives; and if ye are found wanting on the day of your trial, better would it have been for you had there been a millstone tied to your necks, and ye cast into the sea, ere your names be written in the BOOK OF LIFE.*

Elder Sister Agnes put down her basket and gazed round the room. She looked tired, her face gray and lined, her eyes a metal blue. 'Have you ever feared that you would be judged harshly by the *Book of Life*, Sister Polly? Is that why you resist confession?'

Polly looked at her feet. Her thoughts snagged on death, on whether things would have been better had she tied a millstone to her neck. How often she had been tempted. How many mornings she had risen to watch Mama's misery unfold and wondered if it would not be better to die. It had so often seemed the only escape. But then little Ben would clamor to be fed, and the cows would need milking, and her mother would require help gathering in berries, or wild onions, or potatoes, and before Polly could think much more about the freedom granted by the grave, she was through yet another day and lying in wait for what night would bring.

'I cannot say, Elder Sister, how my name will be written.' Polly paused before going on. 'But, though I know it is a sin, I have often thought to die of my own hand. It is only since I arrived here that my mind has been free of such evil ideas.'

The Elder Sister's face softened, to Polly's great surprise, and her voice became kind. 'What could drive a young girl to contemplate such an end?'

'I . . . I suppose it is something that no one so good as you could understand,' Polly replied. Her voice was shaking now and she felt she might cry. She must not show weakness; it would only open a hole in her armor.

The older woman seemed to drift into another world before fastening her regard once more on

Polly's face. 'I believe I know why you came here, Sister Polly. It was fire that drove you away from your home, was it not?'

Polly's heart stopped, then resumed a quick beating. She must tread carefully. She must not tell the whole truth but she mustn't lie either. Why, of late — though she dropped the lamp when her father surprised her — she could not be certain as to whether or not she had truly intended to kill him. She hated him with all her heart. Could she have dragged him through the flames and saved him? Was that her crime: to leave him lying in his bed? She shook her head at the memory of the heat and smoke, the moving ball of fire that leapt from the house and filled that final glance back.

She could not explain any of this. Mama forbade her, and though she did not understand why, she had the sense that her actions could be misconstrued. Arson, murder. If they were pinned on her, she would be hanged. 'Yes,' she answered, looking into Elder Sister Agnes's eyes. 'There was a fire at our house. My mother and Ben and I came upon it on our way home from town. As my mother told you, my father left us. There was no one to save, so we rode away. Rode away and Mama brought us here.'

'Your father,' the eldress said. 'Why do you think he has not come for you? Surely it takes a hard man not to come home after hearing that his wife and children have suffered a fire. And then there is the land. Why would he not claim it for his own and sell the ruin?'

Polly looked to the window and saw that the

afternoon had turned dark. What could she say?

She stared blankly at her eldress. 'I cannot tell you what happened to my father, Elder Sister Agnes. He hasn't come looking is all I know.'

The eldress held her gaze, seemed to be looking beneath Polly's very skin for the answer to what she hoped would be the final question. 'So who will tend to the property now?' she asked. 'Is that why your Mama left you here? So that she might rebuild it on her own? Seems strange that a woman alone would attempt such a thing. With your father merely 'gone,' do you even know if the farm was hers?'

Polly was confused by so practical a question. In truth, she'd not thought for a moment about the farm since asking her mother that first night if it had belonged to Silas. She had been so eager to put behind her the life she once led, she had not considered matters of ownership.

'As it does not apply to me, Elder Sister,' she answered haltingly, 'I know nothing of the law regarding damaged property. Perhaps you could explain . . . ?'

Elder Sister Agnes pursed her thin lips. Her basket was almost finished, ready to take its place as a tool in the universe of useful things. This one had been fashioned with a flat lid that slid up and down the handle so that flowers and leaves collected from the fields and gardens would not blow away, would not escape to rejoin the earth and replenish it. How like the believers, gathered in and bound to such ordered isolation from the World.

Polly sighed and turned to the final page of

her pamphlet, dropping her head in supplication to the rules written out before her. Her candle barely lit the words as she struggled to make them out in the flicker of its flame. She did not wait for the order to read.

It was a poem. She had once loved poems. With words free from precise meaning, they reminded her of dreams. She had found them in books that lined her walls against the cold, books she had borrowed from Miss Laurel, books that had been Polly's secret. Full of poetry, stories, essays — waking dreams so sacred that not even her mother knew of the fullness they made inside her mind.

He never knew. He would have torn out the pages and burned them in a rage. He did not trust those of a bookish turn. He could neither read nor write, scorning the habit, using his hatred of it as a marker to isolate himself from others. He only allowed Polly to attend school because he needed someone who could make the count when buying and selling goods in town. But each day, those hours in the schoolroom — they were the only gift he ever gave her. And then, only because he did not come searching.

Mother Wisdom's Promise. Her eyes could barely focus. Elder Sister Agnes broke her silence only to tell Polly to skip to the final verses.

Now think of this, ye helpless worms!
Ye little specks of mortal clay!
Since at our word all heaven turns,
Dare ye presume to disobey?
Dare ye presume to scoff at God?

And mock and scorn his holy power?
Beware, I say, lest with his rod
He smite your souls in that same hour.

O little children, could you know
The call of mercy unto you,
You'd sacrifice all things below,
And cast off nature clear from you,
The world with its alluring charms
Of pleasure false and vain delight,
Its riches, husbands, wives and farms
Would be disgusting in your sight.

No questions followed, yet Polly could not help pondering what she had read. *Disgusting.* The farm where she last knew a mother and a father. She saw the porch and the narrow front door. She heard the sound of crying, of bellowing, of dishes breaking, of misery. She smelled the choking burn of smoke. *Was he still alive?* Could it have been her father's form bursting through the door in flames? Would he travel the same road as had she to find her here?

She did not understand the poem. She had known no 'alluring charms,' no 'pleasure false or vain delight.' She had known the World to be hard and dirty, a poor and embittering place, her father ruling its domain as Mother Ann ruled Her believers. Had he, like Her, the power to move through souls?

Polly shuddered, and her candle spit as the wick ran out, its flame drowning in tallow. Now, as the only light in the room fell from the lamp by which the eldress worked, Polly stopped reading. She was quiet, listening to the clicking and squeaking of basket switches, the tock of the clock, the slow *creak-creak* of the eldress's rocker, her steady, determined breaths.

'There was a fire inspector who came by your farm,' Elder Sister Agnes said calmly. 'Did you know?' She raised her eyes just enough to catch any reaction Polly might display, but the girl gave her nothing. 'It was printed in a notice. As was your father's name. Silas Kimball. It said that he had died, Sister Polly. In the fire.'

Polly forced herself to breathe though every muscle was a knot and her brain spun to think what else the eldress might know. Her father, dead? Could it be true? What else had this inspector discovered? Were there constables on the hunt to find her and her mother? Could Mama possibly have already been caught?

She thought suddenly of the small gray birds who make their nests amidst pebbles on the ground, of watching one fake an injured wing to distract danger away from its eggs, hopping, body tipped awkwardly to one side, half-spread feathers dragging through the dirt, seemingly an easy prey. She slumped, sliding slowly to the floor.

'Sister Polly?' the eldress asked. 'Child? Can you hear me?' She rose from her rocker.

Polly moaned, opened her eyes, and felt the boards solid and hard beneath her. She was so tired. And her gut — it burned. *How I wish I could rest here*, she thought. *It would be so much easier*. But she knew she must leave while Elder Sister Agnes's curiosity about the fire had temporarily displaced her desire to hear Polly's full confession. She dragged her fingers over the flat surface and imagined her arm as a wing. *Such clever little birds.*

'I am fine,' she said softly. 'Dizzy from the heat, that's all. I haven't eaten yet today. I'm sorry I . . . I never intended to cause alarm . . .'

'It was time for you to take your leave,' said the eldress abruptly. 'You have learned enough for one day. Indeed, more than you expected.' Her voice was as tight as the weave of splints, her changing manner a pattern of light and dark.

'You shall not need a candle,' she said. 'For you, Sister Polly, are full of brightness. Though the afternoon light has faded, you can apparently see where others cannot. Go now and I shall not worry.'

She raised her head and watched her pupil rise from the floor, turn, and make her way carefully down the stairs in the gloom of the narrow space. Polly felt caught, and as she entered the cloakroom and lifted the metal latch on the sisters' door, she was relieved to breathe in the cold evening air. It smelled of open sky and the smoke of a hundred distant stove fires. Hurrying along the icy paving stones, she was eager to find the warmth of one of those fires, eager to be in the company of sisters, eager to wrap herself in the safety she felt as one among many.

Then, she saw it: an inkblot of black in the darkening gloom. Surely her eyes, tired from reading, were playing a trick. Surely the bright gleam of light from the candle, the sudden darkness of the stairwell — they had filled her vision with spots. For if not, then at the edge of the farthest white fence lining the road sat a dark figure atop a horse.

Him. It could not be . . . The wind played with the folds of his cape so that he appeared larger in the billow of his habit. She watched as his horse pawed at the frozen ground, heard a conspiratorial nicker before the rider tugged the reins and urged forward his steed — its chin tucked low to its broad, square chest. *Him. Back from the dead to take her away.*

Simon Pryor

Though it is not far from Hatch to Albion, the winding roads were more difficult to manage than I had anticipated. Icy and slick at top, frozen and rutted at bottom, the hills forced my horse to take each step slowly and with care, and hours spent lurching in my saddle had me feeling stiff and irritable well beyond my years.

Pleased as I had been not two days earlier to be contacted by someone who might lead me to May Kimball and her children, I now felt nervous at the prospect. My study of them and the suddenness with which their fortunes turned put me in square view of what I'd long kept hidden. What had become of my own beloved kin? Eight years is a long time in the life of a man such as myself, let alone that of his aging parents. And though my weekly visits confirmed that they still lived, I also knew that, between living and dying, circumstance can both gutter and flare. With regard to my mother and father — their health, their happiness — I could tell you nothing. I had learned to keep such curiosity at bay, relegating it — like Bluebeard's wives — to a solitary room in my mind. The key has been hidden for so long that it is as good as lost, for were I to open the door to that haunted chamber, I might never leave and put a foot forward again. This much I know about running away: There is but a single direction in which to go.

By now, I shall have made clear the extent to which James Hurlbut rules my small world. Indeed, contemplation of my servitude occasions many a white night — *white* because I cannot slip into dark and blissful sleep. Instead, I lie abed, endlessly re-describing to myself the moment when, as boys, our paths first crossed. How different my life might have been had I never laid eyes on my betrayer.

The scenery around me changed, from rock- and barberry-grizzled fields to a rolling white expanse of snow-swept pasture-land that sloped gently into Albion. I found the town to be little different from most others I have ridden through in my travels about the county, but the sight — a mere hundred yards out — of the Shaker settlement caused me to pull up and gaze a moment from the opposite rise. Neat walls led into fences that ticked along either side of the road, level and regular enough that they looked to have been erected by a master joiner. A net of pathways led from house to house, but with none of the arbitrary crossings of the cow, pig, and sheep trails that determine the erratic jumble of a normal town. Here, everything was at right angles, aligned precisely and cluttered with not a single lazy woodpile or other such example of human haphazardness. The brilliant fields seemed to spread like a perfect quilt around the settlement, laid out with such attention to neatness and order that I found myself smoothing my fraying cape and readjusting my hat before urging my mount down the road and into the center of the village. Despite the dimming light of late afternoon, a clean white-painted house bustled with the comings and goings of oddly dressed men and colorless women, each passing through their own separate doors with never a glance exchanged between them.

I was curious to see the people I'd heard so much about, for I knew townsfolk who, in fair weather, had made Sunday outings to the Shakers' place of worship in order to watch them 'make fools of themselves.' Indeed, I had already heard of several who looked forward to visiting come springtime, when the roads would be more easily passable, so that they might witness the strange utterances of a young girl known to her kind as a 'Visionist.' That her reputation had carried to neighboring towns is testimony to the paradoxical spell cast by these outsiders. Their backwards ways, their songs, and their dances were sources of amusement, ridicule, and, in some cases, suspicion. But their goods — clothing, medicine, household implements, and seeds — were prized. Doctors as far away as France ordered medicinal herbs and tinctures from the Shakers, such was their renown for purity and effectiveness.

I dismounted, tied up my horse, and hoped that I would not be shunned for my obvious otherness. I found little encouragement in the sign adorning what I supposed to be their house of prayer: ENTER NOT WITHIN THESE GATES, FOR THIS IS MY HOLY SANCTUARY, SAYETH THE LORD. BUT PASS BY, AND DISTURB NOT THE PEACE OF THE QUIET, UPON MY HOLY SABBATH. Happily, it was not a Sunday.

For all my discomfort, I need not have fretted. The man who greeted me — his hair cut straight across his forehead as though a bowl had been upturned and its rim used as a guide — spoke cordially, if with strange formality. His language was almost biblical — both in the words he used and the twists to which he subjected them; his dress was the color of wet tree bark; his attitude, patient yet somehow superior.

'I have come at the request of Elder Sister Agnes,' I said in my best and most respectful manner. 'Might I find her here?'

A long pause ensued. Time moved more slowly in this place, though I had the feeling that not a second of the long day was wasted. The man took careful stock before answering.

'My elder sister will be called to her sitting room so that you might have a word. Attend the moment here and I shall inquire as to her readiness to receive.' So calm and self-negating was his manner that his departure to search for the woman he called his sister made barely a ripple in the air. I imagined him as more roadside marker than man, rarely permitted to move himself, yet somehow influential in the movements of others.

I looked about, spooked by the sparseness of my surroundings. The tranquility conveyed by

235

such emptiness is oddly affecting. My own house filled me with the fear that I might someday be buried alive, never to be discovered beneath the detritus of my daily existence. Here, with life described in the most reductive of lines, I was alone with myself — not the best of company under any circumstance.

As luck would have it, before I could commence counting my numerous sins, the marker returned and motioned me towards an inner door situated precisely in the middle of the ground floor of the house. As he opened it, my eyes fell upon a woman — his counterpart, I supposed — standing stiffly beside a straight-backed chair.

'I am Elder Sister Agnes,' she said in a tone colder than the wind that had blown me here.

'Simon Pryor . . . Madam,' I answered.

With a simple wave, she bade me sit in a chair identical to her own yet placed at an unusual distance away. *Does she worry that I might bring contagion upon the good folk of her 'City of Hope'?* I wondered. I found my usual confidence undermined and — rendered mute in the Shaker woman's presence — I waited like a naughty schoolboy for punishment to be meted out.

'I shall not prolong our time together with idle conversation,' she said, settling herself neatly in her chair. Her dress was earth-colored with a high collar that peeked out from beneath a large kerchief. She was not unpleasing to look upon, but her habit was that of a particularly dreary maid. She continued. 'I would like you to tell me what you have discovered regarding the fire on the Kimball family's farm. In particular, I would like to hear what you know about the boy — young Benjamin. The family arrived under mysterious circumstances, and so I asked one of our brethren to look into church records to see what I might find out. As you have no doubt discovered yourself, there is nothing to indicate Benjamin's position in the family — though it appears that he is the only son of May and her husband, one Mister Silas Kimball. I wondered if perhaps *you* might be in possession of a clarifying document?'

Silence blanketed the room. Her letter had already made it plain that she wanted to acquire the land. Indeed, she had written as though she sought to save its very soul by enfolding it into the settlement's existing property. Why she should focus on the boy was a mystery to me. Had she reason to suspect this *Benjamin* to be the sole heir? Is that why she had dispatched someone to search for proof of his birth? Her forthrightness surprised me.

I must admit to a peculiar prejudice, for I did not imagine that such simple people — people who strive to separate themselves from society — know how to dig for clues. I suppose that I should not have found it strange. All it takes is patience and perseverance, precisely the qualities demanded in worship. But from the way she discussed the boy, I began to get the distinct feeling that perhaps the shelter May and her children had taken here was less temporary than I'd assumed.

'A question or two from me,' I said, 'before we

discuss your demands. You appear to have taken great interest in this Benjamin. Am I to assume that he, his sister, and their mother have in some official way joined you in — what did you call it? — *The City of Hope?*'

'I do not intend to waste time playing games, Mister Pryor,' she answered. 'It is *I* who summoned *you*, as you might recall, and therefore it is to *my* concerns that we shall first address ourselves.'

I was not used to having a client run her own case and I did not like it. Everyone who comes to me has a reason — in this sense, they direct the first step of the inquiry. But once they have laid out the facts, they are generally quite relieved to hand them over to me for sorting. Of course, a notable exception is James Hurlbut, but as I have explained, ours is hardly a normal relationship. Elder Sister Agnes would insist on being in charge and — given that I knew next to nothing of the strange world she inhabited — I would have a difficult time wresting control. I decided to concede. As I had little to share, it cost me nothing, save my pride. And clearly, she knew quite a bit more than I about the family that had so possessed me; indeed, she was caring for them.

'Well, as your . . . investigator and I have clearly visited many of the same places in search of information, we are equals in discovering how little helpful official documentation there is for anything involving the Kimballs. And you surpass me by far in terms of what you know personally of May, Polly, and Benjamin. That the boy's birth appears to be undocumented is as much a mystery to me as it is to you. I can only surmise that his family wished it so, since I cannot imagine that people who could barely feed themselves would take on an orphan. Proof of birth cannot be manufactured from thin air — especially not when there is an inheritable property at stake. Had you hoped to use the boy in order to secure his former home?'

If I sought to discomfit her, I failed utterly.

'I do not care for your manner, Mister Pryor, but that is to be expected. Benjamin and Polly Kimball became believers on the day their mother signed their contract of indenture. You are mistaken in assuming that I know anything about May Kimball. Though I urged her to take shelter until she felt stronger, she declined. You'll have to seek her elsewhere. As to the farm, I knew nothing of its existence until I happened to read only a week ago of its having burned.'

'But you feel as though that farm is owed, via the boy's potential inheritance, to you?' I asked. There were so many more pressing questions on my mind. Why had the children been indentured here? Was it against their will? And where did the elder sister think May Kimball had gone? Was she coming back?

I gave no indication of the tumult in my head. I knew that if I wanted to learn anything from the Shaker sister, I would have to stay with the subject that most mattered to her. 'Forgive me,' I said, backtracking. 'Perhaps *owed* is too strong a word. Help me to better understand your reasoning.'

For the first time, she smiled. Not broadly, mind you, but enough so that the corners of her mouth twitched in the general direction of good humor. She actually became quite pretty. 'All property belonging to our believers is passed over when they sign our covenant,' she explained, her tone softening as she seized the opportunity to educate. 'And as Benjamin is happy here, I've no doubt as to what he shall do when he turns eighteen and can decide his way for himself. That he has accepted so readily the renunciation of his flesh mother and sister tells me that he will have the fortitude to remain a Shaker brother. But until then, it is only right that his inheritance be held in trust by a responsible party. We could oversee such a trust. After all, would it not be better to begin working the land now, rather than allow it to lie fallow and fall into the grasping hands of nature?'

I knew well the tactic of claiming kinship to young children who find themselves in a position to inherit property. Still, I was taken aback by the manipulations of so holy and devout a woman as the good Elder Sister Agnes. And that the children would have been forced to 'renounce' the only parent they had left in the world? This detail resonated with particular bitterness for me. How little I knew of her kind.

'Acquisitiveness,' I asked, 'is not considered by you to be a sin, Sister?'

'Not when it serves the collective good, Mister Pryor. I do not need to explain to you what will happen to that land should it be declared

240

abandoned. Every greedy man in the county will bid on it — the higher the offer, the worse the character. Why should we not claim it when it may rightfully be ours through Benjamin? And why should we not work it so that it returns to a productive state, one that would help to provide for not only our kind, but also those in the World who benefit from our industry? The poor who eat our bread, the farmers who buy our seeds, the commoners who wear our cloaks and bonnets, the doctors spread far and wide who seek out the purity of our medicines — they, too, have a stake here.'

Her cheeks took on a wash of pink and her eyes brightened as she spoke. It was as though the very goodness of her intentions brought her to life. I puzzled over her argument. A glance at the settlement had convinced me that these were as industrious a people as ever I'd known. And there was no arguing as to what would happen should she not succeed in her mission to save the Kimball farm from nature's wicked ways. But to view a young child — one who'd known little but misery all his short, brutish life — so narrowly through the lens of the property he might bring. It did not sit well with me.

'And why do you say nothing of Polly Kimball?' I asked. 'Surely she is as likely a potential heir as her younger brother?'

I appeared to have hit a nerve, for the Elder Sister looked down and became very thoughtful before giving her answer. 'Polly Kimball may not be with us for much longer, Inspector. We do not hold back children from going into the World when they are, in some way . . . troublesome. I cannot tell you more. Indeed, I may have misjudged Sister Polly's intentions as well as her character. Let us say simply that it is the boy who seems happiest here. And even if he is only heir to half the property, well, that is better than his being heir to none at all.'

My mind was truly spinning now, for I wondered what Polly Kimball could possibly have done to disturb the formidable Elder Sister Agnes. But I had not a moment to sort through a decent plan now. The best thing would be to leave myself time to think things through, then contact the Shaker sister again, this time on *my* terms.

'You mistake me, Elder Sister,' I said, shrugging and doing my best to show that I was not in the least bit sorry to disappoint her, 'for someone who has the power to determine the fate of the property you seek to own. I do . . . '

A faint knocking kept me from elaborating further on my ineffectiveness.

The Elder Sister looked meaningfully at me, then called for the visitor to enter. It was a young girl, no older than fifteen or sixteen, dressed in the same practical clothes and possessed of the same selfless quality I had, upon my arrival, noticed in the men and women moving about the white house. Tall and slight, she almost appeared to float across the floor towards the sister, bowing her head quickly in greeting.

'You called for me to come and see you, Elder Sister?' she asked. Her voice was soft but steady, and when she looked up, I saw that her face was uncommonly fine-boned, pale to the point of luminescence beneath a hint of straw-colored hair tucked neatly into her cap.

'Ah, so I did, Sister. I had forgotten,' the Elder Sister said, affecting a singularly unconvincing air of confusion. 'Such coincidence!' she exclaimed. 'Mister Pryor, I present to you Sister Polly. Sister Polly Kimball.'

The girl bowed but did not meet my gaze, turning instead to face the Elder Sister once again. 'Is there something I can do for you, Eldress?' she asked. 'Or shall I come back when you are alone?'

Elder Sister Agnes paused before answering. 'No, child, I have forgotten why I asked for you to come. But you must find it interesting to meet the inspector. He knows quite a bit about you, after all.'

As I watched the young sister's face register the remark, it became clear to me that Elder Sister Agnes had meant to unravel this delicate creature. More apparent still was the fact that she had succeeded.

'W-why . . . ,' Polly Kimball stammered before collecting herself. 'Why would anyone concern themselves with me?'

Again the Elder Sister waited and watched the girl's face. 'He has sifted through the dust of what's left of your home, Sister. He is the fire inspector we discussed.'

Polly Kimball turned with uneasy restraint to look me square in the eye. How to convey without words all that I wanted to say to her? That she needn't fear me. That I wanted only to

243

help. That I knew her secret and had chosen to make it my own.

'The fire . . . ,' I said, trying to smile encouragingly. 'It was — '

'That's enough, Mister Pryor,' the Elder Sister interrupted sharply. 'I did not ask you to come so that you could further your investigation by involving Miss . . . I mean, our Sister Polly.'

'Yes, I . . . I know,' I said. 'But as she is here now, I thought . . . '

'What you thought,' Elder Sister Agnes said, 'is of no interest to me. Sister Polly is one of us now, and if there are questions to be asked of her, it is I who shall do the asking. Now, sir, you will kindly take your leave.'

Polly Kimball's gaze fairly burned with terror, blood turning her cheeks crimson and mottling the skin above her high collar. At her waist — elbows snug at her sides, fingers interwoven in a prayer-like knot — her nails pressed into her flesh. I felt it imperative to find some way to speak to her in private. The question was, how?

I realized then that the Elder Sister had made a clever move. She didn't need me to tell her what she already knew about the Ashland property. Why, having met the survivors, she had more of a grasp than I did. It was Polly Kimball who held — and was apparently refusing to give up — the answers she sought. I had been summoned for one purpose and one purpose alone: to rattle the girl.

Now, if she broke — confessed to this conniving woman the truth about how the fire had started — she would expose the both of us.

244

Sister Charity

Little Sister Eudora steps out from behind a corner of the dwelling house to ask the Visionist if she can summon her dead mother. 'It's not been more than a year since she died,' the girl pleads. 'Surely, Sister, she is near enough by for you to bring her back?' The child trembles in the cold, for she has waited outside some time for us to pass. Still, the Visionist can only kneel down and tell her that she cannot summon the dead, that she is but a vessel, one who can only receive, and that it is the Word of Holy Mother that passes through her, nothing else. I watch as Sister Eudora's sweet face hardens like burned sugar. *How quick*, I think, *is the fading of belief.*

Another day. In the shadows of late afternoon, the flare of a lamp in a dark passageway as Sisters Vestia, Rose, and Honora block the stairs up from the kitchen. 'If you are clever enough to call in your angels when the mood takes you,' whispers Sister Rose, 'then why not now, here, where we might all feel their divine presence?' The Visionist remains serene. Challenges born out of jealousy do not pain her as much as the disappointment of a lonely child.

'I wait,' she says carefully, 'as do you, for

instruction. A Vision is a privilege, not a servant. Perhaps your belief will show itself more readily to you when you stop testing mine.' The three sisters regard her bitterly before extinguishing the flame.

Sister Polly is, of late, under the strain of constant scrutiny. The believers wait for her to raise them up. The believers wait for her to fall. Elder Brother Caleb celebrates her. Elder Sister Agnes treats her more coldly by the day. And she? She is distracted, her face drawn and sallow, her body a riot of insults. Dysentery, nausea, cramps, fatigue. She has begun to lose the health she gained when first she came to us, and now, though cleaner and better dressed, she resembles much the same ghost I first encountered only a few short months ago.

The Visions do not help, but seem only to diminish her, as though Mother Ann is consuming Her vessel even as She speaks through it. To be sure, when she comes to the healing room to sit beside Rebecca, they are both at peace as Sister Polly summons a heavenly host of angels to comfort the dying child, for she is dying and my dear sister knows it. But in Meeting, the Visionist has begun, after a long quiet period of months, to regularly transform into a most distraught state — her teeth chattering, arms wrapped tight about her, wild-eyed glares, a stream of words dark in spirit but near incomprehensible. She makes sounds of dread and fear, and though the urgency of her message casts a spell upon us all, we are less sure in our interpretations. At night, when finally she and I are alone, I have taken to reaching for the red book myself — it is hidden beneath my mattress now. Reading aloud the latest adventure, I have come to realize that I no longer look to the stories to transport me, but rather to bring Sister Polly back. Indeed, I barely hear myself anymore, keeping one eye on the words, the other on my sister. She tries to smile when I laugh aloud — the monkey residing in an African's headdress, the discovery of a goat's skull in our hero's soup, even the salty language of a drunken British sailor amuses me now — but there is little joy or wonder to be found in the Visionist of late and I fear that she is beginning to sicken under the weight of our expectation.

I fear something else as well.

In these last weeks of the year, certain of my sisters have found themselves blessed, it would seem, with the gift of Vision. I say this at risk of stepping out of union with my fellow believers, but I have seen how girls of a certain age will narrow their eyes as they gaze upon the blessings of another. And I have watched, even here, the lengths to which they will go to gain such recognition for themselves.

At Sabbath Meeting a week ago, Sister Eliza Henshaw fell into a long spin. A stir of believers surrounded her, watching her gift unfold with childlike glee. For a moment, I was tempted to trust in her. She had always been a cautious believer, one who held her spirit inside and rarely cried out or fell into the physical operations shown by some when they follow their souls into union with the Eternal. Yet on this day, she spun for a great duration — so great that I could see certain of our number wondering if the gift would ever leave her. After some time, she stopped and, as anyone might, swayed and stumbled this way then that. Her unsteadiness led her to take smaller and smaller steps, until finally she fell to the floor in a heap and we began to close the Meeting with our songs of praise and thanks, for in spite of the length of her Spinning Gift, all felt glad for the joy it had brought.

Suddenly, however, it was made clear that her turn as a divine vessel had not come to an end, for she lifted herself to her knees and began to speak in the chanting tones of one possessed. We waited, watching and listening, to discover if the powers of Vision had yet to leave their host. The color of our mood changed, darkening as her words became clearer and rose in pitch until her voice was shrill.

'I cannot hold!' she shrieked as she swayed violently from side to side. 'I am a vessel dashed upon the rocks of truth!' She quieted and looked round with eyes ablaze in anguish. 'And though my crew have abandoned me and I shall be ruined,' she said, whispering now. 'I must speak out. For I have seen two among us coming together in dark corners. I have seen them touch — a brother and sister!'

This revelation brought about great consternation — shouts even — from the believers as they moved in closer to Sister Eliza so as to be sure they had caught her meaning. I stood back and looked at the faces of my brethren and sisters. They were twisted in horror yet strangely locked in their attention to the portrait of carnality she was about to paint. Sister Eliza continued.

'Yes, all were asleep but me, for I felt a chill wind pass through my body as I lay abed and I knew there to be evil close by. I rose and walked silently across my room, opening the door to my quarters hardly a finger's width and peering into the gloom of the hall. This sister, this brother, trusted believers to us all, had pressed themselves into a corner, shadowy but close to where I stood. Oh, hateful was the sight before me! I watched as they moved their hands . . . I can hardly speak of their unholy union, their carnal natures entwined, the pain I felt when I watched their lips meet, their bodies merging in lust, the ugly moan — for it was ugly, my brothers and sisters — the *hideous* moan of the Devil as desire overcame the traitors.'

Her story was greeted by an uproar. Many of the elder sisters and brethren demanded to know who were the sinners. They moved about and stared down every person they encountered with looks of hatred and suspicion. I did not recognize them, for most of the believers I know are full of kindness, of peace and the contentment gained from seeking perfection in work. Yet now, some around me repeated the charges like innkeepers' wives, adding strange and sinful details of their own, details that Sister Eliza had not spoken of in her testimony. It was as if a hive had broken open in the room, the swarm let loose upon us.

'I am directed from a voice on high,' Sister Eliza went on, trying to quiet the throng. 'I am told that I must reveal all in my testimony, for to live with the knowledge of such sin is to sin myself and cover in filth the Heaven we have, all of us together, made here in our worship of Mother. I ask you to believe me, my sisters and brethren: I do so with a heavy heart, for I mean not to be unkind.'

She stopped suddenly, dropping her gaze and drawing up her body until she stood, shoulders squared, chest high, a soldier of righteousness. Then she began, very slowly, to raise her head, her eyes rolled upwards so that she appeared most troubled. Her expression had transformed from one of lively animation to a look as cold and set as stone.

'I saw' — there was a brief jag in her voice — 'Sister Philomen and Brother Luke, saw them curled about each other like dogs! Yes, rutting dogs!' She looked wildly round the crowd standing dumbfounded before her, then yelled in a commanding voice nothing like her own, 'Now make war upon them with your songs, for this is what I know must be done!'

A frenzied search for the offenders began.

'Where the Devil?' several brethren chanted.

'Nowhere here!' That was the answer from a growing chorus of angry voices.

'Where the Devil?' cried the first group once more.

'Cast him out!' replied an even greater number of believers.

A biting wind blew in from one of the doors to

250

the meetinghouse, causing it to bang again and again against the wall, open to the snow-covered field that stretched away from where we had gathered in prayer. We ran to it and saw — small as characters in a children's storybook — the two lovers running. I could not imagine where they would go or how they would survive, for it was bitter outside and they had fled with neither cloak nor jacket to warm them.

My sisters and brethren did not follow, but gathered at the edge of the field and shouted until there was no longer a soul in sight to hear their curses. *Apostates. Reprobates. Backsliders. Flesh hunters.* These are the names we give to those who leave us in shame. Why, I have even heard say that a fallen sister or brother is *naught better than a dog returned to rutting,* or *a swine sweetly bathed but returned to its filth.* All around me, misery ruled. Some wept. Others remained caught up in recounting the backsliders' sins, their recitations serving only to stoke their outrage. But as the empty field echoed back the fury of the crowd, all voices ceased and we fell into lines and filed inside, quiet once more. We had never lost two believers in such a manner. Instead, whether alone, as a couple, or as a small gaggle of betrayers, the weakest of our kind elope into the World more quietly. Tempted by greed or laziness or lust, they leave by night or run from working in the fields when their elders are not watching. With rare exception — the strong and well-learned brethren and sisters being a prize worth finding and fetching back — we allow many to cross over, for grim fates await those who have shown themselves to be wayward. They die in brothels, we tell ourselves. Choke on sinful appetite, suffer the might of Heavenly wrath the likes of which they could never have envisioned. Why? Their lust for flesh. Their carnality. Their bodily greed.

We finished our Meeting with heads bowed, our feet quietly shuffling in time with not a sound to dance by. Sister Eliza was helped up the path by two younger believers while the rest of us fanned out to our dwelling houses to ready ourselves for Sunday supper. It was a holy day but not a happy one, and I felt shaken by what I had witnessed.

'I, too, was troubled in Meeting,' said a small voice, suddenly by my side. 'I watched your face and observed similar discontent. Am I correct, Sister Charity?'

My Sister Polly was speaking, and though she talked of sadness and unease, her tone was a balm on the ringing in my ears. 'You read my feelings adeptly,' I said. 'I have never heard the warring songs sung in this place, although I learned them long ago. Still, I cannot defend such a blasphemous union between a brother and a sister.'

Sister Polly was silent a moment before speaking. 'Were you not surprised,' she said, 'by Mother's choice of vessel? And by the manner in which She chose to have us apprised of such unholy goings-on?'

I stared at the ground, as uncomfortable with my sister's questioning as I was with my own.

'I did not feel that our sister was shrieking

from her soul,' she continued. 'But rather, her spleen.'

She stared at me with the infinite blue of her eyes as I straightened my cloak uncomfortably. I too had thought the Vision to be troubling — less for its content than for the doubts I had as to the authenticity of the seer — but I could not find the words to answer her.

'You know, do you not, that Sister Eliza has looked upon Sister Philomen with jealousy and malice over several weeks now.' Sister Polly placed her finger beneath my chin and raised up my face so that I had no choice but to look at her. 'Have you not noticed that she is in love with Brother Luke?'

I caught my breath and looked about to be sure no one had heard. The evening bell tolled. 'You surprise me, Sister Polly,' I whispered. 'I have never known you to be a gossip, repeating the sinful murmurings of others. It is . . . it is beneath you.'

'No,' she answered, again with an insistence I found most distressing. 'I repeat nothing, for I speak only of what I have myself noticed. I can think no ill of the lovers if they truly loved. *A sin*, you shall tell me, but I cannot see it so.'

Again, the bell. I quickened my pace.

'Perhaps,' she said, hurrying along by my side, 'they were not meant to be believers. Perhaps they should have been allowed to go into the World in peace. I feel sure that they were about to leave us of their own desiring, had not Sister Eliza beat them out in anger. I believe she knew and so chose to receive her gift in time to openly

253

despise and dishonor them. Such hatred has no place here.'

All this time, Sister Polly spoke as though nothing she had said should have shaken me. But I had never heard anyone in The City of Hope embrace a love other than that which exists sister for sister, or brother for brother. Of course, there is the love we feel as believers in union with one another. And there is the love, through friendship, that I shared with her. Already, I had fallen in the eyes of Elder Sister Agnes — because of the markings, yes, but perhaps because of something else as well. I had been late more than once to morning chores for having spent too long reading from the red book the night before. I laughed more than I used to, and often too loudly. And one day I bumped square into my eldress as I skipped down a pathway. She did not need to reprimand me; the look on her face said enough.

Still, I cling to Sister Polly. Our friendship bears no carnal stain. Indeed it is pure as the love between children. For the third and final time, the bell called us in, and as I broke into a trot along the path to the dining hall, I felt overcome by a sudden dizziness. My Polly was so certain in her opinion. Why could I not allow myself the same freedom? I reached up to loosen my bonnet strings. I needed to breathe. But I found that I could not, for when I chanced to glance over at my friend, I felt she was a stranger to me.

'I cannot agree,' I managed to whisper. 'The lovers deserved the wrath they brought upon themselves, for it was Mother who spoke just now, no one else. She was in Sister Eliza's testimony and She was in every curse hurled across that cold, barren field. You of all believers should have been able to hear Her.'

She regarded me with tenderness. 'Of course,' she said. 'You are perfectly correct to think the way you do, my dear sister.' She looped her arm through mine and squeezed it in close to her. I could not help noticing how thin she had become. 'You are ever true and I did not mean to shake you in your faith. Forgive me my weakness. It was a difficult life I lived before coming here, and I used to dream that someday I might find a love that would steal me away. In the books I read, lovers — do not faint, my sweet friend — found one another despite travail upon travail. And I, silly girl, felt cheered by their union. For their happiness led to a blooming within me.' She was still a moment, then I felt her body droop.

A wistful smile tugged at her lips. Had my elder sister been right when she warned that I should not give my heart so freely? That Sister Polly was too fresh from a World of sin to be chosen as a sacred vessel? I almost stumbled at the thought. But, no. Mother Ann would not judge us by our pasts if at our core She knew us to be deeply good. I reminded myself that my sister had not grown tall within the walled garden where I was nurtured and taught. Indeed, I knew little of her life before she came to us. Perhaps it had held such deprivation and despair that she had been *forced* to cling to the raft of idle fantasy — just as I have, at times, needed to hold fast to the roots of my faith.

I calmed myself, remembering that to feel empathy was to experience a kind of grace. But as I turned to smile upon her and mend the rift between us, she cried out, pressing her hands to her stomach. So great was her suffering, I could not help wondering if she was being punished for her rash beliefs.

I dropped to my knees and threw my arms about her. 'Dear Sister!' I cried. 'What pains you?'

She could not speak as I helped her to her feet and half carried her back to our room. I would make excuses for her in the remaining hours of the day and brew her a tea of peppermint and feverfew to soothe her stomach. No one needed to know that she was sick. I had learned well in recent months that jealousy and suspicion prey upon the weak and unguarded, and I knew them to be voracious enemies indeed. No, it would not be prudent for her to be seen as anything but Mother's strongest and most faithful vessel.

Polly

Deep night. Clouded sky. No moon. She heard a commotion in the hallway and her first thought was of her father. Alive, dead, murdered — all ways, he haunted her. But then she caught the orderly cadence of chanting and tried, as she had taken to doing, to remind herself that she needn't fear his wildness here. What habit it was for her to lie in her bed like this: body stiff with fear, ears pricked to the smallest creak. She imagined his attacks as preludes to death. Indeed, she had often wished for it to be so.

Now, she heard the sound of slow footfalls and a low, melancholy song; doors opening and closing; the voices of grown men and women, their feet marching down the long wide way towards the room she shared with her dear friend. She could not help being afraid. Sister Charity sat up in the bed close by and lit a candle, her face white above the delicate red curls still covering her neck.

'The Midnight Cry,' she whispered. 'We must be quick. Stand by your bedside and make ready. They are coming to sweep evil from our chamber. Be steady!'

Polly jumped up with difficulty — the ropes

beneath her mattress had begun to slacken and needed tightening, and besides, her weakness was growing worse. Following Sister Charity's every movement, she whipped the blankets up to cover the indentation made by her warm body as though such intimate evidence that she had lain there was a mark of impurity. It was dark and the cold bit at her naked feet and ankles as she rose to greet the voices at their door.

That day, they had joined in the slaughtering of the hogs, for it would soon be Christmas and there would be fresh roasts in celebration of the birth of Jesus Christ, Holy Mother's partner in Heaven. The harvesting had been a horrid affair, performed with dispatch by a large and determined group of sisters. They exhibited no pity, for the swine had been raised and fed in exact amounts — tallied to the mouthful in daily journals — so that they might be fattened to a precise weight, which, unfortunately for the creatures, they had successfully attained. A quick slitting of the throat did the job, and though Polly had helped to bring animals to slaughter before, never had it been so many and never had the killing taken place in such otherwise peaceful surroundings. In her old life, it had fit naturally into the violence of each day. And, too, there was the power of her ever-present hunger. Here, during her months in The City of Hope, she had been well fed and somehow the chore was made all the more unpleasant because, in so many ways, life had become easy.

She pulled herself from the memory of the animals' warm, dark blood, their terrified squeals. In the shadows of the unbreathing room, Charity was standing close beside her, but Polly could not hear her fierce whispering. A droning had begun in her head, the buzz of a thousand bees; then the bees turned into a crowd of believers, each performing his duty with the same single-mindedness as the insects from which they had sprung. For a bee notices nothing of the beauty of the flower it attends. Immune to such delights, it returns to the hive over and over only to lose itself in the swarm. She felt herself rising, resting upon a dark cloud of moving bodies as though she were separate yet bound in some way to the believers' obsession with work and order and union, their strange expressions of faith, the shame they wielded as a weapon against an endless string of human frailties.

She shuddered. She depended on them, yet she was *other* in her curiosity of mind and spirit. How long it had been since she had sat beneath a tree lost in the freedom of her own thoughts? How long since she'd looked at an apple blossom for its delicate beauty? She had exchanged the chaos of her old life for an existence governed by rules, and though it made for certainty where before she had experienced only brutal unpredictability, she could not forget the girl she had been.

Outside the door, the elders' voices swelled, their steps as thudding and inexorable as those of a creature in a nightmare. The hinges creaked and a draft blew in as they entered, lantern light flooding the room. Its whiteness blinded, yet still they came forward, their voices growing more insistent with every word until they were by Polly's bed, circling so close she could feel specks of their spittle as they sang.

Awake from your slumbers
For the Lord of Hosts is going through the land.

There were six of them — three sisters and three brethren — breath foul with the lateness of the hour, faces distorted by the shadows, standing so near that one of them brushed his arm against Polly's breast as he passed. He raised his eyes to meet hers and it was all she could do not to scream. Was her father here, inside the soul of one of these men?

As the light swept across the hastily made beds and fell on Sister Charity, Polly could see that fear had turned her back into a child. They had come to know each other well, the steadiness of her friend's devotion wrapping round Polly like a cocoon. The security of Charity's love made her feel less fractured and scared; but just as wondrous, she had seen a similar force exerting its power over her friend. Imperious, righteous, and tight at first, then kinder, joyful, and hungry for life, Charity had grown, and to Polly the visions that so excited the other believers were less of a miracle than was the excitement the two sisters shared when a tiger leapt across their path as they lost themselves in reading the red book.

The group's song droned on as though it would never cease. Dressed in their somber brown day clothes, stepping in unison, arms making sweeping motions though none held a broom, they appeared to be playing out a pantomime. Polly would have described it like that to calm Ben, were he with her. But these elders were anything but mirthful as they sang.

He will sweep, he will clean his holy sanc-
  tuary.
Search ye your camps, Yea, read and
  understand,
For the Lord of Hosts holds the Lamp in
  his Hand

On the last word of their chant, they shook their fists and swung their lamps slowly round the room, staring out into the darkness, searching. Then they took once again to singing and stamping — a dark, noisy cloud of foreboding they were as they made their way slowly, sweeping, sweeping until finally the brother who had moved so close to Polly in the dark closed the door and they were gone.

'They have come,' whispered Charity, 'because they are bothered by recent events. Sister Philomen . . . ' She stopped speaking and looked up. The glint of tears shone in Charity's eyes. *Has my support of the lovers caused her sadness?* Polly wondered.

Charity said, 'They want to be certain the Devil has found no purchase here.'

'Then why are you so afraid?' Polly asked. 'There is no evil to be found around you.'

Sister Charity looked away. There was a divide

261

between them; Polly could feel it. *There is no evil to be found around you.* How could she, of all people, say such a thing? Charity had begun to shiver with cold, and though Polly wanted nothing more than to hug her, she did not move. Instead, she felt a wave of nausea wash over her.

Elder Sister Agnes had made it plain a fortnight ago — when Polly chanced to meet Inspector Pryor — that she had more to demand of her; thus far Polly had succeeded in keeping her distance. She could think of only one reason the eldress had shielded her from the inspector's inquiries: She wanted control. For Polly's reputation among the believers was not a burden she bore alone. If she were to be arrested for arson or murder, her plummet from grace would cause havoc in The City of Hope and it would fall upon Elder Sister Agnes to restore faith and trust to the distraught community. Having witnessed Polly's distress when faced with a man who knew her secrets, Elder Sister Agnes's resolve to discover the truth could only have grown stronger. How she would choose to show it was the only mystery now.

The candle flame guttered and died. Even as her head ached from trying to figure out the schemes of others, Polly kept returning to the same thought: *It is only a matter of time before Charity and the rest of the believers see me for who I am.*

'I do not think there is evil here, unless,' Charity said, holding out her mottled arms before letting them fall limp at her sides, 'it is the fun being had by the Devil at my expense.'

Polly moved to sit beside Charity on the lumpy mattress. Snow tapped furiously at the window, for a storm had blown in. 'Your skin has nothing to do with your soul. It is stained by a stubborn malady you have yet to find a remedy for, that is all. Fie on those who make more of it! There is nothing but good in you, my dear sister,' she said, stroking Charity's ginger braid. 'Why can you not see that for yourself?'

She took up Charity's hand and clasped it tightly in her own. *There is nothing but good in you,* she repeated. 'Do not contradict me.' Polly stared hard into Charity's eyes. 'You deserve a confidante who is your equal. If only I were such a person.' She looked down and gently pulled her friend's hand into her lap. 'I have not told you who I am,' she said cautiously. 'On occasion, I have dared to think that I might be good — or at least, *good enough*. But when Elder Sister Agnes regards me with suspicion, she has her reasons. You know this to be true and yet you push the thought away — push *her* away.' Polly turned towards the darkness, her eyes filling with tears. She could not go on.

Charity leaned in and rested her head on Polly's shoulder. 'There is nothing you could say to keep me from loving you. I wouldn't believe . . . '

Polly's voice rose. 'But that's where you are mistaken . . . '

'Stop. Stop talking, please.' Charity stood and faced the window. 'I will not allow you to continue. What do I care for anyone who suspects you? How dare — '

'Quiet now,' Polly said, reaching out for her once again. 'You must listen. It is only fair. Why, look at you! You wear your markings openly. To me they reflect nothing but dignity and strength. You must allow me to show *my* markings now, so that you may gaze upon me and make up your mind about who *I* am.'

'But I know already who you are,' Charity said, turning back to face Polly.

'See me clearly, friend,' Polly answered wearily. 'I grow weaker by the day. How can I say it, Sister? I have taken ill because I am not who you think I am. Every time a believer looks to me for strength, my faith falters. Every time you show me love, I feel myself slip closer to the ground. I am . . . '

Outside, someone began to shout. The sisters turned to stare. Over and over, a single brother called to the believers.

Charity gripped Polly's hand tightly. 'Why would anyone be summoning us in the middle of the night? Do you think they have found the Devil?'

'Perhaps there is a fire,' Polly answered, before realizing what she had said. A fire. The Devil. Their fears were one and the same.

'Go,' she said suddenly. 'You must go and I will be right behind you. I just . . . ' She gripped at her stomach. 'I need a moment to collect myself.'

'No!' Charity said. 'I will not leave you! What if there *is* a fire? I — '

'You must go,' Polly said firmly. 'If you love me, you will do what I ask. Now, run. I shall come and I shall find you, wherever you are.'

Charity looked at Polly, then cracked open the door. Outside in the hall, the sisters were bustling to the stairs. Some of them laughed excitedly, while others — those who knew the tragedies fire could bring — hurried somberly behind as they exchanged worried glances.

Charity looked back at Polly. 'You're sure . . . '

'Please,' Polly begged. 'Please go.'

The door shut behind her friend, and with the hall empty, there was not a sound to be heard inside the dwelling house.

Alone in the room, Polly threw herself down on her bed and grabbed at her skirts, pulling her knees in tight. *Please*, she thought. *Please, no. Not this.*

Her mind was a riot of memory. Mama too tired to carry a pail in from the barn. Mama sleeping whenever Silas left for the fields. Mama . . . grabbing at her skirts as she bent over in pain.

Polly pulled her knees in tighter and rolled herself into a ball. *Why? How many more ways would she have to pay for his evil?* She began to cry — for the first time since she'd arrived in The City of Hope, she began to cry. Not even Ben could make her do that. She'd been strong, but no longer.

When had he last come at her? How long had his child lived inside her?

Sister Charity

Truth. Faith. Love. Union. How does one lead a life that embraces them all? Tell me that and I shall never fear another day. Of late, I feel as though I play favorites from one moment to the next. Faith is my shield, Truth is my cross, Love is my reward, Union is my duty. Each takes its turn blinding, exalting, wounding, betraying, enticing, and enfolding me such that I see nothing in a clear light anymore, feel nothing without also suffering the awareness of its opposite, know nothing without doubting whether I know anything at all.

Rebecca is gone from us, and as I sit beside her body, I weep. I should have helped her die instead of trying to make her live. I should have been brave enough to choose Truth.

Although Sister Polly whispered her comforts, I was the only one allowed near at the end. I alone heard the sole sounds she could make, and oh, they were born of agony! I knew to leave her naked at times so that the air might begin to dry her wounds, but the pain of even the faintest breeze caused her to beg that I bandage her once again. I willed myself to be deaf to her pleas and how she suffered for it. I thought I knew better.

I tried to be good, saving her burns from becoming infected, cleansing the blistered skin then changing her dressings. Sister Polly brought Rebecca her milk-thinned gruel and I was gentle, spooning the food into the girl's open mouth little by little so she would not choke, lifting a cup of water to her blistered lips that she might drink, and then wrapping and rewrapping her skin in clean muslin cloth. When the pain was too great, Rebecca cried out for Mother's mercy, and in those moments, when she could no longer feel Sister Polly's angels about her, I would take of opium and wine and make for her a liquid we call The Laudanum. The drink brought on a sleep so deep that Rebecca's very life seemed to lie in suspension, all pain quieted, all movement made still. Indeed, so like death was her deliverance, she appeared preserved in amber.

I see now that my ministrations were hardly acts of kindness. I know what true mercy is for a believer in such pain. A few drops of the White Poppies mixed into a draught of sugar water to bring her permanent sleep — that is what would have eased her misery. I should have been brave enough.

I think Faith must know there are dogs at its heels, for it has, of late, presented itself in astounding ways. No sooner had it found voice in the curses my fellow believers bellowed across the field at Sister Philomen and Brother Luke, it showed its form in the Midnight Cry, and rarely have I felt so afraid. Just as I had heard of the warring songs but never sung them, I had only been told stories about the nights when elders roamed the houses like ghosts looking to sweep away sin. Truth be told, their dark faces and the sound of their chanting haunted me still. I felt they were after me. Did they sense something amiss in the chamber I share with my beloved Sister Polly?

What does it matter now? I reach my fingers towards Sister Rebecca's face, afraid at first to touch. All I can see are her eyes, set so large and deep that it appears her skull has shrunken away. The skin of her eyelids — soft and papery as I slide them closed — seems too fragile a curtain to black out life. I sink down into the chair by her bedside.

I should have been brave enough to coax death into taking her sooner.

★ ★ ★

The night of the Midnight Cry, we poured forth from our rooms wondering where to run, sure that we were being called to the aid of believers in need. I can hardly think on it now, but I left my dearest friend alone and in pain.

We sped up the road towards the Church Family and, on the pathway that led to the meetinghouse, found Elder Brother Caleb, motioning us to hurry through the storm and take shelter inside. I could not see his face in the driving snow. To be sure, I feared the worst.

Sister by sister and brother by brother, we filed into the meetinghouse and took our places. The very elders who had, not an hour earlier, patrolled our chambers, now stood behind a long table that had been draped with a bright white cloth.

No one spoke, for it had not been made evident whether this was a moment for laughter or seriousness. Even in our uncertainty, we were astounded by the sight before us, for arranged upon the table were tens upon tens of small paper hearts — each about the size of a person's palm, all covered in tiny writing. None of us had ever seen anything like them, for believers were rarely allowed to put pen to paper for any but the most practical of reasons. How then, I wondered, had these glorious hearts come into being?

Entering in a blast of wind and snow, Elder Brother Caleb walked the aisle between us and stopped in front of the table. His cheeks were ruddy from the cold, but also, I think, from excitement. Such a string of miracles as had taken place since Sister Polly's arrival had reawakened in him, perhaps more than in any other believer, a sense of the divine. His ecstasy wafted round him like a flower's heavy perfume, the effect part intoxicating, part overwhelming.

'We have been blessed on this frigid night,' he said, beaming. 'Over the past fortnight, our dear Sister Cora Ann Reed has received a most remarkable gift. Not a one of us knew of it, thus not a one could have predicted that it would be the Cry that told her how and when to bestow it. But tonight, the voice of Our Heavenly Father and Holy Mother whispered into her ear and asked that she present the penned messages you will read on each of these hearts. Every last believer residing in The City of Hope was named unto her, and through her gift, every last one of you will receive the Word.'

He stepped behind the table to join the others while Elder Sister Agnes walked solemnly to the front. Her regard was not the hardened gaze to which we had all become accustomed. Rather, she looked out upon the assembled congregation with serenity, even joy. It occurred to me that perhaps Sister Cora Ann's gift felt somehow more real to her because of the labor it had required, for it was indeed an impressive display of devotion.

'I see nervousness etched into the faces of some of the believers sitting before me,' my eldress said. 'For if spoken to so directly by the Divine, how can we not tremble beneath the gaze of Her all-seeing eye? But I am here to say that you have nothing to fear, for not one of these hearts bears a message of chastisement. We shall call each of you by name, and when you hear it, you may walk slowly to the table and bow down to receive your blessing and be glad.'

Nothing like this had ever taken place. *What blessing*, I wondered, *will be written on my heart?* Elder Sister Agnes had been clear that the gifts spoke not of wrongdoing, yet in my confused state, I could not imagine that Mother's message to me would be a simple one. My body continued to bear the Devil's scrawl, I had favored my beloved friendship over union with my sisters, I had ignored the warnings of the very eldress who created me as a believer, and I had fallen under the spell of the red book. At strange moments, in the most private recesses of my mind, I had even allowed myself to question some of the beliefs I had long held to be set in stone. *Where is Sister Polly?*, I suddenly wondered.

Scanning the crowded hall, I finally found her, her face pallid, beads of sweat forming on her forehead. Was she feverish or afraid? I could not tell, though I knew from what she had tried to say to me earlier in the evening that she and I held the same swirl of emotion within. We were as linked in doubt as we were in love.

One by one, upon hearing their names, believers walked to the table and lowered themselves onto bended knee. The litany was hypnotic, and given the lateness of the hour I found it lulling until I heard my own. Then my heart seemed to flutter awake, and I found myself rising unsteadily from my place and walking towards the table.

Before bending down in humility, I saw that Elder Sister Agnes neither repelled nor welcomed me with her gaze. She simply lifted one of the hearts from the table and placed it in my outstretched hands. I bowed my head in thanks, rose, and turned to go back to my seat.

While others seemed barely to be able to contain their curiosity — reading the slanted letters that leaned across the tiny hearts as if fighting a wind — I could barely look upon the paper in my hands. It felt cool and light, as though it might fly away if I did not pay it proper attention. Still, I left it lie, my hands trembling and growing moist at the notion that I was to receive yet another message. It was true that this one was not from the Devil, but I feared its meaning would be just as inscrutable.

In this moment of uncertainty, I was fortunate to be saved by the utterance of a single name. 'Benjamin,' I heard Elder Brother Caleb say gently. 'Will you come and receive your sacred gift?'

Turning towards Sister Polly — who must have been called while I was lost in worry, for she held her folded heart tightly in her hand — I saw her jaw tense and her eyes go hard. She had suffered mightily for the loss of her Ben. Perhaps if he had occasionally nodded or smiled upon her, she could have learned to show and receive love in small dollops. It is our way, after all. But I know now that the bond between blood relations has its own sanctity. Why else would I feel so palpably the pain that rocks my beloved friend when she sees her brother turn away his head as he passes by on his way to the barn, or the schoolhouse, or his place beside Brother Andrew in the dining hall? She says nothing to me and I know it is because she thinks I cannot understand. But the truth is, I have changed.

On the opposite side of the room, the brethren in one of the aisles stood and shuffled about looking downwards as though a runt pig had been let loose at their feet and no one could see where it might upset next. But then the bodies directly across from Polly parted to make room and Benjamin was suddenly standing so close she could have touched him. He froze a moment, unsure how to move through this mass of people, his brethren crowded as far to one

272

side as he could see, his sisters to the other. He looked tiny and unsure, and I wondered if, in this unguarded moment, Sister Polly would try to catch him up in her arms and if he would fight it. His thin legs shook as he took his first step, then his next and his next until he was near running at the table. Some of the believers laughed softly at how erratically the little boy moved, while others saw only a reaction to the miracle at hand so pure that it knew no regulation, no self-consciousness, no propriety. Benjamin was Mother Wisdom's and the Holy Father's smallest gem, and as such, he received special attention from the elders beaming down at him.

He reached the white-cloaked table and stood before it with his head tucked down so far that his chin touched his chest. 'You may look up, child,' said Elder Sister Agnes kindly. 'You need not fear your heart, for Holy Father cherishes you best of all and sends only his love and gratitude. Here, hold his words yourself and see if they do not fill you with strength.' Slowly, Benjamin raised his head, reaching out his cupped hands as though he expected the heart to turn to water. But before bestowing it upon him, Elder Sister Agnes did a most astonishing thing. She raised the piece of paper up and brought it to her lips, kissing it lightly before placing it in the boy's grasp.

'You have worked hard to be a good believer, Benjamin,' she said. 'You have made many here in your new family glad. Keep this blessing close to your heart that you may draw strength from

its wisdom and truth for all your years to come.'
Elder Sister Agnes was still smiling when she
looked up and found Sister Polly's gaze. She
seemed to be speaking to the both of them.

Benjamin took the paper heart and stared at it.
As he turned and walked back to his place, he
was visible for only a moment before the
brethren shuffled and enfolded him into their
numbers once more and I lost sight of him.
Then, there he was again, his hands reaching up
towards Brother Andrew's chest. He was begging
his caretaker to read the message, and as the
brother leaned down to whisper it in Ben's ear,
the meaning of what had been written upon the
little boy's heart became clear and his eyes grew
wide and serious before melting into the gaze of
one who has heard a most wondrous thing.

The time had come for me to read what Holy
Mother had directed Sister Cora Ann to write
for me. I looked down at the paper in my hands.
It was adorned at the top with a picture of a
dove, as cunningly drawn as anything I had ever
seen. These were the words that followed:

*Blessed Sister Charity, Cherished Daughter
of Holy Father and Mother. Know that ye
are loved. Know that thy devotion is a
Beacon to All. Know well that thy Soul is
true and thy Heart strong. Mother tests the
Strong and waits for the Weak to raise
themselves up or Fall Away. Thou shall
endure thy Trials, which will show thee the
Path of the Devoted such that thou shall
never Fall Prey to Doubt again. Thou shall*

know thy goodness and find it to be sound. Certainty shall be thy Reward, for Mother knows thee to be among the most steadfast of Believers.

I closed my eyes. Mother had seen my doubts and decided that I should be tested until I proved myself to be true. Some of these trials would, I suspected, come as a surprise to me. But the heart told me that one such test was inevitable, and the mere contemplation of it filled me with dread.

The Path of the Devoted. I knew it by another name: a dance called The Narrow Path. The journey along its thin line would be perilous, and I could not be certain as to when I would undertake it. I knew only that its completion would determine my fate as a believer.

Simon Pryor

Cynicism comes as naturally to the sniffer as does wariness to the snitch. It preserves him from underestimating life's capacity to disappoint. I had written to the Shaker sister, asking if I might be allowed to pass even five minutes speaking in private to Polly Kimball. Her reply was swift and short: I would be allowed to meet the girl so long as I brought May Kimball with me. The Shaker people did not permit encounters between men and women, never mind one without a chaperone, never mind one when the man in question was 'of the World.' Though 'of the World' had an appealingly dapper ring to it, I knew that the classification placed me in a caste of the lowest sort. May Kimball, I assumed, would be installed nearby to ensure nothing untoward took place. Now, my task was to find her before her daughter broke down and said anything to anyone but me.

Finding May without revealing her whereabouts to another soul became my mission. She alone would be allowed to speak to her daughter once I explained to her that I would be reporting the fire as an accident. No one except Peeles and the Shaker sister had mentioned the boy Ben to me. I do not understand how a family hides a child from the world — nor, for that matter, why — but clearly it was not as difficult as I had assumed. Of all the parties interested in the land, only Trask appeared the least bit gentlemanly, though his manner could, I suppose, be chalked up to inexperience. It takes practice to become a rogue.

Business, always business, kept me moving forward. James Hurlbut — of whom I'd been blessedly free since handing in my report — had requested a rendezvous, but he had refused to tell me why. I could not resist annoying the man and thus arranged to meet him in the foulest tavern I could find. It was early yet, and though I'd spent the morning writing and delivering an account of my meeting with 'Sister' Agnes to Barnabas Trask — as promised, a letter divulging the whereabouts of both Kimball children — I suddenly felt that I had aged twenty years since the balmy days of summer. Dread and defeat beat upon my bones like the clapper in a church bell, for I worried over what I had to get done before Polly Kimball said anything about the fire to Elder Sister Agnes. The terror in the girl's eyes when she saw me was a clear enough indication that she was hiding something. She knew that her tale, once told, would change everything.

I called for a tumbler of whiskey and then another, hoping to steel myself against the memories that rose up whenever I found myself in the presence of James Hurlbut. The January wind blew hard outside, and the air was so cold that it seemed to freeze one's breath solid before it had a chance to fill the lungs. Still, as he threw open the door to the saloon, it was clear that Hurlbut had taken to heart none of the usual sartorial precautions of winter survival. He was dressed, ever the dandy, in colors gay as a hummingbird — rose satin cravat, blue velvet waistcoat, cream coat lined with a light-hued fur, emerald-green pantaloons, white gloves, and length enough of gold watch guard to have hanged himself. I was, I will admit, particularly intrigued by his hat — a veritable uproar of plumage. Why he should have thought to make such an effort in honor of so low a visit I cannot imagine. Such is the quirkiness of the very rich; they attend to all the wrong things.

'Pryor,' he said, stiffly. 'Face-to-face for the first time in a long time.'

'Master Hurlbut,' I answered, raising my glass.

Though I had never minded the title myself, Hurlbut hated to be called 'master,' for it made him sound like little more than the schoolboy he had once been, his father's youngest son.

'This setting suits you, Pryor,' he replied, 'however much it may disgust me.'

'Better in here than out there,' I said, watching him arrange his clothing about him, a florid shield against the smell of old smoke and alcohol. 'Nothing like a warm tavern on an icy day now, is there?'

'The delights of your place of business interest me not at all. I am here simply to tell you that I require your services once again, relating to the Kimball matter.'

'Ah,' I said. 'And what might you be *requiring* of me this time?'

'I would like you to find May Kimball and bring her to me.'

I signaled to the barkeep for another whiskey. Though I knew he wouldn't take me up on it, I expressly did not ask if my employer wanted anything — he got more than enough out of me as far as I was concerned. 'And if I refuse?' I asked.

Hurlbut stared at his well-groomed fingernails before moving to place his hands on the table and then thinking better of it. He was trying to figure out how best to get what he came for. Oily flattery would get him nowhere, as we knew each other far too well. Infantile rage would make it plain that I'd gotten his goat. He settled on humiliation.

'Never one to come through when it counts, eh Pryor?' His voice dropped low. 'Oh, you laugh at me, but you know well enough how pathetic you are. My lapdog all these years. So long as there's a purse in it, you're a man who'd abandon his own family.'

He let his allusion hang in the air.

'Reminders of the past do nothing to change our present situation,' I said. 'I won't do it. Anything else?'

Hurlbut's eyes blazed beneath his ridiculous headdress. 'You forget how near to your mother and father I reside, Pryor. Do you no longer fear for their well-being?'

'If you make things difficult for anyone close to me,' I said, leaning forward, 'I'll open my little box of Hurlbut keepsakes. Lots in there that could cause you inconvenience.'

He paused, taking a moment to compose himself. 'Strange, you've never threatened me before. It's that May Kimball, isn't it? I had a hunch you'd taken an interest in the woman. Perhaps a more personal one than I'd originally assumed, though she is a bit . . . *mature* for you, don't you think? Then again, well within your class, Pryor. What an old goat you are,' he said, smiling lasciviously.

Dropping his grin, he barked: 'Cramby!'

I hadn't noticed the messenger's dark, stooped figure, lurking in the corner.

'Ready the carriage! Apparently, Mister Pryor has more important things to pursue than his work as an investigator for the humble likes of us.'

The beleaguered messenger looked at me with an odd expression on his face. Hurlbut's back was turned, so the miserable wretch knew he couldn't be seen. Staring into my eyes, he asked loudly, 'Will I be readying the horses for the auction tomorrow, sir?'

Hurlbut pushed back his chair roughly and swatted his gloves impatiently. 'Whatever does that matter now, you cretin. Just do as I've asked and get me out of this . . . hogs' sty.' He grunted as he stood. 'The woman is easily found, Pryor. You just need to know where to look — apparently a talent that eludes you. We'll speak again.'

'I won't look forward to it,' I said, tipping back in my chair and staring him in the eye. Why had

Cramby tried to help me just now?

Hurlbut smiled.

'You are not the only one I can turn to, Pryor. For if there is one thing I've learned, it's never to trust the word of a lone man. Gives him a bit too much control for my taste. The loose ends I may or may not have come across? Well, let us say that it is lucky I have men besides you who are capable of handling them.'

A cold blast filled the tavern as he swirled his cape and stamped out of sight.

* * *

Time had made shabby and mean the town of my earliest days, or so it seemed to one who had last walked its streets as a boy. Even on a winter morning such as this, I remember running through the bustle of the main street, calling out to the shopkeepers, the blacksmith, the town gossips and spinsters as though they were distant members of a large and jolly family. I felt that I knew Burns' Hollow as well as it knew me and, in such reciprocal recognition, discovered the satisfaction of being certain where I belonged.

But I had not come to reminisce. As advertised on the poster Barnabas Trask and I had seen pinned up in the courthouse, today was the day of the town's pauper auction and no doubt the streets were quiet because so many inhabitants had already settled in their places to watch the spectacle. I passed drawn shades and signs reading CLOSED. My horse shied as a mongrel leapt from an alleyway with its teeth

281

bared, but I kept on steadily until the windows of my father's print shop came into view. They were lit against the gloom of the winter day. As I had found him so many other times, he was at work. It didn't surprise me: He was a man who would never participate in such a foul tradition. I pulled my mount up short and shifted the brim of my hat down low over my face. I'd snuck in like a bandit.

Do you think my heart leapt every time I saw my father in his ink-stained apron, older, stooped, standing alone at his worktable? Do you think that the warm lamplight glowing in the windows above the shop made me ache for the embrace of my mother? Do you think that I considered for a moment, knocking at the door and ending my years of exile? Of course. But I had a job to do and found it easier by far to turn sharply in the direction of the Town Hall, where already a line of men, women, and children had gathered, craning their necks towards the door, worried that the room was already too crowded to allow them entry.

There were men of all trades present, for when a son dies or runs away, the father is often left in need of cheap labor. But most of the congregants were spectators, the type to attend hangings on the village green as easily as they did church picnics. I remembered a back entrance to the hall, one my friends and I had used to sneak inside and drink cider under cover from the snow and rain, free of admonishing stares from our elders. Tying my horse to the empty rail, I slipped through the door. I had been wise not to wait with the others, for the room was indeed jammed, a loud burble of excitement filling the air. The smell of so many packed in so tight — their sweat, their breath, the manure on their boots — was enough to make my eyes run, but I found a place by the window and from that perch began to scour the crowd for anyone I might recognize.

No one threw so much as a glance my way, but how their faces blazed memories back at me! There was the winsome Hailey Grant, a clutch of sticky-faced children about her skirts. And by the far window, Jonas Canon, darkly clad and of somber disposition, just as an undertaker's son ought to be. I was hardly surprised to see Zachary Sinclair — with his fine bones, neat habit, and carefully curled hair — accompanied by neither wife nor child but instead by an ethereal equal. And, had I wagered long ago that Solomon Hadley would grow up as porcine and walnut-nosed as his father, I would be pleased with my gamble. *What qualities of my youth could still be found in me?* I wondered.

I turned towards the makeshift platform to study the auction's sad exhibits. If she had not found employment as a mill worker or domestic, May was as likely to be here as anywhere. Why? Because every community has its share of wastrels hiding in the shadows, occasionally risking a plaintive plea for coins or food or drink. Whether or not their begging goes heeded, they are watched and counted closely by more fortunate folk. And, once a year, the strongest of the lot are herded together and auctioned off

— but not in a manner you are likely to have encountered before.

At an auction of paintings — or even cattle — men vie to outbid one another, thereby increasing the value of whatever happens to be on the block. But in small towns such as my own, paupers are contracted to the *lowest* bidders. The winner is the man whose bid reflects the size of the stipend he is willing to accept from the town coffers for taking a beggar off the streets. The less municipal money he takes to cover food, lodging, and clothing, the more of his own he has to put in. And, from the pauper's point of view, the more the bidder has to spend out of his own pocket, the harder the work and the worse the conditions.

The practice — which, in the more free-thinking and sophisticated newspapers, I have seen referred to as the 'New England Method' — filled me with shame. Now, to look round at neighbors I had once admired and watch them grin in expectation was to feel more wretched still. Is there no fixed bottom for us sinking men? Like mud in a quagmire, the ruthlessness of our behavior seems to suck ever harder.

I was thankful, finally, to hear the gavel come down three times sharply on the auctioneer's block. A cheer went up. The games were to begin. First to go was the youngest of the bunch, a haggard girl who can't have been more than sixteen. She seemed to accept what her fate would most likely be and remained expression-less as winking men fought one another for her services. Finally, a sweating, ruddy-faced brute

— too ugly to have found a wife through more acceptable channels — won her, walking proudly to the stage to seize from the outstretched hand of Billy Fowles, town treasurer, the pittance he'd agreed to take in return for ownership of the girl. I was ashamed at my first thought: She was too young to be May Kimball. A hardy-looking woman was up next — far too robust for my purposes — and the expression she wore was fierce. She proved to be fine entertainment, for the assembled broke into hearty guffaws when a meek little farmer bought her for near nothing and was then himself led out the door by the woman he'd won. *Won* is perhaps the wrong way to put it, for it was clear he'd gotten more than he bargained for. Two sisters, indistinguishable in age and appearance, clung with such tenacity to each other that the auctioneer smiled greedily as he pledged to knock them both off the town's dockets if someone in the crowd would venture a marginally low bid for the price of one. They, too, were taken eventually, and as the lot dwindled to the eldest and sickest of the pickings, the master of ceremonies began to bellow louder and more excitedly, hoping to generate enthusiasm. If May Kimball was here, then she was one of the unfortunate leftovers.

They were a miserable lot, headed up by an old woman with a piercing glare. But one stood the slightest bit apart from the rest. She was the thinnest, and though her clothes hung off her body, they seemed warm and well made by comparison to those of her companions. She had once been pretty, though her face had the haunted look of one pursued by misfortune for too long. Her hair was dirty and unkempt, and her hands had the chapped swell of a washwoman's — still she stood tall and held her head high. Why could I not stop looking at her? Where had I seen such hidden grace? Could it be that I had stumbled upon an older, life-worn version of Polly Kimball? Had I found May?

'Six hundred, gentlemen, is Mister Sadler's offer. He will take the last of the paupers and give them suitable provision for a year for six hundred! Six hundred for the lady paupers for one year . . . Going . . . Does anybody say less than six?'

'Five hundred and seventy-five!' called a man seated in the front.

'Come now!' yelled Sadler. 'You can't mean it!'

'Gentlemen,' said the auctioneer anxiously, eyeing the exodus as the crowd began to pull on hats and cloaks and shuffle home for the midday meal. 'Gentlemen! We have another bid from a responsible townsman up front here. Five hundred and seventy-five. Is that you, Mister Bacon?'

The man in front nodded.

'Yessirs, it is!' the auctioneer crowed. 'Mister Abraham Bacon knows all about it — five hundred seventy-five, and . . . going! Now's your chance, Sadler. Can't be helped that another man's come on the scene. The last of the town paupers of Burns' Hollow for one year — five hundred seventy-five . . . '

'Seventy!' cried Sadler. The audience stopped

286

bustling and stared.

'Sixty-five!' countered Bacon.

'Sixty!' spat Sadler, a look of determination in the set of his jaw.

'Five hundred and sixty! Ha!' The auctioneer hooted. 'Oh, down they go! What's a loss to you, gentlemen, is gain to us. A gain to all you who are tired of stepping over these wastrels as you make your way about your business.'

At this, the crowd roared in agreement, but the gig was not up yet.

'Five hundred and fifty-five!' bellowed Bacon.

There was a pause in the proceedings. Even those of a low bent could hardly see their way to keeping this number of beggars alive on so little.

'Five hundred and fifty,' came a gravelly voice that had not been heard before. 'Five hundred and fifty and I'll take the whole lot off your hands.'

Everyone turned and stared at the source of this latest offer as I tipped my hat to further conceal my face. I didn't want to risk knowing the man — or more to the point, having him know me.

'It's Varnum Tanner,' the audience whispered. 'Varnum Tanner!'

'What's he need with a bunch of women beggars?'

'I'll tell you what he needs, if you really wants to know . . . Ha!'

As nobody dared bid below him, Tanner got the contract.

'It's a right tough squeeze,' said the grinning auctioneer, 'to make anything on this lot.'

'And to be humane and merciful about it,' said Tanner with a wink.

'Ain't that it exactly.' The auctioneer nodded. His face had taken on a look of piety so transparent it was difficult not to imagine Lucifer himself waving from behind it. 'Too bad to bet low on the poor devils and be under all that temptation to screw 'em if you don't come out well once the work's done, eh?' Tanner joined in with the auctioneer's lewd chuckling.

From my place in the crowd, I turned and spoke in a low voice to the grinning man standing beside me. 'Who's this Tanner fellow?'

'You from other parts?' he asked. 'Tanner's got the biggest farm in town — well, just outside if you're being particular about it. He'll labor this lot to the death if I know him. He's rich for two reasons: He makes everyone round his farm work hard and he don't owe nothin' to James Hurlbut. Fact is, it's Hurlbut who calls on him for favors. Now *that's* a turn of things for you!'

I turned in time to hear the last of the transaction, the town treasurer singing out from his desk as he counted the money to be paid to Tanner. 'Just tell me,' he roared, 'that you'll be taking the wenches off with you now! They've cost me enough already.'

'My man,' Tanner said gruffly, 'is on the job as you speak, Mister Fowles.'

And it was true. Prodded and yelled at like cattle, the women were being herded off the stage and out the front doors by a hired man, then loaded into an uncovered wagon as the sky grew dark and a cold wind swirled their ragged shawls.

Could Tanner have bought them so that Hurlbut would pay to take May off the man's hands? After all, Hurlbut might not have wanted to be seen *buying* May himself, a woman whose farm he was then going to steal. If for matters of reputation alone, he needed to secure her in a roundabout manner, this was as good a way as any. I looked about the scattering crowd to see if there was anyone I recognized from his gang, but not a face stood out.

Save one.

Barnabas Trask. I was almost sure of it. His hat was pulled down over his head almost as far as was mine, but he'd risked a quick gaze round the room and I'd seen his face. Plunging in after him, I wondered why he was here. Having hired me, he'd had no reason to dirty his hands himself.

But fast as I wove my way, I couldn't catch him and he slipped easily into the throng. He was that sort, never a standout, as common as a sheep among sheep. With a few tips from me he'd have made a good investigator. Our invisibility is as important to us as a clown's maquillage.

The one thing of which I was certain was that Trask's motives would be easy to ascertain, for he was not a savvy man. So I concentrated on making my next move: I had to get to May before one of Hurlbut's men did. I had to follow the wagon to Tanner's farm, slip in and talk to her just as soon as she was alone.

I watched the cart leave. One chance look at a poster had pulled me back to Burns' Hollow. One chance look had likely led me straight to May Kimball. Deep in thought, I walked to the back of the hall, through the door, and untied my horse. Deep in thought, yes — but not so deep that I failed to notice a man slink round a nearby corner just as I looked his way. He'd been watching me. Clearly, May was an object of great value to many of us.

And what right had I, you might ask, to think my reasons for wanting her were any more holy than the others'? I needed May Kimball to cover my lies. I needed May Kimball so that she could help me gum up James Hurlbut's plan to buy her farm. But worst of all, I needed May Kimball to save my soul.

Polly

She arose from her bed and washed away her tears. No more of that, she told herself. Now, with this new horror to keep secret, she would have to redouble her efforts to stay strong. The baby growing inside her tortured her no less completely than had its maker, for it would remind her of him every minute of every day. She should have known he would be devious in finding a way to get her in the end. How long before the believers found out? She smoothed her hands down the front of her dress. She was thin as a stick. Certainly, by the look of her, she did not appear to be with child.

After pulling herself together, she left the dwelling house and walked briskly to the Church Family meetinghouse. How low she felt, how weary. If this was to be another wondrous display of the believers' faith, she wanted none of it. She had begun to find it difficult to join in as they parroted the language of Eskimo kings or spoke in the deep tones of George Washington. This tiny, practical place became a veritable madhouse at Meeting time, and she found herself yearning for release as much from the believers' ecstasy as from their narrow ways. Ah, to read something other than the blasphemous red book. To speak freely to one of the brethren she passed so closely while walking on paths that had become narrow, high-walled alleys of snow. To hold Ben and see Mama again. To take a single breath without being told that it was Mother who'd allowed her to take it. Her sense of what was and was not miraculous was changing quickly.

But the late-night Meeting had been different, wondrous in a whole new way, with each and every sister and brother receiving inscribed paper hearts. True, she felt the air leave her chest as she watched Ben take his from Elder Sister Agnes. But seeing his face lit up with anticipation, how could Polly not have felt glad? Had he not been given more that day than in all the hours of his sorry life? Still, she would never forget that he had been stolen from her, for somehow the ceremony had cemented his place among these strangers. And she had not mistaken the meaning of Elder Sister Agnes's blessing upon the boy. It was an indoctrination: Ben was a pure and solid Shaker now. He had left the World and all who had once loved him.

As to what had been written for her, it was a message as cryptic as scratches on the walls of an ancient tomb. The sheer beauty and fullness of the Vision — more than one hundred tiny hearts! — had convinced Polly that Sister Cora Ann had been touched by something truly divine. But then, if she believed in the messenger, must not she also believe in the message? Polly took her blessing and backed away down the aisle, not wanting to turn on her elders and eldresses, her hand trembling so that she had difficulty reading the tiny writing at first. She saw a picture drawn at the center — a candle, beautifully penned — surrounded by letters that looped across the paper, so small she had to bring the heart in close to read what they said.

You, Sister Polly, came to the Believers from a place of Despair. Still, you appeared as a Miracle, Wondrous Bright. You are not Bound as are they, but fly Between worlds. When we meet in Zion, then I shall send you Down and Down again to the Earth, as many times as it takes to save a sea of Fallen Souls. For you, ever Alone among Many, know Darkness yet are possessed of the Light by which to see through it. This is your Burden and your Blessing.

The ink lines were searing, and for a moment, she felt blinded. But then the words of her blessing began to drift into her mind. *You . . . from a place of great despair . . . fly between worlds . . . When you meet me in Zion . . . alone among many . . . your burden . . . your blessing.*
Her breath returned slowly and she opened her eyes to a room bathed in the golden glow of what seemed a thousand candles. She had known then what she needed to do — was eager, even, to get it done. Looking down at her clenched hand, she saw that like a poppy in darkness, the fragile heart had crumpled shut.

★ ★ ★

293

A week passed. Still she waited for the moment to come. She could barely drag herself through her chores, so tired and sick did she feel. Charity tells Sister Clara in the dairy that Polly is weaving, and Sister Faith at the loom that Polly is in the kitchens, and Sister Lavinia by the ovens that Polly has been called to the sewing room. At the tolling of the last bell on this night, as on so many others, Polly falls onto her pallet, and before tumbling into a troubled sleep, she can feel Charity's worried eyes upon her.

'You are fretting again, Sister,' Polly says in as light a tone as she can manage. 'I shall be fine. You above all people know that these illnesses pass. I just need a full rest tonight. I am sorry to miss our book again. I know — '

'Say nothing more,' Charity interjects. She speaks with uncharacteristic force. 'I am ready. We shall go tonight.'

'Where? What journey have you planned for us? Where will Mister Wolcott take us?' She had begun to see that she could hide inside the red book no longer, for though she tried to pretend it held for her the same joy that it did for Charity, she could not. Charity knew her too well, and though the devoted sister had found the stories to be full of wondrous discovery, Polly now listened to them with nothing but desolation. She was too tired and too afraid — especially now — of what the World held for her. Certainly nothing so warm and miraculous as an Indian bazaar. She closed her eyes and fell asleep.

Hours later, she was shaken awake. 'We must go,' the voice said, and though it was kind and sure, it came to her as if from a dream. 'We will need time.'

Polly rose slowly. The pain in her gut had subsided, and yet everywhere she felt tender and knew it would come again. She did not question Charity. She had hope that her dear sister could help her. No one else could, of this much she was sure. Slipping on the cloth shoes she wore to dance at Meeting, she thought, *Their soft tread shall be put to a different purpose tonight.*

Outside, the floor of the wide hallway that divided sister from brother had been dusted with a fine film of talc. Charity gasped, and Polly realized that in all of the sister's fifteen years in The City of Hope — save for the night the hearts were given, the night of the Midnight Cry — she had never opened the door of her room after retiring. She squeezed Charity's arm and moved in front of her. If they were to do this, it was Polly who would have to lead the way. Swept clean by an elder each dawn before the other believers had risen, the fine powder spelled out in footprints the sins of those who might endeavor to leave their rooms under cover of darkness.

Polly turned and whispered. 'I can get us through. Just curl up your toes and walk on cats' paws. Like this.' She lifted her nightdress and showed Charity her pointed foot. The sister blanched, stripped now of all decisiveness. Polly directed her to tiptoe in front, then stepped in the tiny tracks where Charity had gone before, turning to swirl lightly the hem of her nightdress and so blow the powder back over their prints.

The marks disappeared, and Polly smiled at the fact that their movements could not be traced. For once, she felt free. For once, no one would follow or spy or listen round corners.

They reached the stairs, which gleamed free of tattling dust. Up they climbed to the floor where the older sisters and brethren slept. Past door after door, the healing room lay at the end of the corridor. But there was no talc spread about the older believers' hallway, and Polly wondered why they should be trusted when the younger ones were not. After all, she knew a thing or two about the movements of grown men in the dark. They reached the healing room and Charity lifted the latch quietly before sliding into the darkness.

Within moments of the door clicking shut behind them, Charity lit a candle and pulled an apron on over her nightdress. She felt about atop one of the shelves, took down a brick of dried leaves, placed it on her worktable, and shaved it with a sharp knife. Slices curled under the blade, and when she reckoned that she had enough, she swept them into a dish and placed it on a scale. Polly watched without moving as her friend waited for the bouncing balance to be still, then peered at the weight by candlelight. Back at the table, Charity shaved off two more curls, then wrapped the brick in a paper printed with the words *Lady's Slipper*.

She looked up at Polly and said, 'I have been reading through my journals. It has taken me too long to find a curative for what ails you, but I believe that now I know. I shall mix this with

296

catmint and brew a tea for you to drink. It will bring you calm and ease the cramps. Then I shall make a salve and rub it into your stomach. Will that be all right?'

There is evil in me no salve can cure, Polly thought. *Soon enough, Charity will find that out for herself.*

On the stove, a kettle had been put to boil and soon the room filled with the smell of wintergreen and rhubarb, for no remedy is simple; even the tea Charity poured into a handled cup had been made up of many leaves, drops, and powders. It reminded Polly of a witch's brew, though she knew that the truth was quite the opposite. She looked round the room where she had sat for so many hours calling her angels to Rebecca's side. She understood then that the girl had come into her life for a reason, and since her death, she had come to know why. For the young sister had passed but a few days after Polly discovered her curse. In that time, when Polly had tried to summon her angels, she found she could not. They had left her forever and not even the plight of another could lure them back. Rebecca's faith withered, and so did her will to live. She had discovered Polly to be a charlatan and it had killed her.

In spite of the hot tea, Polly shivered. Bricks of dried Saint-John's-Wort, goldthread, elecampane, and horehound; jars of pine bark and chamomile flowers; tinctures of clove and lavender. There was no dark magic in the liquid made from catmint, lady's slipper, and licorice root that Charity had given her. With such a

297

horror inside her womb, mightn't Polly have needed medicine of a blacker sort? Yearning for her heart to stop racing, Polly lowered her head and drained the last drops from the cup. She would trust her friend. What else could she do?

'I have finished,' she said. 'What now?' Charity was back at the table, this time using a pestle to mash something sticky and strong-smelling.

She looked up and brushed away a wisp of auburn hair from her face. Her cheeks were flushed from her efforts, and though her eyes shone brightly, Polly could see that she was nervous. 'You will find a sheet in the cupboard,' she said absently. 'Lie on that table by the stove and cover yourself with it. Then slip off your nightdress. That is, if you are willing.'

As Polly lay upon the table, she noticed that she had begun to feel sleepy. The room, no longer cool and sharp in the near dark, was warm, soft, and full of distant noises. A log crackled inside the stove. Charity's marble mortar and pestle chimed dully as she scraped the paste she had made into a larger bowl. Polly's mind drifted as she looked about the room, its shelves and cabinets filled with all manner of medicine. The bigger bottles contained leaves and bark and the dried heads of flowers. Then there were the bricks of pressed herbs wrapped carefully in their papers. A blade, some scissors, a pill cutter, strips of clean muslin, several buckets of springwater, the long, cradlelike bed in the corner. Polly took all of it in as the smells of forest and field, tree and flower — now sweet, now earthy, now bitter, now tart

— filled her senses. The room had both awakened her and made her feel that she was sinking into a bottomless pile of feathers. Questions passed through her mind, then drifted away before she could catch them. But there was one she had to ask, for she was drawn to the small dark bottles that lined the uppermost shelf.

'Tell me,' she said, in a faraway voice, 'what is in the high vials, the ones no one could reach without a step-up?'

Charity glanced to where Polly indicated, then looked quickly back to her bowl. 'They are nothing for you to mind about,' she said. 'No one but myself and Elder Sister Agnes is allowed to handle what's in those bottles. They are filled with poisons.'

'But why would you have need of poison in a healing room?' Polly could not make sense of this at all. 'Why would you mix such an evil concoction?'

'I don't expect you to understand,' Charity said gently. She was by the table now, with her hand on Polly's brow. 'It is true: More than a drop and you can kill a grown man. But the tiniest bit, taken over time, will kill the ill inside him and leave him whole.'

'What kind of poison?' Polly asked. 'And what sort of ill? Something in his soul? Something mortification cannot tame?'

'No,' Charity said, smiling now, 'I am talking of wolfsbane, angelica, belladonna, bittersweet, water hemlock, thorn apple, foxglove, hellebore, wild mandrake, opium poppy, burning bush, rue. They won't kill if you know how to give them, and it's not evil they slay, but actual creatures — worms and the like. It's strange, what takes shelter inside us. Now hush your questions and lay quiet awhile. My hands are warm and I've mixed the salve with hot water, so it shouldn't be too much of a shock when you feel me touch your stomach. There, do you see?'

Something warm and slippery was being kneaded into Polly's gut. Charity's hands were gentle, and Polly noticed as she stared up at her friend that she was concentrating intensely.

'I don't feel anything hard,' she said, more to herself than to anyone else. 'That is a good thing. Nor swollen up neither.'

Indeed, Polly's insides seemed to be melting under the heat of the salve and the movement of her sister's hands. Had she discovered the truth?

'I am thinking of September,' Charity said. 'The Harvest Feast. Have I spoken of it before?' She gazed down.

Polly's thoughts had begun to unravel. 'You have never told me,' she said. 'Describe it to me now so that I can close my eyes and picture it.'

'All right,' Charity answered. 'Then you must travel to a holy place in your imagination, as do we. And you must feel it to be real.' Her hands massaged Polly's stomach, and she was silent a moment before beginning her story.

The room spun as Polly floated above the table. Her skin tingled and her mind felt webby and dim. She was somewhere far away — a place she had never been to before — still, she knew her friend was close by, for she could hear her distant voice.

It is the eve before the feast, when sister by sister and brother by brother line up to receive such heavenly garments as they will wear on the morrow. The air is sweet and full of the last smells of late summer. In the meetinghouse, the Elder Brethren and Elder Sisters reach into a golden trunk encrusted with rubies and emeralds and sapphires.

Charity leaned in and Polly felt her warm breath against her ear. 'Do you see it, Sister Polly?' she asked. 'For were you a visitor from the World, you would not. We would appear to rest in our somber frocks, bending and bowing and exclaiming over a celestial beauty you could never understand. But can you, Sister, see it in your mind?'

'Yes,' Polly said dreamily. 'You have made it real. Please don't stop.'

Gathered in our robes, bathed in the rays of the rising sun we gleam as one, a beacon of faith fit to blind all the evil in the World. We circle round the field that empties into a path leading up to our high altar atop the sacred mountain we call Zion. Then we fall into line, two-by-two, marching up the rise singing:

To the Mount we are going
With our voices sounding shrill
And our hearts unite in praises
While we mount this holy hill.

The verse passes down through our ranks and we sing each round in rhythm with our stride. At the summit a celestial feast awaits, laid out in splendor within the five-sided plot of sacred ground. Young Sister Anna sings her song of blessing as she walks the perimeter:

I am a pretty dove
Just come from above
With Holy Mother's love and blessing
I will feed you with crumbs
That will satisfy your souls
And promise of great strength possessing

The feast commences, and as we pass a golden Horn of Plenty and sing songs of worship, all believers spin in the ecstasy of love. Sister kisses sister, brother kisses brother, and we are, all of us, taken up with the laughing gift for quite a time. AH HA HA! How our mirth rings out! We dance and dance and make ourselves merry from drink poured out of golden amphorae into silver chalices as the pleasures of the harvest — dew-drenched grapes, peaches, corn, squash, tomatoes — spill out and cover our table.

'How beautiful,' Polly murmured. 'How I wish I could be there.' Charity continued her ministrations, talking, talking . . .

Yes, but to one from the World who might hide in the bushes and peer at us through *the leaves, our hands, our gullets, our stomachs would seem empty. To that man we might seem only to be engaged in an elaborate pantomime. No chalice, no Horn, no gowns, no food or drink. The interloper would see nothing because ignorance blinds the faithless . . .*

Polly felt she was dancing upon ground that was padded with fallen pine needles. Her arms floated airily at her sides and her feet moved as quickly as the beating of a bird's wings. Everything was beautiful around her. Every soul was pure and filled with happiness. She drank, and the wine deepened the colors she saw before her. She ate, and the succulent juices flowed down her chin. How she was laughing, laughing . . .

'Sister?' The voice came from far off in the forest. Polly could barely hear it among the sound of heavenly voices singing. 'Sister?' It was louder now, and the golden light, the smell of almonds and honey, the taste of fruit on her tongue — all of it faded as the voice spoke again. 'Sister Polly? Are you awake now?'

Polly opened her eyes and the room around her appeared dark and forbidding, Charity's face closed, inscrutable. 'We must leave here. We cannot be found when the morning bell sounds.'

'I saw it,' Polly said, her thoughts difficult to marshal. 'All of it. We were together, dancing and laughing. I saw everything.'

'Come,' Charity said. 'You must come now . . .'

Polly tried to pull herself up from the table. 'No, wait . . . '

'We must go now,' Charity insisted, looking about nervously.

The room swayed as Polly tried again to sit up. 'Do you understand? I am not the interloper of whom you spoke. I cannot be him, for I did see — '

'Hush now.' There was an edge in Charity's voice as she helped Polly up. 'Say nothing and come silent with me now.' Tears trickled down her cheeks. Polly wanted to reach out and brush them away, but she had to keep on.

'I am . . . '

Charity looked hard at her. Suddenly, Polly understood.

'You . . . you,' Charity stammered, hardly able to speak. 'You are with child. I felt it inside . . . ' She turned from the table to hide her tears.

The world quivered as Polly swung down her legs and slid her feet to the floor. She tried to walk to her friend's side. She knew this moment would come and now that it was upon her she could think of nothing but the emptiness she would feel if she lost Charity's love.

'You cannot know . . . ' Polly tried to explain, for she felt her friend slipping away just like the dream of the Harvest Feast. 'How sorry . . . ' She paused and looked about her. Nothing in the room could fix what she had broken. 'I tried to tell you that I was not good enough. I don't . . . '

'Please, stop talking,' Charity whispered, her back to Polly. 'I do not want to know anything more.'

She turned and handed Polly her nightdress without looking at her, then spun away as Polly pulled it over her head. Polly's heart felt as though it had been cut in two. One half was broken over the friend she had lost, the other steely with truth.

'Please, leave me alone,' Charity said. 'I have work and you . . . well, you should not be here.'

'But I have need of your help,' Polly begged. 'Only you can tell me . . . can you give me . . . ' She looked up at the poisons on the shelf.

Charity watched her coldly. 'You think that I would . . . that I would help you cover your lie?' she asked. 'You have stolen everything I . . . everything the believers have given you. How could I have trusted . . . ?' She looked away.

'If I can find no cure in this room, then I shall have to go elsewhere,' Polly said, knotting her hands in shame. 'Please. If you will not help me here, then come away with me.' Her voice quivered. 'Come away. You know now that the World is a place filled as much with wonder as it is malice. And I could protect you. We could live . . . '

Charity wheeled round. Polly had never seen her so angry. 'How dare you suggest first, that I help you hide your sin, then that I *elope* with you? Become a backslider and forsake everything I have held to be good and true? How dare you.' She spat her words.

Ashamed that she had, on top of all of her other failings, asked such impossibilities of her friend, Polly collected herself, walked across the room, and slid into the dark corridor. Eyes closed, she rested her head against the frame as she pulled the latch shut. All was quiet save for the sound of muffled crying.

'Go!' Charity whispered fiercely from the other side of the door. Her voice was frightened, hate-filled, and miserable all at once. 'I know you are there. Go!'

Polly startled and pulled back. As she walked the long, empty corridor, she thought, *We are both alone now.*

Simon Pryor

From behind the corner of a derelict storehouse, I watched Tanner's wagonload weave down the road and out of town. He'd got a horse thrown in for good measure, it seemed, for the poor beast was tethered close enough that I could see one of the women — May, I think — stroking his head as the cart trundled along.

I rode the side streets until I reached the track that led to Tanner's farm. I did not need to hide myself, for I looked like any weary traveler. The main house was situated near town, but its barns lay a sight farther along the road. Though I do not mind the ripeness of country life, it is the privilege of the rich farmer never to be discomfited by the stench of piss and manure on a hot day. For me, the scent brings back the innocence of my youth. Indeed, I have always found the sweet breath of a cow in high summer more delicious by far than any maiden's. Perhaps that is why I am not married.

I approached the horse barn, urging my mount along quickly. The place seemed empty, save for the man who drove the cart, and he left as soon as he had seen to it that the women had been herded into a couple of empty box stalls. I pulled up, swung from the saddle, and led my horse into the hay barn next door. To tie him up was to deny myself the opportunity to beat a hasty retreat, and I knew he would stay. He'd been through this before.

At the mouth of the barn, I stopped to listen for voices. Whispers carried through the air loud enough to guide me to the women. A stable boy had been ordered to keep watch, but I found him slumped on an overturned bucket, wrapped against the cold in a horse blanket, sound asleep. Evidence that Tanner farmed hard? Yes, but then there was also a bottle of cider leaning on the boy's foot. Lucky for me.

Behind him I peered through the slats of a single large stall where most of the women had been housed for the night. I could see them pressed against one another for warmth. Only one sat apart, the aged crone with a witch's nose. In the low light from a nearby lantern — for the afternoon gloom had fallen fast — her darting eyes gleamed. Peering into every corner, stopping only to cover herself with more hay, she was a picture of suspicion.

'Please don't be frightened,' I whispered, chancing to make my presence known. 'I mean you no harm.'

'Who's there?' she barked, her posture suddenly alert and tense. 'Show yourself!'

'Quiet now,' I whispered back. 'I ask only to have a word or two. I'll pay for your trouble.'

For a moment no one moved. Then, as she slid along the wood floor of the stall, the sharp smell of horse urine hit my nostrils. With her face close to mine, I could see the fear in her eyes. I held out three coins.

'You see, I mean to do well by you, Madam,' I said. 'Here, take them.' She reached her filthy fingers through the gate and snatched the money from my hand.

'What's it you've come for, boy?' she asked, fingering the coins.

I had not been called a boy in many a year, and the term made me smile.

'You may feel like a wise old man,' she said, 'but you're just a boy to me. Now out with it. What do you want?'

I looked her in the eye and asked if she knew the names of the women with whom she shared the stall. She shrugged. 'Well, there are one or two I could point out. What's it to you?'

'Can you show me May Kimball?'

She closed her mouth and regarded me with a furrowed brow. 'What's it about this May that's so special? The man who brought us here set her aside so she could be with her horse and now here's you, wondering about her, too. Oh, it's no matter to me to point out where she's been locked up. Not for a little something else in return.'

'Tell me what you know of her,' I said. 'You'll find me plenty grateful, I assure you.'

She said she had heard May mumble of mysterious doings when she thought herself to be alone. Of beatings, of fire, of everything she'd lost. And that horse! How often she pulled his old head to her own and whispered into his ear!

'Horse?' I asked. 'What do you mean?'

'She came in to town like a right farmer's wife, driving a cart with baskets and blankets and the like. Fine quality. The Shakers had given 'em to her, that's what she said. That's how she made out when she first come by. But she couldn't find work, so she sold the cart. Then the baskets. Then the blankets — though with winter at her back, I'd wager she was sad to see those coverlets go. There was a knacker who pegged her horse for the grinder, saying he'd give her a note or two for him, but she near tore off his head at the suggestion. Yessir, she arrived looking like townsfolk — scrawnier but enough of a likeness so's no one ever noticed that she was one of us, only that she'd come from someplace else. 'Course, she should have been warned out with the other unworthies, but that woman can shift herself into all sorts. She's queer that way. That's how come she ended up on the block with us today.'

'You mean she was one of the lucky ones?' I asked, sarcastically.

'You think it's better to be out in the cold?' the old woman asked. 'This time a year, there's not much I wouldn't do just to keep a roof over my head.'

'And the nag?' I said. 'You say she still keeps it close?'

'Put up such a fuss this afternoon when we were being moved that Mister Tanner himself come out and told his man to tie the poor thing to the back of the wagon and leave be. She's in with the animal now. You'll see for yourself.'

Peering up at me mischievously from the

shadows, she granted me a toothless grin. 'Now, I done my part,' she said. 'You stay true and tickle my palm a little.'

'Thank you,' I said. 'You have been very helpful. Can I ask one more question of you? Did May Kimball ever mention her children?'

The crone looked surprised for the first time since we'd spoken. 'I never heard her say nothing of kin,' she said. 'Only that she'd left her old life for a new one and had not a shred of an idea where the wind might blow her. Children, you say? I should have known she'd lost more than she'd ever tell.' The old witch sat for a moment, then poked me sharply. 'Go on, now. She's just there, but I'd approach slow if I was you. Otherwise that horse'll call you out. They've got a tie, I tell you. Stronger than most humans, I'd say. Now, off and leave me be.'

She tore the hem of her skirt in order to hide her money, but stopped when she saw that I was watching. 'Don't you be thinking you'll steal this back. I've a pair of sharp eyes — that, and I'm scrappy, so consider yourself advised.'

Backing away, I checked first to see that the stable boy was still asleep. The single lantern that had shone so weakly across the way shed more light on the stall where May Kimball was sleeping. As I approached, her horse nickered and there was rustling in the hay. Peering over the top, I watched as she arranged herself quickly, sitting with a regal bearing that was strange for one who had suffered such humiliation. She patted her skirts about her on the straw while her nag lowered his head as if to whisper news of my approach.

I will say that whatever comfort the horse's presence might have given her, it cannot have supplied her much in the way of physical fortitude, for now that I could see her more closely, she appeared gaunt and empty. Hung over the set of her expression like a loose cloth, the skin on her face was dull and old beyond its years. But it was her eyes that struck me most. As level a gaze as they possessed, they were dead of all hope.

I slid back the bolt on the door, surprised to find it unlocked. How easily she might have freed herself! Then I entered the stall and knelt down, asking if I might speak to her. She turned from her initial wary inspection of me, looked blankly into the dusty air, and stroked her horse's leg. Again, the nag whinnied — an answer to my request, which apparently disposed May Kimball favorably towards me.

'I know why you've come,' she said. 'You're the law and you've come about the fire.' Turning slowly, she searched my face to see if she'd guessed right.

'I have come about the fire,' I said. 'But I'm not the law.' After we'd spent months looking for her, it was difficult to believe that we were finally speaking. 'Your husband . . . '

She sat up. 'What of him? Lying, whatever he might have said to you. Where's he now?'

Time was running short. I was unsure as to how I should lay out all that I wanted to tell her.

'If he's as bad as I have heard him to be, Madam,' I answered, 'then he is in Hell.'

'Oh, I know Hell, sir,' she said. 'And it's no match for Silas. Where is he really?' She looked at me warily.

'Did you not see the notice in the paper, Madam? He's dead, Mrs. Kimball. In the fire. He . . . '

'Dead?' she said quickly. 'Dead?' She paused as though contemplating how best to react to this last piece of news. 'So you are here about him *and* the fire? Because you don't need to ask anyone else. I'll tell you what you want to know. That fire . . . '

'Was an accident, Mrs. Kimball. That's what I came to tell you. Please listen. *The fire was an accident.* As I have already explained, I am not the law but the law will follow what I say. I am an inspector. A fire inspector. And I have written my official report. *The fire was an accident.*'

'But how?' she asked, trying to find the catch. 'How would you know such a thing?'

'I know because I pored over what's left of your farm. I've been looking for you and your daughter . . . '

'Polly?' she asked sharply. 'What do you need with her? You think I'd say a word about . . . '

I reached for her shoulder then thought better of it as she drew away. 'Your daughter must be told that the fire was an accident, do you understand? As soon as possible. She needs to know that it's all in the report. An *accident.*'

'But Silas,' she said. 'You say he died. That's . . . '

'A *tragic* accident, Mrs. Kimball. Nothing more.'

She needed a moment to take in what I had told her. If she had had her suspicions about the circumstances of the fire — and she would not have hidden herself through the winter had she not — she no longer needed to fear. She was free. Free, perhaps, for the first time in her life.

'You say you've not yet seen my Polly?' she asked. 'Because she needs to know — '

'Yes,' I interrupted. 'She needs to know. I've seen your Polly, but I wasn't allowed to speak to her.'

'Not allowed to speak? By those people?'

'The Elder Sister silenced me. She won't let me see your daughter unless you come with me,' I said. 'Now, if she only lets you in, you can warn Polly. You can be the one to tell her about the accident.'

Her face blanched. 'What about Ben? Did you see him, too?'

'I did not see your son, Mrs. Kimball,' I said. 'But I fear for him as well . . . '

She pulled on my sleeve and looked into my eyes. 'Why? Have they done something . . . ?'

'He's fine,' I answered. 'But I am concerned for the three of you. There are people who are very interested in your whereabouts, Madam. And if they got hold of one of your children, they could threaten . . . '

'Threaten?' she asked. 'Threaten to hurt them? But I . . . I left them far away so they'd be safe from all that. I left them . . . ' She looked down and started to cry. 'Silas tried to kill him,' she sobbed. 'My boy's alive because I grabbed him out of that bucket. Promised Silas I'd hide him,

314

never let his name be written in any records. Now you say there's others who'd do him harm?' She was agitated, tapping her leg with a piece of straw and then passing it through the lantern flame.

My silence was answer enough.

'All this over that cursed farm?' she asked, incredulous. 'That's all Silas cared about. Once he took it into his head that it might not be his, that he might not be able to rid himself of us and sell it — that's why my girl . . . '

'Remember, Mrs. Kimball,' I said quickly. 'The fire was an accident. You've no need to worry about yourself or your girl now, provided we can get to her.'

As she flicked the straw silently back and forth, I worried she might start another conflagration. But there was so much else to think about, I didn't try to stop her. Instead, I went to the heart of the matter at hand.

'I must ask you, Madam. Who is the rightful owner of the farm?'

'*Rightful* owner, you say?' She laughed ruefully, then was quiet a long time. Finally, she looked up.

It was then they struck — two men on horseback, galloping into the barn, headed straight for the stall in which we were sitting like they knew exactly where to find May. One jumped the wall and knocked me down while the other grappled with the latch and threw open the door. May turned away and crouched, scuffling in the hay she'd used as a blanket. Then as one of the men threw his arms round her waist, she screamed. The stall suddenly seemed a tiny space for all that was taking place within it. Her horse reared at the intrusion as the men fought me off and dragged May through the door. I turned in time to see her yanked up onto one of the men's horses as he threw a leg over the back of his saddle and whipped his mount forward. Then the other looked at me — a familiar slab of a face he had. One of Hurlbut's bullies. He slammed shut the stall door, rattled the latch closed, and jumped onto his horse. May's screams and the pounding of hooves faded into the darkness.

I cursed, leaping quickly to my feet as May's horse began to paw at the ground. His eyes were wild and white-rimmed, his nostrils flaring as they emitted clouds of steam in the cold dawn air. Arching his neck and nodding furiously, he hurled his great head upwards and screamed, a piercing call, shrill with panic. Old as he was, he had once been a handsome animal — hardly one I'd call a nag now that his spirit was so plainly on display. Built more for the hunt than the plodding chores of farm work — a rich man's horse is what he'd have been in another life. Benjamin Briggs's horse, I thought, though no doubt just a colt when his master died.

The nag had worked himself into a state, throwing his head this way and that, tilting it sideways to stare down at me with one spooked eye, all the while nickering low and then screeching, backing and starting again and again in the close wooden stall.

'I daren't get near,' the stable boy called out. He had come running from his overturned pail just as the men ran off with May, and now he stood paralyzed by the animal's desperation. 'He'll run harder at the door if I try. Look, he's already cut up his front legs a good bit. Would'na thought so old a horse had that kind of fight in him but he's turned wild.'

My thoughts raced to the stall itself. I needed to get down in the muck of it: Perhaps one of the men had dropped something during the struggle — it was all I had to go on. Moving slowly I met the animal's wild, rolling eyes and spoke as if to a frightened child. I intended to open the door and set him free, if I could only get near enough without spooking the animal into harming itself any further. I extended my hand towards the horse's muzzle, palm facing upwards. There was no stopping myself from shaking. I was frightened, I'll say that, telling myself over and over to keep calm, mind my wits, never drop my eyes from his.

'See now?' I said. 'I won't hurt you. There. You can watch as I take a small step. I shall move just the tiniest bit closer to you. There now. Easy . . . '

I felt for the moist, steamy breath and the velvet muzzle. So close now.

'There, we have done it, see?' We touched, the animal and I, my cold bare hand grazing the soft fur of his elegant nose. We were both easing towards each other, and I felt him beginning to go calm as the trust between us grew.

A scream as his nose whipped away and upwards. The horrid sound of hooves exploding against wood, a sickening crack as he hurled himself down from where, just a half-second before, he had reared up, towering above me. I thought I had passed muster with him, but then he decided to trust in me no longer, for he punched his delicate legs through the stall door, screaming again and again as he pulled his forelegs free of the detritus and reared, this time flinging his limbs so hard that the sound of his leg breaking as it hit the shattered boards was itself alive — moist and hard, pure viscera. I could not pause to think or feel, could not but look at what had become of the noble beast, fallen now but still thrashing, fragments of white bone sharp and jutting from where his leg had all but snapped in two.

My pistol. I reached without thought for the Colt I carry with me yet rarely find reason to fire. Inching my fingers round its smooth, cold handle, I pulled the gun from my belt, acting on instinct, kneeling and leaning with all of my weight to still the horse's flailing head, holding the gun steady against the quivering fur behind the poor beast's eye. Then I fired. One single explosion: all movement slowing in the spray of blood that covered me. A wisp of blue smoke rose from the black hole in his skull.

I could hear little but the echo of my shot, though men had come running and shouting from all directions. They had not yet reached the barn. Raising myself up on quaking legs, I peered around the stall. One of the walls was wet and stained red. But as my focus sharpened, my gaze snagged on a flash of white amidst the dung and straw.

Buried but peeking out from beneath the refuse of the stall was a sealed packet of papers. The animal's frightened pawing must have unearthed it. Lunging over the dead horse's neck, I grabbed for it before others had the chance to notice. Something in crude char was scrawled across the face — May Kimball had put to good use the stalk she had burned in the flame of my lamp.

It read: *TRASK.*

Barnabas Trask? I had no time to ponder his connection to May Kimball. The men were moving in. Varnum Tanner had been disturbed from his bed, they murmured. He was on his way. I backed to the edge of the crowd. My exit would be ghostlike. I had told May about the fire, that much had been accomplished. But only part of my errand was complete, and I felt burdened by memory, death, and the sudden disappearance of another life I had tried to save.

Sister Charity

The wheel spins, my foot on the treadle, the wool feeding out, the yarn twisting thin. It spins without thought from me, the yarn getting longer and longer, all sight of the beginning lost in the loose-combed wool and no end to it either. How I hate the noise in the workshop today — the slapping and creaking of the great loom, the talk, talk, talk of my sisters.

My Polly's womb was hard under my fingers, and had I not slipped a near-full measure of the White Poppies into her tea, she would have cried out in pain as I pressed it beneath my hands. Perhaps I squeezed it so firmly because I wanted to be sure that what I thought I felt was true, perhaps I did so out of hurt and anger. I will say that my thoughts were black. I, who had believed her to be even greater than a Visionist, discovered her to be little more than a rutting farm girl. That was why her mother dropped her here, as do so many. For if a young girl does not abandon her own infant with us — as was my fate — then it is common enough for a mother to abandon a pregnant daughter. Such is the logic of carnal sin: Pass along the shame, hide it as though to put it out of sight is to cleanse the earth of it forever.

No doubt, the girl I had known as my dearest friend had known another in a very different sense. A farm boy? A young man about town? I could not say to whom my Polly had lost herself before coming to The City of Hope, but the imagining of it disgusted me so that it was all I could do not to run from inside the workshop and throw up in the snow. How I wished I could purge my disillusionment with the same ease.

As Sister Polly lay on the table, her mind misted over, could she truly see the Harvest Feast as I described it? Or had she misled me then, too? Like the interloper in the bushes, was she blind to all that we do here? Has she always been blind? It is particularly galling to me that, with her face as pale as the moon, the believers imagine her to be holier than ever. 'Mother's Light!' they whisper when they look upon her. Am I to allow them to fall further under the spell of such a lie, or do I save them from the fate that has befallen me? When is it better to dash faith on the rocks of truth? That is the question before me.

I thought of seeing my dear sister staggering up the stairs of the workshop not three days earlier to help in the sorting of newly dyed wool. She took her place and wound the yarns round the folding wooden swift. Crimson against her blue-white skin, the skeins reminded me of blood. My eldress had been right all along. I was indeed blinded by love.

Now, I spin and spin and nothing around me

holds its shape save the wool I feed into the wheel, faster and faster. My mind travels back, and I am a girl again. Elder Sister Agnes holds my hand, and we are alone in the apple orchard on a cool fall day. I am small enough that she can lift me into the branches of one of the trees, for in it I spy a red fruit hanging high above us, its skin gleaming against the deep blue sky. I am reaching and reaching, though my caretaker's body sways uncertainly under the weight of me and she begins to laugh. We teeter this way then that, all the while my arms flailing. My fingers want only one thing in the world: to claim what I cannot reach.

She asks, laughing: 'Would you not take the one beside it?' I squeal and shake my head. 'The one below, then?'

Again I shake, this time so hard that we career to one side and fall down. She laughs again, and the sound is all the happier for the fact that we are away from the other believers and, for once, my eldress is free to play. It is rare that she indulges in such silliness, and I know somehow that if I settle for an easier apple, our game will end. A strange determination grows within me; I want so much for this lightness between us to endure that I become serious, intractable in my intent. Our mirth begins to dissolve, and though I try to pull her up from the grass, she is tired of my insistence and grows cold and irritable. Fear is welling up inside me, and I want none of it. *Oh happiness, do not disappear!* I cannot imagine when we will laugh again, and I begin to cry for the apple.

'Why do you persist in wanting the one fruit you know I cannot help you to reach?' she asks, her tone suddenly reproachful. 'Are not all the other fruit in this orchard sufficient to satisfy you?' She looks angrily at me, and I know that she is right to be cross. I am being selfish, ungrateful for the bounty that surrounds me. Still I cannot forget the single red apple, the way it looks against the infinite blue of the heavens. My eldress turns and begins to walk quickly up the hill, back to the houses, back to work and the emptiness of union with so many. I want her for my own. I want her to see me more brightly even than she sees Mother. Without her vision, I cannot find myself.

It is a silly tale. I was no Eve drawn to the serpent's urging hiss. Or was I? Did not her apple stand for temptation? And is not temptation the hope that things might be better if only . . . ? My apple — the one I could not reach — was pure hope. And though Eve's brought down all manner of trouble, could mine truly have wreaked the same havoc?

I never allowed myself to think upon that fruit again because it seemed like blasphemy to wonder if hope was such a dangerous thing. To wonder if whatever it was that Eve had sought deserved to be punished with the curse of Original Sin. The notion filled me with shame, for what child would dare to consider such a thing? I gave myself, body and soul, to the believers that day. I recast my heart such that it would allow me to think only of others.

It has been but a few days since I went to the

healing room with Sister Polly. Elder Sister Agnes has been kind since I discovered the truth about my friend. I can fathom not what she knows or how she came to know it — only that she can see that things have changed. She invites me to remember our early years together, but her words ring false and leave me feeling lonely.

You were the first sign that I deserved love.

She is now full of souvenirs I cannot myself recall.

A kind child, always bringing me presents. A bird's nest once. A perfectly round pebble. A silky milkweed pod scaled like a fish!

Strange that I can have erased my memory of love, past and present.

I looked in on you every night and wished for the angels to guard your pillow. Have I not proven myself loyal to you?

I wish I could confess to her: My heart is frozen, my faith intangible as air.

Truth be told, I find the eldress's tenderness harder by far to bear than its stern counterpart. I was never made to understand that her love for me was so full and lush; indeed, it seems as if she is recalling a life led with some other child.

Now, as I sit and work the treadle, the taste of humility is bitter. How dare I imagine that my life before Sister Polly was not enough? That she, above all others, was the prize? Elder Sister Agnes had been right to scold me, for I had chosen one blessed fruit to be better than all the rest, and in doing so, I had dared to imagine that I deserved to possess it.

I spin and spin, and my foot works the treadle

more quickly still. The yarn will break — has broken — and all the sisters cease in their work and stare at me, the clatter of my wheel as loud as the noise in my head. I leave the workshop and make my way to my eldress's chamber. The time has come for me to ask: When can a Meeting be called that I might walk The Narrow Path?

★ ★ ★

The morning of my public trial, the sky dawns dull and gray. Taken aback by the crowd my eldress has summoned to the Church Family meetinghouse — everyone in the settlement has come — I find that I cannot distinguish between faces. Seriousness seems to have turned them hard and heavy, for the believers suspect my faith to be weakening. Why else would I undertake so difficult a test of my devotion?

Walking to one end of the long room, I breathe in deep the air that — even on a cold late-winter day — is hot and damp with nervousness. It will be difficult to stay the path should I become dizzy and confused. If I blink or raise the back of my hand to wipe sweat from my brow, will I waver? And if I waver, how can I hope ever to reach Zion?

The believers walk to the edges of the space and begin to sing the song that is to accompany my every step. In deep tones, more authoritative than our usual singing, they drone:

Precept on precept and line upon line

*We'll walk in the path our Mother has
  trod.
Yea strait and clear straightness the pure
  way of God.*

They repeat the verse, louder and louder,
stamping in rhythm. I place my feet along the
seam between two floorboards. Barely thicker
than a strand of sewing thread, it extends all the
way to the other end of the room. If I step off
while on my journey, I will show my failings.
Then, I wonder, will the others know of the
doubts that so confound my soul?

The dance of The Narrow Path is new to us in
The City of Hope, and so strange. Most of the
sacred pictures that have been received and
recorded — we call them Gift Drawings — are
full of forbidden color, yet forgiven their beauty
for the fact that they represent messages from
the spirits. The Narrow Path is a more somber
piece of business, drawn in black ink over seven
sheets of paper and depicting a pantomime of
penance so complicated as to test the most
devout believer. For several nights, I have
practiced it alone in the attic sewing room. I am
ready to perform its movements while walking
the thin line between floorboards so that I might
be perfect and prove the cleanliness of my soul,
so that I might keep from stumbling, so that I
might reach the end. I tell myself as I position
my feet on the line: *When I reach Zion, all shall
be made clear.*

*Heel to toe, heel to toe, how soft my shoes,
how shaky my balance!* With the balls of my feet

true to the path, I crouch down and scratch at the floorboards, reaching for the invisible pistol to my right.

'Away, pride!' I cry, standing and then pointing the gun at my heart. It is my fingers that explode against my chest (for we have no weapons here) but the force is real to me, and I sway under its power before crouching once more to replace the instrument of mortification.

Heel to toe, heel to toe, how slick my brow! I kneel just a few paces down the path and come upon a tomahawk left for me by the Indian spirits that I might hack at my anger and be free.

'Away, rage!' I scream, rising and thrashing at my arm so as to chop it from my soul. Then towards the floor again I bend low and lay the weapon down.

Heel to toe, heel to toe, how tired my legs! I come upon a field of sharp stones and, ducking to take one and then another, I hurl them against my lust.

'Away, lust and carnality!' I command, for these are the sins I hate most. Then I toss the stones back, stand once more, and continue on my way. The believers' chanting grows more fervent, as though my actions excite in them passions of a strange origin. I try not to listen to their song.

Heel to toe, heel to toe. How loud their roaring as I touch upon pincers, a broom, and a gallows so that I might pluck out sloth, sweep gluttony from my soul, and hang the disbelief of reprobates lest their treachery entice me.

The spear, the axe, the basket full of serpents,

these await me down the path. *Heel to toe, heel to toe.* To the shovel, the hetchel, the hammer, whip, and tongs I must go. *Heel to toe, heel to toe.* My mind grows weary from self-mortification, but Zion shimmers at the end of the thin line and I can almost smell the blossoms on the boughs of its fruit trees. *Heel to toe, heel to toe . . .*

The sound of creaking freezes me in my tracks. What cold wind threatens to blow me from the path of righteousness? Has the Devil come to dislodge me from my purpose? My intention flames out. I cannot move forward. I look behind me to see who is at the door, but as I twist like a fish on a hook, I cannot hope to keep balance, stumbling slowly until I find myself down. The ground veers to meet me; I see a flash of white-blond hair.

She rips off her cap as she pulls open the door, turns and stares at the crowd. Her color is high, her expression furious.

'How could you doubt her?' she hisses. Her skirts billow wildly in the wind as she glares into the faces of the believers. Her voice is low, almost demonic. 'How could you let her doubt herself?'

The believers go quiet at the sight of the Visionist. They are terrified by her wrath. They think she speaks for Mother. I press my cheek to the floor and close my eyes.

Only I know that she is speaking for herself. Only I know that she speaks for me.

Simon Pryor

It was as cold and dreary a ride as ever I'd taken the evening I left Tanner's barn. Flecks of dried blood peppered my hands, and as I gazed out over the snow-covered fields, I felt winter to be endless and unforgiving, a season to stunt the heart. May Kimball gone in an instant, her horse shot dead, all hope of resolution trampled.

I'd stuffed the mysterious packet into my pocket. The manner in which she'd played with the straw, the persistence with which she'd passed it in and out of the flame — at the time, they had seemed the actions of an addled woman, one who was more than capable of setting a fire out of pure madness. But no. Could she have foreseen that she would need the burnt stalk to write me a message? And how had she known about Trask?

The sight of home gave little comfort, save to remind me that it offered a cave in which I could hide from my failures. A drink, a chair by the fire, a pile of miseries yet to be exploited — these were the crude tools I would use to put the events of the day behind me. Then, I would go back to work.

Sitting down at my writing desk, I placed

several sheets of clean paper before me. I am not quite sure what it is I initially planned to write, but I discovered that one is not always in control of the message that spills forth from one's quill. Indeed, the mere act of sitting quietly brought on many of the thoughts I am accustomed to pushing away, my parents appearing foremost in my mind at that moment. May Kimball and I had not behaved so differently in the face of shame. We had sacrificed everything at the altar of a God intent on convincing us that we must pay for our alleged sins by depriving ourselves of the one thing that might save us: love.

I had lost years of the past, but I was suddenly filled with the urge to recapture my future. The words did not come easily, for how does one go about trying to mend so great an undoing? Hour upon hour, I composed and then destroyed each attempt until I came full circle to the missive I had penned on my very first try.

My Dearest Mother and Father —
This letter will no doubt bring you some measure of surprise and understandable confusion. For that, I must apologize. I have never regretted any decision more than the one I felt forced to take in leaving you. I implore you to believe me when I say that I thought then, as I have for all these many years, that I was protecting you.

I have, of late, come to see my life in a very different light, one that encourages me to ask your forgiveness. This is an enormous request, and yet it pales in comparison to what follows. For if you would consent to see me again, I would be thankful beyond measure.

If you feel that you are able, then you may send your reply to the address I have printed on the envelope in which this letter is enclosed. I shall await your answer knowing full well that it may never come. And I shall understand your silence better than you could ever imagine.

I send you all the love that has burned in me since the moment I closed the door on the happiest years of my life. And if this note does nothing save to tell you of that love, then not a word of it shall have been in vain.

Your son,
Simon

Fresh ink blotted and seal stamped firm, I placed the envelope in my coat pocket, intent on finding an errand boy to deliver it come first light. The Hurlbuts had already caused my family the greatest misery possible — they had splintered us apart in a world that demands devotion if loneliness, bitterness, and despair are to be kept at bay. May Kimball, curled up at the feet of the last living creature that could give her comfort, broken, guilt-ridden, alone — she was me. And just as I could not let James Hurlbut get away with stealing her from her children, I could no longer allow him to deprive me of my mother and father. Our fates, May Kimball's and mine, were well and truly wed.

It had finally dawned upon me that our time on this earth is limited, and we are fortunate souls indeed if we can hold even one person close to our hearts, let alone two. Now, though I knew I had to finish what I had started and take May Kimball home, I could barely trudge through another hour without wanting to run back to my own.

It was late, but I could not help myself, reaching into my other coat pocket for the envelope that had been left in the stall. Its broken seal was a pair of interlocking Bs. Benjamin Briggs. I took the papers out of the packet — they were dirty and worn. Someone had read them many times, but I would wait to study their meaning. Instead, my eye sped down the page to the signature at the bottom, and I saw that it belonged to none other than Barnabas Trask. If I could have re-saddled my mount and gone in search of him that instant, I would have. But that would have been unfair to my horse, for it had been a hard day for both of us.

Next morning, with the parcel burning a hole in one pocket and my letter hot in the other, I cannot say that I was happy to open my door to the sight of a twisted and broken soul limping up the walk. Elwyn Cramby, the embodiment of our mutual misery, and worse still, James Hurlbut's messenger.

'Can I have a word, sir?' he asked in a quiet voice. He had traveled on foot, and his bony face was gray with exhaustion. 'I've come a good way with news you'll be wanting to hear. And

. . . well, the news'll be plenty enough for now.'

I thought with some distress about the delay this surprise visit was costing me, but then I remembered that it had been a day and night full of surprises, and that this one had every possibility of being as important as the rest. Waving him in, I took his coat and showed him to a chair.

'Something I've to say first,' he said before he'd even had a chance to catch his breath. 'Your permitting, of course.'

'Say your piece, Cramby.' I was loath to listen long if all he was here to do was parrot James Hurlbut's orders.

'It be about you. About you and that little girl. A long ways back.' He peered at me, knotting his hands while my heart began to thrum in my chest. 'Owe you an apology, I do. Never coming forth, never telling the town what it was you tried to do. I was there, see. I knew. Knew he ran. Knew she was dying of cold and that no one but you had the guts to try . . . to try and save her.'

He stopped talking, and though the content of his confession was confounding to me, equally so was the fact that he suffered none of his usual awkwardness. He twitched once or twice but otherwise seemed squarely in control of his faculties, mental and physical.

'I can tell what you be thinking,' he said. 'Remembering that I gimp around an' don't say much. Did that a long while. Had to. Scared not to. Master Hurlbut, he's not one to leave a man alone. Works you 'til you break. Then you're free.

Been trying just to be free, but been broken just the same. Things he asks of a person . . . and all in the way of breakin' down someone else. It's misery unending, that's what I calls it.'

He looked at me, wondering if I understood, unaware that I understood all too well. About being broken and doing the breaking. About pretending to be someone you're not simply to stay safe — or, in my case, to keep from harm those I loved. Cramby and I seemed to have grown tired of our bondage at just about the same time, and I wondered what it was that had turned him.

'You mean that, all this time,' I started to say, 'you've been . . . '

'Pretending,' he said. 'Acting fool. Bowing and making like I was an idiot. Can't take it. Through's what I am.'

He went on to tell me that he could stand no more of James Hurlbut's cruelty, that he was ready to abandon all duties, and that, if I'd take his word, he had a lot to tell me regarding May Kimball.

If Cramby had been anyone else, I would not have trusted him. But years of abuse had so beaten him down, I did not think it possible for him to possess the wiles necessary to fool me. One needs fortitude to perform believably in a scoundrel's scheme — I can attest personally to that. He knew I had been witness to his public humiliation since we were boys and, what's more, he to mine. This bond was what gave him the courage he showed now, and I was grateful for it.

'She shivers,' he said. 'Cries in a dark room at the back of an office Mister Scales has rented in Burns' Hollow. Fed her my rations before I left — as well as what little they give me to toss down to her like she was a dog. She talks about papers — all the time, *papers* — and now that's all Master Hurlbut can think about.'

'What exactly does he say about the papers?' I asked, eager to glean just what James Hurlbut thought he might find.

'Doesn't know what they're about — and she won't say. But he wants to 'take care of' — that's the phrase he uses — anything what might stand between him and that land. Got two friends. One's a constable who's crook as crook can be. Other's a miller and a gambler Master Hurlbut's got himself in debt with. The three of 'em are in the stew together. Johnny Constable's ready to make sure the land don't go to anyone but Master Hurlbut. Then Master Hurlbut turns around and doubles the price on Johnny Miller, paying off his debt from the overcharge and tossing some scraps Johnny Constable's way. Everyone walks away whistling, right? 'Cept the woman. Be dead most likely by then. He don't care. Just wants to know, *What's in the papers, what's in the papers?* Wants to know if there's some such he hasn't thought of. I don't know what, sir, but he told Mister Scales he needs to know there's neither man nor woman who'll stand in his way once that farm's been put up. Now that he's been told about those papers, he's full of worry, like they held the power of the Lord in 'em.'

'But if he never knew about them before now, why would he have cared about May Kimball?'

'Same reason he wants them papers — so he could make sure she didn't know nothing that might mess him up.'

'That's the only reason he went after her?' I asked cautiously. I wanted to be certain his interest did not extend to Polly and the boy. 'Hurlbut wants the assurance that neither she nor any legal documents stand in his way?'

'Well, just none Mister Scales can't fix, sir,' said Cramby. He shrugged and gave me a knowing smile.

Was Barnabas Trask to be trusted, or was his stake in the outcome of my investigation bigger than he'd let on? Could he be 'Johnny Solicitor'? To be sure, he had seemed as upright as they come, yet he'd done me a crooked turn, hiding his relationship to Benjamin Briggs and thus to May Kimball. Why, he had to have known that she carried his name in her very pocket. What was he up to?

'Can you help May Kimball just a little bit longer?' I asked Cramby. A plan had begun to come together in my head and I needed more time.

'I can and I will, sir,' he answered. 'Think quick, though. She's not long for it.'

'I know,' I said, grasping him by the shoulder. 'And I know, too, that I'm asking you to go on playing fool — can you do that? You'll be helping her, and when it's all over, you and I — well, we'll talk about something more hopeful than the past. I promise you that.'

Cramby nodded and pulled on his worn black coat. As he stood in my doorway, he did not cringe. Rather, his eyes and the set of his jaw showed him to be almost steady as he bade me farewell.

'Tell Hurlbut,' I said, 'that I have the packet. He'll want a meeting with me soon as can be — make sure that you're the one to carry word of his wishes to me. By then, I'll be able to tell you what we'll do to make this right.'

He nodded solemnly, offered me a bony claw, then turned and walked away. At great risk, he'd come to me, and for what in return? I closed the door with a sigh.

Then, I smiled, for there was a time when I'd have thought, *Better his dreams should rest on quicksand than depend upon the likes of me.* Now, with May Kimball's envelope in my pocket, I felt that Cramby and I might have found in each other something akin to salvation.

Polly

The strip of black ash slipped and cut her finger. Though finer and easier to bend than the shaved wood used by the elder brethren, the prickly form Elder Sister Agnes handed to her was stiff and sharp. She knew how it should be woven, for their meetings often took place over the same activity. Even so, this time she was more frightened than before, dropping the tangle, loosening her earlier efforts, forcing her to go back and tighten the weave.

Elder Sister Agnes did not look up. 'With time, you will learn. Perhaps you will learn many things.' The eldress's fingers, strong and bent from years of difficult labor, moved gracefully, the strips dipping under, over, under, over — hypnotic, regular, a dance of thin shafts bowing and rising, humble and rejoicing like believers.

'Always keep your hands busy,' she said, eyes on the task before her. 'Idleness leads to sin and sin to a great fall, even for the gifted among us.' She lifted her face, tilted her head, and stared at Polly.

What can she see? Polly wondered as she struggled to concentrate. *Everything*.

Charity had hardly spoken or even looked at her in the days since their time in the healing room. She had caught Polly once, when her legs buckled under the strain of a spasm in her gut, and for that Polly had thanked her, reaching out to pat her friend's arm. Charity pulled away and nodded briskly. They dressed and undressed in silence in the chamber that had once been so much more than a place for two sisters to rest between the days of hard and tedious work. The red book lay untouched beneath Polly's mattress. Charity hated everything that had to do with their old life, it seemed. She was not trying to be cruel. Indeed, Polly could see her confusion. She imagined her friend clinging to her bonnet, pulling tight her cape, smoothing her skirts, pushing away loose strands of hair, wiping dust from her eyes, clutching the strings of a dozen windblown packages — nothing about either girl's life stood still and calm. Polly felt sure it never would.

And then there was The Narrow Path. How Polly had despised the sight of her friend subjecting herself to such humiliation in front of the other believers! It was all she could do to keep from exclaiming as she watched through the window of the meetinghouse while Charity tortured her body into strange positions, balancing herself all the while on a crack between floorboards. Polly had never been to a circus, but she had read of the tightrope walker's perilous traverse. What was this if not a hateful mockery of such clown's play?

In the end, she could not keep quiet, and as a

result, she made things worse. Bursting through the door (for no one had invited her to attend this strange rite), crying out above the chanting, telling the believers to feel ashamed of themselves — all she had done was to distract Charity from her purpose. Polly watched her fall and only when she'd hit the ground did their eyes meet. Charity's glare had been dark with disbelief. *How much more hatred could she feel?* Polly wondered. It was as though she was convinced Polly meant to hurt her at every turn.

A day later, Polly had been called to Elder Sister Agnes's chambers without explanation. Sitting before her now, she had yet another reason to be on her guard. Had Charity told the eldress that Polly was pregnant? Was it the fire that still agitated her curiosity? She took as deep a breath as she was able and refocused determinedly on her basket form, grateful to have something to keep her hands from shaking.

'You had a Vision the other day,' the eldress said casually, and Polly felt dizzy with relief. This was not the subject she imagined would be of interest, at least not to the eldress. Indeed, Polly barely remembered that it had happened, so full had she been with the misery of losing her friend. And ever since the ministers from other settlements had ceased coming to question Polly, Elder Sister Agnes had made a show of industry when she heard one of the believers asking 'the Visionist' about something of a holy nature. Now, it appeared, she was suddenly curious. 'Tell me what you saw when you circled the tree outside the dwelling house,' she said. 'For though I am certain your speech would have been of a foreign nature to me, I understand from those who know better that your utterances remain filled with meaning.'

The great tree outside the dwelling house. The day after Charity and she had snuck into the healing room, the day after their friendship had ended, Polly found herself drawn to the tree. Round and round it she circled, the icy wind blowing her skirts tight to her legs as she trod through the snow. She had been on her way to the sisters' workshop, the week having been given over to spinning, dyeing, and spooling a new lot of wool. On that day, there were skeins of freshly tinted yarn to wrap and hang in their rightful place. The blue of indigo, the yellows and reds of Nicaragua chips, the blacks and purples of sorrel and logwood, the orange of madder root — these were colors nothing like the faded hues she knew from home. Their intensity in this gray place seemed miraculous.

Despite the pleasure she took in working with the skeins, she had allowed the tree to pull her in, tracing her bare hand over its rough bark. Elder Sister Agnes had been right: Polly had started to sing as she walked, a song she'd never before heard, words she'd never before uttered, her footfalls in perfect time with the rhythm. She was surprised to feel such elation, for nothing about the last several weeks had given her reason to rejoice. Indeed, she had been shaken by so many disturbances. She wished that she could have explained her shameful condition to Charity, but to speak of her father was to allow him into the world that had saved her. For her friend to think her a common slut was bad enough, but for her to know Polly as a girl degraded over months and years — that was a humiliation she could not abide.

Touching the tree made Polly feel as though she had come upon a great source of life and light, grace and truth. She remembered the bark turning into hands, thousands of hands reaching towards her own but never grasping it, only brushing lightly her fingertips as she passed. Whether or not Elder Sister Agnes would have understood the words, Polly had sung of love and friendship. She had spoken of hope. She had spun songs of thanks as she walked, losing track of all time.

Her thoughts veered like racing pigeons in the sky, and like the play of light and shadow on the tilting birds, she found herself transported to another time and place just as suddenly as she had reflected on the tree: the kitchens on a recent wintry morning, where she could still feel the cool counter at which she stood, see the young brethren laughing as they played in the snow just outside, recall the log cart piled high with wood as yet unsplit. She remembered watching as Brother Andrew climbed atop the logs and whistled in the boys. They tumbled over one another with such abandon that Polly had put her flour-dusted hand to her mouth to hide her smile. Joining the pups in their game, Brother Andrew leapt time and again from the cart and fell, ambushed by his charges. The joyful chaos charmed Polly. Was he someone she could talk to about Ben? She banished the thought from her mind. No devout brother would hold a private conversation with a sister, not even if she was a Visionist.

She watched as Brother Andrew heaved himself out of the snow, brushed off his coat, and told the strongest of the young brethren to unload the logs and pass them to where he would split them. Then he lined up the smaller ones and showed them how to toss the wood to one another until they reached the shed, where another band was in charge of stacking it. Polly felt lulled by the roll of each log, the fall of the axe, the arc of the toss, and the puzzling together of all the bits and pieces so that none in the stack stood out from the whole. She was alone in the kitchens, and it had been easy to forget herself in the brethren's industriousness. Then, she caught sight of Ben laughing as he put all his might into throwing a piece of small kindling. He wore a brown coat, dark-green mittens, and a wool cap, but enough of his face peeked out that Polly could see his sweet smile and bright black eyes. The picture filled her with longing and made her stomach seize with such violence that she had to pull away, dropping to her knees. It was of some comfort that she was alone and owed no one an explanation as she lay on her back, breathing slowly and steadily. Now that Silas lived inside her, he had found a way to plague her at will.

The sight of Ben smiling — Polly could not let it go. She raised herself up, wiped clean her hands, and walked towards the door. Who cared what anyone thought of her now that she had lost Charity's love? It was true that when she spoke out during her friend's dance, the believers had listened, thinking it a Vision. They did not hold Charity to her failure to stay on The Narrow Path. They reasoned that Mother Ann had, through Polly, defended her, and thus she was immune from reproach.

But that was in Meeting. What would they say if they saw Polly talking to Brother Andrew? She doubted they would find holiness at work in such a blatant breach of the rules. Polly lifted her head high and opened the door. She wore no cloak as she blazed a path through the snow headed directly for the brother.

It was as if the boys suddenly turned into ice, for they stopped their play immediately and stood stock-still as they watched her.

'Brother Andrew,' she said when she had gotten close enough not to shout. 'Please don't turn away. I need to speak to you. Please. It's about Ben.'

But the brother looked around nervously, then stared down at his feet and said nothing.

'I . . . I . . . ,' Polly stammered. 'I want to know how my brother is. I cannot speak to him, as you are well aware. I just want to know that he is . . . all right. Does he mention me ever? Or his home? His Mama?'

Brother Andrew shifted uncomfortably and remained silent.

'If you will not answer then can you allow me to talk to him myself?' She leaned in and whispered, 'I know it is irregular, but it could be in secret if you like. I wouldn't be long. I just need to know . . . is he happy here?'

The boys had begun to exchange nervous glances. Polly turned and looked at them beseechingly. It was then her gaze finally locked with little Ben's. Her heart fluttered. She smiled shyly and held out her hand.

'Ben?' she said. 'Will you come to me? Just for a moment?'

He stood still. She wondered if he mightn't walk towards her. She hoped . . . But then he reached into the snow, packed a handful with angry force, and threw it at her. The look on his face was one of pure hatred.

'Go away!' he cried. 'Get away from Brother Andrew!' He stamped his foot as he spoke. '*He's* mine! I hate you! *He's* mine!'

Then he turned and ran for the woodshed.

Brother Andrew watched him flee, darting round Polly to follow. All the boys were reaching down now, making snowballs and hurling them at her.

'Go away,' they screamed. 'Leave us!'

Polly could not move, such was her horror. She had only meant to speak quietly to her brother. She would never have put her hand on him; she wanted just to be within touching distance, to be close for a moment.

She shielded her head in her arms, turned and ran back towards the kitchen door. The sisters were at the window now — a crowd of them — and they looked at each other in anguish as she hurled herself onto the floor and began to cry.

No one moved. They had never known a sister

to break ranks and approach a brother. Polly imagined that they were trying to decide whether or not to shun her.

Then one believer stepped forward and bent down to put her arms around Polly. It was Sister Lavinia.

'There, there, child,' she said. 'It's all right now. We all make mistakes, and I doubt you'll be making that one again.' Polly sobbed into her shoulder.

'Thank you,' she said. 'I was only trying . . . he's my brother and he's so young . . . I just wanted . . . ' But she could not finish what she had started, so forcefully did her crying come upon her.

* * *

In the room with Elder Sister Agnes, her mind flickered back to the tree. Circling, circling, suddenly she felt a sharp bite and withdrew her hand, pulling it to her breast and walking faster, her feet now beating a changed time in the well-worn track. The sounds she made were no longer joyful but frightened, frenzied as they tumbled from her mouth. She could not feel the kindness of others but found her fingertips touched by small, leaping flames as, in her mind, fire engulfed the tree until it roared heat and smoke such that she had to step back into the deep, untrodden snow.

How to explain all of this to the eldress.

'The tree called to me,' she said quietly. 'It called with a gentle voice like none I can

346

describe, and I circled round it and started to sing because it filled me with peace and happiness to do so. My song was one of union, not simply here in The City of Hope, but everywhere. It was as though I could touch the hand of every person in the world as they reached out from within the trunk of that tree.'

She stopped and looked up from her struggle to tame the basket that twisted and turned in her lap. Straining to catch the cast of Elder Sister Agnes's expression, she saw that it remained hidden to her. Polly's gaze fell back on her work as she told of the sudden turning to flames, of the burning form of the giant tree as it fanned into the Heavens.

She expected Elder Sister Agnes to keep her eyes on her work, inscrutable as ever. But instead, the eldress jerked her head up and stared, then laid her basket to rest. She seemed afraid to move lest it distract her from choosing the proper words.

'You must know what you are doing,' Elder Sister Agnes said, her impatience barely contained once she decided, finally, to address Polly. 'Do you not realize that there is *someone* in this place who sees you for what you are?'

Polly drew a sharp breath. Was this the moment when everything would come tumbling down? She was surprised to find relief in the thought. Ever since the believers had placed her on a pedestal, a part of her had yearned to be exposed. And ever since she had set the farm afire — how could she have believed for one moment that it had been an accident? — that same part wished for the law to find her and get it over with. She knew what the consequences would be. She would be taken away from the only place she'd ever felt happiness. She would be forced to admit to her crime, exchanging The City of Hope for a jail cell — or worse, the noose. Even so, if she were revealed as nothing more than a farm girl with a past as foul as a rat's tail is long, she might finally find peace.

She stared hard at the eldress. Could it be that she had aged in the short time since Polly had known her? Her face seemed etched with deeper lines, her skin stretched tighter across her cheekbones. She could not be much older than Mama, and for the first time, Polly noticed how similarly broken they were by the toil of their difficult lives, toil that brought the years on fast for women the world over. Perhaps because Polly knew that she had little left to lose, her heart was suddenly full of sympathy for Elder Sister Agnes. After all, she sought only the truth. If Polly gave it to her, would her confession remove from the eldress's shoulders the burden of protecting the believers' faith?

The believers. Polly could imagine their faces if only they knew. She could hear the swelling of their angry voices. To bear the message that they had been duped — Elder Sister Agnes would never want to be the one to do that. To tell them that they had placed their faith in a fraud — this was not a fate Polly would wish on anyone. She bowed her head and continued her work, unable to think of an adequate answer to the eldress's accusation.

'You have surely read or heard of something like this Vision before?' Elder Sister Agnes said. 'I ask with great seriousness, have you not encountered this burning tree before?'

'I . . . I used to see a great tree in my old life, an oak,' Polly stammered. 'I imagined its leaves to be red. I imagined standing beneath them and raising my arms until they shimmered and shook. There were thousands of leaves, whispering, trembling over me and I felt full. It never caught fire, though. It never bit my hand with burns. It never frightened me. It was where I needed to go. Can you understand?' She stopped speaking. An image of flames filled her mind, and though she closed her eyes, she could not help seeing the burning figure tumbling from the blaze of the farmhouse.

Elder Sister Agnes rose from her chair and walked slowly to a tall cupboard built into the wall and fastened shut. She paused before opening it and taking out a brown leather-bound book, which she clutched to her chest as she turned and walked back towards Polly.

'You have heard tell of the *Book of Secrets?*' she asked. 'That is its common name. It is a sacred text to any believer who knows of it — the story of Mother Ann's life and beliefs as remembered by those who knew her. When I was a younger sister, we read it freely so that we might learn from her greatness. But it was decided, after some years, that should the book find its way into the hands of the World's people, its tales of purity and redemption might be misread. Out of fear that the book might cloud

349

our mission, every copy in existence was collected and guarded by the elders of the communities. No one in The City of Hope has seen this book for many a year. Do you understand?'

'Yes,' Polly answered faintly. 'I have only heard believers whisper its name. I do not know what it says.'

The eldress paused before speaking again. 'Well, you shall now be allowed to see why your most recent Vision has startled me so.' Sighing, she turned the printed pages, edged brown with age, until she found the passage she was searching for. She looked up sharply and pushed the open book at Polly.

'Read,' she ordered.

And James Whittaker sat down by the roadside in darkness to eat his victuals and saw America as a large tree, and every leaf thereof shone with such brightness as made it appear like a burning torch, representing the church of Christ, which will yet be established in this land.

Polly looked up from her recitation. 'I don't . . . '

'You don't understand?' asked Elder Sister Agnes briskly. 'Nor, I must say, do I. There is something about the way that you came to us that keeps troubling me. It was hardly unusual, at least on its surface. I myself was a refugee from the World's cruelty, though that's of little consequence here. There was a fire, that much you — and the investigator, of course — have told me.'

Polly's hands slipped again as she tried to bend the wooden strips to fit the basket form. What else had the investigator said? She tensed in her chair.

'You are hiding something from me,' Elder Sister Agnes continued. 'I warned you, when you arrived and impressed the believers so deeply with your first Vision, that their faith in you carried with it responsibility. Now that I have watched you embrace their trust so fully, I wonder how great your past sins would have to be to justify my crushing of their adoration. Perhaps it would be simpler if I just gave up my doubts and joined them?'

Polly felt the color drain from her face. *Confess, confess, confess.* Those were the only words she could hear inside her head. But she shook off the temptation to speak. If she could hold on for just a bit longer, perhaps she could devise a better plan.

'We have been a comfort to you, Sister Polly, have we not?'

The question was so simple, it stunned Polly. 'Yes, of . . . of course,' she stammered.

'And to your brother as well?'

Polly thought back on how clearly he had shown his hatred of her. Still, she could not help admitting that yes, he too had benefitted from his time with the believers.

The elder sister smiled. 'I think Benjamin is a true Shaker. You, however, do not appear to be as taken with our ways. Would you say that I have described the situation correctly?'

'I would say that Ben is a child, Eldress,' Polly answered, more quickly than she intended. She knew that she had to mind her every word. 'By that, I mean that it is difficult to determine one's faith at so young an age.'

'Ah, but I cannot agree. Your own dear Sister Charity became a devout believer when she was younger by far than Benjamin.'

'Yes, but — begging your pardon, Eldress — she was as good as born here, with no one else but you and the believers to love and feed and teach her. Ben has a real family. A mother and a sister . . . '

'Yes,' the eldress said, pushing hard at a particularly thick shaving, one that refused to fall into the weave. 'Once, he had a flesh family like the one you describe, though I am struck by the person you choose to leave out. A father.'

'No,' Polly said, feeling dizzy as she answered. 'I mean, yes, a father. It was unintentional . . . that I left him unnamed.'

Elder Sister Agnes was quiet a moment. Polly's hands hurt, the air inside the room felt warm and close, she did not know if she could hold up much longer before spilling the whole truth.

'I am curious about the circumstances surrounding Benjamin's birth,' she said, her manner strangely coy all of a sudden. Polly felt unnerved by the agility with which she seemed to flit from subject to subject. 'He was fully your brother, yes?'

'*Is* fully my brother, Eldress,' she answered. 'Yes.'

'Is he recognized as such?'

Polly stared at her. 'You would have to ask my mother about that. I imagine that he would have been treated like any child who comes into this world.'

'Surely,' the eldress continued, 'there was a doctor present. You would have remembered that. Did he not ask your mother and father to sign your brother's name into some sort of record?'

'I remember no such person,' Polly answered, though she was lying. 'Many a baby is born without the aid of a doctor. I'm sure you've delivered your share even here.' Polly lost herself in memory. What had his name been? He had helped Mama, hadn't he? And then later, when Ben had almost drowned, he'd come again.

She looked up and saw that the eldress's face was dark with anger. Polly had known that births taking place within the settlement were not something Elder Sister Agnes would wish to discuss, but she did not want to go on talking about the day Ben was born. And anyway, Polly had heard stories. Whether they arrived in The City of Hope already with child or found themselves in that position after some time here — desire will out in the coldest of climes — at least a few young girls had come to the eldress in search of aid. Polly might have done so herself had her circumstances not been so complicated.

'Do you take me for a midwife, Sister?' Elder Sister Agnes asked, her blue eyes glinting.

'I . . . I meant nothing of the sort,' Polly answered. 'Only that you are respected and possess knowledge when it comes to healing that no one else — not even Sister Charity — can claim. Why wouldn't any sister who found herself in trouble seek you out? To birth her baby, if it was not conceived in . . . ' Polly was treading on slippery ground, but she forged ahead. 'And if she showed genuine contrition, she would know that you have the capacity to forgive and teach the moral path through compassion, as you are so often called upon to do concerning matters of a different sort.'

Elder Sister Agnes rose from her chair and walked to the window. 'You show an impressive knowledge of such things for one esteemed by so many for her purity. I believe that you are quite a different sort of girl than the Visionist you are thought to be. I have suspected it from the first. But tell me, Sister Polly, how badly do you want to leave us?'

Polly felt the floor drop from beneath her feet. 'I . . . I don't understand why you would think such a thing. I . . . '

The eldress held up her hand. 'Hush, child. Hear me through. You are ill, that is no secret. 'Tis true, you may be suffering from some sort of ague, but I know that there are many things that sicken both body and soul. Secrets, for example.' She turned to face Polly, but Polly stared at her feet waiting to hear what Elder Sister Agnes would say next.

'I have an idea — one that might serve everyone, even those who know nothing of the real truth. Even *myself*, who knows only that there is more to know. You say that your mother is the only person who could tell me what I seek to understand about Benjamin's birth. If I could speak to her, then I could see my way to helping you leave with her. You met the fire inspector, Mister Simon Pryor. Indeed I believe he caused you some alarm. He has asked to meet with you privately, you know.' She paused, the better to gauge Polly's reaction. 'I have, against all of our rules, accepted — on the condition that he bring your mother to me.'

Polly's mind raced. She could leave without having to run. But what awaited her outside The City of Hope? How she wished she could be free. She longed to see Mama again. She would be allowed to slip away from this place without a fuss. By some miracle, would she be able to persuade the inspector to let her disappear? Perhaps then she could begin anew. Such a dream was barely conceivable. She looked the eldress in the eye.

'I will meet with the inspector,' she said, trying to keep her voice from shaking. 'And I will leave quietly with him and my mother.'

Elder Sister Agnes could not hide her satisfaction. She brushed her hands briskly down her skirt. 'You will doubtless be missed,' she said, 'but the actions of the Divine are impossible for mere mortals to comprehend, and every believer here in The City of Hope understands that. Just as you appeared out of nowhere, you will vanish. There is a certain Heavenly symmetry to it all, is there not?'

Polly nodded. The eldress had laid out her plan with such calm, it was as though she had been thinking it over for weeks. But there was one more detail to discuss. 'Ben,' she said. 'He would have to leave with us.'

'Ah,' said Elder Sister Agnes. 'There you are mistaken. When I said that Benjamin was a true Shaker, I did not speak idly. Look,' she said, turning to her writing desk and taking a sheet of paper from one of the drawers. 'It is true, we do not normally invite so young a believer to commit himself to us fully, but he is . . . a simple soul. And a gifted one. We saw fit to make an exception, and he has quite happily joined us in law as well as spirit. You see? He made the mark of an X beside his name in our Covenant just yesterday.'

Polly stared at the paper, then looked up.

'But he is a child,' she said fiercely. 'He knows only that he has been fed and kept warm and not had to live in fear.' She stopped, afraid that she had revealed more about their other life than was prudent. 'He has been shown kindness at the expense of the love of his own mother. He understands nothing of covenants. He could not even write his own name! You wonder if he exists in the eyes of the world? How can you claim that such a mark as this means that he exists as a 'true Shaker'?' She had run out of words. Was life nothing but loss upon loss? 'You cannot have my brother,' she said firmly. 'I will leave if that is what you want. But you will not take him from his own mother, from me. He *will* leave with us.'

The eldress's voice was soft. 'I do not believe that he will, do you? Am I alone in noticing how he behaves when he sees you? Do you think that

I was not informed as to what happened when you tried to speak to him?' She paused to let her words sink in.

Sounds began to fill Polly's head. Of children singing so loudly, she had to raise her hands to her ears to block them out. It was a song she'd heard coming from the schoolhouse one day during her first weeks, and it had haunted her since.

Of all the good friends that I ever possess
I certainly love good believers the best:
So good and so pretty, so clever they feel
To see them and love them increases my
    zeal.
O how pretty they look
How pretty they look!
How clever they feel!
Of all the relations that I ever see
My old fleshly kindred are furthest from
    me:
So bad and so ugly, so hateful they feel
To see them and hate them increases my
    zeal.
O how ugly they look!
How ugly they look!
How nasty they feel!

It took all her strength, but she drew herself up to face the eldress. There could be only one reason that Elder Sister Agnes cared so vehemently that Ben stay behind. Silas was dead, isn't that what the eldress had told her? So Mama would inherit the land. And if the land was Mama's, she would leave part of it to Ben.

Elder Sister Agnes did not simply want to take her brother from her; she wanted his share of the farm as well. Poor Ben. Whether as an X on the Shakers' Covenant or a blank entry in the town rolls, his existence — or apparent absence — meant only one thing to everyone except Mama and Polly. Land. He'd nearly been killed for it; now he was to be stolen. Polly felt sick.

'You think that if you keep my brother here, it entitles you to take the farm,' she said. 'You think that if you can get my mother to prove that Ben is her son, then you can present him — a true Shaker — as the eventual heir to at least half of the property. Is that the reason you are so intent on keeping him?'

'Yes,' she said, matter-of-factly. 'Benjamin's gifts are many, as I have said, but one of them is the land he brings with him. You needn't make me out to be a thief. We have the means to bring back your farm. Whatever you may think of me, I have no interest in hurting you. I seek the betterment of all believers, and as such, I have thought long and hard about your future. I offer you mercy, do you not see that?'

'Mercy?' Polly said. 'Taking a child from his mother? Taking my brother from me? Is that what you call mercy?'

Elder Sister Agnes's eyes hardened as she lost her patience. 'Do you not remember the morning you arrived? Your mother gave you and your brother to us. She signed papers of indenture. You are lucky that I am so lenient as to consider breaking that pact where you are concerned. I do so only because I sense that it will be best for my fellow believers.'

She stopped herself, took a breath, and stood down. 'You hate me now, Sister Polly,' she said, sitting and taking up her basket once again. 'But someday you will see that I was right. I will come and find you when the inspector brings your mother to me. Please take heart in the thought of that reunion.' She looked up. 'Now, go.'

Polly wanted to say so much more — she owed it to Ben — but she could not find the strength. She halted before opening the door to leave.

'Elder Sister Agnes,' she said. 'How did you come to be a believer?'

The eldress looked up, startled. Then, evenly and clearly, she spoke.

'I was not wanted elsewhere, child. I arrived barren, beaten, and of no use to a single soul in the world. That is how I came to be a believer. Does that answer your question? You see, I hide nothing from you. I am not afraid of the past.'

Polly looked down at the floor and nodded. Her shame was complete.

Simon Pryor

After my revelatory conversation with Cramby, I set out to find an errand boy to deliver my letter and went in search of Barnabas Trask, his signature as emblazoned on my mind as it was on the papers I carried. I did not know if he would continue to try to mislead me as to his interest in the property, just as I did not know how he would greet the news that I was aware of his association with May Kimball. I expected to discover yet another worm in the wood. After all, even the Shaker sister had proved more manipulative than her humble trappings would have led one to suspect. So much for spiritual purity.

'Ah, Mister Pryor,' Trask said as he opened the door, a look of surprise on his face. 'I knew you were a diligent man, but I should never have expected you to deliver your reports in person. Come in, come in.'

I thanked him for the invitation and apologized for startling him. 'I've a matter of some importance to discuss with you, and I'm afraid that I did not think it wise to wait for a formal appointment.'

His smile did not waver as he took my coat,

360

but as he hung it on a rack in the hall, I noticed that confusion had darkened his brown eyes. Looking round, I saw that his study was not so very different from my own, though the leather and dark polished wood of the desk lent it an air of propriety distinctly lacking in my jumbled library. The place was dark and warm and woody with paneling, but as my eyes adjusted to the lack of light, I saw that the furniture had become rather threadbare — the leather armchair cracked and scarred; the desk full of gouges that had never been attended to; the dark red carpet worn in a track from the door to the fire to the desk and back again. Perhaps, I thought, the place had once contained the offices of an older and more successful solicitor.

Yet Trask's surroundings suited him — a country lawyer, seemingly honest, hardworking, with never enough cases to allow him to become lazy. Seating myself opposite him by the fire, I stared into his face and saw a man not so very different from the person I had once hoped to be. Then I reminded myself that I had good reason not to trust him; perhaps Trask and I had followed more similar paths after all.

I dispensed with pretending to believe in the character he had initially presented. The signature on May's papers had been straightforward enough. Why not let it do the work? I took the envelope from my pocket and held it out.

'Are you familiar with this, sir?'

His was not a gambler's face. When he glanced down at what I held in my hand, his cheeks reddened and his eyes opened wide beneath his furrowed brow. He drew a sharp breath and, for a moment, seemed unable to find his voice. He knew precisely what the packet was about, and I was glad for it.

'However did you come by it?' he asked, as wary as I had been bold. 'May I look?'

I handed the sheaf to him. He studied it, turning the envelope over in trembling hands.

'Benjamin Briggs's seal,' he said, almost as though he were speaking to himself. 'After all this time, who would think the wax would have stuck?'

'It is indeed a wonder, sir,' I said. 'Now, if you don't mind, please enlighten me.'

He eyed me from head to toe, no doubt curious as to what my interest was beyond seeking to advance my case. 'Can I ask you first,' he said, 'whether this means that May and her children are safe?'

'I'll tell you soon enough,' I answered. 'It's complicated. Please, sir. Indulge me.'

He heaved a sigh. 'By now, you've no doubt come to the realization that I knew the Kimball family — I'm sorry to have concealed my connection from you. I didn't see another way to . . . well, as I knew for whom you usually work, I wasn't sure whether or not I could trust you.'

'Ironic, wouldn't you say?' I noted dryly. 'But of little import now. Go on.'

He opened the packet and held up the document. 'And, as you can see, my father knew Benjamin Briggs.'

'Yes, sir,' I said. 'I have been made aware of that.'

He coughed as he looked down. Trask was not comfortable with having passed himself off as someone he wasn't, and I liked him all the better for it.

'Benjamin Briggs and my family were well acquainted. Indeed, I believe I was as close to being a son to him as anyone. My father — after whom I was named — had been his solicitor. Briggs last saw him not long before he . . . died.' There was a moment of silence in the room; then he spoke again. 'He was in an awful state. He'd noticed Silas changing as he grew, knew there'd been something wrong, knew he'd done nothing to protect his own daughter . . . When he found out May was pregnant and had married out of shame, it tortured him. He ordered Silas to leave. That wasn't long before the accident.'

'So these papers,' I said, 'how do they fit in?'

'Well, as you can see, it's Briggs's will leaving May the farm and everything in it. He didn't know what was going to happen to her once he died, but he wanted to be certain it would be she who'd have control of all of his property and not Silas. So he wrote what's known as a 'sole and separate bequest.' It's common enough, though most folks are pretty backward when it comes to these things. They assume that, as it did in the past, everything always goes to the man. No longer true. Less and less so, in fact.'

'So Silas had no claim whatsoever? And this here — 'free from the debts of her husband.' That protected May in some way as well?'

'That's right,' said Trask. 'No matter how

363

much of a reprobate Silas became — racking up debt, drinking, gambling, name your vice — there was no way anyone was going to be able to put a finger on that land to pay off what he owed.'

I thought awhile on this. Briggs might have assumed he'd locked things up tight, but I doubted he'd ever met a man like Hiram Scales. As long as May owned the land, then May stood to lose the land — if Scales got hold of Briggs's will and had his way.

'You look troubled,' Trask said. 'Pryor, please tell me about May and the children now. I ask out of concern for their welfare and for no other reason.'

I paused. I wasn't certain as to where I should begin, so I chose to build from bad to worse. 'Well, as you saw for yourself,' I said, shooting him a significant look, 'May Kimball was bought at auction just yesterday. What you don't know is that I followed her to the horse barn where the man who bought her was keeping her. And I spoke to her — that's how I came by this.'

Trask stared at the envelope and turned it over. 'And why is my name scratched here with a piece of charcoal? Seems awfully crude . . . '

'It was a piece of burnt straw,' I told him. 'May wrote that, just before she was kidnapped.'

'Kidnapped!' he exclaimed. 'You mean right then and there? In front of you?'

I looked down. I was not proud of having failed to protect her once I'd finally found her. 'That's right,' I said. 'James Hurlbut's men.'

'Why would anyone . . . ?'

'I believe you hold the answer in your hands, sir,' I said.

'This ancient document? What can it possibly have meant to anyone save May — and possibly me?'

'Speculators,' I said with a shrug. 'James Hurlbut must have had an *intuition*. He had a feeling that if there was anything he needed to know about the land — any surprises he'd want to wangle free of before it went on the block — he'd get them out of May. These papers are exactly what he hoped he'd find.'

Trask was speechless for a moment. It hardly seemed surprising that his next impulse was to suspect me. 'And you, Pryor?' he asked carefully. 'What is the genesis of your involvement in all this?'

I hid nothing. 'I'm afraid that, as you already know, I have been called upon to serve James Hurlbut a number of times over the years, as an investigator and facilitator of sorts. I'm not proud of the association. But suffice to say, I have reasons that are nowhere near as unworthy as the acts they force me to perform. Just as you did, he hired me to investigate the fire at the Kimball farm — a labor that has led me to secure the very packet you now hold in your hands. The situation worries me, I'll be frank. From what I know of Hurlbut — which is more than I care to admit — I think that this farm is something he wants badly enough to . . . Well, you said it before, when we first met. May Kimball is in danger and the sooner she can be rescued, the better.'

Trask looked as though he still needed convincing as to which side I was on. He bade me continue.

'Not long after he approached me,' I said, 'you appeared on the scene. So you see, in no uncertain terms, I am here on business.'

'And yet you have chosen to return the envelope to me,' he said, looking perplexed. 'What can you possibly have to gain by expressly going against Hurlbut's wishes?'

I hesitated a moment before uttering the truest words I had yet to speak. 'I despise the man, sir. And I have seen and heard described the misery of May Kimball's life several times over. I want no part in stealing what could be her last chance at turning her fortune around. Now, if I have answered your questions to your satisfaction, let us return to discussing the contents of the packet.'

He turned, got up from his chair, and stood gazing into the fire. Something was on his mind.

Finally, he made his way to a cabinet across the room, took a key from his pocket, and clicked open the lock. 'I've a few things to show you, Pryor. And if your object is to scuttle Hurlbut's plan, then I believe you'll be glad to see them. I'll warn you now, there's a bit of a story attached.'

'I've got time,' I said.

He smiled as I beckoned him back to his chair.

'Here is the first,' he said. 'I've held it in secret for more than six years now.' He handed me a single page of sworn testimony. The signature at the bottom — firmly marked and accompanied

366

by Trask's familiar seal — was that of Mister William Peeles, my drinking partner from the squalid Ashland tavern.

I, William Peeles, do solemnly swear in the presence of solicitor Barnabas Trask Esq. that on this 11th day of March in the year 1836, I aided in the birth of one Benjamin Briggs Kimball, Jr., born alive and healthy of May Briggs Kimball and Silas Kimball this very morn.
Signed, William Peeles

I looked up expectantly.

'Peeles came to me directly from the birth,' Trask said. 'Silas had threatened to kill the boy unless May left him, for all intents and purposes, invisible to the outside world. Peeles, being a decent and perceptive man, knew well enough to go along with the scheme while Silas was watching, but he also knew that the boy would be out of an inheritance if there was no record of his birth. He wasn't a doctor, but he'd birthed the infant and was willing to swear to it. He never told May what he'd done. He feared Silas would find a way to beat it out of her.'

'So, May doesn't know about this?' I asked.

'No. I never told her. Peeles asked me not to. Said if anything ever happened to May because of what he'd done, he'd never forgive himself. But now that Silas is dead, I see no reason for her . . . '

'Well,' I said, 'clearly you've never met a Shaker by the name of Elder Sister Agnes. May shouldn't be told about this until both of her children are free and clear of those people.'

'Is that where they are?' Trask asked. 'May put them with the Shakers? That's . . . well it's a sad irony, that's all.'

'Why?'

'Because when Briggs came to my father, he told him that he'd discussed the Shakers with May. Just wanted her to know they were there, and that she needn't feel any shame if she ever had reason to go to them. Funny how things come full circle.'

'Isn't it though,' I said. 'Lucky she paid him no heed — well, in one respect, anyway.'

'Why's that?' Trask asked.

'Because had she signed up, she'd have lost that land her father went to such lengths to secure for her. The Shakers would have made her give it to them, as part of their 'covenant.''

'Hmm,' Trask said, looking pensive. 'Well, there's no point worrying about that. Here. Exhibit B.'

He handed me a second document. 'What's this?' I asked, genuinely confused. 'It looks like a deed. A deed signing the farm — *May's* farm — over to . . . you.'

Trask shrugged. 'She didn't trust Silas — not for a minute. Once he started acting strange, once he started beating her in earnest, once he attempted . . . '

'To murder Ben,' I said, finishing his sentence. 'Go on.'

'Well, she came to me behind his back and said she wanted to put the land where he could

368

never get it. The children were too young for her to pass it on to them, so I suggested that she deed it to me.'

'How convenient,' I said, sarcastically. Perhaps Trask was the crook I'd suspected from the beginning — just sharper than I'd given him credit for.

'That's not all I suggested,' he said quickly, handing me yet another document.

It was a trust agreement. It said that as soon as Polly came of age and Trask deemed her to be in a good position to take charge of the land as well as Ben's interests, he would promise to sell it back to her — for one penny. And if she ever fell into the same misfortune as had her mother, then he was to hold on to the property and manage it in such a way as to benefit both Polly and Ben.

May had not left her children unprotected at all. Indeed, she'd shown remarkable foresight. With Barnabas Trask as the legal owner — even if only temporarily — no one could put a finger on the farm. Ruined as it was, the property would be there for the taking just as soon as the Kimball children were ready to receive it.

'Now that you know the whole story,' said Trask, 'do you have any idea what you are going to do with the information?'

I was uncertain at first how to answer. The instinct to guard my thoughts and actions had deepened over the years. Now, it paralyzed me. What was I going to do? Between them, May and Trask had beaten a formidable villain in the form of Silas Kimball. But were they any match for James Hurlbut? Or, for that matter, Elder Sister Agnes?

'I believe, sir, that Briggs's original — and now defunct — will could be traded for May's safe return. Then, once she is back in safe hands, she will accompany me to the Shakers and tell them that Ben's birth was never recorded and, as such, that he is useless to them. It's what she believes to be true, after all, so I've no doubt she'll be convincing. Finally, it's my assumption that, having determined neither child to hold great promise as a 'believer,' the Shaker sister will release Polly and Ben from their indenture and the family shall, once more, be reunited.'

'Very neat,' said Trask. 'But how will you find May?'

'I have my sources, sir,' I answered. 'One important detail: Do you have a second copy of Briggs's will? One with an unbroken seal? It will be more convincing to Hurlbut if it looks clean and official. The envelope May held onto for all these years — well, it's pretty worn out.'

He reached into the cabinet and handed me his copy of the sealed will. He had something else he wanted to say to me.

'You know,' he said, 'I tried to persuade May to leave the farm. I told her that she and the children could live in peace and safety here with me, but she would not come. I think she was afraid of what Silas was capable of. In the end, helping her to secure the farm was the only thing I could do for her. Seems so little, really. Given the horror of her life.'

'But it wasn't so little, as it turns out,' I said,

standing up and heading for the door. 'It's not just saving her life now — it's saving her children's as well.'

I smiled and held out my hand. He shook it firmly.

'You know where to find me, should you need any assistance,' he said.

'That I do.' One final question buzzed about my head like a mosquito. I turned to Trask. 'Why do you think May carried around her father's old will?'

He looked pensive, and a little sad. 'I imagine she just wanted to have a souvenir to remember him by. That, and it was the last thing anyone ever did to protect *her*.'

I could not help feeling a familiar melancholy sweep over me. My mind traveled far away to that solitary house on that solitary hill, the door to my roomful of regrets thrown open wide. May had seemed such a broken woman, yet she'd managed to care for her kin anyway. Could I have done better looking out for mine?

Polly

The bottle was small and cool in her palm. She reached beneath her pillow and pulled out a slip of paper. It had been torn from a book. Trembling as she tipped the page towards the window, Polly began to read.

The intestines should be kept moderately soluble during the cure; for this purpose the purgatives of the more stimulant, or drastic, kind are found most efficacious, as jalap, black hellebore, scammony, aloes, mercury, bitter apple, &c. these are found to influence circulation and promote the discharge: in addition to which horehound has been much extolled by the French. Hellebore has also been used in the form of tincture, but its action is violent, and if given in a full dose, is found to purge too roughly and profuse.

At the bottom, Charity had written just two sentences.

The tincture of Black Hellebore is made to be drunk in four small sips over two days.

Morning, night, morning, night.

That was all. She had not even signed it.

Polly looked back over the strange text. Though the title at the top had been torn through, she could still make it out. *Menstruation Obstructed.* So this was how the other sisters were told to bleed their wombs. She shuddered and looked once more at the bottle.

So small, such dark liquid, just four tiny sips to out Silas from her body. It was all she could do not to drink it down then and there. Charity's note told her to be careful, but Charity's concern was not for Polly. It was for the believers. They must never know that their Visionist was a whore. They must never know that she took poison to kill the child inside her. If this purging was to be done, it was to be done quietly.

Polly crumpled the page around the bottle and shoved it back under her pillow. Cold and empty, her room felt like a cell. Now that she had the means to force the curse from her body, the moments until it was done stretched endlessly before her. She knew the bleeding would be dangerous. Too much, too fast, girls died from this all the time.

She took her cape from the peg in the hall. She felt weak, it was true, but she needed to work in order to clear her head. Besides, her presence was required in the sisters' workshop. There were seed packets to be made, and they were far behind in fashioning the number they hoped to have ready in time to sell to the World. Spring seemed farther away than ever, yet the months were deceiving. It was almost the end of February.

Polly's thoughts swirled as she walked along the path. There were so many things she needed to sort out. When would the inspector and her mother be coming for her? Elder Sister Agnes had not mentioned the day. Why was he so keen to see her, this Simon Pryor? The only reason she could think of was that he meant to arrest her. Had Ben's birth been recorded? She'd never wondered before, for what child thinks of such things. If it had, she would need to warn Mama to say nothing about it. It was imperative that Elder Sister Agnes be convinced that she had no reason to hang on to Ben, that he was illegitimate and could thus bring the believers no promise of property.

Then, there was the child inside. With every passing hour, she wanted more fervently for it to be gone from her womb. She could not figure out how old it might be, so often had Silas forced himself on her in the months before she came to The City of Hope. If she left things for too long, the cure would kill her. Yet she could not take the poison here, for who would help her if it all went wrong?

She stopped. She would go to Elder Sister Agnes and ask when the meeting would take place. That would determine everything.

★ ★ ★

Polly stood in the doorway of the eldress's workroom. She was breathless from her walk to the Church Family meetinghouse.

'Why are you here, Sister?' the eldress asked. 'Visiting me is all well and good, but do you not have something more important to occupy your time?'

'I need to know when the inspector and my mother are coming,' Polly said. 'If I am to leave with them, there are . . . things I would like to do.'

Elder Sister Agnes regarded her closely. 'Things? What things? Are you planning a final Vision? Something for the believers to remember you by?'

Polly closed her eyes. 'No,' she said sadly. 'Nothing like that.' Her legs felt weak and she wished that the eldress would invite her to sit. She could feel a cramp coming on. She fought it, did not want to bend over and clutch at her stomach.

'Sister Polly?' the eldress asked. 'What is wrong? Come sit by the stove. You look quite unwell.'

Polly crossed the room and fell into the chair that the eldress had indicated. She was tired, so tired.

'What is it, Sister Polly?' the eldress asked. Her tone was not hard. 'I can assure you that you'll feel better for telling me.'

Polly looked up with tears in her eyes. What did it matter anymore? What did anything matter? She was leaving. There was no punishment the eldress could mete out that would be worse than what the World might do to her.

'For all the time I've been here,' she said. 'You have wanted me to confess, Eldress. Well, here I am. You needn't worry that I'll let down the believers. You have determined a plan to keep that from happening. And Charity. You cannot be displeased that she has come to hate me. All that's left is for me to help you understand why.'

Polly sat up as tall as she could and told the eldress everything. About her father's vile ways, the fire, the fact that she'd left him to burn, her last glimpse of him rolling out of the flames, and finally, the child. She told the eldress everything and it was a relief.

Elder Sister Agnes did not say a word throughout the whole of Polly's confession. Indeed, the few times that Polly dared to look into her eyes, she noticed nothing but sadness. And when Polly had finished her story, Elder Sister Agnes looked away towards the bleak light coming through the window and still she kept quiet.

'You must despise me,' Polly said. 'Perhaps more, even, than you thought you might.'

The eldress turned to look at her. 'No, Sister Polly,' she said. Her voice was barely audible, and she turned away a moment before continuing to speak. 'How could I despise one who has been so unfairly cursed?'

They sat in silence, and for the first time, Polly felt calm in the eldress's presence.

'I . . . I had to get Mama and Ben away,' she stammered. 'I don't understand what happened after that. I suppose I intended to set the house on fire. I hated him, I won't lie. I — '

Elder Sister Agnes interrupted her. 'You say that after you settled your mother and Benjamin in the cart, you went back into the house carrying a heavy lamp?' she asked. 'To look at him one last time? What did you hope to see?'

Polly thought a moment before answering. 'I wanted to . . . remember him. Not as he always was, screaming and beating Mama and . . . well, I've said what else he did.' She stopped, suddenly ashamed.

'Go on, Sister Polly.'

'I wanted to remember him weak, vulnerable, like a child I could have done anything to. Like he saw us.'

'And the lamp,' Elder Sister Agnes went on. 'You say he startled you and you dropped it.'

'Yes,' Polly said. 'But I think now that I must have meant it. That it was no accident.'

'Why would you think such a thing?'

'Because, while I believed for a moment when I first came here that maybe I was . . . good, I have since discovered how capable I am of deceit, of the worst form of treachery. I have realized that I am rotten and that I must have meant to . . . murder him.'

Elder Sister Agnes stared out the window again before looking back at Polly. 'I disagree, Sister,' she said. 'I think that the lamp slipped from your hands as it would from anyone's. I think that there was a sleeping man on the bed before you, and with the flames leaping around you, you realized that you were not strong enough to drag him out. You are guilty of nothing save finding yourself in the middle of a dangerous tragedy.' She paused. 'What are you going to do about his child?'

Polly's cheeks reddened. To hear mention of her disgrace only made her feel more disgusted by it.

'I . . . ' She turned and stared into the eldress's eyes. 'You will not approve, Eldress.'

'Tell me anyway,' Elder Sister Agnes said.

'I have decided to . . . out it from my womb. I cannot abide his presence in me. My father's. I . . . ' She turned her face away.

Once again, the eldress paused before speaking.

'It is dangerous, you know. If that is your decision, you will need a doctor to help you through.'

'I know,' Polly answered. 'That is why I came to you in the first place. To find out when I would be leaving.'

The eldress thought a moment. 'I do not want to draw attention to the inspector's visit. We both know what is good for the believers as far as your departure is concerned. I think it best that they see neither Mister Pryor nor your mother in any special way. We have had an increasing number of people from the World visit the Sabbath Meeting since you arrived here. According to the new rules sent out from the Central Ministry, we should not allow them in, but as there is always the chance that one or two of them will join us having seen our worship, the elders here have decided to . . . quietly follow our own counsel in the matter. Perhaps the inspector and your mother could visit from the World this coming

378

Sabbath Day. They could sit in the gallery with all the others; then you could slip away with them after Meeting is over.'

'But you wanted to speak to my mother,' Polly said. 'About Ben. When?'

'I am of the opinion,' the eldress answered, 'that under the circumstances, it might be better to have that conversation at another time. Given everything you have told me, I think it prudent to concentrate on you for the time being.'

Polly looked at her skeptically. 'At another time?'

Elder Sister Agnes smiled. 'You must trust me, Sister Polly. I have suspected you all the time I've known you, it's true, but not because I am wicked. I need time to think about Benjamin. I promise, I will speak to your mother, and we will try and find a solution that leaves everyone happy — including the boy.'

Polly nodded. There was little more she could say. She sighed, feeling she had failed her brother yet again. 'I am late for my duties in the sewing room,' she said as she stood, not sure quite how to take her leave. Then, to her great surprise, Elder Sister Agnes stood up and approached her.

She seemed to want to reach out and touch Polly's shoulder to comfort her. But then she pulled back at the last moment, unable to complete the gesture. 'You must wait before taking the . . . medicine,' she said. 'I have not asked how you got it, but I have my suspicions, and thus I have no doubt that you have been instructed as to how you should use it. Pay that advice great heed, Sister Polly. Your life may depend on it.'

'I will,' Polly answered. 'I will time my actions with care.'

They stood together, not speaking. Then the eldress said, 'Go now and be gentle with yourself, Sister. You deserve to feel at peace.' And with that she turned away. As Polly pulled shut the door, the last thing she saw was the eldress's back, bowed by the burden of all that she had so tenaciously sought to be told.

Simon Pryor

I had been overwhelmed by the scope and implication of what Barnabas Trask had revealed to me, so I did not greet the sight of yet another tightly penned note peeking out from under my door with great enthusiasm. It was from the Shaker sister, and I worried that she was writing to tell me she had changed her mind and would no longer allow me to meet with Polly Kimball. Something about the woman rubbed me the wrong way, and I believed as fully in her power to disappoint as I did in her piety.

But I could not have been more wrong: She requested that May and I come to the Sabbath Meeting that was to take place in just a few days. From there, she wrote, we could slip away with Polly, unnoticed by the other believers. She made no mention of Ben, but there was no time to worry about that now. I had not a second to lose in securing May Kimball.

'James Hurlbut shall receive his documents, but only once I can be assured that May Kimball is alive and, if not exactly well, then at least no worse than when he kidnapped her. Is that clear? Sunday morning . . . seven o'clock. On the road to Albion just beyond the signpost.'

These were the orders I delivered to Cramby when he came calling the next day with a note from James Hurlbut, demanding a meeting.

'The town is not large,' I assured him, taking the note, scribbling my reply and bustling him out the door. 'You shall find the spot easily enough. Just make certain that in the days remaining, the woman is given ample food and rations. Blankets, too. I have written in my note that I shall inspect her myself. Her well-being is the hinge upon which this door swings — you must see to it that Hurlbut understands that.'

'We shall be at the meeting Sunday morn, sir.' Cramby's hand shook as he took back the dispatch and thrust it into his pocket. 'The minute the lady glimpses daylight again, I'll have bowed before James Hurlbut for the last time.'

His gaunt face glowed with anticipation before a shadow crossed and it went dark. 'S-sir,' he stammered, 'before I leave, I've something to give you you'll not be pleased to see. Found it on Scales's desk this morning. Your boy must have been caught on his way to delivering it.' He reached into his pocket and pulled from it the letter I'd written to my mother and father. 'I don't know what you penned here, sir — I'd never read it,' Cramby said, looking down in shame. 'But it was open when I found it.'

'Are you saying that Hurlbut may have seen this?' I asked.

Cramby's silence was answer enough. I looked at the crumpled paper — now that I understood what May Kimball had done to take care of her children, it seemed a pathetic attempt to bridge years of absence. Worse still, Hurlbut knew of my desire to see my parents. Could he find some way to make them suffer? I could only hope that he would be too interested in getting his hands on May Kimball's land to think about it.

'Thank you, Cramby,' I said. I was glad to be made aware of what purchase my enemy had on me. It was to my advantage to be prepared. 'You've done me a great service, one I shan't forget. Now, be off. We've a net to weave.'

He turned and left me, not a glance back. Just walked briskly towards a new future so close at hand he could practically smell the varnish.

★   ★   ★

Sunday morning dawned foggy and seemed to want to stay that way, almost as though the weather itself knew there were strange doings afoot. I was glad for the damp shroud, for I had arranged to meet Hurlbut along a busy stretch of road near Albion, and I was not eager to negotiate with him in front of a procession of travelers. Our rendezvous was to occur early enough that I might continue on in haste to the Shaker Sabbath Meeting. There, with May Kimball by my side, I would secure the release of at least one of the Kimball children. In time, perhaps Trask could find a way to break the boy's indenture; for now, I was ready to take what I could get.

When I woke, I had the sense that I had been ambushed by daybreak, and I all but faltered beneath the weightiness of my situation. A woman's family and livelihood — if not her life — hung in the balance, and I had only an aged deed to offer in exchange for my prize. The paper's value came not from what it *actually* said but from what it could be *made* to say through the wily manipulation of Hiram Scales, Esquire. He was a man for whom birth certificates were generated to be reborn, deeds to be undone, and wills to be robbed of all will. He was a dissembler of genius. How, I wondered, would Trask — a mere lamb of the law — measure up against such a wolf?

The line of crooked constables and lawyers Hurlbut had assembled — to say nothing of my doctored report — assured his success in winning the property at auction. May Kimball and her children, should I be lucky enough to bring them back together, would have not a penny to their name and nowhere to go. That, at least, is how I hoped it would appear to James Hurlbut.

I dressed in the better of my Sunday suits, for it was modest and somber and I thought it would help me fade equally well into morning mist and midday piety. My day was fuller by far than usual, and as I climbed onto the bench of my covered carriage and urged my horses forward, I felt the grip of jangling exhaustion.

Up and down the now familiar road to Albion I traveled, and though it was still near dark, I felt I knew every bump and curve along the way. Finally, from a distance, I saw Cramby standing on the side of the thoroughfare in the appointed meeting place, his dark coat hanging off his frame, a black-clad scarecrow. I rolled up and greeted him with a curt nod.

'I've been instructed to inform you, Mister Pryor,' he said loudly and deliberately, 'that the carriage bearing the party of interest will arrive soon as the lady can be coaxed into it. She's all a-fright, but when she comes, you'll have your inspection. My master says he hopes you'll be pleased with his keeping of her.' His face was grave as he bowed and then blinked significantly at me upon rising. I, too, had a part to play, and so I heaved my most irritable sigh and made a show of pulling my watch from my pocket and tapping upon its face.

'I was specific as to the time of our meeting, Cramby,' I grumbled. 'But then your master has never troubled himself with the convenience of others, has he?'

'Don't know what you speak of, sir,' Cramby answered, ever the good soldier. 'Mister Hurlbut, he's as good as his word. That's truth for you, and if you don't mind, I'm not keen to say more, sir.'

'Well, Cramby, you're right about that — the man is certainly as good as his word.'

Cramby pursed his lips in a dramatic display of disapproval, and I knew he was trying to signal that we were being watched. Deceit breeds mistrust, and one does not become a rogue like James Hurlbut by relying on the honesty of others.

I turned and climbed atop the driver's perch once more. Perhaps the impression that I might lose patience and leave would hasten Hurlbut's

385

arrival, for he desired what I carried in my pocket as badly as I wished for May Kimball to be situated safely on the seat behind me, wrapped in the blankets I'd brought and eating the bread and cheese I'd packed into a sack before I left.

Minutes later, his carriage lumbered into view and pulled up short beside me. I peered through the fringed window to behold one of the strangest pairings I have ever seen. For there sat James Hurlbut dressed in his finest frippery while May Kimball — a study in misery — sat as far from him as possible wedged into the opposite corner. The lush red tufted velvet of the seat only served to highlight the impression that, in all but body, she had entered another realm. Her eyes stared in the general direction of Hurlbut's three-button shoes, her face a blank and colorless curtain of despair. It was as though every muscle in her expression had given up, refusing to support emotion of any sort.

Three sharp raps from the silver head of Hurlbut's stick indicated that he sought my attention. Fearful he might catch a disease of some sort from the sorry company with whom he shared his carriage, he'd covered his mouth with a lace handkerchief and was thus quite difficult to understand when he spoke.

'You've had your look,' he said. 'Now pass me the packet so I can read it through in private. Then and only then will I have Cramby hand over the lovely lady for whom you have pined so assiduously. You'll find yourself thankful for the fresh air of the driver's bench, I'll wager you that. The packet, if you please.'

His short fingers emerged from the tips of his demi-gloves like pink sausages. I detest the cultivation of uselessness that is so popular among the rich — their overripe appendages and soft middles; their pale, unmarked skin; their sagging jowls. They labor over this display of weakness, for it announces their immunity from struggle, thereby — they presume — placing them above the common man. I enjoyed watching James Hurlbut suffer a moment in the cold.

'I cannot agree to your terms,' I said, waving my hand dismissively. 'For how can I trust that, should she stay beside you in the carriage, you will not take the envelope and be gone. On the other hand, should you force her to wait outside, she'll freeze. Let us conduct this exchange like gentlemen. I shall stand well away from my carriage. Please instruct your man to help May Kimball into it and cover her with blankets. Then I shall wait beside you until you have studied the papers and found them acceptable.' I hopped down from my bench waggling the packet in front of the window. 'And you'll not forget my purse, I trust.'

I trusted nothing of the sort, but strode away anyway without acknowledging his reply. Presently, I heard the door to his carriage open and turned to see Cramby helping May Kimball down the step. He bent towards her, holding her arm, encouraging her along and then tucking the blankets round her after he had walked her to my trap, helped her inside, and pressed the bread

I'd brought into her hands before quietly closing the door. Then he strode, head down, to the other door of Hurlbut's carriage and held out an arm to support his master, who placed a foot daintily on the frozen ground and looked round at the bleakness of the surrounding countryside. The wind toyed so roughly with his maroon topcoat, feathered felt hat, and curled locks that I could easily picture him rising up and flapping away. With a scowl, he managed to sort himself out, and eyeing the dirt of the road before embarking on the perilous journey that would land him at my side, he took his first hesitant step.

'As always, Pryor,' he remarked, 'it appears to delight you to cause me the utmost inconvenience. Had you not in your possession — by sheer chance, I might add — something of great interest to me, I would never have agreed to your terms. Now, shall we attend to the business at hand? No doubt you are eager to continue your chat with Mrs. Kimball, the one that was so rudely interrupted the other afternoon.'

I said nothing. I did not need to: The paper in my pocket spoke for me. Affecting the most magnanimous smile I could summon, I gazed upon Hurlbut's despised form for what I sincerely hoped would be the last time.

'Now that you have seen your quarry,' he huffed, 'such a lovely thing, is she not? — it would be decent of you to deliver me mine. I shall feel much relieved when I can hold the envelope in my own hands.'

Like a glutton forced to endure grace when a

sumptuous meal rests just inches from his maw, Hurlbut hated nothing more than to be kept waiting with satisfaction so close at hand. *A little flattery might be in order*, I thought, for it would draw out the minutes and force patience upon him.

'I must say that I am impressed as ever,' I said, my voice oily with sarcasm, 'with your ability to bring the world to its knees and, indeed, its riches to your feet.'

He regarded me with something close to hatred. 'You are still the same contrary creature, are you not, Pryor? Never at peace with your level in life, always scratching about to raise yourself out of the mire? Guilt can be . . . *so crippling*. My forgiving nature almost makes it tempting to pity you. Almost, but not quite. It came to my attention that you wrote a letter — a very touching one at that — begging your mother and father to take you back. Do you not realize that you can never return? I do apologize, but that was our boyhood agreement, was it not?'

He stuck the needle in with great precision. Still, I had grown calluses to equal his expertise, and thus we remained impervious to each other.

'I am pleased to hear you mention my intercepted letter,' I said. 'For it brings to mind one condition I neglected to mention with regard to our little exchange. You shall see the back of me once this is done, now and forever. I should have fought you from the first, when we were young and you were still clumsy in your bullying ways. If you wish to have the packet, you must promise never to put a hand towards directing misfortune my family's way. I have recently been made aware of a witness to your cowardice on the day your sister died. Now that your father is old and infirm, I don't know that his opinion matters much to you anymore, but I, at least, would find some satisfaction in setting the record straight.'

I had not expected my pale threat to make much of a difference to Hurlbut, but his face went white at the mention of a witness, and he nodded rather more readily than I would have expected. His trouble, whatever it was, must have been greater than I realized for him to accede to my demands so easily.

Then he gathered himself together and shrugged unconvincingly. 'It would only be a bother to me to make your old mother and father miserable now,' he scoffed. 'And you've proved to be of little real value over the years. I believe I'd get better service from an errand boy for most of the things I demand of you. So, Pryor, though I don't expect you'll bow before me in gratitude, I grant you your freedom. Run along home. But first, fulfill your end of the bargain — and quick, before I take it into my head to change my mind.'

I took my time reaching into my pockets, checking first one and then the other before holding the envelope just beyond reach, forcing him to lean in before he could snatch it out of my hand. A leather pouch full of coins dropped to the ground at my feet. 'Pray, what do you plan to do with your treasured farm, sir?' I asked innocently as I bent to pick it up. 'Lead a simple country life?'

He looked at me with disgust before turning his attentions back to the packet. 'I plan to invest in the future, Pryor,' he answered. 'The past is a tar pit. Industry's the thing. I want to see land put up to work as hard as those who put up with working it. You know, I spoke to the farmer who owned the Ashland property before he died in that *accidental* fire. Strange, the timing of things. He was going to sell it to me — said he just had a few family matters to see to first.' Hurlbut sighed at the memory, tapping the packet impatiently on his thigh as a smirk washed over his face. 'Wish now I'd offered to take the girl who was watching us. You understand. To lessen his load a bit. A pretty thing she was — flaxen-haired under the grime. Alas,' he said, sighing heavily, 'the father was a greedy brute — probably would have asked quite a price for her. At least now that he's gone, his land will come cheaper.'

'Ah,' I answered. 'Couldn't get the girl, so you went for her mother instead, is that it?'

'Your insults tire me, Pryor. Pray leave me in peace to examine what you have so triumphantly traded for the *rescue* of a vagrant. I'm just sorry the lady doesn't come dragging a coffin behind her. You'll be in need of one within the week, I can assure you of that.'

He tore at Briggs's seal — cracking it and sending bits of chipped wax flying — then pulled the paper from its fold, held it close to his face, and began to devour the words that spilled across it. All was quiet at first, save for the occasional impatient snort-and-paw of one or the other of our horses. The morning light was growing brighter and it filled me with strength and optimism for the coming hours. That is, it did until I heard May Kimball's shriek carried eerily on the wind. She had been watching us from my carriage, and the sight of the envelope held fast in Hurlbut's grasp caused her great distress.

I made a move towards where she sat, but Hurlbut grabbed my arm and shook his head. 'Not yet, Pryor,' he said with evident pleasure. 'I don't mean to delay your reunion, but I need more time to be certain that what you have brought is the thing I need.'

I hated using her this way, but perhaps May's cries made the paper seem more valuable. Hurlbut passed his beady eyes back and forth over each and every line as I held my breath. Finally he sighed, tucked his prize into his coat pocket, and patted it smugly. Without another word he spun away and fairly skipped back to his carriage, clapping twice to summon Cramby. His door snapped shut, and Cramby clambered onto the driver's bench, cheeks flushed with what I could only assume was triumph.

For my part, I thought it best to stay in character to the last so I indicated nothing in return. Indeed, as I walked back to my carriage, which rocked with May Kimball's sobs, I felt my legs wobble beneath me. Checking my pocket watch, I saw that there remained just enough time to take my passenger to the travelers' inn in

Albion, where I had arranged to pay a young woman to help May Kimball bathe and put on a dress I had procured from a former client. It would be a miserable fit, I was certain of that, for it came from the storage trunks of my dear, full-figured spinster, Elvira Drean. Her quest for a suitable man gave her scant use for simple frocks. My gain, I say: Mistress Drean's delusions allowed me to ensure that May Kimball was clean and comfortably clothed when she accompanied me to the Shaker Meeting. I wished I could avoid having to bring her at all, but Elder Sister Agnes would turn her back on me if I did not deliver my end of the bargain. Besides, I no longer felt safe letting her out of my sight. As it was, the day ahead was full of uncertainty. I could leave nothing to chance.

Polly

Strips of muslin from the attic workroom — they were soft but how much blood could they hold? She would need so many that she feared another sister might detect the theft. Then again, what did that matter now that she was leaving?

Polly bent over and sucked her breath in sharply. The child would not out easily. She had taken but a single sip of the Black Hellebore at daybreak. She had tried to hold back, but she could stand not a second more of Silas's presence in her body. And, she had told herself, it was Sabbath Day morning; she would be gone before nightfall.

But she never imagined that the tincture would act upon her body so quickly. The bleeding had commenced, and though it had been less than an hour since she stuffed the first strip up under her dress between her thighs, already the cloth was soaked through. She bundled up another and held them both beneath her skirts, squeezing her legs together. Tearing at the thin fabric used for making the shadow forms of dresses, she remembered standing still for the first time on a wooden box as the young seamstress took pin after pin from her pursed lips and, beginning at Polly's wrists, worked her way up each of her arms, down the sides and darts of her figure, then along the edges of the long skirt and hem. Wrapped in white cut to fit her body, she had felt special for the first time in her life. She had entertained the notion that she was possessed of the gifts the believers had assigned her. *Stupid girl*, she thought now. The muslin dress form and the heavy cotton and worsted wool frocks that had followed had been nothing more than costumes — ones she'd had no right to wear.

She understood better now Charity's and Elder Sister Agnes's warnings. The Black Hellebore could kill her — why, as she tasted its bitterness, she had almost wished for it — and after that first sip she sensed that she had set into motion a convulsive process, one that would be painful to the end. Worried that, once they were reunited, her mother would try to talk her out of taking the medicine, Polly had begun the purge earlier than planned. It was not that Mama would ever want her to birth Silas's child. It was that the alternative was so dangerous. May would have seen the baby brought into the world and then disposed of it rather than risk watching her daughter die from trying to bleed it out. Polly had taken her first sip here, in The City of Hope, because she knew that once the bleeding started, someone would have to get her to a doctor to help her through. As another stab of pain pierced her gut, she wondered at the wisdom of her reasoning.

She hoped she could last through Meeting.

That was all she had to do. Then Mister Pryor would throw a cloak over her and walk her to his carriage. She would be gone from The City of Hope, and the believers would never realize how or why. That was how the eldress wanted it.

She looked at the floor beneath her feet and saw that a single drop of blood had fallen. *I am in Fate's hands*, she thought. A cramp bent her double. It was hard not to think back on Silas's face. Such a laugh he seemed to be enjoying at her expense. She could hear him, the slap of a single word. *Whore*. She tore at more of the muslin.

Though she would not speak to Polly, Charity had slipped another vial under her pillow since she'd delivered the Black Hellebore. An elixir named White Poppies. Made from pods of white poppy, Madeira wine, and sugar water, the potion was boiled down to a syrup 'impregnated with opiate matter and uncertain in strength.' So read the recipe, written out on aged paper in the nurse's journal to which Charity often referred when mixing medicines. Polly remembered it well, for it had been the tincture Charity had asked her to make for Sister Rebecca when The Laudanum was too strong. Indeed, Polly wondered if there had been poppies in the tea Charity had given her the night they had gone to the healing room together. The liquid had helped her escape into the story of the golden robes and the procession to the sacred mountaintop. It had opened her mind so that she could see everything Charity described and believe her every word.

Her sodden dressing needed changing, and as she pulled her skirts awkwardly round her thin hips, she bound several strips in a kind of harness about the tops of her legs. She knotted the cloth tightly and thought, for the first time since she'd heard of it, how the young brethren soaked such lengths in freezing water before retiring, wrapping themselves as she did now to discourage carnal desire from poisoning their souls as they slept. She had found the muslin harnesses amidst their damp sheets on many a morning and washed them, as was her duty, hanging them to dry by the stove while closing her mind to their intimate nature. The irony was not lost on her: that she should bear closer witness here to the private lust of men than would ever have been required of her among the people of the World.

She did not believe that she would bleed more than could be held by the handfuls of cloth she thrust into her apron. As another swipe of pain moved through her, she jerked her hand from her pocket, dislodging her thimble. It had been a gift from Charity, who had scratched POLLY in neat letters around its rim. Polly was never without the finger cup, but as she watched it roll away in a great arc, she felt too awful to get down on her hands and knees and pick it up. No matter now. One of the sisters would find it after she was gone. Perhaps she would use it to keep from pricking her own dainty finger as she sewed her countless loops and knotted her countless knots.

This was how Polly's time in The City of Hope

had been marked: in tiny gestures — the kneading of bread, the sweeping of floors, the collecting of eggs — tasks that took place not simply in the kitchen, the hallway, the chicken house, but under an endless sky of faith, blue as the ceiling beneath which they danced and sang inside the meetinghouse. The hugeness enveloped every sister and brother day upon day upon day. Little marked by change, protected from the disturbances of a world they refused to acknowledge, full of infinite small acts, each believer's life was a ticking down of purpose as meticulous as a merchant's count.

Polly held her breath, bent down, and wiped her blood off the floor. Knocked on its side, out of reach beneath the woodstove, her thimble looked as defeated as a fallen toy soldier.

She passed the rest of the morning lying on her bed, but she knew that eventually she would have to rise and ready herself. Now, she had but a few moments to change her dressings before joining her sisters and walking to the meeting-house. In the last few hours, she had almost fainted from pain and loss of blood several times, and now, as she took the vial of White Poppies from her bodice, she finally allowed herself its sweet relief. Folding and packing tight the muslin strips, pinning them to her strange harness, she felt a wave of grief wash over her with such power that she swayed as she shut the door to her chamber and turned away from the room she had shared so happily with the only friend she had ever known.

I must keep moving, she thought. The White

Poppies were on her side it seemed, for the pain lessened with every step she took. She managed the stairs, and by the time she reached the bottom, she was floating. Nothing could touch her now. She entered the sitting room of the dwelling house, pale but resolute.

'Why, Sister Polly,' said Sister Honora. 'We were worried about you. What, on this Sabbath Day, can have engaged you for so long?'

Polly looked up and faced the sister who spoke. 'I thought I had forgotten my thimble in the sisters' attic,' she said. 'Had I left it, I am afraid I would never have found it again. So I went to retrieve it. I am sorry for keeping you so long . . . '

She pulled her mind back from the daydream induced by the White Poppies. It had been a stronger dose than she realized. She would need to be vigilant.

Elder Sister Agnes eyed her a beat longer than usual. 'Indeed,' she said quietly. 'Now, if you will indulge us, Sister Polly, the Spirits await, and though they are eternal, their patience is not.'

Polly nodded and began walking as quickly as she dared, holding her skirt from behind lest the blood begin to show through her garments. Above her the sky looked heavy and gray, as though snow might be coming. The cramps swept through faster now, so she slowed and tried to breathe out her pain. She was certain that once the dancing had begun, she would be able to hide her distress. She willed her strength into every step she took.

Was all of life pretense? she wondered. Even in

this holy place, did anyone see another for who they really were? Did the believers know their own souls? How mistaken they had been to trust her. How selfish she had been to let them. And yet had not both benefitted from the game? Charity spoke often of the better life that had blossomed since Polly's arrival in The City of Hope. And until this latest and cruelest curse, Polly had felt herself healed by the strength of the believers' conviction. If, somehow, her presence had made it possible to work and worship in peace and union, how could matters have gone so terribly wrong?

The line of sisters entered the meetinghouse, and though all of the believers were silent, she could hear the din made by the World's people. Many had come today — for they had heard tell of the recent Visions — and they seemed to await the spectacle with boisterous anticipation, speaking loudly with an ease and oblivion Polly could not understand. Did they not realize that this was a holy place? Could they not hear their own cacophony and know it to be an affront to Mother and Her Spirits?

The sisters and brethren arranged themselves into two lines facing each other, and she drew in her breath, forcing herself to look just beyond the brother opposite her, stamping her feet and shuffling to and fro, away and then towards the string of brethren backing and advancing in unison before her. It was easy to fall into step. She knew the songs and movements as well as did the most practiced sisters. The flow of the dance soothed her as the believers wheeled and rocked in their somber patterns.

She felt the blood begin its slow trickle down her leg and adjusted her petticoats beneath her skirts. Floating in a White Poppy haze, she did not notice when the dancing came to an end and all had gone quiet save a lone sister's voice.

A believer was having a Vision, Polly could tell by the cadence, the lilting slowness that marked the sound of one who finds her soul filled with light. A fortuitous moment of deliverance, she thought, for it would animate and distract the others. Her gaze fell upon the crowd in the spectators' gallery. The visitors, seated on benches, appeared to be from another land. Some of the women had rouged their lips and bared their breasts in a manner that shocked Polly. Men decorated themselves in the colors of parrots and peacocks, pictures of which she remembered seeing in books when she was a child. Could she have forgotten the ways of the World? These sinners looked absurd, drawing such attention to themselves. Like a spoon beating an empty tin cup, their titters rang nothing like the full laughter of the believers. She wondered for a moment how she could go back to living a life of such feeble purpose.

A sharp cramp reminded her that she had no choice now. She knew she must go, and as her eyes scanned the crowd, they snagged on the face of the inspector. As Elder Sister Agnes had promised, he was there. Her heart sank at the thought of what he would say. He appeared to be looking straight at Polly, his face filled with . . . was it pity? He nodded, and in the slow reverence of the gesture, Polly detected something she could not name. Perhaps it was the White Poppies at work, but it seemed to Polly as though he was trying to communicate with her. She shook off the thought; she must concentrate on the hours that lay ahead.

The crowd — enraptured by the Vision in progress — did not notice her swooning. So much the better. All eyes were on the sister, all ears on her trancelike chanting. As distantly as it echoed in Polly's addled mind, the voice was familiar. Polly moved into the mass, craning her neck to see. How the sound haunted her — sad, mellifluous, intimate.

Charity.

The White Poppies had wrapped a kind of gauze about Polly's head, and the words came through muffled and unclear. Her friend was speaking her name. Why? The voice began to rise in pitch; the bodies of those around her grew tense. What was she saying? Polly forced herself onto the balls of her feet, stretching in her soft dancing shoes. Charity had finally been blessed with the gift she deserved. She would know holiness in its full glory, and the force of her goodness would be made plain before all the other believers. *Here*, Polly thought, *was a true Visionist. Here was a believer deserved of Mother's faith*. No one was more steadfast. No one Polly had ever known was possessed of a soul so pure.

Her ankles went weak, and she had to stand down. The air pulsed with foreboding as the believers parted and cleared a path. A faint smile spread across Polly's face. She meant to show her friend her love, but a glance at those surrounding her proved something was amiss.

Charity swayed as she spoke. 'And the angels said, 'The one you have known to be the holiest Visionist, the first ever to appear in your midst, is not to be trusted.'' Eyes flashing, Charity stared at Polly as she continued. 'Yes, my brothers and sisters, I speak the truth. The Holy Mother's angels appeared before me and said, 'She hides a filthy secret within her flesh and worse, within her heart.'' She paused, and there were shouts of protest from within the tight knot of believers. 'And then further, Mother's angels, they bid me listen to Sister Polly when she sleeps, for only then, they said, would she reveal her true nature. And what did I hear? Our Visionist's real voice! Carnality rules her soul! Why else would she have been made ill in past weeks? Punishment! Concealment! My brothers, my sisters, she has indeed acted as a vessel, but I ask: Whose message has she borne unto the faithful?'

Charity looked fiercely about her as she spoke. Before she could utter another word, one of the brethren cried out, 'Whose servant is she, Sister Charity? Pray, tell us now so that we may know the truth!'

The room fell silent.

'Why, the Devil's is whose!' Charity hissed. 'He is her master. He sent her here to deceive. To wreak havoc. He used her to speak his gospel in this holiest of places. She breathes his Evil and lives for his Word. She is no believer! Look! She bleeds with his child!'

A clamor rose from the gathering of believers while in the gallery the spectators had grown quiet. All faces were turned towards Polly. Red-faced, teeth bared, eyes blazing with hatred: The believers came at her so suddenly with their wrath that it hit her dull and hard as a wood splitter's mallet.

'Who is this creature?' bellowed one of the brethren. 'We must drive her hard away!'

'Yes!' cried another. 'Oh, damn her Devil!'

'Yes,' answered a chorus of angry voices. 'Damn her Devil! Damn her Devil!'

Polly kept her gaze on Charity, for without something to focus on she knew she would faint. Her friend's eyes had filled with tears, her chin quivering violently as she stared back. Polly could only beg silently, speak as they had spoken so often before without words or gestures. But then her friend was gone again. Eyes narrowed, Charity screamed, 'He is here! He stands among us! He must be made gone!'

Polly's legs trembled at the force of the roar that rose up around her. The believers were closing in, and though she searched the crowd frantically, her mind was confused and her vision blurred. The inspector was leaving, attempting to push past a woebegone woman who was crying beside him. It was Mama. Were they leaving without her? *Wait!* she wanted to cry. *Take me from this place!* But no one would have heard her over the melee.

Blood dripped down the insides of both of her legs now. No matter. The men and women of the World were standing, shaking their fists at Polly, laughing, mocking the believers. In a brief moment of clarity, Polly spotted a door. She crept towards the opening. It was, she saw to her dismay, the Brethren's Door — even now, the rules of this place sought to bind her — but she shook them off and inched nearer.

She was almost there, just a few more steps and she would be able to reach the latch and make her escape. But the believers turned and looked back, one of them sounding the alarm with a great yell. She could not recognize his voice, for all of their shouts merged into a chorus of righteous indignation. All save for Charity, whose cheeks, Polly saw, were slick with tears, whose mouth hung open as though aghast at the scene she had created. Polly looked away and, with a force she did not know she possessed, threw herself at the door and onto the stone step outside.

Then she was bolting, stumbling towards the carriages that lined the road. The cold air cleared her head and blew strength into her legs as she willed herself forward, straining to make it to the closest buggy. She was closing in, was almost there when something caught her eye and fairly froze her midstride: The figure of a man moved purposefully ahead of the crowd, chasing her at a dead run. Polly's heart seemed to stop, for though she could not see his face, he seemed horribly familiar. Thin, wearing a dark hat and cloak, he stood in high relief against the splashes of color worn by the other visitors.

She gasped, tripped, rose, and tripped again. She knew she was hallucinating, for it couldn't be her father. Yet the mere thought of him had conjured his form and blocked all else from her mind. His darkness was poised to descend, and Polly's skin prickled in anticipation of his touch. Breath thickening in her lungs, she moved forward on legs that could barely carry her, and in the last moments when she could still feel ground beneath her feet, she rolled her eyes heavenwards and begged for her angels to come.

She felt his arms close round her as the world went black, and distinct from the din that rang out around her, a single voice echoed inside her head as she felt herself slowly fading away.

'Polly,' it whispered. 'Polly, I am here to gather you home.'

Sister Charity

Sister Polly climbed down the stairs slowly, and I knew she'd sipped the poison. The sisters standing around me hissed and burbled like a pot of porridge. They could let nothing she said or did go without comment. They observed her every move as children watch a bug caught in a jar.

I cannot judge them for it. I myself could not help from studying her in that moment, a watchman whose eyes never close, whose ears can hear the movement of a clock's hands circling round the hours. Was it really her thimble Sister Polly went to retrieve? The thimble I gave to her? That was her excuse for making us wait.

Time had run together over the last several days, and just as I could no longer remember when my skin shone white before the markings came, I could no longer remember life without Sister Polly. All these winter months, I had thought one balanced the other. My markings were the work of the Devil; my friendship was a gift from Mother. Had not Sister Polly entered my life just when I needed her most? Was I not being offered a chance at salvation?

The answer, as I now see it, is yes. Salvation was dangled before me, a stick waved teasingly in front of a dog, and I leapt for it. But it was never intended that I should be saved. The Devil, just as he drew upon my skin, was having his fun. He gave me Sister Polly that I might dare to hope I could, someday, be pure. He infected my heart with love for one who was bound to betray me.

Though we imagine it to be mild, the truth is more beastly than we are taught. Lies slither silently and leave things where they stand while Truth crashes about, breaking down what once seemed unassailable. Since the night in the healing room, I kept my racing thoughts to myself. I stayed awake trying to plan what it was that I should do. I lay listening to her moan. Down the dark hallways of my mind I ran, seeking all manner of action. What if I did this? What if I did that? What if, what if, what if.

Suddenly, I knew the path I must walk. It obliged me not to take up weapons against evil — no tomahawks or stones. I am done with such tests. My new course was no gentler, for it leveled destruction even as it sought to save. I had to follow, and it led me to denounce her.

★   ★   ★

In the weeks after Sister Polly's last Meeting, it was my eldress — of all people — who made me to understand my mistake.

'She was subjected to great cruelty before she came to us,' Elder Sister Agnes said. I was not accustomed to hearing her express sympathy for

408

a girl she had always treated with suspicion. 'People do not come here to escape circumstances that are happy.'

We sat alone, sewing in my eldress's workroom. For me, time had split in two: the months before Sister Polly left, and the months since. 'What cruelty?' I asked. 'She never spoke of it to me.'

My eldress knotted her thread and snipped the end with a scissors. 'She had a father who would not . . . leave her alone.'

I was quiet as I pulled my needle in and out of the cloth before me. My task was the sewing of initials onto handkerchiefs for the brethren. 'He beat her?'

'He may have,' she answered.

'And was there a boy?' Once upon a time, those words would have been too embarrassing for me to utter. Not now.

Elder Sister Agnes was silent. Then, 'No, there was not.'

'Well, there had to have been someone who . . . '

My eldress stopped sewing and looked at me. 'Her father. The child was his.'

I put my sewing ring in my lap. I could barely breathe, so great was my disgust.

'Her own father?' I said. I was naive and had never even imagined such inhumanity was possible.

'She was not who you thought she was,' my eldress said, as though the statement might comfort me. 'But she was not who *I* thought she was, either.'

Is anyone who we think they are? I wondered. *Are you?*

My hands shook as I tried to resume my embroidery. 'Did she die?' I asked, struggling to keep my voice from cracking. 'After she left us?'

Elder Sister Agnes was quiet as she worked. 'I don't think it will do you good to think about her anymore, dear Sister Charity. You loved her and were a good friend to her. But she is in a better place now, wherever it may be.'

There was much my eldress had not told me, of that I was certain. She had not become the woman she was by being indiscreet. She did say that, in the end, Polly came to her and confessed, but she never shared with me the substance of her confession. And I never asked. The finest layer of dust had settled over that part of my life, and I felt, somehow, that to disturb it would be to visit further insult on the strange months of my awakening.

I wondered how much Elder Sister Agnes knew about my full role in the events of Sister Polly's last day, for I kept secrets as well. I never mentioned the Black Hellebore to her. Did she realize that I had made the Visionist bleed? That it was I who near killed her? Indeed, for all I knew, my friend *was* dead from the hemorrhaging and Elder Sister Agnes just didn't have the heart — or mind — to tell me. The blood — its profusion had stunned me.

My beloved Polly carried her father's child and I never knew.

How this haunts me as the brown mud of March yields finally to April's tentative green. All

410

month, I hetchel the flax and card the tow. I spin more mops than could cleanse the Earth. Now, to making soap and cleaning the houses I should turn, for spring is upon us. The young brethren, freed from school, stack stone after stone, thrown aside to make way for the plowing of the fields. Brother Benjamin works among them. The fences must be stood right again after the weight of the winter snows; the planting of hardy crops must begin — corn, beets, potatoes. How low we stoop, how hard we toil in our service to Mother, particularly so in these months of renewal.

My fingers bleed from the labors I perform. I wrap them at night and still the white bandages are soaked red by morn. It is said that ruffians from the World pulled Mother Ann through the mud by her ankles so that her skirts might rise and reveal her sex. It is said she was beaten by angry mobs. It is said she suffered such a horrid fate as only a woman can know at the hands of men. Thinking on her perseverance and faith, I disgrace myself worrying about my own blistered hands. Thinking on what happened to my Sister Polly, I can scarcely allow myself a drop of pity.

Why can I not be the girl I was when I heard the music of my beliefs in the whirl of the spinning wheel, the boil of the distillery cauldrons, the crisp cutting of medicinal pills? My blessings and prayers I once counted in every stitch, for oh, did I sew my soul into the seams of our city! I was both dust and broom, sheep and yarn, grain and bread.

No longer. The strange thing of it is, my markings are gone and my skin is now as white

411

as a linen kerchief. I am pure enough even that Elder Sister Agnes asked me to replace Sister Columbine and take up my *rightful* position as one *destined* to be like her someday, an Elder Sister. My 'Vision,' you see, was thought to have saved the believers from ill-placed faith. I was said to have outed the Devil and shown Sister Polly for who she truly was.

Of course I said yes to my eldress. I want no more attention than I had already gotten, and to refuse — well, let us say that no one would ever forget it. But I will never be like Elder Sister Agnes, for I am surly with disillusionment.

Indeed, I have my own idea as to what really erased my markings. I believe they left me when I gave up trying so hard to be good. Funny, all that time I thought that if I could only be a better believer, they would disappear. But that is not what the Devil wanted at all. He wanted to kill my faith, and once he succeeded, his work with me was done.

I ask myself: Had I known the burden of the Visionist's past, would I have been merciful? Just as I refused to hear the truth when she sought to tell it, I did not seek it when she sought to conceal it. My penance? It surrounds me. I sing, dance, perform my chores as though already dead.

In the sisters' attic, I stand under the massive eaves of the dwelling house where she claimed to have gone in search of her thimble before the final Sabbath Day Meeting. She told a half-truth when she said she had dropped it, but I knew that she never went back to get it. In the dark, the night after I drove her away, I came here, dropped to my knees, and felt along the floor. I could not rest until I had found it.

It lay beneath the stove. How cold the tiny cup felt in my palm. Icy and sharp, smelling only of tin. I ran my fingernail over her name. It had taken days for me to scratch it neatly with my needle. *If she is capable of hatred*, I thought, *then may she despise me. If she can curse, then may she fill the air with furious noise.*

I have since returned often to this place. Now, I look round and I see everywhere the order of our lives. It is printed in the numbers labeling each drawer, built into cabinets under the slope of the roof. It is in the rhythm of pegs dotting the walls. It is mapped out in the straight paths far below me. It thrums from every last one of our buildings, huddled close. Were there brethren and sisters about, I would see them walking in lines from one colored shelter to another — sure of their place within this safe, sealed world.

I alone rebel, for in the back of the highest drawer in the attic, I have hidden the red book. I don't show it to anyone, but I am no longer ashamed to read it when I am by myself. Sister Polly proved to me that to open a book is to step into another world, a place I had assumed was hateful and full of sin. I always thought the red book was dangerous because once inside the stories it told I never knew if I would be able to get out. And how could I foresee what temptations awaited me? How could I know what words I might read that would forever change who I am? But in the end, I was wrong

— about everything. For it is what happened *outside* the red book that made me different. And, in the end, it is the red book that takes me back to myself.

I open the small attic window and a damp breeze blows in. How much of my life I have passed in this room, folding the clean sheets and blankets, then tucking them neatly away. Sewing and darning and laughing. In these sad days, it is here, closest to Heaven, that I feel most at home.

I sought to punish Sister Polly, but I try to comfort myself that I sought also to save her. I even dare to think that perhaps, if she was pure again, we might . . . What does it matter now? As she bled in Meeting, I saw how the Black Hellebore was gutting her and I knew that my plan had to succeed; I knew she must be flushed out into the World and taken to a doctor. We could not help her here. My means were clumsy and deceitful — I watched her bleed, stumble, and fall — but I believe that I truly meant to save her.

Sitting so close to the high window, I close my eyes and dream the same thing over and over: the pine burial board is straight and smoothly cut, the winding sheet white and clean. They lay my cap upon my head and place my collar about my neck. I wonder: *Will my cloak repel the chill?*

The psalm that whispers in my ear says this:

Oh, that I had wings like a dove!
I would fly away and be at rest.

414

That is my wish. To fly — my body tumbling to the stones below, my soul soaring to Heaven that I might rest my eyes upon Sister Polly, that she might forgive me, that we might once again laugh together in the world unseen.

Simon Pryor

I have come to the end of many stories only to wait for them to begin anew. No tale stands alone, for just as one cannot speak of the future without paying due reverence to the past, one cannot sing the ballad of a single life.

Permit me first to crow from the rooftops the demise of James Hurlbut. A wondrous thing, the comeuppance of a scoundrel. Scales's legal meddling could not defeat May Kimball's determination to preserve what was rightfully hers. And Trask? Well, we are a wily lot, even the good among us.

My *former* master had planned to take ownership of the Ashland farm and sell the land at profit enough to cover his debts, for his creditors were many. And he'd had good reason to fear that I might ask Cramby to speak out about what really happened the day Millicent died. Disgusted with James's profligate ways, Amos Hurlbut had threatened to cut his son out of his will and give everything to James's brother. Cramby's story would only have steeled the old man's resolve.

As it was, having lost the opportunity to acquire the Kimball farm, he continued to gamble and lose — everything, as it turns out, including any chance of inheriting his father's money. It is sad, in its way, but you'll forgive my glee in reporting that, destitute beyond recompense, my nemesis is now locked in debtors' prison. I doubt that his miserable end has occasioned much pity. Indeed, I cannot imagine a soul who'd lift a finger to help him.

As to what transpired in the Shaker meeting-house that blustery Sabbath Day, I can only, even now, profess utter astonishment. May Kimball, clean and newly dressed, accompanied me with great dignity in spite of all that she had endured. We made an odd couple, it's true, but once we had seated ourselves with a clear view of the proceedings, I wondered at the world of difference between the worshippers' selfless presentation and the brassiness on exhibit in the audience. The Shakers were a different people, from a land no commoner could ever understand.

When the dirgelike singing commenced, it had a quieting effect on the gallery, the song severe yet hypnotic. Such humility before 'Mother' — as the worshippers called her over and over — cleared with a sharp slap the senses of those whose true religion demands that they fall on bended knee before wealth, gossip, and fashion. I heard mocking whispers and stifled giggles, but considering the rudeness that had been in evidence when first the crowds sat upon their benches, we eventually evolved into a respectful, if ridiculous, flock. For one cannot help feeling self-conscious when faced with the discipline

417

demonstrated by such a serious and, I must admit, dreary tribe.

The dances began to quicken and the songs to rise in tone and feeling. Men and women who had just moments before seemed half-dead of virtue became possessed by righteousness. They shouted and stamped, skirts swirling as the women turned, men jumping and falling to the floor, their bodies akimbo. And even as their spiritual fervor distanced them from anything I had known in my own sinful life, I recognized their faith to be a most powerful force.

So distracted was I by this performance, I almost forgot to seek out Polly Kimball in the fray. Though thinner and paler since last I glimpsed her, she was easy to spot. She had been in a panicked state the first time I laid eyes on her — certain that I sought to expose her, whatever her role may or may not have been in the Ashland fire. I did not really see her that day; I was too upset by my failed attempt to reassure her. Now, with her eyes halfway closed, she swayed in a world of her own making. The effect was mesmerizing, and when finally she looked up at me, I felt caught in her spell.

It was then that I noticed that the performers had quieted, their attention directed towards the otherworldly voice of a girl chanting something I could not understand. Movement around her slowed, and I had the sense that her utterances held great weight. The Shakers clenched their fists and looked angrily from one to another as her speech intensified and her voice grew louder. Then the dancers parted so that a path became visible, one that appeared to lead straight from the speaker to Polly Kimball. In tones accusatory and cruel, the girl seemed bent on inciting rage in the other worshippers, and it wasn't long before they were all glaring at Polly and crying out for what they termed the 'warring songs.'

I knew that May and I needed to leave before the situation became more frenzied. Busily pushing my way through the crowd, I never witnessed Polly's escape. I remember only that once I had made it out the visitors' door and set off at a run towards my carriage, I saw her stumbling across the icy yard, a bloodstain spreading over the folds of her skirt. It was then that I noticed a second figure — a man dressed in a dark streaming cloak.

Trask, bless him. I had my own difficulties to contend with, for May had glimpsed young Ben in the crowd of outraged worshippers, and though she gasped and hurled herself towards him, I would not let go of her hand. I was not about to lose her a second time, no matter how ferociously the Shakers jostled us. From afar, the sight of Trask catching Polly up in his arms as she fell filled me with relief and gratitude. He was spry and strong, carrying her as though she were no heavier than a feather bed as he closed the distance between us.

'Pryor!' he shouted. 'Make room for her in the back and ready the horses. We must leave before they can stop us!'

Leaping onto the driver's bench, I whipped the horses into motion while Trask hoisted Polly onto the seat beside her mother. The girl was finally safe. From his seat next to me, Trask turned towards the women behind us and reached out a hand to stroke May's shoulder.

'Hello, May,' he said. 'I'm glad to see you again.'

Save for the thundering of hooves, a deep silence fell over the inside of the carriage. 'Barnabas?' May asked, her voice a hoarse whisper. She looked at him as though she could hardly believe he was there. 'So Mister Pryor found you after all.'

Trask nodded, his eyes filling with such sorrow that, upon gazing into them, May burst into tears and buried her face in the folds of his cloak. 'There now,' he said as he wrapped his arms about her. 'I'll take care of you from here on. Hush your crying, poor sweet May.'

Rarely do forks in the road present themselves as literally as did the one that faced me at that very moment, for when I wrenched my attention from the reunion taking place in the lurching seat behind me, I saw two signs on the road before me. One pointed towards the town from which I'd fled, the other towards the one where I'd hid myself ever since. I pulled on the right rein and urged the horses forward. There was only one way for me to go.

★ ★ ★

In the weeks that followed, May Kimball and I did not leave Polly's side as she lay feverish, in and out of consciousness, in the very bed I had occupied as a boy. I had chosen wisely the road away from The City of Hope that strange afternoon. My mother and father, gray-haired and diminished by the passing of the years, seemed almost to have been expecting us, and after seeing to it that Polly was taken in and made warm, my father ran to call the town doctor away from his Sunday supper. The man did not attempt to mask his grim view of her condition.

'I've seen too many girls,' he sighed, 'shamed into inflicting torture on themselves. She was fortunate not to have died within hours of starting to bleed.' He closed up his bag and turned to take his leave, a quartet of pale, worried faces blocking his path. 'I'll do all that I can,' he said, looking into May's eyes. 'But you would do well to prepare for the worst. It's only right you should know the truth.'

We watched him go in silence. Then, with Polly having been administered to as best we could manage, Trask and I left to find quarters in a nearby inn. May was in good hands with my parents. As for me, I hugged them each good-bye with the promise that I'd be back in the morning, and we parted as though we'd never been torn asunder. There is nothing more to say on the matter.

Burns' Hollow is where I have stayed and made caring for others my purpose — for now. Despite the doctor's bleak prediction, Polly Kimball refuses to die. All I can say is that she must have an angel on her side; no other girl could pull through such an ordeal. And though May grows stronger with every sign that her

421

daughter is healing, she does not forget Ben. For he is part of another broken circle, one she gives her all to making complete again.

Over the course of daily visits to the Shaker enclave, she tries to coax him back. Indeed, Elder Sister Agnes surprises me by attempting to persuade the boy herself. Trask drives May out to see him, and every time, she comes back crying; Ben will not leave his new home. Perhaps one day the child will change his mind, that is what I tell her. I know that if anyone has learned not to be surprised by what the future holds, it is May Kimball.

For my part, I can only describe these months as nothing short of miraculous. As the days lengthen and the land begins to trust in the constancy of the sun, life opens in more ways than I could ever detail in these simple pages. It is not just that grass grows tender in the fields, that violets and strawberry flowers carpet the village green, that the scent of lilac and roses fill the air. Those are but a few of the common wonders I allow myself to behold after refusing, for so long, to acknowledge their fleeting beauty. Where once they seemed a sign that nothing lasts, now they fairly glow with a different meaning — that the opportunity to begin anew presents itself over and over, in infinite ways. Complacency, I now realize, only *seems* to be the easier path. In truth, it is much more of a struggle than is the act of moving on.

As I keep watch at Polly's bedside, I listen to her nightmares and hear of the torment she has suffered. That she had become Silas Kimball's

422

prey as had her mother before her. That she had seen him tumble from the burning house. That she was haunted still by the fear he had survived and was coming to find her. She does not speak often of her time with the Shakers. But in calmer moments, there is one word she utters over and over. *Charity, charity, charity* — a prayer, perhaps, in praise of the kindness they showed her.

As she grows stronger and we begin to converse, the enchantment she casts over me is all-consuming. It is not merely that her mind is quick and curious. Nor, I must add, that she has bloomed into a girl of dazzling grace and loveliness. It is more profound than that, for the honesty she displays disarms me of all cynicism, heals all bitterness, forges faith where before there was nothing but a void. She is possessed of great strength — how else could she have survived the trials of her young life? But there is an ethereal quality about her, a well of empathy and beneficence. One feels forgiven in her presence, seen, understood.

I imagine that God acts upon his faithful in a similar manner, though I would hardly know. Indeed, I must sound foolish to even suggest that she is, in some manner, divine. The simplest explanation is to say that she acts as a balm on my confused soul, and so soothed, I have allowed her to know me. That my years on this earth have been marked as much by deceit as by decency; that she has been both ground down and idolized; that both of us have learned to vanish from life even as we look it squarely in the eye — these are the paradoxes we share.

And, oh, the glorious bewitching! Time speeds up and stands still; the ground gives way and is made firm; my heart breaks open and is, once more, made whole.

I cannot know whether she will ever entrust herself to me. To expect such a thing would be indecent, for why should she put her faith in any man after all that has happened to her? I can only tell you that I am besotted, a sod like any other, at the mercy of cliché and the threadbare language of exaltation. How can this peculiar devotion have been conceived if not in a fever dream? For it is born not of furtive glances, nor clever remarks, nor the shiver of an unexpected kiss. I have played my part in all manner of delightful flirtation and never felt more than a halfhearted flutter. But this, this love lifted from the ashes, abused, abandoned, afraid, misread, discarded, half-dead — like those who enter into it, it is broken. Yet beautiful, so very beautiful.

Acknowledgments

This book would not exist without the help of my agent and friend, Dorian Karchmar, whose ability to guide, inspire, counsel, and console is apparently limitless. Cheers to you, Suzanne Gluck, for putting us together.

Reagan Arthur made clear her vision for *The Visionist* from the moment we first spoke; ever since, her enthusiasm and creativity have been miraculous, and I cannot thank her or Michael Pietsch enough for changing my world.

With her keen eye, sharp ear, and unerring sense of how stories should unfold, Laura Tisdel is a writer's best defense against herself.

Jessica Leeke, adept at bucking me up while toning me down, took a chance on this book, for which I will always be grateful.

Tom Dyja told me the Shakers were worth writing about. He was right.

Alex Sichel, my earliest best friend, inspired everything I know about love between true companions.

Alice Truax midwifed *The Visionist* into being; Greg Villepique, Shannon Langone, and Jayne Yaffe Kemp taught it some manners; and Keith Hayes gave it serious style. Leon Friedman and Simone Blaser took care of me.

Given that a period novel is nothing without accurate period details, deep respect and gratitude are due to Glendyne Wergland, author and

Shaker historian; Lesley Herzberg, curator of collections, Hancock Shaker Village; Christian Goodwillie, former curator of collections, Hancock Shaker Village; John Demos, Samuel Knight professor of history emeritus, Yale University; Ted Widmer, former director of the John Carter Brown Library, Brown University; and Jayne Ptolemy, social historian and researcher extraordinaire.

Maura Finn: How strange that you, of all people, taught me everything I know about 'The Narrow Path.'

Reading is one thing; seeing, another. The following Shaker sites, as well as the knowledgeable people who work at them, provided crucial visual and factual information: Hancock Shaker Village, Pittsfield, Massachusetts; Canterbury Shaker Village, Canterbury, New Hampshire; The Watervliet Shaker Historic District, Colonie, New York; and the Enfield Shaker Museum, Enfield, New Hampshire.

Thanks from the bottom of my heart to Maggie Howard, scrupulous editor and champion; Wesley Gibson, peerless teacher; George Kalogerakis, Tony Goldwyn, Val Coleman, Katharine Ohno, Amy MacDonald, and Margot Herrera — adroit readers; Lisa Craig, booster of spirits; and Elissa Schappell, lifesaver. No one, E. — not even you — could dream up a more stalwart comrade-in-arms.

My parents, Sidney and Brian Urquhart, have been inexhaustible sources of support, encouragement, advice, astute critical commentary, and, above all, love. It's obvious, I know, but I couldn't have done this without you.

Theo and Simon, you are my blessed tethers to what's really important.

John, how to even say it? You set me loose in the world and I came home with this book. I owe you everything but can offer only my profound — if at times prickly and inscrutable — love. All of it.

Bibliography

When I began researching this novel, I knew three things about the Shakers: They forbade sex, they made beautiful furniture, and they shook. Thanks to the following sources, I now know a lot more.

Books

Andrews, Edward Deming. *The Gift to Be Simple*. New York: J. J. Augustin Publisher, 1940.

— . *The People Called Shakers*. New York: Dover Publications, Inc., 1963.

Andrews, Edward Deming, and Faith Andrews. *Work and Worship Among the Shakers: Their Craftsmanship and Economic Order*. New York: Dover Publications, Inc., 1974.

Beale, Galen, and Mary Rose Boswell. *The Earth Shall Blossom: Shaker Herbs and Gardening*. Woodstock, VT: The Countryman Press, 1991.

Castleman, Michael. *The New Healing Herbs: The Classic Guide to Nature's Best Medicines*. New York: Rodale Press, 2001.

Faber, Doris. *The Perfect Life: The Shakers in America*. New York: Farrar, Straus and Giroux, 1974.

Feintuch, Burt, and David H. Watters, eds. *The Encyclopedia of New England*. New Haven: Yale University Press, 2005.

Francis, Richard. *Ann the Word: The Story of*

Ann Lee, Female Messiah, Mother of the Shakers, the Woman Clothed with the Sun. New York: Penguin, 2000.

Herbrandson, Dee. *Shaker Herbs and Their Medicinal Uses*. Albany: The Shaker Heritage Society, 1985.

Herzberg, Lesley. *A Promising Venture: Shaker Photographs from the WPA*. Clinton, NY: Richard W. Couper Press, 2012.

Humez, Jean M., ed. *Mother's First-born Daughters: Early Shaker Writings on Women and Religion*. Bloomington: Indiana University Press, 1993.

Larkin, Jack. *The Reshaping of Everyday Life: 1790–1840*. New York: Harper & Row Publishers, 1988.

McCutcheon, Marc. *Everyday Life in the 1800s: A Guide for Writers, Students & Historians*. Cincinnati: Writer's Digest Books, 1993.

Smith, Archibald W. *A Gardener's Handbook of Plant Names: Their Meanings and Origins*. New York: Dover Publications, Inc., 1997.

Sprigg, June. *By Shaker Hands*. New York: Alfred A. Knopf, Inc., 1975.

Stein, Stephen J. *The Shaker Experience in America*. New Haven: Yale University Press, 1992.

Swank, Scott T. *Shaker Life, Art, and Architecture: Hands to Work, Hearts to God*. New York: Abbeville Press, 1999.

Wergland, Glendyne R. *One Shaker Life: Isaac Newton Youngs, 1793–1865*. Amherst: University of Massachusetts Press, 2006.

— . *Sisters in the Faith: Shaker Women and Equality of the Sexes*. Amherst: University of

Massachusetts Press, 2011.

— . *Visiting the Shakers, 1778–1849.* Clinton, NY: Richard W. Couper Press, 2007.

Wessels, Tom. *Reading the Forested Landscape: A Natural History of New England.* Woodstock, VT: The Countryman Press, 1997.

Other Sources

The Drawing Papers 2 — Heavenly Visions: Shaker Gift Drawings and Gift Songs. New York: The Drawing Center, 2001.

Filley, Dorothy M. *Recapturing Wisdom's Valley: The Watervliet Shaker Heritage, 1775–1975.* Colonie, NY: Town of Colonie and the Albany Institute of History and Art, 1975.

A Juvenile Guide. Canterbury, NH: United Society, 1844.

Koomler, Sharon Duane. *Seen and Received: The Shakers' Private Art.* Pittsfield, MA: Hancock Shaker Village, 2000.

Paterwic, Stephen. 'Mysteries of the Tyringham Shakers Unmasked: A New Examination of People, Facts, and Figures.' *Historical Journal of Massachusetts* 31, no. 1 (2003).

The Peg Board 4, no. 3 (1936).

Shaver, Elizabeth D., ed. 'Fifteen Years a Shakeress.' *Galaxy*, March 1872. Reprinted by the Shaker Heritage Society, Albany, 2000.

The Youth's Guide in Zion and Holy Mother's Promises. Canterbury, NH: United Society, 1842.

Theses

Finn, Maura A. 'Guided by Vision: The Ritual,

Theology and Function of Shaker Gift Drawings.' College of Wooster, 2000.

Wergland, Glendyne R. 'Women, Men, Property, and Inheritance: Gendered Testamentary Customs in Western Massachusetts, 1800–1860: or, Diligent Wives, Dutiful Daughters, Prodigal Sons, Westward Migration, Reciprocity, and Rewards for Virtue, Considered.' University of Massachusetts, 2001.

Film
The Shakers: Hands to Work, Hearts to God. Directed by Ken Burns. PBS Home Video, 1989.

We do hope that you have enjoyed reading this large print book.

Did you know that all of our titles are available for purchase?

We publish a wide range of high quality large print books including:
Romances, Mysteries, Classics
General Fiction
Non Fiction and Westerns

Special interest titles available in large print are:
The Little Oxford Dictionary
Music Book
Song Book
Hymn Book
Service Book

Also available from us courtesy of Oxford University Press:
Young Readers' Dictionary
(large print edition)
Young Readers' Thesaurus
(large print edition)

For further information or a free brochure, please contact us at:
Ulverscroft Large Print Books Ltd.,
The Green, Bradgate Road, Anstey,
Leicester, LE7 7FU, England.
Tel: (00 44) 0116 236 4325
Fax: (00 44) 0116 234 0205